It is an odd thing to begin a story part-way into its third act, so we beg the reader's faith that with this tale's unfolding, time will make plain and all will understand what I have come to learn in making myself a chronicler of the extraordinary account of two great families...

Theodora would not have it any other way

Serinda
Justinian and Theodora

A novel by Daniel Cirignani

Ahwatukee, Arizona
Adriatic Memories
2018

Published by
Adriatic Memories
Ahwatukee, Phoenix
Arizona, USA
Second edition

Library of Congress
Catalog Card Number: 2018952007
ISBN: 978-1-949235-06-7

Edited by Gail Wade
Spanish audiobook narration by Leonor Lavado
Cover and art by Nikki Cirignani

Available in translation

Spanish translator	*French translator*
Paola Hernández	Marion Bilger

Printed in the
United States of America
Set in Cambria

Permissions and Sections Licensed

Cover	"Zeugma Mosaics", Turkey Author: Bulent SARI Mosaic dated to the mid-sixth century, popularly known as "The Gypsy Girl of Zeugma" and preserved at the Zeugma Mosaic Museum in the Gaziantep, Turkey Fotolia photo reference: #2419631 Paid image used with permission under extended license
Cover (Background)	Pixabay – Purple Silk Shiny, image 668054_1920 Image used with permission
Tabula Peutingeriana	Austrian National Library Reprinted with permission Tabula Peutingeriana 1200 AD (copy—original ~410 AD) Web Link: http://data.onb.ac.at/rec/AC13945113
Tabula Rogeriana	Folio 14 Bibliothèque nationale de France Reprinted with permission
The Secret History	Excerpts from *The Secret History* by Procopius of Caesarea produced by Ted Garvin, Project Manager; Keith M. Eckrich, Post-Processor; the PG Online Distributed Proofreaders Team, "LITERALLY AND COMPLETELY TRANSLATED FROM THE GREEK FOR THE FIRST TIME", "PRIVATELY PRINTED FOR THE ATHENIAN SOCIETY:

Permissions and Sections Licensed
(Continued)

Other maps   Other maps are the work of the author

Justinian and Theodora on Social Media and the Web

Website	Serinda.com
	and
	JustinianandTheodora.com JustinianoyTeodora.com JustinienEtTheodora.com
Facebook and Twitter	Facebook.com/JustinianandTheodora Facebook.com/JustinianoyTeodora Facebook.com/JustinienetTheodora
	@dcirignani
Audio editions:	Search for Serinda on iTunes podcasts!
	Soundcloud.com/JustinianandTheodora Vimeo.com/JustinianandTheodora YouTube.com/JustinianandTheodora
	JustinianandTheodora.com/Audiobook
	(Audio editions only available in Spanish at the time of print for the first edition)

Foreword to the first edition of Serinda

About "Volume III, Part I, Book 2" – *Serinda* is the "B-story", that is: the second story to the main "A-story", of the third volume of what will be a three-volume series that follows the lives of one of the most evocative power-couples in history: Byzantine Roman Emperor Justinian and Empress Theodora.

A full account of their lives requires that we begin loosely with their parents, about sixty years prior to the events described in *Serinda*—and shortly enough we'll return there and start from the beginning.

But not yet!

One of my purposes in releasing the third installment of the historically-based epic of Justinian and Theodora prior to the others is to introduce those of us occupants of the 21st century to the world of the sixth, and in so doing to shake willing readers from our snug, modern complacency so as to open up the world that Justinian and Theodora belonged to.

As the cliché goes, their world "shares a planet" with ours, but at times and places it occupies a different universe altogether—a universe which in comparison to our own was one they experienced as immanent, enchanted and providential. The Divine was present everywhere and in everything, magic was as operable a force as any other physics or mechanics, and while destiny and fate were sometimes known, sometimes unknown, they were always irresistible.

Let's encounter Justinian and Theodora as real people. One cannot get to know them unless one understands the world as they experienced it. In *Serinda,* we will depart from the materiality and mechanism of the 21st century and step into the immanence and Logos of the sixth.

I have a second purpose too for this ordering, which for now will remain undisclosed, but it will be exposed as the stories unfold.

To reach as many people as possible, we are making the first audio edition of *Serinda* available universally, online and free of charge to everyone.

It is my hope that in so doing you will find yourself in possession of a compelling story—one that is well-researched, thoughtfully-written and which has the ability to channel the reader into the lives of its subjects. For me, this project is a "love letter across time and space" to the two remarkable individuals who form its center.

Follow us on Facebook and keep up with latest events at:

Facebook.com/justinianandtheodora

Audio production may lag behind written editions, but readers can find audio versions as we make them available on Vimeo at:

Vimeo.com/justinianandtheodora

I sincerely hope you find the story of Justinian and Theodora and the people they cared about as enthralling as I have and that it is as enriching for you as it has been for me.

Best wishes,
Daniel Cirignani
4 March 2018
Ahwatukee, Arizona

Acknowledgements

In writing this book I was fortunate to have as a friend Gail Wade—just the person capable of navigating the narrow line between subjective critique and friendly demure that marks the constructive feedback an author needs from his editor, and to boot: a fellow well versed and practiced with fiction, language and always ready to push towards the 4-minute mile of creativity.

I am profoundly appreciative of my translators, Paola Hernández and Marion Bilger, who have been both reliable and patient through the process of bringing part 1 of Serinda to launch.

I regard it as a special fortune that this project led to a crossing of paths with Leonor Lavado—whose care, labor and dedication is in self-evidence in the remarkable quality of the Spanish audiobook.

I am thankful to my son who set aside time and was patient while his dad learned his way through some of the more modern technologies for media and production. Special thanks too are called for, for my niece, Nikki Cirignani for her superb work with the cover and other art which stands on its own bringing Anastasia to life.

Lastly I would like to thank everyone who was supportive at any time during the ups and downs on the way to Serinda including those who "kicked me in the ..." along the way—Joseph Perry, Tyler Gentry, Andy Krals, Jeff Barth, R.J. Ramirez, Piero Fioravanti, Kent Bertrand, Tom Leegstra, Kim Gomez, Rick Boomer, Fred Graef, Kalpana Porwal, my brother John and sister-in-law Diane and my sisters Kristine and Jennifer, the latter who helped with some of the business challenges particular to bringing a French translation to market.

Contents

Foreword to the first edition of Serinda 10
Acknowledgements 12
Contents.. 13
Location of Maps.. 14
Conventions for Chinese Language in this Series.................... 15
Partial Cast – Book III.b, Part I 18
    Part I – Byzantium **22**

Chapter 1 The Hidden Agendas of Doors................................ 26
Chapter 2 A Solitary Light.. 32
Chapter 3 The Orphan Seamstress... 38
Chapter 4 Saturninus 49
Chapter 5 A Notary is Diverted to Hermonassa...................... 58
Chapter 6 A Battle Goes Badly in Lazica................................. 98
Chapter 7 Ambition of the Looms... 150
Chapter 8 The Storage Chamber 166
Chapter 9 The Balance Scales.. 175
Chapter 10 The Hànyǔ Interpreters of Dalmatou Monastery
.... 188
Chapter 11 The Visitors in the Apokrisiarikion...................... 206
Chapter 12 Balaneus Divina.. 224
Chapter 13 The Consistorium 249
Chapter 14 The Chrysobull of Propontis Tower.................... 309
    Appendices.. **325**

Time and Chronology As Justinian and Theodora Knew Them
.... 326
Glossary of Byzantine and Some Chinese Terms................... 330

Location of Maps

Psamathia Quarter in Byzantium.....................................39-40

The Disputed Region of Lazica...60

The Augustaion in Byzantium....................................228-229

Conventions for Chinese Language in this Series

Serinda is a fictionalized account of an early, historical cross-cultural encounter and the accompanying industrial espionage that transpired between the Greco-Roman, Byzantine Empire of Late Antiquity during the reign of Emperor Justinian and the Liang-Dynasty of the war-torn China of the same era. Serinda takes its name from the word the Byzantines used for China.

Sericum is the Latin word for silk and though use of Latin was already undergoing precipitous decline in Rome's eastern capital as it gave way to Greek, it remained the language of government. Contemporary maps of the era stretch as far east as India. Knowing little about what was beyond India except that the mysterious fiber silk originated there, Byzantines of the time combined Sericum with India and assigned to this unknown country the name Serinda—as if to say, "Silk India".

Serinda—China as sixth-century Byzantine Romans knew her, was a land beyond India, shrouded in mystery, from which originated the sublime silk—a treasure so valuable no law or prohibition could stop Justinian's subjects from paying fortunes to their enemies, the Persians, to acquire it. Actual court records that have been preserved, written by Justinian's secretary Procopius, inform us that at the behest of some monks who made his audience, Justinian commissioned a party to travel to China and retrieve the secret of the manufacture of silk—a mystery to Mediterranean people for as many as two-thousand years before his reign.

Procopius describes this land as "north" of India, and provided the extremely low acuity with which cartography was then understood we would be justified to make little of this, noting that China was more correctly east or northeast of India—but Procopius's determination may also be accounted for due to the flattened orientation of the best maps of the era where— by flattening an image of a spherical globe onto a 2-

dimensional surface, east-and-west was sometimes pressed into north-and-south, and vice versa.

The party Justinian commissioned did make it to China—and thereafter it returned to Byzantium with the secret of making silk—the silkworm! And her eggs! All of this is recounted for us by Procopius.

In relating a fictionalized narrative of the events of this amazing encounter it is necessary to make some account for China, the nation and its language, and this proves no easy task and became by itself a subject of some research to make this novel possible. Here follows a summary of findings as well as conventions adhered to throughout.

The language: Hànyǔ, Chinese – 汉语/漢語– isolating the exact language spoken by residents of Liang Dynasty southwestern China in the 6th century produces some significant challenges. The earliest written Chinese are bone inscriptions from the 13th century BCE and Chinese as written in this period through about the 2nd century BCE is broadly described as Old Chinese and the inscriptions that come to us from the 2nd century BCE to the 3rd century AD are regarded as belonging to the Classical Chinese period. The events of Serinda occurred during the Middle Chinese period which is generally described as about the 6th century until the 10th century AD, so these events fall during the earliest period of Middle Chinese, just prior to the publication of the Qieyum rime book in 601 AD which demarks an important anchor in our understanding of the historical development of the Chinese language. Besides time, however—China, then as now, was a vast geographic landmass beset by sophisticated ethnic, political and martial complexity and it is difficult to know today exactly how dialects and languages varied in use and adoption from one region to another. A peculiarity with Chinese is that the written language, being symbol-based, doesn't tell us much about differences in use and pronunciation from one region to another.

The visiting monks in Serinda hail from the Liang Dynasty of southwestern China which borders in the south with modern Vietnam. This milieu took place in the wake of the Eastern Han Chinese period—a sort of intermediate period around the 2nd century AD until the 6th century AD when Eastern Han Chinese is understood to have bridged the transition from Old Chinese to Middle Chinese. We are in debt to a scholar Yang Xiong (53 BCE – 18 AD) who at that time compiled a dictionary, the Fāngyán, (方言; literally meaning "regional speech") highlighting the dialectical differences between six regions of China. That is fitting because not only does the period of Eastern Han Chinese fall in the same time wake, but geographically the region is reasonably co-present with the holdings of Liang Dynasty China which occupied what is southwestern China today where the contemporary dialect is Southwestern Mandarin.

Another candidate for a term Serinda's Chinese monks may have referred to when describing their native tongue was putonghua, "common language", but because we presume their language to be particle to the concurrent spread and adoption of Hàn, we presume for the purpose of this book that the spoken language of Liang Dynasty China could be described as Hànyǔ – "Han language", though it may be that contemporaries and locals described their tongue with a different identity and we stand to be corrected if that is shown to be so.

For purposes of convention, for the remainder of the text, we will presume the use of Mandarin when describing Chinese people, places or things or when otherwise representing Chinese linguistic practice.

Partial Cast – Book III.b, Part I

Anastasia	An orphan and seamstress at Saturninus, 12 years old, 8- or 9- in memories and recollections—she is good with embroideries and the drawloom
Vesta	An Italian nun at Saturninus whose father, Priscian, a wealthy merchant, endowed to Saturninus some drawlooms, a recent entry to the textile industry of Byzantium, of whose use Vesta is an expert
Cyra	Hegumenia, the female head of a monastery or nunnery, who is also something of a businesswoman
Cyril Fuller	A merchant of moderate wealth in Byzantium and a trader in textiles
Alexander	A young monk at Dalmatou, son of Nestorian Christians, his mother Persian and his father Syrian, he is quadri-lingual, received a Persian education at Nisibis and is loaned out to the eparch as a mitotes—a regulator responsible for quality, weights and measures
Simeon	A boullotes installed under the Eparch by Theodora to whom Alexander reports – a corrupt miaphysite bureaucrat in the service of Peter Barsymes
Didyma	Nun, at Saturninus; key holder and courtier for Cyra
Thaddeus	Mentioned—the archimandrite of Dalmatou
Joseph Nios	Oikonomos (something like an accountant) of Dalmatou

Clement	Minor character – a fellow monk with Alexander – educated, sits at the sigmata; he is from Italy
Phillip	A diakonetai at Dalmatou—an illiterate monk tasked with manual labor
Callinicus	Cubicularius to Emperor Justinian and *praepositus sacri cubiculi*, the highest-ranking eunuch in the emperor's service and a member of the Consistorium
Stilicho	Scholae palitinae and attendant to Callinicus
Peter Patricus	Magister Officiorum in Justinian's Consistorium—supervisor of foreign affairs, custodian for ambassadors received in Byzantium from foreign states, responsible for translators and interpreters, diplomatic missions and the "Bureau of Barbarians"—role is akin to a modern Secretary of State or Minister of Foreign Affairs
Peter Barsymes	Comes sacrarum largitionum, Count of the Sacred Larges, in Justinian's Consistorium—in modern terms: the Minister of the Public Treasury
Flavius Arabissos	Armenian notary assigned to support administration in the war in Lazica
General Bessas	General reassigned from Italy to Lazica
John Guzes	Tagma commander sent to quell a revolt in Apsilia
Terdetes	Traitorous Lazican chieftain of Apsilia
Vistahm	Persian vizier and ambassador at Apsilia
Euphrates	Eunuch presented by Terdetes to John Guzes as a gift to Justinian to show rapprochement
Natan and Rava	Jewish tanners from Byzantium who maintain a shop outside Hermonassa

Dudai	Natan and Rava's father who stayed behind in Byzantium
Loris	A cousin of Arabissos who survived the plague
Arsaces	Armenian general and tagma commander; a former conspirator in a plot to murder Justinian who, in the aftermath, received Justinian's forgiveness
Paphos	A trumpeter in Arabissos' tagma
Orbicius	Veteran soldier in the Lazica campaign serving in Arabissos' tagma, a confidant of Arabissos
Rufus	An officer in Arabissos' tagma
Lao Yi	Elder Chinese Taoist monk ambassador
Hui-Shen	Younger Chinese Taoist monk ambassador
Justinian	Emperor of Byzantium
Sophia	Daughter of Comito, Theodora's older sister, and General Sittas, her husband
Antonina	Long-time friend and survivor of Theodora, feared everywhere by almost everyone

Serinda

Part I – Byzantium

551 AD The 196th Year of the Twelfth (Byzantine) Era

Byzantium as depicted in the Tabula Peutingeriana – a copy of a 410 AD map of the Roman Cursus Publicus (Latin: "the public way"; Greek: δημόσιος δρόμος) which depicted the entire known world and the Roman road-system that connected it from Britain to northwest India and Ceylon as these extreme locations were understood in the Greco-Roman world; Eratosthenes of Cyrene, the chief librarian in the School / Library of Alexandria (d.194 BCE) had used trigonometric computation based on the sun's angle of elevation to accurately compute the circumference of the earth to 252,000 stadia—40,074 km, within 66 km of the estimates of the most modern technology, so it was generally known in antiquity that the earth was a sphere—nevertheless the ancients had not developed means to express their geographical knowledge topologically so the Tabula Peutingeriana expresses the earth in a flattened manner that often presents north-south orientations (such as the Italian peninsula) as though they were east-west.

(Opposite page)

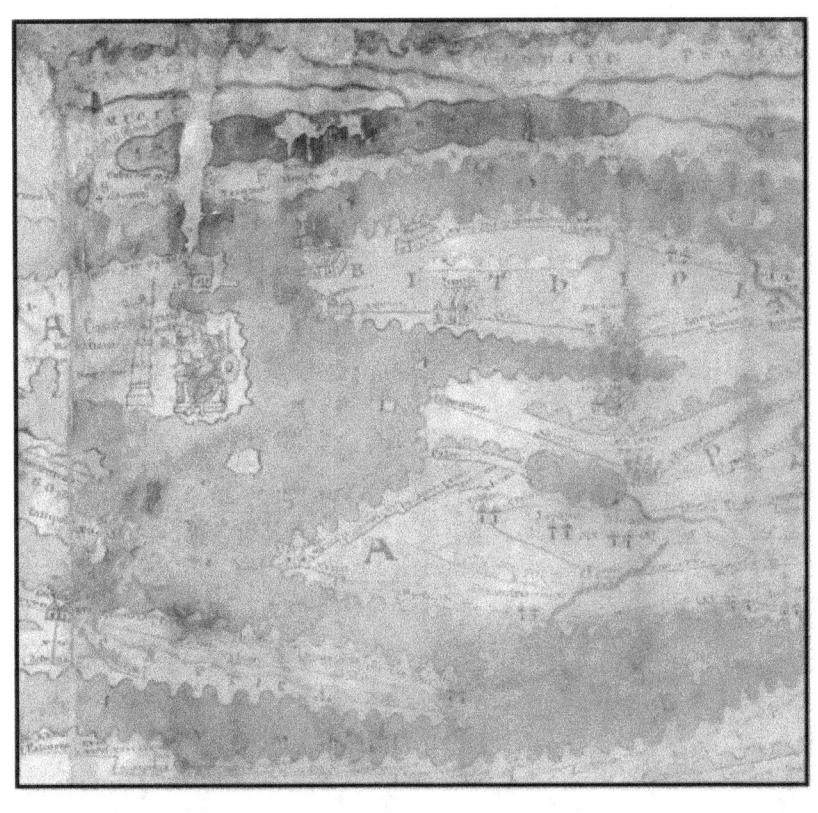

Approximate location of Byzantium on the Tabula Rogeriana – a map commissioned by Roger II, the Norman king of Sicily, to the Arab geographer Muhammad al-Idrisi, in 1138 – in its original form north is south, so this image inverts the map to make it recognizable to modern cartographic intuitions; the copious writings of Cosmas Indicopleustes attest that the Byzantine sense of geographical space was improving over the late Roman times of the Tabula Peutingeriana though it is improbable Byzantine cartographers had arrived at the level of sophistication expressed in the remarkable al-Idrisi map.

At about this time certain monks, coming from India and learning that the Emperor Justinian entertained the desire that the Romans should no longer purchase their silk from the Persians, came before the emperor and promised so to settle the silk question that the Romans would no longer purchase this article from their enemies, the Persians, nor indeed from any other nation;

for they had, they said, spent a long time in the country situated north of the numerous nations of India—a country called Serinda— and there they had learned accurately by what means it was possible for silk to be produced in the land of the Romans.

Procopius of Caesarea
History of the Wars
Book VIII, Chapter XVII

Chapter 1
The Hidden Agendas of Doors

But as the mind progresses and through ever greater
and more perfect diligence comes to apprehend reality...it sees
more clearly what of the divine nature is uncontemplated.
For leaving behind everything that is observed, not
only what sense comprehends but also what the intelligence
thinks it sees, it keeps on penetrating deeper until...it gains
access to the invisible and the incomprehensible

Gregory of Nyssa
Life of Moses

There were doors everywhere at Dalmatou Monastery.

Most of the time they were closed

That is to say there were doors everywhere one could
find oneself lingering about the grounds or participating in the
order, and everywhere one could look, and yet almost every
door was closed almost all of the time.

Mundane people, we share a mundane plane and we
take for granted that doors and the placement of doors "makes
sense." Indeed, we find as a rule that doors can be relied upon
for this, and they "make sense" so often that it is required that
from time to time a door must be placed just such that it
"makes no sense," so as to shake us from our complacency that
we may be reminded that all along, we assumed quite
improperly that it is something put upon doors to satisfy our
expectations by being present when we think they should be,
absent when we do not expect them, open when we need, and
closed when we require.

But doors are not ordained to respect human expectations. There are no terms written in the Platonic contract between doors and men that stipulate that they situate themselves only in places that abide our rules and the order, laws and designs, those of the gross material plane Providence decrees we – both doors and men - temporarily inhabit together. Doors—like beauty, numbers, and virtues—are not material things; and doors, like beauty, numbers and virtues, invade our material universe and operate according to the intentions of their own designs. Doors arise, exposing behind them secrets and vistas, treasures and dangers, according to a reason that exceeds our limited dimensions. The only thing separating us from our own fate is a choice:

> *Open the door,*
> > *pass through*
> > > *and find one's Fate with Providence*
> > *or pass by*
> > > *and leave destiny undisturbed*

Much has been written and much more has been said of the preternatural visitations of angels—those celestial messengers of the Divine and the Logos—sent to interrupt the affairs of the living with words of prophetic insight. But, angelic beings operate in unexpected ways, and it is the occasional door in the occasional place where no door should properly be, through which is sometimes conveyed a message—indeed behind which may lie destiny itself, a fate available for the one who is paying attention.

Let us consider the ways of doors so that we might divine at their intent when they sometimes deviate from expectation.

The front of a home or building should have a door into which one can make entry. The back of the same should have a door out of which occupants may access a yard or other expanse. To the sides of buildings we normally do not place doors. There, windows or enclosed walls are preferred, but every so often a door may be required to access a basement or attic or in some buildings as a means of overflow or urgent exit, or to access a patio, but even such doors, to human expectation, make sense. Doors belong in places where we have something to keep and in others where we seclude one mode from another:

> An area to work
> > An area to recline
> > > An area to visit
> > > > An area to enjoy views and
> > > vistas
> > An area to rest

Behind doors, we keep things we wish to hide, sometimes because we wish to save them for another time, other times because we wish to save them for other people, and often too because they are needed to preserve things we cannot destroy or let go, but which we cannot yet directly face and therefore must keep safely behind a door until the appointed time.

Recognizing all of this, in Dalmatou Monastery the placement of doors from any distance would strike a viewer as most odd. Dalmatou was nothing if not large, and there was plenty of space for all the activities to unfold in the areas that were not enclosed by perennially shut doors. That there were so many doors and that they were so seldom opened was enough that anyone who bothered to think long about it should have deduced that so many closed doors decidedly did not make sense, *unless* there were hidden places strewn about the monastery.

But how odd—to conceal a hidden place behind a door in plain sight.

Perhaps we are given to think that clocks and the division of time is a matter that is relatively new and characteristic of cosmopolitan modernity. If so, we are quite mistaken. Clocks, like doors, were never ordained to the service of men and so were not content to abide the lumbering progress of mankind's science. It was not centuries, but millennia before mechanical clocks made their debut in Western Europe around the time of the Renaissance that they imposed themselves onto the human world to lay their agendas into action.

From earliest antiquity the aqueduct builders of the Mediterranean and the underground qanat builders of Persia devised water clocks that were reliable, sophisticated, and widespread. From the coasts of Spain and Algeria, across the Mediterranean's seaside cities, through the Levant and Persia, and all the way to India and throughout China sophisticated people devised sophisticated ways to cut and divide, order and outline the passage of time.

They did not do this because of the genius of Swiss clockmakers or the inventiveness of western pioneers. Even water clocks were not the inventions of men. Eons before erudite observers first arranged two water basins so that one rose above the other, rhythmically dripping water through a hole carved in the top basin to fill the bottom, until empty, dew dripped from leaves and water from rocks, marking the moments and then the hours of morning passing to noon—all the while the moon cycled round the earth and the earth round the sun and the zodiac across the night's sky. None did so on account of the agency of men—no. They did this because the Logos required it, for clocks abide Time itself, they do not abide the timelines of men.

The circumscribed lives of the monks who lived in Dalmatou, as well as the nuns and orphans in the adjacent buildings of Saturninus, followed an order that functioned on a clock with hourly cycles within daily cycles within weekly cycles within seasonal cycles and repeated themselves throughout the liturgical year.

The effect of this was that most everyone knew where they should be, when they should be there, who they should be there with, and what it was they should be doing. Aligning oneself and one's activities with the order always entailed going to this door or that, and usually most people were so busy keeping their time and place in the rule of the monastery that it was remarkably rare that anyone might question that this or that odd door was never seen open.

When we divine the intent of a door, it pays to bear in mind that the same things may lie behind insensible doors as are often found behind sensible ones because doors' purposes are uniform, while their intent is inchoate.

As with sensible doors, behind insensible ones we find objects we wish to preserve or use at another time, places where one mode is secluded from another, secrets we sometimes wish to hide, and matters, sometimes dark, which we are not yet ready to face. The difference between that which is kept behind a sensible door versus one which is insensible is not the substance of the article or space so concealed; the difference is the purpose.

The Teleos of the Door

And Teleos belongs to the Nous, the Divine Intellect.

Doors, following their own agenda. That which makes no sense from the mundane standpoint of human reason may be, when viewed from the standpoint of eternity, essential.

When three dimensions and chronological time—limited by finitude and materiality—fail to order themselves according to intentions of providential purpose, a door is so often found in an unexpected place, a place that makes no sense whatsoever, and that door acts as a portal to possibility.

A sage may have had in mind clocks and doors when he disclosed this to his followers:

We must not argue from earthly frames to those of the celestial system whose sustaining soul is not the same, whose space is not the same, whose conditions are not those which make restoration necessary in this realm of composite bodies, which are always in flux*

Under reason known only to the Cosmos itself, the man or woman, boy or girl, who deigns to pass through an insensible door, a door with no proper reason to be present, but which offers itself to be entered, has matured of earthly life and passes ahead of the rest of us, to destiny.

---

* Plotinus, Neoplatonic philosopher, d. 270 AD; *Second Ennead*, First Tractate, Chapter 8

Chapter 2
A Solitary Light

Psamathia Quarter
Byzantium

Tuesday evening
Trite, "Third Day", by Byzantine reckoning
Well past apodeipnon, the hour after sundown
Later in the first watch

28 March 551 AD
Julian Calendar

A service door straddled the unmarked line that separated Dalmatou from her sister institution, Saturninus, which was distinguished from every other door primarily for being undistinguished in every way except one: *Its hinges were placed opposite those of every other door on the east face of the building.*

This door shared the east face with several others, and some of these were open from time to time, often enough open and often enough closed that the periodicity of their opening and closure made it all the easier to never notice that this oppositely-oriented service door was hardly ever opened all the way—rather most of the time it was cracked open just a bit as if to let in a draft but keep out daylight and any curious solicitors, and in this respect it had the unusual quality of being open, but only partially so, most days – even on days when other doors were closed.

Anastasia had at times seen the monks working inside one set of open doors in what was clearly a workshop, although she could not be sure what they were doing, and it was not permitted for her to approach them and ask. Certainly, it did not look like anything secretive, and if she had to guess her guess would have been that the monks working on this side of the building were tailors busy making and repairing shoes. Another door, she was quite sure, opened to a descending staircase and a storeroom for their wares, which was also entirely unsurprising as everyone was aware that there was a basement for such things.

It was this straddling door that had fixed her curiosity, but she rarely saw anybody move into or out of it, and there were no cycles or hours in the order that caused any of the resident monks, nuns, or orphans to go in or out from it. Obviously, someone kept to an hour and would pry it open and then close it again at some appointed time, but she never saw whoever it was who did this.

Once when she was eight years old, she snuck by and peaked inside, and what she saw mostly disappointed her. It seemed that the mysterious door opened to a wall.

The door began to preoccupy her and the mystery of it became a fixation. Her thoughts and even her dreams were haunted by questions, *why would any door open to a wall? If it just opens to another wall, why does anyone bother to open the door at all, let alone every day?*

Half the time she guessed many of the doors throughout the complex probably opened to walls, but people just left those doors closed. This door was odd. Someone kept cracking it open—just a little—almost every day. Her obsessive thoughts about the door at times became cynical and precocious.

Did the wall need a lone beam of sunlight to read by?
Perhaps its bricks were complaining of cold?

*Why the meticulous care to open and close the door
every day for sake of a wall?*

Her curiosity piqued, she decided to explore. Exploring strange doors at the monastery was oddly more possible for a diminutive orphan child than for any of the adults who resided there. The irony of this was that opportunities to peak behind closed doors presented themselves to her, and on account of this she seemed prone to get in trouble.

She did not really know why she got in trouble so often, but when she did she was sent outside where she was expected to sit on a portico which faced north towards the Mese. The older nuns who punished her would occasionally conspire to amplify the punishment by making her sit there for a long time, but they did not seem to think about the fact that this meant no one could watch her unless it was their intent to join with her in punishment.

By way of these lengthy and sometimes frequent expulsions, it became easier for her to sense the timing and cadence of when she might be checked in upon. She began to take to slipping off and finding her way in and out of the less explored corners of Dalmatou. While it was true that she was forbidden to approach the monks or speak with them, she learned soon enough that the monks themselves were usually so occupied with either their work or the order of the monastery that they could not really be troubled to question why an eight or nine-year-old girl might be roaming about. In fact, she came to suspect that her appearances and visitations were quietly welcomed by the more gregarious brothers as not unpleasant disruptions of an otherwise predictable monotony.

So it was no surprise that during one of her punishments she sated her curiosity about the open straddling door and moved down the portico to walk up to the edge of the east face of the building past the door that opened to the basement. From there, she slipped into the interior between the open straddling door and its oblique wall.

That is when she discovered what the door really served to conceal—a narrow hallway.

It was so narrow that she did not think many adults could fit through it unless they turned their bodies sideways and walked forward while facing the wall itself. Still a child, the matter was nothing for her; she was able to slip right in. When she did, she saw that while very little light came in from the open door to the hallway—where it was mostly caught in a circular pocket large enough for an adult—the space was nevertheless well lit by oil lamps that hung above, separated from one another by about six paces each. This could only become clear to someone outside, however, if they entered the door entirely while still leaving it cracked open only a bit to keep out the exterior light which could only illuminate the pocket, because their eyes, adjusted to the sunlight outside, would otherwise not perceive the clear but dim lights of the lamps which led ... somewhere. Until now, as she had only seen the door open by day when the sun was out, she could never have noticed the gentler lamplight that illuminated the narrow hallway.

Following the length of the hallway she found that it terminated at a narrow, circular staircase. When she ascended the staircase it rose to a balcony rail that she was able to walk along until it closed into a narrow air shaft. She deduced that its purpose was to ventilate the inner areas of both Dalmatou and Saturninus. She began to get a sense of what the architects had in mind here. At some level of awareness she had long perceived that air in the monastery moved from east to west. It was apparent now that this was by design since the placement of the door on the east wall set it in the direction of the Propontis where regular ocean air currents were reliable. The cool, salty wind would be caught by the divot of the partially-opened door, enter the building through the hallway, and from there it was forced into a narrower airshaft which created pressure so that it could ventilate the building. The pressure, she guessed, compelled air to move from the east to the west. It also served to make sense of why the door was propped open so often and it settled the mystery of why it was oriented on its hinges in the opposite direction of the othes—the door itself served as a wind-catch, redirecting wind from the hallway and into the air shaft.

Slinking her way through the shaft she was able for the first time in her life to orient herself to the opposite point of view of the air vents, which had from time to time comforted her when she was in the stuffy living space on the other side.

The access to the air vents also made it possible for her to listen in on conversations that she never otherwise would have been able to hear. Most of the time she did not understand the conversations, but it was clear to her often enough that some of those she listened in on were not expecting to be heard, least of all by a furtive eight- or nine-year-old girl concealing herself in a nearby ventilation shaft.

A tower rose above Dalmatou adjacent to this east-facing wall where Anastasia had seen the monks' workshop. While it was inferior to the much larger dome that was more centrally located over the building, the dome was oriented north towards the Mese relative to the tower which itself was oriented both east and south. For this reason the dome did not block a view of the Propontis for anyone in the top of the tower. The tower itself was part of the monastery, so neither Anastasia as an orphan nor any of the nuns who watched over her could have had ordinary access to it.

Exploring the air vent, Anastasia discovered that it opened to a small storeroom that was placed part way up the tower. A staircase passed through the storeroom, and Anastasia discovered that by climbing it she could make her way to the top. It was by this means that she was able to enjoy a beautiful view of the seawalls of Byzantium that separated

Psamathia from the ocean, as well as the ocean itself and all the ships that would sail to and from the city's many harbors.

Anastasia was twelve now and she had discovered all of these mysteries about the eastern service door years ago. She had grown since then, but she was still able to fit through the air vent. It so happened that this evening before bed she had made Vesta angry and was banished outside to the portico where apparently Vesta expected her to sleep overnight. She was almost ready to do it, to lie down on a bench and try to make a pillow with her hands, when she saw a flickering light illuminate corner of the building. She realized that this must be from the hallway lamps, until then concealed by daylight, which lay behind the peculiar door that opened to a wall.

She decided she would not sleep outside this evening and let the light beckon her to find her way to the top of the tower where she was sure she would find nobody. Perhaps to protect themselves from the sometimes-cold winds that would enter the tower at night, the monks kept thick linens in storage up there in chests. She could fashion a small bed for herself and sleep indoors, with a view to the orange flickering glow of the nighttime metropolis of Byzantium. Tonight, she decided, she would sleep in the tower, she could return to the portico when the sun reliably woke her with its rise—Vesta would never know.

Chapter 3
The Orphan Seamstress

The manufacturers of silk and garments had for many generations been a stable industry of Beirut (Berytus) and Tyre, two cities of Phoenicia. The merchants who handled these and the craftsmen and artisans who produce them had lived there from time immemorial, and their wares were carried from there into every land.

Procopius of Caesarea
The Secret History

Saturninus Nunnery and Orphanage
Psamathia Quarter
Byzantium

One Day Earlier
Monday, Deutera, "Second Day" by Byzantine reckoning
Trite Hora, "Third Hour"—Midmorning

27 March 551 AD
Julian Calendar

Anastasia was established on a loom inside the antechamber of the nunnery's trapeze, the latter of which doubled as a day chamber where the convent's nuns as well as orphans such as herself conducted manual labor. While she worked weaving linen thread through the loom her thoughts strayed to the peculiar name of the nunnery: Saturninus. It was a curious name for its ability to conjure images of a Roman, pagan deity which did not at all seem appropriate for a nunnery. In years past, it had never occurred to her to be troubled by these things, but of late—since her twelfth birthday—questions like this posed themselves more and more.

Dalmatou Monastery, to which Saturninus was attached, was also not named for a Christian saint as was custom. In fact, it was not even named for its own location, which was more generally called Constantinople at the time St. Isaac had founded it shortly after Emperor Constantine moved the capital there from Rome two hundred years ago. Instead, the monastery's name brought to mind the Dalmatian coast facing the Adriatic Sea and Italy.

Image on following page

Psamathia quarter of Byzantium

Southern branch of
the Mese

Psamathia

Sea of Marmara

The Mese

Golden Horn

Bosphorus

N

Rasophore[+] Vesta was from Italy, and as long as Anastasia had known her, Vesta had always been mean to her. Anastasia did not really question it much as she simply understood that this is the way things must be. She had never been far beyond Saturninus. In fact, the Psamathia quarter in which it was located represented most of what Anastasia knew of the outside world. The Dalmatian shores of the Adriatic Sea did conjure to mind visions of high waves crashing against tall rocks under blue, cloudy skies, which Anastasia took to be a much grander version of the same spectacle as the Propontis outside the seawalls of Byzantium that she had seen once when she had the privilege to accompany Saturninus's hegumenia (the head of the monastery), Cyra, to meet linen merchants, the othoniopratai.

Othoniopratai brought their wares down from the Black Sea to Byzantium from Kerasous or sometimes north from Dacia, but most often up from Strymon in Macedonia. Linen fiber from Dacia and Kerasous was the best, but with restive and unpacified barbarians in the north and the Persian war in the east, they were the least reliable and most expensive. Most of the time the orphanage would make do with linen from Strymon.

The tower of Dalmatau was high enough to see south to the Propontis, but Saturninus was positioned on a northerly slope facing away from Dalmatau towards the Mese at the base of a lower slope of Seventh Hill, which curved back up again for a final rise. At the top, Dalmatau stood over the remaining drop to sea level where it was possible to view the water and remind its residents of its founder's beloved

---

[+] **Rasophore** (Greek: ρασοφόρος), title given to an eastern orthodox nun, in the modern era of the lowest rank, but less stringently so in antiquity—the name is derived from a napless woolen cloth garment out of which developed the cassock—the title is used in a similar fashion to "sister" in Latin / western monastic convent traditions

Dalmatia—the reason for its unusual name. Anastasia relied more strongly on her memory of the harbor to guide her dye and embroidery than the more ambient, ever-present, and nearby Propontis.

Othoniopratai routinely sold their wares to a vestioprates such as Cyra and Saturninus whose charter ordered the nunnery and orphanage to support Dalmatou and its monks, a mission it rose to by processing raw linens to produce clothing and other textile products that were distributed to the city's population. Anastasia knew that Cyra harbored ambitions to have Saturninus recognized as a serikoprates—a merchant of fine, processed silk textiles, but these lofty ambitions were tempered by two uncooperative realities. For one, monastics were not supposed to have ambitions and were expected to remain content with whatever was the station to which Providence had them preordained. For another, the eparch, the capital city's governor, who at least in the city was second only to the emperor, forbade merchants from holding both designations of vestioprates and serikoprates at the same time. No one had written the rule book on how one bridged the distance between vestio- and seriko-, but unless one began as a wealthy merchant from the steppe, the only means of entrance to the linen enterprises was to establish oneself first as a vestioprates, learn the ropes, and make connections from there.

To get around these obstacles the hegumenia, Cyra, was always careful to transfer and distribute credit for her ambitions to the humble nunnery and the monastery whose prayerful work was supported by their enterprise—an approach which embodied the dual virtues of removal of her own ego and others' suspicions about said ego from the agency of ambitious action. It was improbable the highly ranked masters of Dalmatou would fault such a plan when adequately deficient of ego, and it even created an opportunity for the civil authorities to favor or disfavor the church. While a short-term advantage was occasionally to be had by such officials in delaying the realization of ecclesiastical objectives, in the long run their success was always a reliable bet. In this regard, as to the enforcement of linen regulations, Saturninus had to its advantage that the mitotes of the eparch responsible for inspecting the quality of linen in Psamathia just so happened to be a monk by the name of Alexander who resided next door in Dalmatou.

Anastasia drew on her memory of the Propontis and its waves beating against the city's walls outside the Harbor of Julian. She tried to expand the vision in her imagination as she worked the weights on her drawloom—the only drawloom in Psamathia—and the principle reason Cyra had for hoping that Saturninus would be promoted to a serikoprates. She was too young to remember that not long ago – quite inside the living memory of most adults - there had been no drawlooms. The drawloom made its first appearance in Byzantium no more than fifty years earlier, which seemed like a long time, so one would expect there would be more of them, but the device was complicated, bulky, and expensive.

Furthermore, a factor that prevented them from catching on despite its extraordinary utility was that most of the older nuns did not want to touch one!

They preferred to work with the traditional style of warp-weighted looms. Anastasia understood that the warp-weighted loom was truly an ancient artifact. She had seen frescoes, cast in pagan times, that depicted women working with such looms and she was told by her elders that those women of old had plied their trade long before Sparta, Athens, Thebes, and other Grecian city-states bound together to turn back a Persian invasion more than a thousand years earlier. Cyra once told Anastasia that legend held that the warp-weighted loom had been introduced to Greek society many thousands of years before by the ancient seafaring people of Crete who had sailed deep up the Danube River, far to the north where they acquired the loom from an unknown people in a mountainous land called the Alpes.

With warp-weighted looms, a seamstress had to weave fabric from the top of the loom thread by thread and line by line to the bottom, walking back and forth and managing warp threads in bundles that were tied to hanging weights that held the thread taut. When the seamstress would reach the bottom of the available warp, she would lift the completed section of the linen back over the top of the beam and then unwind warp threads from the weights. The principle was straightforward, but weaving patterns with such a loom represented a challenge because identical patterns had to be woven separately of one another so rarely were two linen's patterns exactly alike, even when uniformity was the seamstresses' intent.

Not helping matters for Cyra was the fact that the older nuns seemed possessed of bottomless reservoirs of energy to defend the warp-weighted loom's ancient honor. This was unfortunate because the drawloom, at least to Anastasia's reckoning, was a significant improvement that made it possible to weave complex patterns that might have taken forever to complete if the warp-weighted loom was a seamstress' lone tool. The drawloom is composed of two sets of shafts called harnesses. A bridge is set on top of a floor loom and an extension is placed at the back, which creates depth where a seamstress could operate with her weave. A second harness of pattern shafts is set inside the loom behind the first harness. The second harness made it possible to mechanically repeat a pattern after the first press of the pattern had been completed.

The pattern Anastasia was working on was for a grand banquet tablecloth to decorate the home in Third Hill for a merchant, Cyril Fuller, who had commissioned the weave to Saturninus. A talkative man, Anastasia had overheard him many times chatting away with the hegumenia carrying on at length about his travels to distant lands. More than once,

Anastasia's ears perked up when she heard Cyril invite Cyra to his home for an occasion with guests. The rules governing social interaction between nuns and other monastics with all the varieties of people—rules specific to every possibility of gender, class and rank—were complex, and Anastasia did not kid herself into thinking that she knew them all. Still, she felt quite certain that Cyril was crossing, or at least testing, some definite social line to invite the head mistress of a convent to a social occasion in his own home. Indeed, most of the time when she observed men and women conduct commercial transactions with one another, such as when Cyra had her along to the Neorion, a mercantile market at the Harbor of Julian, there were usually eunuchs on hand who would oversee and sometimes assist in the administration of customs.

There was no eunuch in the convent though, and when merchants came here to do business they dealt directly with hegumenia Cyra. Cyra tolerated the many ways Cyril seemed to push the boundaries of the appropriate. It could just be that he brought a lot of business to the convent, either himself or by way of others whose weaving and textile needs he would send their way—good business after all kept buildings maintained and food on the table and so was a quality all its own. Then again too, Anastasia was not sure, but she had a sense that Cyril's antics really were not altogether unwelcome by Cyra. They added some color to life and Cyra always appeared to be in better cheer on days when Cyril paid visits.

Knowing what she knew about Cyril, Anastasia imagined the tablecloth in his home adorning a grand banquet table in a great dining room. He had asked for a pattern of waves crashing against tall rocks on a long shoreline with a lone double-masted merchant ship battling the sea's foul temper. It was not hard to picture Cyril entertaining guests and regaling them with stories of his adventures in far-off lands; Anastasia's tablecloth would serve as an ideal prop.

She continued making adjustments to the drawloom, passing new yarn through the eye of a heddle, then lowering it. She added more weight to the second harness, tightened two cords, loosened a third, and was about to make a final adjustment to the bridge when she was startled by a yell.

"You're doing it wrong!"

It was Vesta. This came as no surprise. The older nuns all preferred their warp-weighted looms, and on this matter Anastasia's youth seemed to count to her as a blessing. Anastasia had never got used to weaving with the old, warp-weighted looms, and as early as she could remember ever beginning with the crafts of spinning and weaving, her work had almost always been done with a drawloom—this very one.

Weaving with a drawloom required a partner, but the operations of the weave could become so mechanical that it was sometimes easy to forget that it was a person and not a device that operated to one's opposite, a fact for which Anastasia was grateful because Vesta was her partner. Not only that, Cyra had acquired the drawloom from a Persian merchant in the years before the plague, when the Romans and Persians were still at peace. It may even be that—despite all its utility—one reason why the drawloom still had not really caught on among the extensive textile community in Byzantium was that the long war made trade with the Persians a difficult matter.

Anastasia did not know much about Italy and anything else beyond the Adriatic, but she knew Rasophore Vesta, and she knew she did not like her. She did not really think it all the way through, but she had a sense that if she did not like Vesta and Vesta was from Italy, then she must not like Italy either. Italy was to the west. If she ever left this place, she sighed and breathed out softy, "let it be east."

Vesta was nine years older than Anastasia and she was a novitiate, not an orphan. They had been paired together for four or five years now and it was Vesta's erstwhile assignment to train Anastasia in the crafts of spinning and weaving with a drawloom. Given that enmity that had existed between the girls already when Vesta was sixteen and Anastasia just seven, it might have been an unusual pairing. So far five years of working together had done nothing that would make Anastasia think the match was auspiciously appointed. She imagined that for most children their earliest memories must be the kindness of a mother or father, or cheerfully playing with siblings and other playmates. For her, the earliest memories were of Vesta, and of Vesta being mean.

Vesta was the youngest daughter of an Italian silk merchant named Priscian. He was from the southern city of Taranto and did a lot of business with Antioch where he had access to unusual Persian goods just such as the drawloom. Vesta was his youngest daughter and custom usually required that fathers find suitable mates for their older daughters. Because Vesta had the misfortune of being the fifth daughter, Priscian had decided to reduce his burden by sending her off early to the convent. Anastasia and Vesta were not on such terms that she might have felt comfortable or even would have wanted to ask Vesta how she felt about her father's decision, but enmity or not Anastasia was possessed of sufficient empathy to suspect that Vesta was bitterly resentful of her father for consigning her to this fate.

It was common practice that when the wealthy gave sons or daughters up to the care of a monastery they would surrender too some kind of meaningful donation. Very often this was straightforward coin, but in Priscian's case, and despite his commercial success, he was running short of fluid currency on account that he had hosted lavish weddings for his two eldest daughters for he took to be to be merit-worthy, socially advantageous and status affirming matrimonial unions. With two daughters yet remaining to be married, even the wealthy Priscian had been short of hard currency.

In lieu of a monetary endowment it was often acceptable to provide the monastery with a gift in kind, especially if the gift held promise for its own commercial utility. It was by this means that convent Saturninus came to be the only monastic community in Psamathia to be endowed with the drawloom, and it was in the person of then fourteen-year-old Vesta that her father Priscian provided the necessary expertise to put it to its proper use and so it was ordained that the young orphan girl Anastasia would be trusted to an older tutor's care, a very mean older tutor, to become one of the first mistresses of the drawloom.

It was early aptitude Anastasia had shown between the ages of four and six that had caused her to stand out in Cyra's mind as one who held promise for embroidery, and Anastasia suspected that even these many years back a younger Cyra was already dreaming of a future with silk. It was by this set of coincidences that as early as Anastasia could be trusted to take needle to thread that Cyra, in her wisdom, paired the young six-year-old orphan girl to the tutelage of her sixteen-year-old senior—the young nun Vesta who would go on to teach Anastasia, while barely tolerating her existence. They had been together ever since, and so, for what must be the millionth time (Anastasia had long lost count), Vesta laid into her.

"Yeehuahgah!" The noise she made was both guttural and loud. "I don't know what you were thinking," snapped Vesta. "If you don't match the pulley cords to the necking cords, we can't repeat the pattern."

Chapter 4
Saturninus

During the reign of Justinian, those who lived in Byzantium and other cities raised the price of their silks, on the plea that at the present time they were dearer in Persia, and that the import tithes were higher. The Emperor pretended to be exceedingly indignant at this, and subsequently published an edict forbidding a pound of silk to be sold for more than eight gold pieces; anyone who disobeyed the edict was to be punished by the confiscation of his property. This measure appeared altogether impracticable and absurd. For it was not possible for the merchants, who had bought their wares at a much higher price, to sell it to customers at a lower rate. They accordingly resolved to give up this business, and secretly and without delay disposed of their remaining wares to certain well-known persons, who took delight in wasting their money upon such adornments, and to whom it had become in a manner an absolute necessity.

Procopius of Caesarea
The Secret History

Alexander stood with his back against a white mulberry tree in the colonnaded portico outside the business entrance to Saturninus. Like many other shops that lined the Mese and its nearby side streets, Saturninus had a service window, but unlike most establishments with such a feature Saturninus's window was more often uninhabited than not. But in the extraordinary taxis[*] of Byzantine society, even in an uninhabited service window served a purpose, and that was especially so when the shop in question happened to double as a convent.

Hegumenia Cyra was apparently busy with other matters, and under ordinary circumstances all the nunnery's business was transacted through her. Alexander imagined that in any shop that did more sales, Cyra, like most in her position, would be forced to delegate administration of every day transactions to this or that official as was the custom in most institutions about the city. Indeed, it would have been altogether customary for Cyra to appoint an oikonomos to manage the property, income, and expenses of Saturninus. But she kept the title to herself, along with that of hegumenia.

The products of Saturninus were most often sold in bulk and most often then either to civil or church authorities. In rare exceptions, they usually involved a premium, custom artifact chartered by a wealthy merchant. Alexander supposed the low volume of transactions contrasting with the significant bulk of the goods sold probably accounted for Cyra's ability to excel as both an executive of the nunnery at the same time as operational master of its finances. This arrangement, like Cyra's dual role as an accountant and executive, was unusual, and if Alexander thought much more about it, he expected it might trouble him; for the moment he could not quite articulate why. One way or another, the arrangement certainly had an effect.

In the first two centuries after Constantine moved the capital of Empire to Byzantium, the Psamathia quarter was home to any number of wealthy and aristocratic families. However, in recent decades, most houses of import had moved closer to First and Second Hill. Most streets, colonnades, and agoras north of the West Mese were built

---

[*] Taxis – Greek τάξις – "arrange" or, as a noun, taxis is an order – refers to the arrangements and ordering of society

about packed earth, but Saturninus stood atop marble pavement. Saturninus was above a four-step rise that led to a sheltered area behind an elaborate gate, arguably the most ostentatious feature of an otherwise appropriately humble nunnery.

The gate bore a highly worn inscription that would have been undecipherable to a newcomer, but Alexander knew it to read "Πύλη τοῦ Σατουρνίνου" (the Gate of Saturninus), named for the wealthy benefactor and devotee of Saint Isaac who had endowed Dalmatou. Beyond the gate in the sheltered area was a patio that enclosed the service window; two centrally opening, sliding wooden, batten doors of modest design; and a waiting bench, which though made of stone showed all the signs wear and tear—it got a lot of use. Clearly, much sitting had been done here. Alexander even detected an indentation where many a sandal's sole nervously pressed and turned away, creating a divot in the concrete. Many people it seems whiled away their time waiting on Cyra. Perhaps to ease the waiting customer's burden, an elaborate mosaic decorated the floor. Not surprisingly, the image featured St. Isaac, the founder of Dalmatou, who was surrounded by four corners with each corner depicting the symbols of the four evangelists: the winged man for Matthew, the winged lion for Mark, the winged ox for Luke, and the eagle for John.

The mosaic packed a lot of complexity for the either the erudite observer and student of religious art or the bored waiting customer who might watch the hours slip away in hopes of Cyra's quick return. Behind St. Isaac, stretching out to his left hand towards the winged man, seemed to be a line of shadows, each the silhouette of a man. Down his other side but also to the left was what seemed to be a bush or reeds that hid lion cubs at their base. Off to the saint's right but below his feet extending towards the winged ox was an altar. Finally, to his right and above were separating clouds exposing the sky and sunbeams passing between them. Alexander knew all this so well he could picture it in his mind even though he stood now on the street away from the patio with his back to the mulberry tree. That is just how long he had already spent waiting on earlier occasions.

He was well known to the nuns and orphans who lived and worked with them; he was on a first name basis with nearly all of them, but it would be quite inappropriate for a man to walk into the nunnery unescorted and to engage in un-chaperoned social contact with its female inhabitants no matter their personal familiarity. This was made more so, not less so, by the fact that he too was a monastic.

"No one can serve two masters?" Well, perhaps it was written somewhere, Alexander mused. The nunnery with its linen industry represented one form among many that the varieties of monastics had scoped out since the time of Saint Anthony so as to provide the coin necessary to the continuous operation of spiritual enterprise. Rural monasteries often engaged in agriculture and animal husbandry and some urban monasteries owned property with apartments and shops and supported themselves off rent charged to their occupants. But it was not at all unusual that younger sons of well to do families found themselves established in vocational contemplation of the divine and not always by way of their own election. Nevertheless, these monks tended to create a high concentration of literate and educated young men among the holy.

Alexander understood that just two centuries earlier opportunities for advanced education in the world that surrounded the Mediterranean were comparatively many. As recently as the reign of Zeno, there were no less than eight institutions of advanced education: Alexandria's ancient school and library of mathematics and astronomy, the Alexandrian Catechetical School of St. Clement, the ancient Academy of Athens, the Catechetical School of Antioch, the Library of Caesarea Maritima, the University of Constantinople, the School of Edessa (which his grandparents had attended but which was closed by Emperor Zeno due to its alignment with Nestorians), and a school he knew from personal familiarity as he had grown up nearby—the Law School of Berytus.

Surely there had been many extraordinary accomplishments during the reign of the present Emperor Justinian: Africa, Italy, and Hispania—lost to barbarians in the previous century, had all been returned to the order of the imperium. But, while all of the schools that closed had not closed under the hand of Justinian, it was nevertheless true that since Zeno and up to the present time six of the eight had closed their doors to aspiring students. Of these seven institutions that had served as the light of civilization during a time when traditions that man had kept for thousands of years were slipping beyond memory, only two schools remained to this day: Berytus and Constantinople. With the intense pressure of the nearby Persian war, Alexander had his doubts Berytus could remain open much longer. As for the University of Constantinople, Theodosius had endowed it well, and all emperors since— Justinian included—continued to support it. Given to his straying thoughts, Alexander wondered if it were possible that one institution alone could bear the weight of educating the entire world.

There were four options available to the aspiring scholar if Berytus or Constantinople did not work out. There were schools in Gondishapur, Ctesiphon, and Resaina, which were fine as long as a Greek or Latin could make himself transparent in the Sassanid Persian Empire—a tall order fraught with risk. If those did not appeal to him, there was also the option of studying at the School of Nisibis, which depending on the month of the year might be in Byzantine hands, or Persian. A student just had to survive the periodic overruns and shifts in power. Arguably, the first three were safer bets. It so happened that Alexander, son of a Syrian father and Persian mother, had made the latter proposition work out and had finished his studies in Nisibis.

Persian education was not exactly what one expected from a Greek education. The Greek tradition of education that stretched back to Pythagoras, Plato and Aristotle, was preserved in the Roman-Latin world and indulged in a peculiar process of engaging a tension between a high value placed on inquiry, in constant contraposition to an ancient, lingering suspicion of innovation. To Persians, even a thousand years later, Greeks were still newcomers and the Persians considered themselves the bearers of an older, Zoroastrian tradition that was said to stretch beyond dark ages of ancient times to the era of the Egyptian pharaohs and Persian teachers held innovation up to sharp critical review, while working tirelessly to consolidate, record and systematize knowledge from both the east and west.

The relatively uncritical placement of inquiry in Greek education was a quality that arguably is what made education so dangerous when it fell outside the administrative hands of the government or the church. The present authorities seemed to be in a process of bringing the precocious tendencies of educators under their liege. On this score, it might be the case that the very reason education still thrived in Persia was that the more heavily centralized Sassanids were a century or two ahead of the Romans and Byzantines when it came to controlling what happened when a pupil received an education.

When Justinian closed the School of Athens twenty-three years earlier (when Alexander was two years old), the philosophers and teachers there fled to Nisibis and took refuge under the protection of the Persian Emperor Chosroes. It seemed at first a good arrangement, but it did not hold together. The philosophers had returned to Byzantine lands long before Alexander began his studies there. As contested as Nisibis was, it would have been a hard place for many Greek or Latin students to survive. The increasing lack of tolerance for Nestorians had led thousands, like the Athenian philosophers, to flee east, and many had taken up in Nisibis;

there was a safety of sorts in numbers. Alexander did not sense that at Nisibis he had received an education in the spirit of inquiry that his father was wont to speak of, but it was an education which had imparted literacy, numeracy, and high culture—and that was something.

Either way he knew that with so many schools closed it was falling on the monasteries to carry an ever-increasing burden for the needs of education to serve the vast, cosmopolitan, Mediterranean world where industry and complexity required knowledge and knowledge remained in tight supply. This was not altogether a bad thing as monasteries had already become a concentration of the literate. When they could be distracted for a moment from thoughts of the divine and brought to tend to more material affairs, the provision of education was often a useful form of industry; it was offered as a valuable service to the sons of wealthy families. After receiving payment from such families for these increasingly scarce services, monasteries were in a unique position to return the newly educated labor of their student monks back to the grateful, paying services of government, military and commercial interests. A virtuous cycle!

The arrangement was not without problems though. It was a process that kept making more monks who were educated and more educated and who also happened to be monks.

This brought Alexander back to the problem of two masters: administration, records, accounting, taxation, archiving, and chronicling; the arbitration of disputes, the construction of ships, the maintenance of harbors, and every facet of civil engineering for two hundred cities with running water and two thousand more communities connected by paved roads. These are all matters that required the able hands and minds of armies of literate men and, often enough, literate women! If the state had a role in the demise of a millennia-old tradition of Greco-Roman advanced education, it seemed an unintended side-effect was to fix the state into unprecedented dependence on the church for almost every imaginable sort of knowledgeable labor.

If the kings or tyrants of old required strategic advice uncorrupted by the delusions of human ego, vice and ambition, they always had the oracles, and if they did not like what the oracles had to say it was easy enough to ignore them. Nowadays, if any city's curiae wanted to keep latrine sewage out of public cisterns they had better be on good terms with the bishop! Alexander's own elders in the monastery insisted that many of the teachers in Alexandria and Athens were dangerous and often times still pagan if not outright heretical—this was not an unproblematic stance from Christian leaders when these schools remained the premier centers for math, geometry, architecture and hydraulics.

Alexander regarded his masters' proscriptions on educators and education. Perhaps they're right, he thought, as who was he to question the scandal of heresy or the curses of the old pagan ways—but, he recollected, it had been said that the physicians and physicists of Alexandria had known a means of ridding buildings of miasmai by use of an aeolipileii[ς]—miasma[φ] was suspected by many to be the cause of the plague that had ravaged the entire world not ten years hence, a scourge that brought death to millions—but

---

[ς] **Aeolipile**, a bladeless, radial steam turbine engine described in the 1st century by Hero of Alexandria, and/or Vitruvius, a Roman architect and author of De Architectura; the word is derives from the Greek Αἴολος and Latin pila and translates as "ball of Aeolus", the latter being the god of air and wind

[φ] **Miasma**, a theory of epidemics which held that they were caused by "bad air", or miasma, also known as "night air"—though technically in error as physicians in antiquity did not know about bacteria or germ theory, it was nevertheless structurally accurate conception

Alexandria's teachers while vaguely tolerated had nevertheless been silenced. If suppressing these things had meant closing the schools that could teach mechanics to keep water clean and air free of plague, this was a high, worldly price to pay for the stability of empire and the safety of the soul.

For the moment, anyway, it all worked out, "As long as they close schools, they're going to need monks...could be worse." If Alexander was a monk in a rural monastery, he would likely be sweating in fields or fermenting hops. If the government had a better supply of secular regulatory officials, then he might have the unhappy duty of collecting rent from the tenants of properties of this urban monastery. Happily, when he was not tutoring young monks on the harmony of Aristotle and Plato or otherwise occupied in the important business of meditation and prayer, he was able to offer his services as a mitote on behalf of Dalmatou to the eparch of the city. It was in that capacity today that he found himself visiting his sisters at Saturninus and not in the status he held in common with them as a fellow monastic.

With no warning there was a sharp "smack"—Alexander was startled from his thoughts by the crash of a door being swung open and smashing against its own hinges.

"Alexander! Oh Alexander. Alexander, I am so sorry to have kept you waiting so long," it was Cyra.

Chapter 5
A Notary is Diverted to Hermonassa

...catapults should be used to hurl the so-called incendiary bombs ... hurl fire bombs and stones at them.

The Strategikon of Maurice
Written—6th Century, Byzantium
Suspected Author: Emperor Maurice
(r. 582 – 602 AD)

...the Medes nevertheless sustained severe losses, both in battle and owing to the difficulties of the country; for, as I have said already, Lazica is a country almost inaccessible, owing to its rocks and precipices.

Procopius of Caesarea
The Secret History

Over a month earlier
Suania, in north east Lazica

Somewhere outside Scanda
Behind Persian lines
Friday, *Paraskeve by* Byzantine reckoning

February, 551 AD
Julian Calendar

"I'm a notary," Flavius Arabissos mumbled under his breath; his thoughts carried on, *a god-damned notary! Who the hell needs a notary in Suania?* he asked himself rhetorically while feverishly piling dry dirt atop a bladder that oozed a layer of what looked to be a blackish tar at some of its seams. The air was moist, and in the heat of battle no one would recognize the pit for any more than a muddy jetty if he did his job right. It was important to keep it dry, so the trick was to create the appearance of mud, but avoid water. This was best achieved by a few strategically placed leaks in the bladder, followed by digging and dirt-piling, then flattening, stirring, and scrambling the dirt and dirt-tar mix with other rocky or plant surroundings as best as he could.

He was dirty and sweaty and, thankfully, almost done. He thrust the shovel into the dirt, took its handle by both hands, and leaned on it to help himself upright while catching his breath.

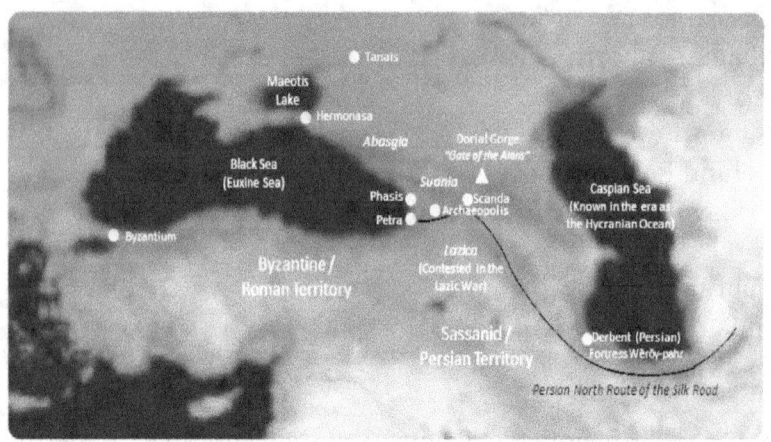

The disputed region of Lazica [++]

His Roman first name, that is his Roman birth name, was Flavius, but he was generally known here as Arabissos, the Greek name of the city in Cappadocia where he was born. A hundred years had passed since the legendary western general Flavius Aetius banded together a motley alliance of Alans, Burgundians, Saxons, Franks, and Visigoths—as well as the tattered remnants of the western Roman army—and, in a final, desperate punch, sent Attila the Hun and his noxious hordes packing at the Battle of Maurica in Gaul. To this day, proud, new parents from Hispania to Syria, from Egypt to Libya, still kept the tradition of naming their first sons for the general, an understandable sentiment that was not without complications. The tagma to which Arabissos had been attached suffered a characteristic problem that arose from this widespread affectation: a third of its members shared the same first name.

[++] The contested region of Lazica that was the center of exhaustive fighting between the Persian and Byzantine empires - in contrast to other contemporaneous wars in the fertile, populous regions of Italy, North Africa, Asia Minor, Syria and the Levant, Lazica was distinguished for being a cold, rocky, mountainous wasteland – but one with promise of a frontier northern route to the Silk Road that might break the Persian toll monopoly

The memory of Attila still burned. Many grandfathers and great-grandfathers claimed to have met the Huns in battle and lived to tell, so it was a kind of balm for the sting of the trauma the Huns inflicted for everyone to be reminded that the "last Roman," Flavius Aetius, could, and did, defeat them. Yet it came to be a paradox of sorts that the living legacy of Flavius Aetius surviving in the forename of a large fraction of the empire's men, served to raise all manner of aggravations, *especially* during battle.

Too many Flaviuses was confusing, particularly under fire. To remedy this, soldiers and auxiliaries such as Arabissos, who tended to hail from all over empire and yonder, took to calling one another by their town or city of birth. There was actually a kind of wager going among the troops that the first Flavius to distinguish himself in combat would be re-christened Maurice, in honor of the Battle of Maurica that gave rise to their common identity. Arabissos could not hope for this honor, however; he was a notary, not a soldier, and his role in the tagma was at best described as that of an auxiliary.

Born almost fourteen years earlier to an Armenian family in Cappadocia, Arabissos figured his mentors in Byzantium probably told themselves they were doing him a favor when General Bessas requested administrative support to supplement the baggage train of his expeditionary assault against the Persians after he replaced the prior *magister militum per Armeniam*, Dagisthaeus, a Goth who until then commanded the campaign against the Persians in Lazica. Such thinking was silly of course. What anyone believing him to be going "home" did not understand is that the Lazi, Lazica's locals, were *perhaps* cousins to the Armenians, but the latter, Arabissos thought, were hopelessly provincial people who had been cut off from surrounding communities as far back as anyone knew. This was never a case of sending him "home." No, it was sentencing him to hard time in the bush.

He considered this while reflecting on the fate of General Dagisthaeus. After some early successes at Phasis and the Hippis River, Dagisthaeus managed to lose the coastal fortress city of Petra to Persian control. Justinian rewarded him for this failure by sending him to fight the Ostrogoths in Italy. Arabissos had not completed his education, far from it, but he understood that the Goths who had settled in Asia Minor were not the same as the Ostrogoths who vexed Italy, but they were still Goths. *A Gothic general to lead Greek Romans in the war to eject the scourge of Ostrogothic occupation from formerly Latin Italy?*

He wondered how that worked.

Perhaps the relationship between Asia Minor's Goths and the Ostrogoths in Italy was like the Lazi and the Armenians? Cousins, but distant and often fighting cousins who were more knowledgeable in one another's ways but had no love to lose all the same? One thing was certain, after losing Petra, Dagisthaeus would be more welcome in Italy than anywhere among the Armenians, the Lazi or the poor Greek Roman soldiers Justinian had sent to fight in this godforsaken place.

Emperor Justinian replaced Dagisthaeus with General Bessas, who he recalled from Italy to finish the work Dagisthaeus started in Lazica and correct where he had erred. Bessas quelled the Abasgians well north of Petra on the other end of Suania from where Arabissos currently toiled, and thereafter laid siege to Petra and retook it.

While Dagisthaeus was uniformly despised by the soldiery, the Lazi and the Armenian auxiliaries alike, Bessas was originally seen as a controversial replacement. Arabissos' role as a notary put him in an unusual position of being a young man who enjoyed a peculiar proximity to the heights of military command, and this proximity brought with it some insight. Though it was true that Bessas was elderly—almost eighty, a truly shocking age for a field general who would normally be expected to be energetic—Arabissos noticed that Bessas seemed endowed with a strategic acumen, a maturity that, as far as this fourteen-year-old notary could tell, was two or three levels above his subordinate generals. Bessas had confided in him that while the army had taught him to fight, it was during his time serving under General Belisarius in Italy that he had learned to win wars and then so, to win wars when both underfunded and under supplied.

There was sense to this. When he first arrived in the Byzantine stronghold of Archaeopolis with strict instructions from Justinian to retake Petra, Bessas' lieutenant generals were appalled at the instructions he gave them to divert an expeditionary tagma to the rugged, exhausting, northern mountains of the Abagasians. Many even suspected that the reports of a local revolt were a ruse to justify the move and, as close as he was to command correspondence, Arabissos sensed these suspicions were not entirely unwarranted.

Shortly after Bessas' arrival in Archaeopolis, it was reported that a certain Lazi noble, Terdetes, made himself a traitor and handed the fortress of Tsibilium in Apsilia over to Mihr-Mihoe, the commander to whom the Persian Shahanshah Chosroes, the "shah of shahs," had entrusted with the war effort. Arabissos had seen this fortress with his own eyes, and it was a remarkable sight to behold. Even in Byzantium he had never seen anything like it before, and he expected he would never see anything like it again.

It stood atop two cliffs, each almost a staggering 1,300 feet above a deep river gorge below. If it hadn't been handed over to the enemy, it would have been impregnable except to the mightiest hosts of armies. Some dared wonder out loud what it even meant that Terdetes had handed the fortress to Mihr-Mihoe, when the latter's strongholds in the war around that time were on all of the most far-flung outposts on the opposite ends of Lazica from where the fortress was located: Scanda, Sarapanis and Petra. It was true Mihr-Mihoe kept some armies stationed in the various corners around Lazica, but their positions only served to make Terdetes's move more suspicious as none of them were anywhere near Apsilia. Militarily, giving the fortress to the Persians seemed to gain the Abagasians little, and accepting it seemed to profit the Persians even less.

Normally, a fourteen-year-old notary would not have much insight into these things, but Arabissos had seen it all up close and knew the skeptics were onto something with their doubts about Tsibilium.

It was sinking in with Arabissos that while everyone understood a massive army and a full frontal assault, precious few of Bessas' lieutenants and none of his many critics understood that by taking Phasis and the Abagasian coastal towns of Pityus, Anakopia, and Sebastopolis, Bessas had cut Petra off from resupply or reinforcement by sea—it was already effectively sealed off by land. A considerable army was brought to lay siege to Petra when Bessas finally ordered the long-anticipated land attack, but it was small units of marines who slipped in under the cover of night and undermined the enemy from behind that made the city's re-conquest relatively bloodless.

Recapturing the city of Petra was one thing, a rather quiet affair all considering. The fortress of Petra, that was another matter entirely. It had long been a powerful citadel that belonged to the king of the Lazi before it fell into the hands of the Persians. The manner of how the citadel fell and how Bessas had it razed to the ground related to the other reason Emperor Justinian had risked the scorn of his critics and surprised everyone with the appointment of an eighty-year-old general to oversee the Lazic War, a general who seemed to have an odd sensitivity to the importance of administration and minor bureaucratic offices—such as notaries, like himself.

John Guzes

John was his Christian name, but Guzes was Lazi. He had served with Bessas in Italy and knew the territory of Lazica and Abagasia.

But that was only one thing that made Guzes important. Guzes also knew tricks...tricks he had taught Arabissos.

Tricks that involved fire.

When General Bessas was informed of Terdetes's treachery, he did not seem all that much bothered by it.

His lieutenants were in a fury. "Traitor!" Arabissos recalled one blurting out reflexively as he lurched forward from his chair and pounded the table with both fists. After the dusk cleared from the first outburst, another asked, "Can we make an exception to custom and bring back crucifixion?"

Others went on to exclaim,

"The fortress at Tsibilium!"
"Have you heard how high it stands?"
"Is it even possible that that's built so high? *Who* built it?"

Agreeing with one another at the enormity of the treason, they began making plans while Bessas, their commander, simply looked on.

"We will need to double our forces, and double them again, just to retake it."
"Who can send an emissary to the Emperor? Surely he will understand we need more tagmas."

Against all their fury, Bessas was nonplussed.

His answer to their protests and the apparent problem presented by Terdetes was to send John Guzes to quell the Abasgian rebellion.

And to do so with only *one* tagma.

The fervency of the objections Bessas' lieutenants made to this was only matched by the contradiction, which could not possibly had come closer in time. Bessas ordered John to Apsilia with one tagma that he also immediately numbered to be of two hundred soldiers-strength. Tagmas could vary in size from two hundred to four hundred, and they were designed to deliberately vary in size from one another, in contrast to the legendary, earlier Latin legions whose number was universal and uniform. Uniformity of sizes initially gave Roman legions all manners of advantages in what was already now—ancient forms of battle. Roman generals knew precisely the size of their contingents, standard plans of supply and resupply could be established and mastered, and tactics and training for tactics could be systematized with individual and groups standards established so that generals were assured of their units' mastery and the units themselves were self-confident and full of morale. Compared to the motley, comparatively disorganized hordes the legions often faced they made for a coldly efficient war machine.

But in later years Rome faced more and more enemies who were careful not to engage without first understanding its ways of war and uniformity as a strategy proved susceptible to certain vulnerabilities. One feature the Persians were early to exploit was the ease with which it was possible to estimate the size and strength of Latin armies. Varying the size of tagmas kept the enemy guessing and added uncertainty to the choice of where, when, and how to engage. With variable-sized tagmas, the enemy was always taking a chance of underestimating the size of an army when it inevitably elected to face the tagmas in battle.

When Bessas announced his orders to John, one lieutenant immediately protested that the soldiers should not be detached for this mission at all—they were required nearby, to assist in the inevitable assault on Petra, which was the Emperor's stated objective after all. Bessas took a moment to quiet the objecting general and assure him that reversing a rebellion in Apsilia was a necessary step in the path to the final objective of retaking Petra and eventually expelling the

Persian menace from Lazica, and he entreated that the general should trust that Bessas understood their objectives.

No sooner had he finished speaking as another lieutenant spoke up, this time horrified that Bessas was prepared to send a detachment that small on a mission so fraught.

Bessas assured the general that the assignment was adequate. While the contradictory objections of the respective generals were evocative enough to Arabissos as he watched silently, he nevertheless found much reason to sympathize with the second general's concerns and to feel anxiety at the paucity of Bessas' reassurance because, breaking with all expectation: *he was assigned to join John's detachment!* Did they need a notary to certify and seal the recapture of Tsibilium after leveling it? Or would it be to take dictation of the terms of the under-manned tagma's surrender?

Neither. Probably more likely to certify their own soldier's inevitable death certificates. Arabissos mused.

Moments earlier the matter had been abstract, now it was personal.

How was a two hundred-man tagma going to capture a two-towered fortress at 1,300 feet? Would they exercise some clever tactic Guzes or Bessas had learned from Belisarius in Italy or Africa? A secret weapon? Surely not a frontal assault and, Arabissos sneered to himself: a lot of luck to them laying siege at the base of the mountain with a unit that small. Ingress and egress would be seamless, especially at night.

It took some time, but the picture came into focus as it became increasingly clear that Guzes' mission would include none of those things. What Arabissos had not expected was that when they finally arrived in Tsibilium and met the erstwhile rebels housed in the sky-citadel there, the encounter unfolded less as a military campaign and turned out to be more of a meeting.

A meeting, as it were, as if between old friends, over drinks, with a large fire, and lots of food and warm embraces. Moreover, this banquet was held in the full presence of the Persian vizier, who Arabissos came to suspect was the only Persian presence with two feet on the ground in Apsilia. As the poor vizier looked on helplessly, Guzes proceeded to "convince" Terdetes of the wisdom of restoring himself to Roman rule.

Terdetes put up an argument, the details of which were difficult for Arabissos to recall, but the substance of which clearly left the impression of being more about appearance and show than content. The argument was that Apsilia was right to separate from Rome on account of something to do with unfair taxation and those interminable wars with the Persians. The argument between Terdetes and Guzes had an element of comedy to it. One could be forgiven for thinking it put on, rehearsed. Surely it was as much for the benefit of Bessas' lieutenants who were on hand to witness so that a consensus report would be made that Terdetes capitulated to Roman entreaties for reunion. Besides that, Guzes and Terdetes seemed to be toying with the pitiable Persian emissary who at turns interjected to emphasize this or that argument in favor of rapprochement with Persia while demanding the immediate ejection of the Byzantine Romans from the premises. At other times, he was simply aghast and left speechless at the near obvious show, yet he was too horrified at his own vulnerability to admit it as a farce.

The discourse inevitably concluded, and Terdetes was persuaded by Guzes to mend fences with the Romans and the Lazi ruler, Gubazes, Terdetes's local superior who also had representatives present. So convinced was he on concluding the argument and conceding to the wisdom of his Lazi brother-in-arms, Terdetes summarily ordered the titular Persian vizier in residence of Tsibilium, whose name was Vistahm, ceremoniously cast out the banquet room window before all of the guests and into the Kodori River below.

As a token of rapprochement with the imperial seat and a symbol of appreciation to the Romans for their patience and understanding at the fickleness of the Abgasians, Terdetes presented John Guzes with a eunuch, Euphrates, said to be legendary for the voice he could give to the songs of the mountain people here—to be offered as a tribute to Emperor Justinian upon their return to the capital. When this expedition was concluded, Arabissos was expected to accompany Euphrates, now in Archaeopolis, back to Byzantium to conclude the transaction. A jolt of apprehension shook him whenever he remembered this; the return to Byzantium could not come fast enough.

Still a youth, Arabissos shuddered thinking about it. He then laughed at himself for shuddering at a memory safely tucked away in the past, even while at that very moment he occupied a plot of land that would soon be the scene of a new blood-letting battle, of which he was sure to be near the front lines.

He shook his head and wiped sweat from his brow. Eight months prior to arriving in Tsibilium, he had been notarizing the most mundane legal documents and bills of sale in Byzantium for linen, leather, and such. It had been a long journey from Byzantium to Tsibilium. That day he had watched a senior official of the Persian Empire tossed 1,300 feet to his death in the white, raging, gurgling rapids below; his body and screams disappearing into a whitish stew.

All of this was unexpected. Unexpected that a far-flung mountain fortress in Apsilia would be handed to over to the Persians without blood or so much as a proper reason. Unexpected that General Bessas saw no need to request additional manpower to support its recapture. Unexpected that he would delay the operational imperative—an assault to retake Petra—while tending to the matter of a fortress arguably outside the zone of contest with the enemy. Unexpected that a single tagma of minimum size would be sufficient to return the fortress to sovereignty. Unexpected that it would be settled by a jovial argument between cousins, and unexpected that the reconciliation between the Apsilia and the Romans would be solemnized by the ceremonial catapult of a high-ranking Persian Vizier from a balcony window into torrential river currents raging leagues below.

Mismatched expectations did not even stop there. Upon Terdetes's rapprochement, rather than return to Archaeopolis with the rest of the expeditionary unit to join the larger army and get along with the recapture of Petra—a unit he now knew to be impossibly suited to capture a castle-fortress perched on mountains a quarter-mile high, he was instead asked to continue on northwest with John Guzes and a small detachment that proceeded along the coast of the Euxine (Black) Sea to the city of Hermonassa. Arabissos could not imagine why this excursion was necessary or why he had been brought along.

Hermonassa was an ancient community believed to have existed before the earliest Roman times. It sat at the southwest mouth of a narrow straight that connected the larger Euxine Sea with the northerly Maeotis Lake. It was a primary trade center that connected Byzantium and the Mediterranean beyond with the vast and largely unknown lands to the north, still often referred to, inaccurately as Scythia, which continued to be important source for furs, exotic animals and when it was not a good season, barbarians.

Hermonassa, though founded by Greeks, had passed out of Roman hands almost two centuries prior in the catastrophes that followed the Battle of Adrianople and fell into the hands of the Alans. Briefly controlled by the Huns, it had since technically passed back to Byzantine, Roman control, but once there it was clear to Arabissos any such control was no more than "influence," and even that was only if one allowed for the most charitable stretch of the term. Hermonassa, as far as he could tell, was an altogether lawless place; that did not necessarily mean it was a violent place. Indeed, for a hamlet inhabited by **Abasgi**, Laz, and Romans as well as a surprisingly sparse but still real assortment of Alans and Huns, it was remarkably peaceful—if peace could be said to coexist with chaos.

Perhaps it said as much as one needed to know about the remote nature of the place that this town of four or five thousand did not even rise to the status of a mayoralty. For its own self-governance, the various and sundry mercantilists who established themselves there elected an administrator of sorts. In this regard, they were civilized, but the title they gave to this official, their presumptive governor, was *fisherman*.

As they made their way about Hermonassa, John Guzes' purpose in bringing Arabissos took on a more discernible form. Indeed, some shape could begin to be detected as to why unarmed troops of civilians such as himself had been a peculiar priority to Bessas in the first place.

Guzes was looking for something. He had need of merchandise.

A product. A product, apparently, that could be found only in and around Hermonassa. The manner of seeking the product proved to be as mysterious as the product itself. Guzes specifically set Arabissos to the task of finding it, but at all points along the way he was altogether sketchy about what it was Arabissos was so ordered to procure.

Hermonassa was not small, but it was not that large of a community either, and the presence of a Byzantine military detachment, no matter how diminutive and lightly armed, in a far-flung port under only the most nominal control and which was clearly accustomed to only the softest touch of the government's long hand, did not go unnoticed by the locals. To the contrary, word of their presence spread quickly. People wondered at the designs behind their presence. Suspicion abounded.

Passing through?
Checking in?
Looking for someone particular?

Or, what they all feared most...
Here to stay and assert some manner of control?

To this end, the nearly utterly random purchases Guzes kept sending Arabissos off to acquire both took a toll and got him wondering if his own role in the exercise was that of a decoy and even further, if he was a decoy whose role was to deliberately spread disinformation. Guzes sent him after lamp oil. After that, tar. After that, pine resin. One of his errands was, deliberately he suspected, a fruitless excursion to purchase heavier paludeamentums (cloaks fastened at one shoulder) for the tagma since the climate was cooler than for what they had been equipped. John eventually settled for civilian coats and Arabissos purchased every remaining one in Hermonassa. People began to understand him as the visiting tagma's commanding officer's errand boy and they started to think of the visiting officer as just visiting.

This was exactly how Guzes wanted it.

With a fourteen-year-old notary as the most visible face of the imperial presence and with an increasing sense that the presence was surely transitory, Arabissos noticed locals began to take less and less notice of that presence and became decidedly more comfortable with it. It reminded him of what someone once had said, "It was a long and hard military campaign in Italy, and we've learned many things, military things, and they aren't at all what you would expect."

Arabissos had almost all he could stand of the exercises in pointless procurement when Guzes sent him on what would prove to be his final excursion—this time to the tanners. By now, few noticed or talked about the latest mission or its underlying conspiracy of the imperial tagma's fourteen-year-old notary.

Unlike all of his previous projects, this one made great sense. Of course he needed to see the tanners! The journey from Archeaopolis to Apsilia and from Apsilia to Hermonassa was long and crossed much rocky and wretched terrain.

Everyone would need new boots, so the words slipped almost effortlessly off Arabissos' tongue when Guzes ordered him to the tanners.

"Boots sir? For the whole company I assume."

"Boots?" Guzes answered him with surprise in his voice, as if he hadn't even thought about it. "Ha! No."

"For what then?" Arabissos retorted, virtually with a sneer that familiarity at this point allowed, but rank would have frowned on. "We've worn out our soles marching from Apsilia. What else would we need from tanners?"

Guzes considered him ruefully, then chuckled a bit more before answering.

"Well, it's not an altogether ridiculous idea."

Ridiculous idea! Arabissos thought.

"Before we set ourselves back to Archeopolis surely we can replace soles, but that's not what we need right now."

"I see, sir. What should I order from the tanners then?" Arabissos asked.

"Bladders," Guzes answered.

"Bladders?" Arabissos responded, the confusion obvious in his voice.

"*Leather* bladders," Guzes clarified, drawing out the first word for emphasis.

"Alright, sir. There is a tanning shop by the port, not far from where we're quartered..."

"No," Guzes interrupted. "Not that one."

Arabissos raised an eyebrow at this. Hermonassa was not a big place, and he had seen most of it with all the errands he had run. What was Guzes talking about?

"There's another shop I want you to use. The one near the port services sailors and relies on the sea's winds to carry away the scent. The shop I need you to visit is not so close. It's set outside the town, northeast, towards the mountains. The tanners will be expecting this order, but you'll need to take a horse and a baggage mule. It's a long ride, and the bladders you'll be returning with will be heavy. I'm sending a guard with you."

"A guard?"

"Two"

"Two?"

"Yes, you're still young, and you'll have merchandise on an open road."

"Ok, ..." Arabissos started before Guzes interrupted.

"And, I misspoke—it will be seven".

"Seven guards!?"

"Seven baggage mules".

In Arabissos mind the words were forming as "what the hell?" even as his mouth was reflexively stating "if you say so, sir, but I think I'll be fine without a guard."

Guzes brushed off this comment and continued, "There's another thing, Arabissos. These tanners won't sell their product to anyone. These are...*special* bladders. You will need the code word."

Arabissos' heart skipped a beat. *This hasn't happened before! Guzes had never given him a code-word for a purchase. What was the meaning of this?*

"What is that, sir?"

"You."

"The word," Arabissos asked, "...*you?*"

"No," Guzes answered. "The boy...the young man...Arabissos, the person, in the flesh...*you.*"

Arabissos was perfectly perplexed.

"You are the code word, Arabissos—your very person. The tanners, their names are Natan and Rava. Tell them John Guzes sent you. They are under orders to sell to no other person."

At the mention of these names, Arabissos felt himself flush and his jaw almost dropped to the floor.

"Wha-wha?" Arabissos could hardly form a sentence. "Rava and Natan!? T...t...tanners?"

A curious smirk unraveled across Guzes' cheeks while Arabissos tried to wrap his mind around this.

"Rava and Natan, sons of Dudai?"

"Yes," Guzes answered. "The very men."

"Tanners. Jewish Tanners. From the Vlanga quarter, in Byzantium?"

"Did you didn't think we brought you here to buy lamp oil and notarize bills of sale?"

"I...I'm sorry, General Guzes. I just don't understand."

Guzes considered Arabissos a moment before proceeding, "Well, as you said, Dudai is a tanner in the Vlanga quarter, or so I am told; I've never met the man myself. But, Rava and Natan—his sons, yes—they have...uhhh...an *auxiliary* office out here in Hermonassa."

"What?" Arabissos slowed down as he tried to speak; pieces of the puzzle were starting to come together, but too many were still missing. "Just a year ago, I notarized their boulloterions and certified they'd paid taxes on their leather."

"A year ago, that's right," Guzes said, "and, correct, you made acquaintance with them", Guzes spoke as if he knew all about this.

"Well," Arabissos said, "yes, sir I did. Natan is older, twenty I think, but Rava is just a year or so older than me. We got along."

"Correct. And they remember you. Which is why you were selected when Bessas asked for administrative support for Lazica, and it is why you have been brought to Hermonassa with me."

Arabissos could scarcely wrap his mind around the implications of the fact that so much of this was planned, in so much detail, so far in advance, so far away, and that he, still many years short of autexousion**, was central to these plans. What were these designs he was a part of?

** Emancipation of a minor under Byzantine civil law

"But why? Why me...why them? Why are they...we, here?"

"In so many words, son," Guzes said familiarly. "It's about the scent."

"The scent?"

"Tanning is a profession that is prominent, if not infamous, for its scent. Most find the scent of tanning revolting and nearly anyone who has a choice in the matter does everything in their power to put as much space as possible between themselves and a tanning shop. That may seem to be a bad thing. Buuuuut, ... if one wanted to conceal something, especially something that also had a prominent scent—one could see how tanning may be advantageous because the scent discourages curious eyes from taking a closer look. No one wants to be around the scent of a tanner's shop, which is nice, and because we have need of merchandise, we also don't want anyone else around our merchandise."

"Yes, sir," Arabissos replied, "but—any town has tanners. Why Natan and Rava? Why did they have to come so far from their father's shop in Byzantium?"

Guzes answered as if continuing where he left off, "On the other hand...the scent is a double-edged sword. One cannot easily hide a tanner. People notice when you open a tanning shop, especially in a locale that already benefits from the presence of one."

Arabissos held his gaze, confused.

"Natan and Rava are Jews. There's a tanning shop in Hermonassa, but in such a community the needs are great and no one will object much to the addition of a Jewish shop, especially if they are courteous and open their shop a distance away from the existing order, outside the town."

Guzes allowed a moment to pass while this sunk in.

"But that's not the only reason I selected Natan and Rava."

"*You*, selected them?" Arabissos asked.

Guzes went on, "I selected them because they know you."

"Me?" Arabissos asked, incredulously, thinking to himself *why the hell do they care about me?*

"They will recognize you and know without doubt that they can sell their product to you."

Arabissos stared blankly.

Guzes continued, "There are not two of you. *You* are the password.

"It's a good thing no accident befell you on the journey to get here. They are not authorized to sell to anyone else. They cannot even sell to me—they don't know who I am after all, anyone could show up with a cape and officer's insignia claiming to be John Guzes. There is only one Arabissos from Cappadocia who is fourteen years old."

While they carried a certain a logic of their own, none of Guzes' answers would close the loop of questions that plagued Arabissos; they only opened up more.

He remained completely confused and considered Guzes blankly.

"They knew you'd be here before you did Arabissos. They left Byzantium about the same time you did, but they sailed directly here and established a shop on orders of Justinian himself."

"The emperor!" Arabissos blurted, almost as if horrified.

"A new tanning shop in Hermonassa would have attracted attention. A Jewish shop, as long as it was raised far in the outskirts, on the margins, would shock no one's sensibilities. Frankly, a Jewish tanning shop was long overdue in Hermonassa. How else could anyone get a shoe repaired on Sunday?"

* * * * * * * * *

Rava wore a thick coat that weighed heavily on his lanky body as he stepped out the back of the shop and into the shed. The shed itself was enclosed against the back of the shop on three sides so that the shop's walls made for a four-sided enclosure. The three other sides were constructed from wooden planks, which were assembled together deliberately so that they would be open to wind and light from the outside to illuminate and ventilate the semi-outdoor workspace. A wider opening between the wooden planks was placed at eye level so that Rava had a view of the rough landscape surrounding him outside and beyond.

The shed was arranged so that it came together at the far end in the center wall opposing the shop where a large divot was carved in the lower base of the wooden wall. At the center was a wide stone basin that drained out the divot and down an embankment to a stream thirty paces below. At the edge of the basin and laid in a few other places about were several tubs that, from where he stood at the doorway between the shop and the shed, mostly brimmed with pools of water interlaced with the projections of rocks peaking above the pools' surfaces. Rava approached one of these that was next to the basin presently.

He gripped in his right hand a tough leather pouch that contained ash. Hermonassa was a coastal town, but his and his brother's shop was at the base of quickly rising highlands not far inland. Wind blowing down the mountains tended to keep conditions cold, and in cold conditions it was often necessary to soak a hide for more than the usual three days before the hairs on the hide's surface would be ready to "slip," indicating that a soaked hide was ready for the fleshing stage. Adding ash to the water helped to move along this process. Rather than set down his pouch of ash, he removed a glove, submerged his hand into the cold water, and tested a hair. To his surprise the hair slipped. He tried another; it slipped and still another. Drying his hand against his pants leg, he replaced his glove and was pleased that he would not have to use the ash. He stood for a moment and set aside the pouch on a table, which acted as a workstation behind him.

He returned to the tub, removed the rocks that had been placed on the hide to keep it submerged, set them back at the same table, and proceeded to lift the tub and drain its watery contents into the basin so that he could remove the hide. Taking the hide from the tub, he wrung it out thoroughly flushing out the water that soaked it. It was just as he was stretching out the hide again to make it ready for the fleshing beam that he heard a commotion. The dogs were barking out front, someone was approaching the shop.

The interior of Rava and Natan's shop was built over packed earth and divided into three parts. At the rear and adjacent to the shed was a workroom where they did their tanning. At the front was a service bench that doubled as a location where Rava and his brother might dine and take breaks or service customers. Above the service bench was a loft where, for a while, the brothers slept while they established the shop until operations got going; the place stopped being suitable for any purpose but work.

With some money from the investors in their project, they had contracted a few of the villagers to build a small dormitory a short distance away, which was where Natan was probably still sleeping. Rava noted this to himself and wondered at it. It was uncommon for customers to come so early in the day. Ordinarily, they might start off to the shop from town around this time or later in the morning, which would have them arriving towards noon or sometime in the afternoon.

As he strode his way towards the service bench, he could see that the prospective customer had already let himself in and was removing his outer coats and placing them on the hooks that Rava and Natan had installed there for that purpose. Compounding the peculiarity of the time of day for this arrival was that he was quite a youngish-looking man. The toughened, tan exterior dress had concealed below it the looks of one who was more of a scholar than the ruffian sort Rava was accustomed to in these parts.

Rava could hear commotion and the sounds of whinnying and men corralling their horses from the partially opened front door. The visitor was not alone. Though he was of slight build, it was immediately doubtful his companions outside were as well. The light was dim inside, and his eyes adjusted to the outdoor light where he would have been working a moment before. He had already allowed a smidgen of anxiety over this unlikely arrival to build up before he came up to the service bench; the visitor came fully into view. He wore a scarf about his head, surely to protect from the wind and cold on the ride from the town to the shop. A clavus rounded the top of the scarf at the tonsure—certainly this young man was not a senator anywhere—so it probably suggested equestrian status, which made sense; he clearly arrived on horseback.

The customer let down one shaft of the scarf, leaving the majority of its body in place on his head and moved to face Rava. As he did so, recognition came over Rava and his cares were immediately put to rest. He spoke without skipping a beat, before the customer could remove the rest of his scarf, "Are you needing new boots, notary?"

A wide smile crossed Arabissos' face from one end to the other, though just one side peaked out from behind the half-hanging scarf.

"Would that I was here for boots man," Arabissos exclaimed, not bothering to introduce himself.

"But," he said, laying his face down to his palm and bobbing his head back and forth dramatically, "as God is my witness I am here under the order of my master to return with one hundred streptons." Arabissos stated the last word with sarcasm and went on rolling his eyes to the ceiling and shrugging his shoulders in a way that conveyed bewilderment and unjustified familiarity.

"Bronze tubes!" Rava bellowed in answer. He parried, "If you came from Byzantium to Hermonassa looking for amber, fur or down—well, you're in the right place, but if you walked all the way from town to a tanner, well I've got leather for you sir."

"I was told one hundred streptons, bronze tubes," Arabissos said, and he shrugged his shoulders as if helpless.

"Hmmmm," Rava regarded him.

"Someone might have mentioned something to me about you and your unusual order. Can you tell me...did your master give you a word?"

"A word?" Arabissos replied.

"Yes," Rava said, "a word that might help...jog a young tanner's memory. I'm still new to this kind of work, like you apparently."

Arabissos widened his eyes, "Indeed."

"Aaaannnnddd?" Rava slightly bowed forward, opening his palms on either side towards Arabissos.

"It isn't a word you require," Arabissos said.

To this, Rava lifted one eyelid inquisitively while Arabissos stepped back and unwound the remainder of his scarf. The joke was in the open. The two young friends, after over a year apart, embraced.

The three old acquaintances sat around the table in the small dormitory that Arabissos and Rava had transferred themselves to after their reunion. Rava had woken Natan who had since joined them at the table; they shared some warm tea.

They each exchanged stories of the unlikely and circuitous routes that brought them together at Hermonassa. Two young, unmarried tradesmen from the Jewish quarter and a superlatively young notary from Armenia, a year ago they were together in the capital, and now, by separate paths, they were together again at the northernmost outpost of the empire. For their part, Rava and Natan had had the entire year to let the reality of it settle in with them, but Arabissos was hard pressed to wrap his mind around the level of forethought that was required to bring this all into being, let alone the meaning of it all.

Three years ago he was still playing children's games. A year ago as a junior notary in the capital of empire he had fortune to make company with two lads, about his own age, tanner's sons. Now the three of them broke bread together in a hovel on the rugged outskirts of a rugged town that was only nominally civilized. *How had this all come to pass?*

He puzzled it over while enjoying tea with his old friends and his thoughts wandered to an evocative conversation he'd held with General Bessas.

* * * * * * * * *

General Bessas had been recalled from the western front in Italy to turn matters around on the eastern front in Lazica. Most of the time he was learning from his elders and straining to master the various tasks they would throw in front of him, but sometimes being young and not having many assumptions did prompt Arabissos to think of questions the adults around him did not seem to bother asking.

"Why Lazica?" he asked the general.

"What?"

"Lazica? Why are we fighting the Persians in Lazica?" Arabissos persisted.

He did not press many adults with the question, but they all answered the same way when asked the first time...and usually the only time.

Some responded with a chuckle, some with a shrug, but always, "Romans have always fought the Persians. We were fighting the Persians *before* they were Persians."

"But that isn't the point!" he cringed at his last word— a bit too presumptuous. He had to draw himself back or risk offense.

"Well, what then? You asked a simple question. It's a simple answer. The Romans and Persians are ancient adversaries. How is it odd that we fight?"

Arabissos was exasperated. "We can fight the Persians in Syria or Palestine...where there is a proper border, and trade, and irrigated land worth having. Isn't that about the only place the pre-Triumvirate ever fought them?"

"Or...Armenia...seems like they've learned a taste for Armenia. Even Sinai and Arabia."

It did not matter who. His interlocutor would just be staring at him about now.

"All of these places make sense to fight the Persians. Why *Lazica*?" He tried to emphasize the last word without raising his voice.

Bessas said nothing, so Arabissos tried again.

"Any place...anywhere else at all that we could fight the Persians would make more sense than Lazica. It's barren; it's rough. There are no roads. The people are primitive. It's bitterly cold. And even though it takes longer to trek from one end to the other than it takes to arrive at the place from Byzantium, it's not even big. It's just hard. Barren, cold, and hard."

"There...is...*nothing*...here...in Lazica!"

"So, what are we fighting for? And why so hard? Doesn't the emperor have more pressing concerns. Aren't there wars to fight over lands where real Romans live? Like Italy, Sicily, Spain?"

Bessas remained silent but didn't say or do anything that would suggest Arabissos was out of form or should stop, so he continued.

"Heh," he smiled and shook his head. "Wouldn't it be easier—good strategy even—just to give it up? The Daugava waterway can be reached through Hermonassa, and there won't be Persians anywhere near there soon. We could move the army and secure Armenia from threat and let the Persian

Shah exhaust himself chasing ghosts in Lazica with no one firing a bow."

Bessas offered a shrug to this, the barest wince of his brow, this child knew something of strategy.

These questions had troubled Arabissos, but no one his elder ever seemed to ask or question these things.

While Lazica seemed like a prime opportunity to retreat and succeed while "failing," it was only that much more odd that the seemingly more lucrative western front—where the empire stood to gain all that Italy had offered her a thousand years hence until barely a hundred years ago when it was overrun by barbarians—was to give up its general because it was apparently so important that matters be turned around in Lazica!

On arrival from Italy, what an unusual general the elderly Bessas immediately proved to be. With the inexplicable priority placed upon his transfer from the western to the eastern front, the talk along the Milion was that Justinian would raise a whole new army for Bessas—if Bessas said that's what it would take to conquer and secure Lazica ... such was Justinian's confidence in his general, Bessas had only to say the word and it would be done.

And after a sense, Bessas did ask for an army, and true to expectation Justinian gave him what he asked for.

A civilian army!

An army of clerks, logothetes, regulators, notaries...people like Arabissos.

And so he found himself here in Lazica—or in Hermonassa today—Abghasia again in a month maybe. To Lazica he would return; that was abundantly clear now if it had not been before.

The crude outlines of Bessas' unusual stratagems did take on more clarity and sometimes because Bessas himself would take a moment to settle the doubts of the confused young man he had taken into his retinue. After a heated meeting with some generals where Arabissos had been asked to scribe as secretary, he was completing his notes and requested a clarification from Bessas. Seizing the opportunity, he added, "If I may, sir?"

"Of course you may...what is it?"

"What am I doing here?"

When Bessas did not answer immediately, Arabissos went on. "You could have asked for a regular army. The emperor would have put his wars on hold and raised one or recalled one from Egypt and Libya. Why me, why us? What document can I stamp that will turn the tables and gain an inch for the emperor in Lazica?"

Bessas stood up. They stood together in a tactical tent. Naturally, the general's tent was spacious and had all the best accoutrements one could ask for if one was going to be out at the business of war; it was designed with flaps that could be pulled aside to create a window when desired. Bessas walked over and pressed aside the flaps allowing in a beam of sunlight, which shone on the ground beneath, and spoke as he tied the flaps against the side of the tent.

"Before we recruited you, you did some work in the palace?"

"Yes, sir."

"And you had privilege while you were there to meet General Belisarius."

"ye..." Arabissos started to say, but Bessas continued, talking over him.

"...and Narses, Theodora's pe...uh...Theodora's eunuch general." Arabissos' mind had already filled in the unspoken word with "pet," but he said nothing, unsure of where Bessas was going with this.

"Belisarius, he is a young man, do you think?"

"Well," Arabissos said, "he's much older than me, and older than the average soldier. I think he seems appropriate to a general's age, to lead men."

"Huh," Bessas grunted. "You are so young."

Bessas held Arabissos' eye then went on. "Belisarius has been leading men as Justinian's general for over twenty-five years. When I first served under Belisarius, he was ten years older than you."

Bessas waited a moment for that to sink in.

"And Narses...a 'beardless one.' They all look like children no matter how old they get."[ψ]

"The Italy we were sent to is not the Italy that left the empire when Diocletian created the Tetrarchy. Italy has changed since those times. The Ostrogothic yolk, the effect of the Ostrogoths on Italy, has been...odd."

"Odd, sir?" Arabissos inquired.

"Normally, a conquering tribe or army subjugates the people it vanquishes, or sells them into slavery, if it doesn't decimate them entirely. It's always been this way. But the Ostrogoths in Italy had done nothing of the sort. They enslaved no one. They certainly didn't decimate Italy—rather, they left the place quite well intact! The odd thing about the Ostrogoths as conquerors was that they knew that the Italians had something, and they wanted what the Italians had. While they came as conquerors, they were conquerors 'bearing gifts' so as to woo the vanquished people."

"That—the Italian's *knowledge*—was what the Ostrogoths wanted. They wanted the Italians' knowledge more than they wanted anything the Italians possessed. It is easy to take the possessions left behind by an enemy you have massacred. It's another matter, upon installing oneself as another people's lord, to cleave away from those people secret knowledge they keep locked away only in their minds."

Arabissos had never heard anything like this. *What was Bessas talking about?*

"What was that sir...what knowledge...what do you mean?" Arabissos interjected.

[ψ] Beardless one—a Byzantine epithet for eunuchs

"Civilization."

"What?"

"Civilization. Young man, for over two hundred years, from the Rhine in Germania to Thrace, the other way to Spain and this way to Armenia, Goths and Alans have pressed themselves up into Roman society. On every border our armies have strained to hold them at bay, but their aim has never been to destroy or replace us. Their aim was to become *like* us."

"In Italy, they finally had that opportunity. Italian government, teachers, administrators, ha!...notaries like you...the Goths wanted to learn the arts of civics, and so for the most part once they established themselves they left the body of Italy unmolested."

"I understand what you're telling me general," Arabissos said, while still doubting his own words, "but I still don't see how this answers my question. Why do you need administrators here...in Lazica? Lazica has never been a civilized place."

At this, Bessas turned from the view he had held at the tent's open flap and walked over to Arabissos when he answered.

"Generals like Belisarius and Narses," Bessas said, "they know how to do what generals know how to do. They know how to win battles, to win wars. They know how to do this when poorly equipped and when armies are undermanned. Belisarius, in particular, has been doing this so long because he is good at *winning* wars. Justinian fears him, but he keeps him around because he's so good at it."

"The problem arises that war is won...by *destroying* things."

Arabissos looked on. Bessas took a minute to ascertain if he might see what he was getting at.

"Italy wasn't broken," Bessas said, "Italy was just under the thumb of the wrong rulers. But we could not win Italy without breaking it. We broke Italy east, and we broke it west. We broke it in Sicily in the south, and before we are done we will break it in the north. Belisarius retook Ravenna and left her fairly unscathed. That would be saying more if it were as true of human bodies as it is of concrete buildings. Not many of our Latin brothers are still there in Ravenna. It was almost entirely depopulated."

"We *will* win the war in Italy. Narses was sent to replace me, and I've no doubt he will finish my work and drive the Ostrogoths back to the mountains they arrived in from. His soft face conceals behind it a hard heart that knows no pity for the misfortune of Goths. When they are done, having won the war for Italy, we will have laid waste to the land. We will win back Italy for Rome...but we will achieve that by crushing underfoot what remains of Rome, in Italy."

A moment passed, Arabissos said nothing. Bessas walked around to the seat of his desk and leaned over it with both arms set on its top.

"The Emperor has ordered me to Lazica because, like any old general, I too know how to win wars—we retire when we stop winning wars, but he selected me," Bessas paused. "He selected me because of what my eyes have seen, and because I, like our emperor, learn. Even this old mind, it still learns new things," he tapped his head as he continued.

"I am among the sad few who have learned that it isn't enough to win a war; it is not enough to be an effective destroyer of things, a destroyer of men. Italy, when she is returned to Mother Rome, will be a depopulated husk. The Emperor embarked on the conquest of Italy believing that her return would pay for itself. It's clear now it may be a hundred years before she can pay back the war ransom it cost to recover her. He doesn't want to make that mistake again. He can't afford it. That's why he sent me, here."

At this, Arabissos involuntarily flinched. Everything Bessas had said up until this moment had made sense, and then it all crumbled to dust with the last words.

"*Here*? Sir?"

Bessas stood up erect, "Indeed. Have you not followed me young man? You had looked as if you'd understood."

"Yes, ye..." Arabissos' voice cracked a bit, "begging your pardon, sir, it's just that..."

"Just that what?"

"Well," Arabissos went on, "Italy was the center of civilization for a thousand years before Hadrian. Rome, Palatine Hill, the Senate, the Via Apia, everything...it all started there. But there's, there's..." Arabissos struggled to find words to express himself in the short time he knew he had, "There was civilization to ruin, to destroy, with war, in Italy. But, but...we're here, in *Lazica*." He had to restrain himself on the last word and not be caught yelling at the general.

"There's *nothing* here in Lazica to destroy. You can't lay waste to it." At that, he knew he had pressed the boundaries of rank too far, but he was in too deep already. He thought he may as well break form and gestured out the open tent flaps, "You could destroy it a second time over and it'd make no difference. It's already a wasteland."

Bessas walked over to him and met him face to face.

"Notary, you're more inquisitive than you'd led me to worry just a moment ago."

"And, what's more, you're right. Lazica is a wasteland. But it isn't what Justinian sent us here to destroy that matters. It's not enough that we drive out the Persians. We are here, you and me, for what comes after."

Arabissos met this with a blank, puzzled gaze.

At this, Bessas dismissed him, "Finish your report. I'll expect copies for each of my lieutenants in the morning."

* * * * * * * * * *

As they sipped their tea, Rava prepared a fire in a small hearth.

"What, I wonder," Arabissos said as Rava and Natan listened, "had they already sorted out Terdetes' plot with the

89

Persians at Tsibilium when they sent me with Bessas to Lazica, or did that come up along the way? I guess—if it had not, I'd of been sent up here with Guzes to meet you both either way, but it had to help matters in Apsillia that Guzes and Terdetes are acquainted."

"Whatever their plans though, you see it made sense don't you?" Natan answered. His voice was still raspy from sleep and cold air.

"Well, kind of, but there are five thousand notaries in Byzantium. Why me? I—I'm fourteen years old for heaven's sakes!"

At this and quite unexpectedly, Rava and Natan alike broke out with completely unselfconscious belly laughs as if Arabissos had just said the most ridiculous thing—when in fact he was altogether sure it was both a perfectly reasonable question without a note of false humility. Their laughs were so loud he could almost sense his guards outside regarding one another at what must be taking place inside while they were locked out in the cold. He had been taught not to fret such things. They were guards—they were muscle. He was here on a mission, and the information of the mission—the contents of the strepton he was to acquire from the tanners—weighed many times the guards' weight in gold. They would just have to suffer the cold.

His mind returned to his amused friends.

"What? What's so funny about that?"

The belly laugh had warmed his throat, and Natan spoke over Rava to answer, his voice now both smooth and loud, "They chose you...because of us!"

The answer was perfectly cryptic, perfectly unhelpful, and as far as Arabissos could tell, as amusing to the jovial brothers as the question that evoked it.

At this point he did not see a reason to press the matter, so he just remained in his chair sipping his tea until the two got over their laughter and were able to address him again. Rava finished up by getting a fire running and seated himself by Arabissos with some tea; his face besmirched from one end to the other with a smile that seemed it could fall off either side.

"Arabissos," Rava said, his voice coming down to a moderate tone but his face still beaming, "we're going to have to come back to the matter of the number of streptons your master asked us to provide. That part might be a problem. But, we mean no offense, it isn't us." He looked a bit strained and turned to his older brother, "How can we make our friend understand?"

Natan's eyes peered sideways at Rava, then back to Arabissos. He peered his eyes upward to the ceiling for barely a second as if considering then started, "It's because you are so junior that the eparch assigned you to our father's workshop.

A tanner ... leatherwork, the higher-ranking notaries and boullotes ...think of all the things they'd rather inspect and certify and sign and regulate! Jewelers, bankers, tavern keepers, linen work, and..."

"Taverns!" Rava broke in to add with deliberate redundancy.

Natan continued as if uninterrupted, "No one wants to visit tanners, so they gave the work to a fourteen-year-old and lucky you! And lucky us!"

It still did not make sense, but Arabissos kept with them, sipping his tea and nodding for Natan to go on.

"Bessas and Guzes fought together in Italy, and Bessas learned from Guzes that there is a...a...substance that's found in the mountains, here, outside Hermonassa, and they used it in battle in Italy. To devastating effect I'm told. But, as far as anyone knows, it can only be found here."

"A substance?" Arabissos inquired.

"Yes, a substance. Ahhh, how would you describe it Rava?"

"Well," Rava answered, holding his tea cup with two hands on the table, starring into its contents for a moment while he thought. "It's thick, but liquid, like a tree's sap. We have to treat it actually, to make it work right...we dilute it so that it's a consistency somewhere between olive oil and tree sap, but it has the look of tar. The army likes it to be kept inside the streptons you were told to ask us for. We are never permitted to let it be seen...not by the townsfolk, not by other merchants, not by tanners, not by the guards outside."

Rava looked up from his cup and met Arabissos in the eyes, "Actually, we're not even supposed to let you see the contents. We were told to sell you the streptons, but that no one should peer inside; they didn't say to make an exception for you."

Natan started after Rava finished this, "And that's another thing about this all. Bronze streptons are ideal for containing the substance and moving it around, but when used...what's the word here..."

Rava finished his sentence like someone used to it. "Tac-tic-ally," he enunciated, "Right," Natan started again. "Tactically. When used tactically, it's often best to transfer the substance from the streptons to large leather bladders."

Arabissos' head fell. His chip bounded off his chest when it came up again, and he asked, "Bladders?"

"Why yes," Natan answered, "you look surprised."

Arabissos shook his head back and forth and replied, "Yeah. I know. It's just that when Guzes sent me on this mission he said that the key thing I needed to get from you, was bladders. It made no sense to me. Boots—that'd of made sense. Hell, even the streptons, if he had started with the instruction, that would have made sense too. But..." Arabissos struggled for the words, "It is as if the whole point of the mission, after a month of running about this town throwing the merchants and smugglers off the scent of why we were here, after trekking five hundred and eighty stadia beyond Tsibilium, which was originally supposed to be our whole reason to go to Apsilia, was so that I could get leather bladders from the only Jewish tanners outside of Hermonassa!"

Rava and Natan both smiled, but neither of the jovial pair seemed wont to laugh outright at what Arabissos, until this moment, thought was something like a punch line. They both looked back at him; he returned their gaze, tilting his jaw off-kilter to his right and gesturing with a bare nod.

When one spoke, it was Natan again. It seemed the pattern of their discourse was to leave more sensitive matters to Natan. Arabissos had a feeling whatever he said was going to be sensitive.

"Arabissos' business has been growing in Hermonassa, or so we're told. We've only been here a year as, but even in the time we've been here the town has grown by as much as a third. In just a year, one or two thousand have arrived. Transients mostly, but there's a lot of commerce taking place, so no one would notice if a pair of Jews showed up in town and opened up a tanning shop. Normally in a small, remote place it might be noticed, but truly here—I think even the tanners at the port, Florian and Balimber the Hun, they had too much business to keep up with. I think even they welcomed us; now they can sleep!"

"And, you may be too young to understand, but it isn't just that we're tanners that they assigned us to you, it's that we're Jewish."

Indeed, that much probably was true, at the ages of twelve and thirteen, when he was essentially an apprentice and barely not a child anymore, this young man from Armenia did not completely understand the significance of sectarian distinctions.

Natan went on, "No one would think anything of it if two Jewish tanners moved into a growing community and set up shop outside the city where they wouldn't bother anyone by being there. That our father taught us well and that we can tan good leather made us all the more welcome. We have been here a year without drawing an eye. And while we were here, we were asked to prepare the contents of the streptons. While that's not exactly tanning work, let's say that many features of tanning work are well suited to the problem. The substance in the streptons must be in part concealed there because its scent is so strong at close range it can actually overcome a man, and, well...scents, need I say more? Then there's the matter of tactical delivery as we said...leather proves to be ideal."

"So, you see, it is that you were chosen for this job, because of us—because you weren't any notary, you were *our* notary. I mean, I'm sure General Bessas needed a notary for something, but any notary wasn't going to do. It had to be the one notary the secret Jews he'd sent to Hermonassa would recognize."

After a minute Arabissos responded, "Ok, ok. I think I'm seeing it now. But just one thing. You said that this substance, I assume I will not be told what it is called," both brothers were nodding over their tea, "You said it has to be...diluted...you said, in order to work right?"

Rava nodded, "Yes."

"Alright. I know this is supposed to be a secret, but when it works what does it do?"

Arabissos waited a few seconds to gauge their answer; he could tell they both looked pained at keeping it from him. He went on, "I mean...we came five hundred and eighty stadia from Tsibilium alone, and this plan, with me, with you—they made this plan before any of us were even sent here. It had to have been made at the Great Palace, at the highest levels. Come on...friends," he said, allowing a bit of inquiry into the last word. "Surely, when it works, it must work something a—mazing! Right?"

Rava and Natan had a way about them where they would cast each other glances and gestures—waves of the hand, flicks of the eye. All of these together made for a nonverbal language that could make a guest feel like he was talking to a two-headed twin. This time they did not look at one another and made no motion towards one another. It was as if they had already had the matter planned. Each nodded his head in unison. Rava answered, "The reason for the bladders has to do with pressure. Part of the secret is in applying pressure, and you can do that with a flexible leather bladder but not so much with a bronze cylinder." Rava turned half-way towards his brother and went on, "Natan will distract the guards with an errand. I'm going to retrieve something from the shop. There's an embankment that flows down to the stream out the back of the shed behind our shop. Walk down there. We'll both be by and find you shortly."

* * * * * * * * * *

As Arabissos' horse trotted along the train back to Hermonassa, one of the guards trailed slightly behind him and to his left. They were both followed by a train of seven mules, each pulling a cart. The second guard trailed them behind. Two of the mules were intended to pull the bladders, and the remaining five had been intended to pull twenty streptons each in their carts. As it were, there were only forty streptons to be purchased, so Arabissos decided to divide them evenly in blocks of eight and stack the bladders over them, covering them with sheets and blankets.

Natan explained that there had been still more to the elaborate ruse of how they ended up here in Hermonassa on this mission. As part of their inventory, they had carried with them several chests of "wine," although instead of amphoras, which might contain wine, the chests contained streptons; they took up about the same cylindrical space in the chests. They were supposed to have received one hundred, but there was some confusion or mix up, and before it could be cleared their ship had to depart, so all they had were forty.

He had tried to wash and wipe his face, but every time he sensed his sweat; he could feel the ash being pushed from his pores to the surface. He had no means of being able to tell how obvious or not it was to the nearby guard. What could not be hidden and what probably could not even be explained by the tanning shop, was the scent. It was all about him—in his clothes, his shoes, his scarf, his skin—and he especially smelled it in his hair. How could one describe this smell?

Burning

The *smell* of burning. Oily burning.

Before today, maybe in childish myths of his imagination he could have conjured such a stench, maybe. However, he had never before now thought such a thing possible. What Natan and Raza showed him, changed everything.

Guzes was not going to be pleased that he would return sixty units short. Arabissos guessed his tanner friends would be visited by additional representatives of the commander before they departed and returned to Lazica—these representatives would not be old accomplices. He wondered if their explanation of the shortfall would find purchase.

As they pulled into the main thoroughfare of the town, he tended to think it was all for the better. For one, the forty bronze streptons tended to shift in their carts and clank loudly against one another. *One hundred. God, just the thought.* They would have been an orchestra and would have drawn unwanted attention. Seven mules with cloths and leather bladders come into town from the tanners; mostly this had the look of a garrison equipping to leave—something everyone living here probably took to be a welcome development no matter how well the visiting soldiers had minded themselves. The locals were unlikely to question evidence of the garrison preparing to leave.

Arabissos thought that he now knew why Bessas did not ask Emperor Justinian for another army to quell the fighting and expel the Persians from Lazica.

Forty streptons of *this*.

He realized he did not know what it was called, but *this*—if placed right, he thought—may as well be two armies. He again sniffed the scent that clung to his skin.

Chapter 6
A Battle Goes Badly in Lazica

They had at the same time been attacked by pestilence, which carried off the greater part of the troops, and many died from want of food and necessaries.

Procopius of Caesarea
The Secret History

The battle cry, "Nobiscum," which it was customary to shout when beginning the charge is, in our opinion, extremely dangerous and harmful. Shouting it at that moment may cause the ranks to break up. For because of the shout, the more timid soldiers ... may hesitate ... while the bolder, roused to anger, may rashly push forward and break ranks...The result is that the battle line is uneven and without cohesion...

The Strategikon of Maurice
Written—6th Century, Byzantium
Suspected Author: Emperor Maurice
(r. 582 – 602 AD)

Arabissos was still too new to combat to know much, but he did know a few things—and among those few was the uniform, categorical contempt veteran officers had for soldiers and units who would yell, whoop, and wallop their battle cry before a charge. Absolute disdain. Far worse than a routine matter of poor discipline, the battle cry occupied a special nadir for being an act either of ignorance, announcing one's manifest lack of readiness to be in the very position one must be in order to have cause to yell it, or arrogance—arrogance can get a whole unit killed. Arrogance throws aside the simplest lesson of so many lessons the Romans had learned as they honed the art of combat against their worthy Persian adversaries in interminable wars of attrition.

Or, it was simple, impudent childishness. It seemed that nearly every soldier was a grown-up boy, a boy who had been raised playing a game of Roman soldier where the depth of his imagination could be likened to the depth of a spoon—invariably he played out fancies of great Roman legions rushing headlong into battle plains. Few understood that when legions won a traditional, set-piece battle on a plain it was through concentration of discipline and strategy. Fewer still understood that many of Rome's greatest victories were not really on battle plains at all, but were achieved through sophisticated tactics that deceived the enemy and got under and around his defenses—like Scipio Africanus turning the tide on the Carthaginians in Hispania or Flavian when he harassed Cannibal all about Italy.

In this latter case, the battle cry was worst. It amounted to a grown adult playing out his most childish playtime fantasies at just the most fatal imaginable time.

The veterans were unanimous: Don't ever use the battle cry!

That is why Arabissos knew this was not going to go well.

There was lots of time to talk about anything when making one's way from Archeopolis to Tsibilium or from Tsibilium to Hermonassa, and back again. Some days, people would ride for hours and say nothing, but other times a mood swept over and soldiers and officers felt social and passed their time telling stories. Not surprisingly, many of the veteran soldiers had interesting stories to tell.

That was a whole part of it: Veteran soldiers. There were too few of them.

The plague had started almost ten years earlier in Egypt before winding its way around Sinai and the Levant through Syria and up through Asia Minor, and then it swept on to Byzantium and beyond. Fortunately—if that were an appropriate word for such a travesty—it did not just "fork" left on the way, but it progressed in both directions as it came up out of Africa, wreaking as much havoc on the Persians to the east as it did the Byzantine Greeks and Romans to the west.

That was fortuitous because the plague badly weakened the Byzantine Greeks. Things would probably be different, much different, if it had favored to spare the Persians of its wrath.

Most Byzantines would not bother to think about the indiscriminate aspect of the plague—though it was most certainly that. The plague knew nothing of tribe or nation but claimed man and woman, Roman and Persian, Christian, pagan, Zoroastrian, and Jew with equal ferocity, and against which there proved no viable defense anywhere by anyone, save time. Arabissos had been three and four years old when Armenia was overcome. Normally, that would be too young to remember much, but it was impossible not to remember the plague. His grandparents, a pregnant aunt, two uncles, and several cousins were all infected; only one of his cousins from among them, Loris, survived. When he was still four, he did not know much about the Persians to worry or fret that they too might be scourged with the same tempest. Today, at least for that, he could be grateful. The Persians were here, here to fight. *They, like we, are few.* He thought. He had that to be thankful for.

Besides being few, the armies tended to be young and inexperienced; veterans who had survived earlier phases of the war and the plague were prized. Unfortunately, one disadvantage of youth was not so much error as it was foolish error. The temptation to respond to a fool making the battle cry—when time and time again the veterans had trained recruits not to do this—was such a simple reaction. A battle cry was a human mistake, not an act of God; it was a preventable mistake—a mistake that got men killed.

"Nobiscum!"

One soldier started it. *A cavalryman?* Arabissos watched and wondered where the cry came from. The battle cry went up and down the line; once started it was nearly impossible to stop. The first line, then the second:

"N-o-b-i-s-c-u-m!"

Who?

Who was the goddamned fool who started this? Arabissos wondered.

Arsaces?

Arabissos shook his head.

No. Couldn't be.

The man seemed a barely competent commander, but he could not be that incompetent—unless he was playing for the other side.

Arabissos drove the idea from his mind. Not because it was impossible...quite the opposite. While he had learned so much from the wildly unexpected assignment of accompanying a military campaign to Lazica—when he had not two years earlier began as a young, inexperienced apprentice notary in Byzantium where it had been hoped he could leverage his bilingualism and education to secure a desk job in the city where popular Latin was in almost total disuse, but remained the language of government—there were still many things Arabissos did not understand. Just three years earlier, when he had been eleven years old, a general, Artabanes, formulated a conspiracy to overthrow Emperor Justinian, and Arsaces was a key co-conspirator.

The conspiracy was uncovered, and Justinian resolved the crisis by forgiving the two conspirators. Not only that, but Justinian summarily appointed Artabanes the *magister militum per Thracias* and assigned Arsaces to act as a lieutenant general in the war against the Persians in Lazica. But, things did not end there with this three-time compounded oddity. Arsaces and Justinian already had a history before the conspiracy. Arsaces, who was, like Arabissos, Armenian, was an Armenian of Parthian descent from the noble Arsacids family, which fled to Armenia when their control over Persia was usurped centuries earlier by the Sassanids. In principle, this might make Arsaces an ideal leader to resist Persian encroachment in Lazica, except for the problem that Arsaces was a suspected traitor who was believed to have conspired with the Persian Shah Chosroes in the lead up to the war to work a deal on Lazica that might lift the Arsacids family. Justinian learned of this and had punished him with public embarrassment.

The best Arabissos could make of it was that the emperor probably thought the assignment to the wretched wastelands of Lazica to fight a war against his erstwhile Persian co-conspirators was a sort of poetic justice, but it seemed a justice that did not make much account for the likely more loyal garrison Arsaces would necessarily lead in the fulfillment of the affair. Justinian was a survivor of the plague that had claimed the lives of many of Arabissos' family. There were many who suspected that the combined traumas of surviving the plague and the loss of his beloved wife the Empress Theodora—also three years ago—had taken a toll that had been too much and that the emperor's erudition and judiciousness had been erratic ever since.

He tried to suppress his suspicions about Arsaces, which he kept telling himself were mere figments of imagination that haunted him, but Arsaces the man and physical presence would do something to pique them again. There were not many factors the tagma had in its favor, but it did have in its corner the option to choose the location of the battle—and when to fight. These were important choices that could be leveraged for advantage and they were planned accordingly.

The Persians had control of Suania where they were now located. This expeditionary unit was intended to harass Persian garrisons and keep them under stress until a larger plan, which Arabissos could not be privy to, was undertaken to break the Persian vice and drive them out. From time to time a Persian vasht, a small division, would be mobilized to expel Arabissos' small tagma. The tagma was expected to be on the run and the Persian orders were to drive it out or destroy it. The Persians could be counted on to proceed against the tagma if the tagma appeared to be backed up against a cliff. The Persians, who would think they had backed the outnumbered tagma into a corner, would feel emboldened and advance though the line of Roman archers, who would have the high position at the top of the cliff. The Persians would be assured that through their greater number they would crush the balance of the Roman positions as they pressed it under the precipice.

And then they would experience a surprise.

It was all a good plan. On even ground the tagma was barely a match for a Persian unit at least twice its size. With at least one archer line positioned above on the cliff, maybe two, the match was much more even. The infantry simply had to appear to be slowly giving ground, then escape up the crevice under cover of arrow fire, and with the Persians in position...but no. Arsaces would not have it.

He ordered all three files of archers to the ground. "Formation," he said. "Battles are won on excellent application of formation." Against all sense and good advice, he made his orders clear—no archer would shoot from the cliff. That the problem this created was compounded in its effect by the secrecy of the mission did not matter to Arsaces. The soldiers did not know there was an escape route!

There was some reason for this. If the soldiers knew the plan, it made it all the more likely the information would fall into the hands of a spy. Soldiers were not privy to the reasons of strategy.

But electing not to position the archers on the cliff, even in the last moment before the battle when the significance of their position would be manifest to the tagma's infantry and when the Persians would be too committed to extract themselves even under recalculation of the outcome of the skirmish, meant that the entire tagma did not know this cliff had been selected specifically for a very well-concealed gently vertical crevice, wide enough to take two files of men to the top of the cliff and to safety. At a time of great chaos, when it would be most difficult to telegraph a "flee" order— let alone to communicate that soldiers should flee specifically to a location that was selected for its difficulty in spotting—is exactly the time when someone would have to give the unfortunate order that all units should retreat directly into a wall of rock.

Arsaces knew better. He always seemed to know better. This time, he would tell no one and keep the archers level, where they would have no advantage at all against greater numbers because "formation."

The doubts Arabissos harbored and the utter hopelessness of doing anything about a general who had already been convicted and forgiven of conspiracy— conspiracy to kill the emperor—was crushing.

Arabissos clenched his teeth.

Never mind.

Someone, perhaps Arsaces, had invoked the battle cry.

The sight of altogether predictable ensuing chaos made Arabissos shudder. The shudder was not on account of anything unexpected. Instead, he cringed on playing eyewitness to the disastrous details of what was about to unfold, of what the veteran officers described so vividly on the way to Hermonassa.

The tagma's soldiers were young, many untested. They had no proper business on this detachment in Suania, but that was another matter. In any case, he—a fourteen-year-old notary—already had more battle experience than half the tagma. He watched the predictable wreck unfold.

Many of the soldiers in the front line, for the first time facing actual combat, wavered; they hesitated. Every third man, every fifth man, did not have to hesitate much because the bolder in the line behind them were already breaking their ranks.

They were breaking their own line!

The horses had been positioned at the flanks. Their positioning was deliberate with larger, heavier specimens placed first—the better to batter through the enemy with lance. The lighter, more nimble horses were behind—the better to flank and attack from the outside with bows. Bows were a dicey matter with Persians already, especially horse-borne bows. Many centuries of painful lessons were written in blood on the battlefield, not only with the Persians but with the Alans, Goths, and especially the Huns. Roman armies who had in long-gone eras been the unmatched masters on the battlefield of uniform mass, ponderous momentum, infantry, and sword had reformed to learn a new way of war: War based on speed, agility, and diverse units. These units were diverse in number and function—units of lance and spear, sword and archery, infantry and cavalry...cavalry and mobile archery. Hard lessons in strategy and tactics had turned constant wars of attrition and, in the latter times, wars of regression into what now seemed to be increasingly favorable campaigns. But even with the significant advances in archery—in the construction of the composite bow itself and its use on a moving horse—the tradition of mobile archery was ancient among the Persians; small errors could turn the minor advantage the Romans had fought so hard to achieve into devastating vulnerability.

It was with some horror that Arabissos watched the same pattern unfold on the flanks with the mounted lancers and archers. Horses did not differ so much from men when it came to temperament, and some of the forward horses hesitated on hearing the cry. Their riders whipped them and, being obedient animals, they moved but not before a few bolder beasts from the archery line behind burst through.

One...two...three...four...

"Five!"

Arabissos could not stop himself from saying the last count out loud. They were as good as dead—lucky if they got off a shot before being minced by the forward lancers on the Persian side. He could see from the bodies of the mounted archers that they knew their predicament. Two furiously tried to pull back their horses; one leapt! He jumped off his horse! Arabissos glanced behind to his right to see if the depotatoi, medical corpsman, witnessed this.

They had. They sprang into life. At least they were paying attention.

The mounted archer, if he could be retrieved—which was unlikely—would surely return with broken legs, a few broken ribs, and a dislocated shoulder.

Arabissos watched the depotatoi sweep into action. All but two of them at least were veterans, and they were carefully arranged for that. That depotatoi were primarily selected from among the best soldiers—naturally most of whom would be veterans—at first struck him as odd; he guessed now that he had felt that way because his reflexive assumption was to think that the best soldiers should be in the business of killing and aggressing. A soldier who trotted along with him on the way to Hermonassa explained it to him this way:

> "If you were stuck, debilitated beyond the line or inside enemy lines, not dead—yet!—but stuck... immobile, unable to save yourself, and separated from your garrison, who else would you want coming for you but the best soldiers?"
> "Isn't it the best that you want, or if not then, might it as well be *nobody*?"

Put that way, it was hard to argue with. While this tagma was a regrettable, motley mess, he could do nothing but admire the small band of depotatoi, marveling at how they worked in practiced, swift cohesion.

Probably before the archer went down, they had already deduced the breaks in the forward line. Two, two-horse teams shot through these openings on opposite sides. It was a bubble of competence rising confidently into the air over a sea of novitiate chaos. One team was entirely diversionary. A horse with lance sped ahead directly to the line of the dismounted archer while the second, a mounted archer, kept his rear flank. The pounding, determined gallop of the lead lancer caused hungry Persian soldiers who were advancing on the fallen archer to alter their focus of attention and fix it on the inbound warhorse. As their attention locked on the lancer, one and then two in rapid succession became prey to the arrows from the mounted archer behind.

That—Arabissos thought—was the way it was supposed to work! But it did not because of the goddamned battle cry!

This archer was well trained in all the three points of his craft:

Accuracy—two Persians struck—check.

Force—two Persians down—check.

Rapidity—two more arrows were in flight.

Four arrows in less than a minute!

One found its mark in a Persian shoulder. He was not dead, but he stopped being a threat to anyone. The other arrow wreaked more havoc for missing than it might have had it found a mark—splitting through the ranks of what was now a confused forward squad. Two of the most forward soldiers not yet struck ducked for ground, three in the rear froze, and one of them turned tail and ran into the shield of an advancing adversary in the second line.

As all of this happened, the second team came around on the other side to Arabissos' left in two arcs. The first horse raced on a narrow arc that terminated at the location of the fallen mounted archer. A second pair of stirrups dangled from the back of this lead depotatoi's elongated saddle. His job was to carry the wounded. The second horse galloped on a wider arc, clearing a path that dared the enemy to try to close in. As the horse sped along its wide arc, the mounted lance on the first team of horses sharply turned left so that now the two horses from the two teams were racing towards each other.

At the distance Arabissos stood, it appeared that they would collide. It was hard to take his eyes off of them—their combined speed so great, their size so broad, their mutual target: each other. He sensed that the spectacle must have transfixed the enemy as well. It was designed for that. Much of military work, he had learned—especially in this era of fast, mobile units—was intended to conceal movement from the enemy. Paradoxically, one of the more effective ways to achieve this was to divert the enemy's attention with grand displays, especially when arrows were flying and swords were swinging.

This display was intended to open space for the double-stirrup horse and the ground team to retrieve the fallen soldier, but it did not need to be limited to that. If they were wise the rest of the infantry should have been seizing this moment while the whole enemy advance slowed in the face of the spectacle. Sadly, he suspected it more likely that if they weren't mired in self-ambulatory confusion brought on by their own boorish battle cry, this unit's infantry was probably as spellbound by the depotatoi's show as the adversary.

As the two lancers seemed to come together, merge, and then come out from either side, the depotatoi with the extra stirrups closed the distance to the fallen mounted archer. It was only at this moment that Arabissos even noticed the two dismounted depotatoi who had been approaching the wounded directly, but from the ground. This display of the mounted corpsmen had many effects and created a distraction so the groundsmen could make contact with the wounded was one of them. These two groundsmen, surely, were the non-veteran depotatoi. They had probably distinguished themselves sufficiently for the corps but were assigned relatively uncomplicated roles in its complex choreography. They ran in a single file, one at front and the other at rear. Each carried a rope that was tethered front and rear to a leather gurney; they held it just above the ground between them as they moved. Each of them crouched low while they sped in the linear-most fashion towards their fallen comrade.

The fallen archer had enough of his wits about him that he expected this. Arabissos could see that he had taken one arm and crossed it over his chest, holding the opposite shoulder in his palm. Neither leg seemed to move of its own...they were both probably broken. Bracing himself with the weight of the crossed arm, the archer heaved in one direction, drew the full force of his weight back on the other, and teetered himself up on the side.

It was just in time. The double-stirrups cavalryman had drawn back his speed to time his arrival with the groundsmen. As the three converged on the fallen, the two lancers crossed paths again at frightfully close distance and passed one another. They seemed to slow down just barely enough to turn inward— back towards the Byzantine ranks— then buckled. The one to Arabissos' left turned again sharply, the horse's two feet lifting off the ground as it whinnied. The rider beckoned his horse into a 180-degree turn; the stop and turn provided time for the other lancer to gain distance on him in what was now the same trajectory. Fully reoriented, the two riders were now both coming around for another circle—this one more narrowly drawn. Both rode clockwise and split from one another by half the circle's circumference, forming a sort of narrow wall of protection around the rescue team.

All the while, the mounted depotatoi archer had slowed to a trot. He was still off to Arabissos' right and to the right of the center of action. He did not dare stop moving, which would be an unnecessary act for cavalry that would make himself an easier target. Now, rather than rapidly firing, he aimed and quickly re-aimed, making it clear to the opposing side that the first Persian to interfere with the rescue would be the next Persian to die. Arabissos sensed that the enemy line understood that the archer held them in a silent pact: he would agree not to shoot and spare their lives for a chance to take a pound out of the Roman infantry, so long as they didn't interfere with the rescue.

Finally, the two groundsmen and the double-stirrup cavalry converged on the fallen. The groundsmen pulled the gurney up the wounded man's side. Aware of their efforts, he let go of the upward tilt he had established himself in and fell into the gurney. While the groundsmen secured and lifted him, the cavalryman pulled up astride the three and oriented his horse directly back towards the Roman line. For the first time, he brought the horse to a stop; it was the first time Arabissos observed a stationary horse since the affair had started. Holding himself in the saddle by his stirrups, he leaned forward and down towards the groundsmen who pulled the gurney taut. They were prepared to give it a "heave-ho!" when one of them gestured to the other groundsman and the mounted rider.

He noted their rapid nodding and watched while the groundsmen, instead of lifting the wounded soldier onto the saddle, rope one side of the leather gurney through both of the free stirrups, pulled it back behind and closed the loop into itself—tying the rope back to its source on the gurney.

There was a whistle, and in the same moment the horse was off—galloping not at full stride but quickly—towards the Roman line. The groundsmen went running close behind.

This was dangerous. Ground conditions were perilous, and it was anyone's guess what the poor fallen archer might be dragged through in the final dash to safety. They had to make a quick, battlefield call and must have assessed that he had broken too many bones to risk lifting him to the saddle—a wrong move might have been a sure death, making a vanity of all their efforts.

Once the four, including the fallen archer, had cleared the circle of defense that the lancers kept drawn there was another whistle. Arabissos could not tell where it originated, but both the lancers and the archer responded, breaking their formation and falling back to the line. A moment later the rescue team was behind the line and then the mounted team.

All of this was expensive. The choreography was that of a team that continuously trained. The formation Arabissos had just observed, he knew, was one among many the depotatoi had trained for, and if need had arisen they could have signaled for an alternative formation during the same rescue.

The team was selected from among the best and most experienced soldiers in a tagma. It might seem a luxurious indulgence to concentrate so many of the best military assets into rescuing the fallen, but this too was something a bored officer explained to him on the way back from Hermonassa. All soldiers were expensive. Expensive to recruit, suit, garrison, move, and train. Any lost soldier had to be replaced— requiring a duplication of what was already a high cost.

Archers were all the more expensive. Their equipment, naturally, and the arrows in particular were disposable, in contrast to sword, shield, spear, and lance—all of which could be reused. The training for archers not only was expensive, but it was limited. There were only so many trainers, so many schools, and so much time between conflicts. It was not just a matter of cost—value came into play. Legions in the old republic or Latin empire made limited use of archery, preferring large infantry formations and their lumbering, churning momentum combined with artillery that was terribly intimidating to the contenders of the day, but which was still bulky and slow.

As the value of momentum gave way to the advantages of agility, archers had proven their value on the battlefield.

An archer might disable five enemies before an infantry made contact—and the archer did not even have to hit the enemy to achieve this! Given a simple hail of arrows, to raise one's head was to volunteer it for the release of the next archer's draw; it was enough to neuter an enemy advance. As long as arrows remained in good supply, one could multiply the loss of such an asset by the number of minutes in combat. Now—all of that in mind—consider the value of a trained and effective *mounted* archer, which not only required an archer trained to shoot on a moving horse, it requires a horse trained to carry an archer.

All of this still did not account for the effect on morale. Units of soldiers were social bands—human beings with complex reasons for being in the military—and no one could say why everyone or anyone fights, but men would fight for each other. Losing the human bond took a toll on a unit. A unit of twelve may be reduced to half its value for a loss of two. On the other hand, the soldier's confidence that every effort would be made to recover them in case of injury steeled their determination in conflict and cultivated a dedication to their superiors.

A good corps of depotatoi was a precious asset, a sound military investment. Their work was so important that the corpsmen were guaranteed a nomisma for each soldier they rescued.

The stupendously executed rescue was like a beautiful, crystalline bubble that rose out from the torrid, chaotic dissembling that unfolded on the battlefield before him. What started with a fool's invocation of the battle cry was quickly disintegrating into the setup for a rapid tactical withdrawal...if they were lucky.

The broken forward and center lines converged on one another during the charge. The effect of this was hard to understate; lines were trained to operate as a unit. Earlier legions were a sort of slow advancing, grinding cube that would churn its way through disorganized enemy armies. It had been almost a millennium since the last time Latins had fought like barbarians, throwing disorganized masses of lone sword and ax-wielding warriors into a battle plain. Like legions of yore, the units remained organized and operated as a unit, but gone were the square formations of identical legionnaires. Infantry fought together but in carefully arranged and diverse units.

Leading the units—but far off to the edges of the battle on both sides—were the standards, flags held high above the line of sight whose purpose was to provide visual cues to infantry locked in confusion as to where the line of battle was, and whether it was moving forward or falling back. Behind the standard bearer was the trumpeter who relayed calls from the commanding officers. Most soldiers could not retain a sense of auditory perception in the heat of battle to register a trumpet call no matter how loud and clear, that is except for the most experienced veterans who had opportunity to learn to discriminate the sound of the trumpet from the chaos of battle.

Commands for soldiers' units and individual actions were telegraphed by standard bearers through the placement of flags and streamers on either side of the battlefield. The trumpet's real purpose was to retain cohesion between both sides of the battle line and signal flag bearers to change colors or manipulate their streamers, which in turn were observed by military commanders, the detarchs and hekantontarchs, who would relay or facilitate the orders to their units on the ground.

Within the battle lines, order was critical. The first lines were armed with lance and shield, the second sometimes with sword and shield, and the third and subsequent lines with bow.

As it were, all were factors that lent plausibility to Arsaces' insistence on the importance of formation. Vexing still, but plausible.

In an orderly advance, the enemy did not get close. Lances would take out enemy swords and axes before they met the advancing line. An arrow from the third, fourth, or fifth lines, which fired in continuously rotating volleys, met the odd adversary who broke through—that is if he was not diced by spear or sword in the second file. The transition from legion to tagma had been slow and painful, a necessary change to meet the challenge of Persian archery and barbarian cavalry, especially Hunnish. But, by this day, the tagma had developed into a potent killing machine. In theory.

The killing efficiency of the tagma was intimately connected to its ability to fight cohesively—as designed—as a unit. This capacity, expensive to learn and expensive to train, was achieved by practice through lessons written by survivors in the blood of their fallen brothers. However, its achievement evaporated almost instantly when some damn, hotheaded fool yelled, "Nobiscum!"

When the lines broke order, it was too often swords from the second line that got ahead of lances in the first.

And almost with that, it was over.

Swords did not keep the enemy at a distance, which is where the enemy needed to be in order for the line-formation archers to have clear lines from which to shoot the advancing Persians. Scattered between the lancers were vagabond swordsmen. The archers shot together, and every archer fired, regardless of whether they had a target. The reason for this was to harass the enemy with a continuous hail of arrows and limit his freedom of movement—even if it was impossible to land an arrow on a specific man.

With no lines to aim through, this forced almost all the archers to aim over the forward lines' heads. At first this tactic was not immediately useless since it put pressure on the Persian lines from above, but once the Persians—with an able commander and effective battlefield communication, as this unit damnably had—detected the consistency of the hail, then they could adjust by advancing hard forward. Essentially, they would be placing themselves inside the archers' firing vectors and very nearly render three lines of expensive archers useless to battle.

Without archers to get their back, the infantry manning lances and swords at the front found themselves effectively outnumbered. Add to that the fact that these were most inexperienced soldiers; a rout was shaping up before Arabissos' eyes.

The second line that had merged into the first was minced, and the Persians were advancing into the first line that had merged into the second. This line included in its number many of the more timid soldiers who had given way at the battle cry. Interestingly, the second line seemed to hold its ground a bit more effectively than the first. The soldiers who had not advanced were the more disciplined and ordered those who were retreating to fall back into line, which opened lines of fire for the archers. In the meantime, the trumpet was sounding. Overhead, Arabissos could see the standard falling back, acknowledging that events were not proceeding as they hoped.

The open lines of sight for the archers were a blessing, but the rate of fire had dipped. The three rows of archers were arranged so that the first line stood in front of a row of shields. The second knelt a bit higher so as to shoot from above the shields planted in the ground. The shields in this way served as a guiding device that led the second line to fire above the first line's heads and reminded the first line to keep their heads down at all times. The third line stood upright.

When a fall back was ordered, the first line of archers had to move to the rear, safe behind the shielded second and third lines. This preserved valuable archers from exposure to the weapons of the advancing enemy, but it also reduced the rate of fire that the front lines could rely on to suppress the same enemy advance.

Looking beyond, it was clear too that things were not going much better for the cavalry flanks. Cavalry operated in teams—like the depotatoi, infantry, and archers. Cavalry were not sent in to battle as automatons, but their functions were carefully balanced between lance and archer. Several well choreographed and interminably drilled patterns were put to use in combat to maximize their effectiveness. Veterans claimed that a small band of effective cavalry who had mastered their patterns could out-fight four to six times their number in combat. They were insistent on this. Twelve horses (with nine lancers and three archers) could stop as many as sixty when the twelve were orchestrated and the sixty ran as lone warriors.

The math of it was spectacular, but there was a weakness. If something broke the choreography, if the orchestration of pattern was disrupted, a superbly drilled cavalry regiment could be reduced to twelve individuals. By the self-same math, they might find themselves twelve individuals aligned against forty four mounted warriors. The ancient legions almost always operated according to a master order of battle, but the tagmas were designed to be semi-autonomous. They may all work towards the same goal, but they were free to judge for themselves the most appropriate tactics for their situation. When several tagmas were deployed on a battlefield, if one tagma erred or was overcome, the other autonomous tagmas could come to its aid.

Out in the wastelands of Lazica and staffed in the aftermath of the plague, it was too common—Arabissos learned—that tagmas fought alone. One error was all it took.

He watched the two flank regiments of cavalry, both in disarray, in open retreat.

"Goddamned, battle cry," he muttered under his breath. *Goddamn you, Arsaces*!

What had a moment ago looked like a semi-orderly fallback was rapidly descending into a rout. There were so many bodies from the first line strewn across the battle's seam that there was no hope that even the best corps of depotatoi could retrieve the wounded. From across the field, Arabissos made eye contact with a soldier in the second line. He could see the question in the soldier's eye, asking himself if he should break ranks and flee. He caught the eyes of a second; this one just as he plunged his lance into the chest of a Persian adversary. The soldier took a quick look around him—victorious in one instant, but on all sides surrounded. Arabissos could feel the weariness of the man who had to hope he could extract his lance and use it again before himself falling victim to an enemy's tip.

An overwhelming and cold shudder came over Arabissos, he was disturbed to his core. It felt like a cold throbbing in his heart that dropped into his belly. How was this going to go? Was he sick?

He thought he was going to be nauseous and was preparing to throw up, but it was not nausea. Something inside him clicked. Something took over his senses.

He was not even sure what he was doing when he found himself already doing it. He turned, strode in three menacing strides over to the trumpeter, planted his face into the trumpeter's face, and yelled, "Call a cavalry retreat! A full cavalry retreat! Do it, now!"

The trumpeter, barely older than he, looked at him aghast.

"Whah!? Who...who the hell are you?" He was finally able to protest—knowing the answer to his own question was exactly its point.

He was about to tell Arabissos to go to hell or his station; Arabissos did not wait. With both hands, he grabbed the trumpet from the orderly's hands and yanked at it. As the trumpeter had in no sense been expecting this, it readily came free. "Give me that!"

Arabissos leaned as close into the young man's face as he could. Their breath combined as he spoke.

"I need the Persians to follow us into the bomb."

The trumpeter's eyes grew wide with astonishment, if not understanding. Arabissos, who was not altogether tall, stood on his toes to raise his own stature while trying to drive his face down over the man, urging him to crouch into a submissive position.

"We planted a bomb. I don't have time to explain—you must do what I say!" Arabissos knew that if the cavalry retreated the Persians would believe that the tagma was routed. They would let the cavalry flee and try to finish off the infantry against what they believed is an impassable wall of rock. The infantry needed to follow him across the bomb and—when they are clear—he would detonate it.

By now, the trumpeter's knees were bending while Arabissos lurked above him, the trumpet he had taken partially raised.

"B-bomb? De-detonate?" The young man stammered.

Arabissos asked, and felt himself foolish for not knowing this earlier, "What is your name?"

"Flav..." he started, then corrected himself, "Paphos. I...I'm from Crete."

"Paphos," Arabissos started, "we have almost no time. You must take a lit torch and light the fuse when I give the signal."

The confusion and fear in the trumpeter's eyes were palpable. He struggled to answer, "But...General Arsaces...on what authority?"

Arabissos had no idea if it was his wit or just the wave that had caught him up, but he did not hesitate. He knew it was this moment or never. He lifted the trumpet sideways, like a club, to take it like a bat to Paphos's head.

"The general is out *there!*" Arabissos yelled.

"For all you know he's already dead and soon we will be too. If you don't order the cavalry retreat, I will – and I don't know how to trumpet, so who the hell knows what it will say!"

He gave the claim three seconds to sink in and then went on, gripping the trumpet, ready to swing, "And that will be *after* I take this to your bloody head!"

"Ok! Ok! Give me the trumpet...I'll do it!"

In a flash, Arabissos brought the trumpet underhand pressing it into Paphos' hands. He did not have to wait to see if he would keep his word; he knew that he would. Arabissos already turned and was striding towards the torch, which he extracted from its post while Paphos blew the cavalry retreat.

Returning to Paphos with the lit torch, Arabissos handed it to him as he heard the flank trumpeters by the standard bearer repeat the order. He could already sense confusion in the third line of archers at the retreat; he knew what they were thinking: *We are already doomed—why order the cavalry to abandon us?!*

He tried to drive it from his mind. Commanding Paphos, he pointed to a rocky embankment and exclaimed, "There. The bomb is laid there. I will lead the infantry across to the other side. There's a wedge beyond the cliff where they can escape. I won't have time to explain; you must convey this to the third archer file for me. Tell them that they will need to provide cover long enough for the lancers and others to get across the wedge to safety."

"When the archers withdraw—that's the moment. You must light the fuses quickly. The fuse is at the flag by the baggage train—that's a one-minute fuse—but if it doesn't ignite you must light the fallback fuse at the armament tent— that one is only a fifteen second fuse and it's hopped full of oil. It will burn hard. The fallback fuse will be dangerous, by that time the ground will be crawling with Persians."

"Assume the worst. Strip off your clothes, all of them—be completely naked. Throw blood on your body. Run like you are crazed and wounded, not in a straight line—do *not* act like you are concealing yourself—if you are lucky, they will ignore you. They'll think you are a child and save their ire for the soldiers. They will expect and kill a uniformed trumpeter, but they'll be too busy to notice fleeing children. You must light the fuses *in order*, do you understand?"

Paphos looked at him with a gaze of astonished acceptance.

"You can do this?"

Paphos nodded.

"One more thing," Arabissos added.

"Don't light either fuse until the Persians are clear of the armament tent. They must be in position to receive the blast. Not too late, not too early."

Arabissos did not wait for another question, though he was sure Paphos would have many once he had any time to think about the absurdity of situation. No time.

He ran for the nearest horse and grabbed a flag. A moment later, he was astride. He made two loud clicking noises, shook the stirrups, and struck the horse's behind. It was off.

With one hand holding the flag, the horse's forward burst momentarily threw Arabissos off balance; he only regained it by allowing himself to over-turn in the direction flag-wise so that his free hand passed over the saddle's horn. Gripping it, he pulled himself forward and fell towards the pommel so he could use the force of his own gravity to take hold of the strings and guide the powerful animal galloping beneath him.

Forthwith, he rode the horse headlong between the second file line, which was in an advanced state of wreckage, and the archer's line. He barely had time to think that he had put himself in the line of fire when he did the only thing he could; he waved his flag as frantically as possible and yelled, "Follow me!

"Follow me now!"

He had to hope that with the longer delay between arrow volleys that there would be enough time for the archers to notice his interruption and hold their draw.

"Fall back!" He yelled. "Everyone!"

A stray arrow slipped past his head. He felt a stray hair pluck from its roots at the force of it. He braced himself—no more followed.

"Fall back to the cliff! Fall back!"

By now he noticed that two thirds down the line was mostly in confusion, but the archers had held their draw.

There was no time to explain, no way to explain—all he could do was hope the soldiers would honor the flag he carried, if not his person; he carried no rank, no insignia.

A trumpet blared.

It was Paphos! He was sounding the retreat, this time for the infantry.

Thank God, Arabissos thought. He elected not to think any more about it.

He did not know how to use the flag to signal a retreat. He had seen it done, but flag signaling, especially during battle, and especially from the seat of a horse, was an art and a craft. He tried from his memory of it, but then he quickly gave up and instead drew the horse to a stop, reversed it, and faced the lines of archers who were now giving him their attention.

Standing up in his stirrups, he locked his knees and planted all of his weight down center. As he felt himself come off balanced he tried to use the weight of the flagpole to re-secure all the while lifting it as high as he could with two hands and waving.

"Follow me! Follow me! Fall back...to the cliff!"

Knowing few would hear him in the chaos of battle, he nevertheless yelled, this time to the archers nearest him in the probably vain hope they might pass the word as far as it could go.

"There's a crevice! There's a crevice in the cliff—use it to escape!"

Then, once more he swung the flag and yelled, "Follow me!"

At that, he fell back into the saddle, leaned forward, and grabbed the strings with both hands while holding the flag off to his right. He kicked the horse's sides with both legs from the stirrups—"Heeya!" Once again, the horse was off. This time he galloped the horse back down the line to where he started, slowed down towards the edge, and turned it, coming around the rear of the entire tagma's line.

"Follow me," he yelled, kicking the horse as it ran to center then righting it; he motioned the horse in the direction of the cliff face while easing it to a fast trot.

The word had spread. He was heard. The tagma was in a retreat and following behind. He glanced off to his left looking from one landmark to the next until his eyes fell on the naked, muddy body of a racing Paphos who carried a torch in his left hand. *Thank God he had wits about him to remember the instructions!* He was running to the tent...the first fuse. Once the fuse was lit there would be one minute if it kept its light. There was not much time.

"Hurry!" Arabissos yelled.

122

He arrived at the armament tent and stopped his horse. He began waving the soldiers through. They passed in an unruly line while the lancers and a small band of archers worked to slow the Persian advance.

Arabissos was waving them through and pointing to a large rock outcropping. "There, there, behind that rock! Find the crevice and take it to the top of the cliff. You'll be safe there!"

He was about to repeat himself when one archer intruded himself into his space. Arabissos could read by his insignia a that he was a *dekarch*, a commander of ten.

"The trumpeter said we are to guard you."

It was only in this moment of proximity—especially so while his stature was enhanced from his presence on the back of a horse—that the dekarch could see who and what he was. Arabissos tried to ignore the questioning and astonishment revealing itself in the man's eyes and instead regarded him for a moment in confusion. He then remembered the chaotic details of his own half-baked plan.

"Yes! Take a position opposite the muddy knoll by the rock. The crevice for escape is just beyond. Form a line and hold the Persians as long as you can so everyone can escape. We must lure them to the cliff where they'll think they have us cornered."

The soldier hesitated; Arabissos knew it was the doubts about his identity, his rank. Quickly, he thrust his flag at the soldier, hoping it would settle the question. He yelled, "Do it!"

Arabissos could almost see a "snap" in the man's head. He turned and began barking orders at his unit. In a moment, they were clearing the knoll—eight of them, four on four, taking position. Two others, including the dekarch, directed retreating soldiers behind the rock.

Out of the corner of his eye, in his far periphery, he caught the glimmer of a naked body moving quickly but running wide-paced, almost as if a giant were stomping on ants—the direction was towards the armament tent. Paphos! Any other time it would be a comical sight.

Now was his moment. Arabissos had to draw the Persians in without appearing to draw the Persians in; he had to look like he was addressing himself to the Roman line, not the Persians.

Arabissos pulled his horse up to a position off to the side of the archer dekarch's line of fire and in between the fleeing line of retreating soldiers and the remnants of the lancers from the second line— who were doing their best under the archers' fire to slow the advancing Persians. The goal now was to direct as many Persians near the knoll as possible. He had to get the lancers to safety while drawing in the Persians without spooking them and he had to act quickly—Paphos would be lighting the fuses any moment.

His position was dangerous; he was making himself an obvious target for a Persian arrow. He was able to maneuver the horse to keep it a trot ahead of the Persian infantry advance, but if an archer decided to loose an arrow any second might become his last. Fortunately, they were leaving him alone. He wondered why and looked above...*Thank God!*

Overhead, hails of arrows were coming from the top of the precipice where he had sent the archer lines. They had made it, apprehended the situation, taken position, and were doing their jobs!

With such a novice unit, Arabissos had come to appreciate that one could not always assume that soldiers could be counted on to do their jobs. Confused archers in flight might find themselves at the top of the cliff under order of command but having found themselves there they might not be completely clear on *why* they were sent there. In their confusion, it would not be surprising if they loitered about until an officer gave them an order.

Arabissos had thought quickly to devise the half-baked plan that was now irreversible in its execution. But no matter how fast he had thought, he had not thought that far. It was impossible for him to have considered every contingency or possibility. War countenanced nothing but the best of plans—that was true—but in the heat of battle fortune reigned supreme. Sometimes misfortune reigned, such as the infantile scream of an ancient battle cry. Sometimes fortune took the day—as with the arrows hailing from over the cliff head and landing atop the advancing Persians. Finding their unit under a hail of arrows, the Persian archers, who were until that moment providing backing for their own infantry line while it advanced, were now forced to adjust their fire to answer the archers above and provide cover. So far, at least, they had more important targets than an oddly positioned unarmed horseman with a battle flag.

He wished he had a trumpet. Thankfully, the line was not very long, and by his position alone he had brought much attention to himself. He pulled the strings on his horse up to his chest and lifted his stirrups, bidding the beast to turn in small circles and kick up a cloud of dust while he lifted and swung the flag. Trying not to cough, he yelled, "Retreat! To the outcropping, retreat!"

He knew that no matter how loudly he yelled the words, they would be dim in the hum of battle and confusing. The best he could do was to add, "Follow me!" He burst forward with his horse, running back down the line to its edge, rounding it, and coming back up again on the center in the rear. He slowed once more, spun the horse, lifted the flag, and repeated, "Follow me! Retreat!"

As he strode the horse towards the outcropping against the precipice he glanced over his shoulder to see that the remaining soldiers had heard. Indeed, many were in short trot, following after him. In their arms they carried what they could, but then he saw something that disturbed him. Others. *What the hell?* Others were trying to gather equipment; they were afraid to leave equipment behind. They thought they were going to need it to fight again!

Once more, he gathered up the strings and drew back against the stirrups to spin his horse. "Leave your belongings! Leave your belongings, leave the equipment!" When some soldiers looked up at him in confusion, he dropped all sense of military decorum and just yelled, "Ruuuunnnnn!" Then he spun the horse once more and continued his lead until he reached the edge of the outcropping where he stopped.

A soldier arrived on foot a moment behind. Presently, he pointed the soldier around the rock face towards the entrance to the crevice.

"There. I need you to stay here and wave on the men. Keep them going through that crevice. It's urgent that you be fast. When the last man passes through follow him—don't wait for me. I'm going to create a diversion. Do you understand?"

When the soldier nodded, he motioned his horse back toward the string of men, urging them to keep moving as he passed each column to where the line thinned out to nothing.

There he was. Standing on top of it. He could tell from the odd patches of conspicuously dark mud here and there that this is where he needed the Persians. He had no way of knowing what the Persians made of the Romans disappearing into what moments earlier appeared to be a cliff face, but he needed to be sure they did not have too much time to think about it. On his horse, he could keep his distance from the lancers at the Persian front line, but he was minimally armored. What if a Persian archer took his attention from above and noticed an oncoming cavalry?

Ordinary cavalrymen wore full-body armor, a thorax, or if agility was the greater concern then lighter protective coverings called klibania. The infantry were covered in kabadia, long quilted coats, but Arabissos was a notary.

He had to be grateful the tagma saw fit to suit him with a linen corslet, which he wore under his chiton that had been stiffened using a compound of wine and salt. The soldiers laughed at his skepticism when they gave it to him, insisting it would be strong enough to repulse an arrow. Observing the body of a fallen soldier the depotatoi had not collected as it disappeared behind the Persian advance, he seriously doubted their claim more now than he did when he first heard it.

No matter, the gauntlet was cast. He had no weapons, just the horse and the flag. *It worked when the depotatoi did it*, he thought to himself. *May as well try it out*. He had exhausted other options; the only option he had left now was show.

Kicking the sides of his horse with two feet, he pulled back on the strings yelling, "Go!" and it was off. He rode the horse into a full gallop, headlong into the Persian front line. Hesitation would have been death. What he was doing was absurd. Apart from the distraction of the Roman archers overhead, the only thing protecting him was the confusion of the Persians who must be wondering what demon had gripped this suicidal horseman, or else what did he know that they did not? Still holding the battle flag, he did what he could, swinging it somewhat into the advancing wind so the flag would catch onto the pole; he dropped it in front of him so that it led like a lance.

So far so good—no archers had targeted him yet. With seventy-five pous separating him from the Persian line, he veered his horse just left so that he would come to head off the edge of the alam, the Persian battle standard. His target was in reach. His heart was pounding. The wallop of the horse's gallop vibrated through his body as he yelled in a long, drawn-out holler. Finally, he came to fore and pulled back on the horse's strings, "Sstteeaaddddyyyy boy!" He hung on tightly as the horse's forelegs came upwards—their momentum so strong he could almost feel the giant drag a few inches on his hind legs below.

Then, when the horse had reared to its peak and Arabissos made contact with the fleeting instant of maximum height, he pulled his right arm back. As the horse came down on four legs again, he followed through, more plunging the flag than hurling it, drawing his palm downwards as he opened it and released the pole, giving it not just thrust but spin.

For a slow, finite instant, the flag and pole flew through the air. The horse shot its head and kicked. Arabissos' hands fell to his sides, his grip broken on the horse's string. All eyes of the Persian lancers, which a moment ago had been on him, followed the trajectory of the flag.

It touched its mark.

No one…not one had seen it coming, until seconds ago, not even Arabissos.

Almost as if through the hair standing up on his skin, Arabissos sensed that even the archers—on both sides—had paused their volleys.

With the apparent fury of a suicidal cavalry charge, it was revealed to be a symbolic attack on the Persian battle standard by an unarmed notary in a chiton with a hardened linen corslet beneath.

In midair, there was a crack as the head of the pole made contact with the alam. Their mutual force repelled once another. The alam came off of the hinges that supported it on a wooden pole; the flag came unfurled. Both fell to the ground.

The silence was broken by a voice that came from somewhere near the armament tent.

"Ruuunnn! The fuse…the fuse! RUUUNNN!"

It was all he needed to break the spell.

Before the gravity of it could settle in, he turned the horse around and was on the way back to the cliff face. It took a second more for the Persians behind him to get their own grip on the matter. What followed he had to more feel and sense than see.

With no helmet or armor, all he could do was point the horse in the direction of the rock outcropping and drive it forward while burying his head in the saddle, covering his ears on both sides with his arms. Lances were being thrown at him but the horse was already surpassing their range.

Arrows were flying overhead—in both directions. The archers above were doing what they could to protect him, which was not much. It was not likely that an arrow would hit another arrow in midair, but the multiplicity of cross-purposed arrows might make the Persian archers' aim more difficult.

Then he felt it—the one thing he had decidedly feared.

It came as the oddest collusion of sharp and blunt and it struck him in his side—in his soft abdomen on his right, below his rib cage. Arabissos had done enough battle to know that the sense of the pain usually came after the blow that delivered it. The pain would come later.

Tentatively, he lowered his right arm from his heart down to his side and pressed his palm up against where the arrow had landed.

He felt around.

No arrow.

No wetness.

It isn't wet?

"I'm not bleeding?" he asked aloud and risked lifting his head to see.

There was an indentation where the arrow struck and a sharp rip in his chiton. A half second later, he saw a broken arrow tip caught between the saddle and his waist. In the vibrations of the horse's gallop it was bobbing up and down, probably doing more damage in a scratch to his ass than it had done against his side, against his hardened linen corslet!

It worked.

"I'll be damned," he said to himself, amazed.

At about this instant, the horse came to the rock outcropping, and he slowed the animal, turning it.

He leapt from its back, grabbed its strings from the ground, and beckoned it to follow him up to the crevice where he slapped it and drove it so it would follow the path to the cliff top.

He knew he could follow the horse to safety, but if either of the planned fuses failed there was one last fuse that he could light from under the precipice. It was the option of last resort and it meant taking cover in a small hole he had dug in a space that was about to be between hell and a rock face. If the two fuses failed, in a moment the Persians would find the crevice and all of this would have been for naught.

Yelling once more for the horse to keep going without him, he turned around and ran back to the edge of the outcropping. The pace had slowed, but two or three arrows hit the rock face. The Persians were making sure that no Roman stuck his neck out.

Crouching as low as he could, Arabissos peered around the outcropping in the direction of the armament tent. So many Persians had run past the tent that it was blocked from his view. From his perspective, there was no hope of seeing a lit fuse, but then something else caught his attention.

On a hill beyond the Persian lines, beyond their backs, at a higher level on this hilly Lazican terrain, there was a figure. It was the figure of a young man who appeared more muddied and covered with ash than clothes. He was jumping up and down as high as he could and waving his arms frantically in the direction of Arabissos as if to say "Run!"

It was all the signal Arabissos needed. In one motion, he twisted and thrust forward with both legs—he took air. He was not running— *flying* into the safety of his shallow hole. He drew his legs up to his chest, covering and cradling his head in his arms and plugging his ears as best as he could.

Just as John Guzes had taught him.

* * * * * * * * *

In war, most of the time, numbers lie. At least, that is, numbers reported by men.

"Half killed."

"An army destroyed."

Usually it is not wrong that there was much destruction, but battles were won more often by exhaustion than by killing. Dying is simply the most present measure that the advance of exhaustion had taken too high of a toll. Exhaustion through hunger, through thirst. The exhaustion of battery, of advance, then retreat, then advance again. The exhaustion of elation followed by disappointment, followed again by thirst. And then wounds. Wounds, compounded by exhaustion, may as well be fatal.

An army reduced by one-tenth of its number from death, and another half of its number from exhaustion, was a defeated army. One for the victor's history books. One that would be remembered as "half" destroyed.

There were no exaggerations today, Arabissos thought as he surveyed the crater that opened into the space where five minutes ago there had been a muddy knoll.

This Persian army, not less than twice the size of his two-hundred-man tagma, had been destroyed.

Utterly destroyed.

It is true that a few cavalry and baggage units in the rear flank had been far enough back to witness the carnage and flee before anyone could stop them—that was probably a good thing.

The report they would deliver to their commanders would metastasize into debilitating fear that would be an asset to the Romans going forward.

John Guzes' mission to Hermonassa had supplied Bessas with the materials he needed to reduce the hardened walls of the citadel at Petra to pebbles and rubble—a fact that no doubt was well understood by the Persian rank and file. That was achieved through the use of siege engines whose actual intent was to distract the citadel's defenders so that civilians, like himself, could dig. The civilians Bessas had requested from Justinian in such large numbers—to the astonishment and frustration of the entire Byzantine officer class and Lazican nobility alike—frantically worked with shovel and cart to dig holes out from underneath the citadel's foundation and replace dirt and rock with bladders filled with Guzes' incendiary potion.

Until now, as far as the Persians knew, that was a tactic of stationary warfare. They had not yet seen it deployed on the battlefield. This was a first. The incendiary potion could be mobile. What was more likely too is that the surviving witnesses could not have told whether the explosion came from the cliff above or if it came from a bomb buried beneath. The survivors must have been so shocked it would not surprise Arabissos if they reported to their superiors that the Romans had a dragon in their company.

Of course what the Persians also did not know was that when it came to this deadly superweapon, the Romans were almost out of rounds. The Hermonassa plan had called for one hundred casements, but as Arabissos learned from Natan and Rava, they could only produce forty. At least the Persians did not know that.

For now.

Above him, infantry—archers and lancers alike— loitered at the top of the cliff, observing the landscape Arabissos walked about at level: bodies, body parts, fallen weapons, ash, small plots of fire.

Behind him, soldiers were returning from the crevice and spreading out. Surely. They were under orders from Arsaces to do a more formal survey and make a report.

A report, Arabissos thought. He started making a report to himself.

Nearly the entire first file—lost. The second, sufficient to retreat, but it was a rout. Perhaps as much as half their number. Of the cavalry and archers he estimated as many as eighty dead.

Eighty.

Out of two hundred.

He could not exactly ask rhetorically, "For what?" There he stood atop the answer. More than four hundred Persians were dead, a crushing defeat against the enemy's morale that should pay itself back for months to come.

Most generals would reckon this a great win. Five enemies dead—not exhausted, but dead—for every Roman fatality. The way the generals saw it, eighty dead was the cost of doing war, especially when winning.

But Arabissos knew better.

It didn't have to be this way.

It didn't have to go this way.

Arabissos knew that if the archers had been positioned on the cliff ahead of battle...if the order of battle had properly advanced...if no one yelled the damn battle cry... Mistakes had been made, and it is true that mistakes happen. But these were mistakes that should not have been made.

Soldiers joined the army, learned to fight and learned to survive, in battle and in war—that was their objective.

Arabissos had never intended to be here at all. He had intended to be a notary, an educated, literate, notary, in the capital, in Byzantium—not digging holes for incendiary devices in far-off, cold, desolate, Lazica.

But even when it was not grammar and rhetoric or geometry and harmonics, even when it was not the classical subjects of Greco-Roman education, he was teachable. From veteran soldiers who had survived a second tour of the most brutal war under brutal conditions while also coming through the plague, he too learned the art of war.

He stood and looked at the dead, sensing the movement of officers striding slowly past him. He looked ahead at where the Roman line had been, at the carcasses that littered the line.

"This was preventable," he said out loud.

"What?" someone asked, startling Arabissos.

Turning, he saw that it was Orbicius. *Flavius* Orbicius was one of Arsaces' better lieutenants. In a private moment, he could probably be pressed to be a better general than Arsaces.

Arabissos relaxed and answered his question, "I said that this was preventable."

Orbicius, fifteen years Arabissos' elder, replied, "Wars result in killing, son."

It was ever so slightly patronizing, and in this moment Arabissos was not ready to be patronized. He turned and faced Orbicius, shoulder to shoulder, eye to eye. "No! This...was...preventable!"

Surprised for a moment by Arabissos' assertiveness, Orbicius loosened what could be taken as a forgiving grin, "Alright. You are the hero. You tell me...how was this preventable?"

Hero.

He ignored the thought and answered, "So many things. The battle cry. That *battle cry*, Orbicius!" At this, Orbicius nodded. The smile drained from his face, along with some color. "And the archer placement—we could have placed some, at least a detarch, at the cliff and still not compromised the third file." As if his inner imp got hold of him, he went on not bothering to look to see if Arsaces was near as he said, "There was *no* excuse for that! None."

Orbicius gave way a bare nod, perceptible only to Arabissos.

"And the second line—they should *all* have had lances. I know it's disputed and some argue for sword but honestly, if the first and second file are lined in a checker and the archers have the back...to get through the first line to the second without killing off the first would mean suicide for an archer. For sword...the second line had to close and expose themselves while also making it difficult for the archers to aim."

He went on, "You and I know the only reason anyone still supplies swords is we haven't enough equipment. We have the wrong equipment...or not enough equipment. It would be better to wait, fight with the right equipment, and win every time than fight and lose just because we have the wrong equipment.

"Think about it. What is the rush? This is a wasteland here. If we're going to fight and possibly die for a wasteland, why not at least wait a few months until they can send proper equipment?"

"Men," Arabissos said, pointing at where the infantry files had made their stand, "Men lie dead...*not* because we had to fight. We *chose* to fight here. We chose this fight, in this place, on this day. We *chose* this. It would be another thing if the Persians had us cornered in siege back at Archeopolis, but out here...this was our battle to choose. And we chose to fight it *without* the right equipment. And now, because we didn't have the right equipment, because we treated our soldiers as disposable and refused to place them on high ground that properly was ours...we *chose* to fight on unfavorable terms. Those men," he pointed, wagging his finger as if enunciating with it, "Those men are dead. Those are our comrades."

He could see a glimmer between Orbicius' eye and nose. *A tear?*

Arabissos finished his point, "And training. *Training* man! Did you see our depotatoi?"

Orbicius nodded.

"In battle, men are afraid. You—you soldiers—you are in the battle. You are trying to calm your fears.

But from where I stand, back at the observation podium, I can watch. I can *see* what's happening. Men who are taken by their fear cannot fight. Men who command their fear do not think—they act. They act on what they have been trained to do."

"And this is as true of the adversary as it is of us. The adversary is but men! They are afraid. They are either afraid and immobile or afraid but in command of their wits so that they act on their training. What if every unit *trained* until it fought—like the depotatoi can retrieve the wounded? What would that even take? A year? Daily training for a year?"

"And is that so much? Imagine an entire tagma that could fight like the depotatoi. Think about it!" Orbicius held his gaze a moment as they stood in silence together.

Arabissos finished, "A well-trained tagma...trained to the skill of the depotatoi. A tagma half this size would have been twice as powerful, and very few lives would have been lost to lay waste to this Persian host."

"Victory," Arabissos groaned, "isn't victory when it costs too much. This cost too much."

For a moment, Orbicius and Arabissos stood together surveying the crater, their fellow soldiers, the fallen.

Finally, Orbicius faced Arabissos again and spoke, "Perhaps the gods had a fate in mind for you in sending you to Lazica with us, notary."

The gods.

It was an odd thing to say nowadays. The land abounded with heathens, but the armies remained primarily soldiered with Christians. True, Stoicism remained popular in the soldiery and there was the rare hold-out Mithrain, but either way—even if it was just a figure of speech—it could get Orbicius in trouble with the wrong set of ears.

"And what fate do you think that is?"

"We soldiers," Orbicius said, "We learn these things, and we keep them to ourselves. They are lessons, personal lessons, which keep us alive. We keep the lessons and the lessons keep us." "You are a different case. You observe the lessons. You watch them, their effect."

They regarded each other. Arabissos shrugged his shoulders slightly as if to say, "*And...*"

"Veterans can teach new soldiers, but where do the lessons go when we retire?"

"How many decades did it take us to learn to fight this way? How many generations of veterans did it take to learn that we couldn't fight the Persians, *and win*, with the old ways? We couldn't fight and hope to win if we had gone on fighting the way they used to, with the old legions? Lessons pass slowly when they only pass from ear to ear."

Another moment passed before Orbicius went on, "Write it down, Arabissos. Write a book. Write so that others can learn what we learned. That is why the gods sent you here to us, notary. Write. Write what you told me. Write what you learned...what *we* have learned."

"That is your fate."

* * * * * * * * *

The collection of the dead had occupied the afternoon, and the camp had to be relocated upwind from the killing field. It was late when the tagma set down to dinner. Torches lit the camp; soldiers and baggage train orderlies sat on rocks and logs like they were tables. They sat about a large, central fire whose warmth was a welcome and comforting contrast from the bitter cold of the Lazican night. A logothete was distributing the opsonion rations. Arabissos sat on a large boulder with Orbicius; another officer, Rufus; and Paphos, the young trumpeter who had lit the fuse. He had since bathed and found a spare chiton to replace his old one.

Midway through dinner, Arsaces stood on a tree stump and addressed the soldiers, congratulating them on their victory. He recited the names of the fallen who by now had been named and accounted for. When finally, as he seemed he was about to close, he stopped.

Arsaces was nothing if not difficult to read. Arabissos wanted to say that what followed seemed forced, but he could not tell. Maybe it was not Arsaces; maybe it was him.

Either way, Arsaces proceeded to congratulate certain soldiers by name: the depotatoi, the fallen mounted archer, the detarch who led and commanded the archers at the cliff, some cavalry he recognized for events Arabissos had not witnessed in the chaos and confusion, and the lancer who guided the retreating second file up the crevice to safety.

Next, with what for Arsaces passed for a smile, he beckoned Paphos to join him by the fire.

Paphos, who had been all smiles until now, jumped from his seat on a log and approached Arsaces, who stepped down from the higher log by the fire. He gestured for Paphos to take his place, which he did.

Turning and addressing the mostly seated tagma, and now with what no one could mistake as anything but a smile, Arsaces had these words—the warmth of which even affected Arabissos:

> "Gentlemen, I have fought, sometimes with some of you, in Armenia, in Lazica, in Africa…with Romans, with allies, with barbarians, and I have seen many things in a long time. But today would be the first, and—if Christ is merciful—the last when I was made to witness a battle won on account of the decisive deployment of *male* nudity."

At this, the entire tagma broke into laughter. Rufus about choked on what he was chewing. Paphos, for his part, could barely hold his balance on the log; Arsaces had to raise his own arm so Paphos could steady himself. Their laughing was only interrupted when an officer raised his voice above it all, addressing himself to Arsaces personally, "Oh, but General Arsaces! Sure…sure it's an unusual phase of the moon when male nudity wins the day but tell us about the times you led armies to victory on the basis of *female* nudity."

After the tagma enjoyed another laugh, Arsaces directed Paphos down. He returned to his seat, and as his eyes followed Paphos back to the boulder where they sat, they met with those of Arabissos. Arsaces didn't have to say anything; he just nodded as he and Arabissos held eye contact and indicated now was his time. Arabissos stood and approached. Once again, Arsaces gestured—for Arabissos to take a position on the log.

He did, and the tagma took on a moment of silence. Everyone stopped eating. Arsaces simply stood there considering Arabissos, saying nothing. After a moment, Arabissos was not sure what was going to happen. That he was sure he was going to be honored momentarily stoked his anxiety.

Arsaces did not speak. Instead, he took two strides backwards, stood upright, and saluted Arabissos.

The gesture had an immediate effect. At once, the entire tagma stood. Everyone stood in salute of Arabissos.

While they stood saluting, Arabissos heard someone say something. It was Paphos.

"So say I, a Flavian! I, Flavius Paphos! I name him Maurice. Maurice of the Battle of Maurica. Who seconds me?"

About the tagma there were affirmative grunts and ayes. Arabissos looked at Arsaces uncertainly; he could not believe this was happening. He was not even a soldier! Was this out of order? Had the young Paphos committed him to a well-meaning but embarrassing public guffaw? Arsaces glared back at him, with an iron certainty—he should stay his place on the log.

"I, So say I too! A Flavian. I, Flavius Rufus, name him Maurice. Maurice of the Battle of Maurica. Attila flees again! Who seconds me?"

Again, grunts, ayes, and a few whistles.

Finally, approaching in the flicker of the fire light, was Orbicius.

Walking slowly up to the log where Arabissos stood, Orbicius carried himself in a way that drew everyone's attention to him. The noise quelled. Orbicius stood below Arabissos, then started.

Orbicius did not shout but spoke so that Arabissos heard him as he approached.

"I, So say I too! A Flavian. I, Flavius Orbicius name him Maurice."

He turned and faced the standing tagma, "Maurice of the Battle of Maurica!"

Orbicius extended a hand to Arabissos who instinctively took hold of it. Flexing, their strength lifted Orbicius up to the log where he stood together with Arabissos.

Taking Arabissos' right hand in his left, Orbicius lifted it up in the air with the fire blazing behind him, calling out to the tagma, "Attila flees again! Long live Maurice!"

The tagma exploded in cheers. Soldiers were standing on the logs and rocks that they used as tables. Some threw weapons or cups into the sky. Eventually, their cheers settled into a chant.

"Long live Maurice!"
"Long live Maurice!"
"Long live Maurice!"

* * * * * * * *

Maurice, as he was now being addressed, trotted on his horse alongside the baggage train as the tagma made its way along a primitive road—more of a marathon fox trail back to Archaeopolis. Their orders provided for two objectives: One, was to harass the enemy before the October cold set in, making it too difficult to fight and then return to Archaeopolis. The other: Use Guzes' incendiary bladders to rout and demoralize the enemy.

With two-fifths of its fighting number lost, this unit would be leaving the Persians to roam free and un-harassed in Suania this summer. There were yet many months of life left in the season, so perhaps Bessas would be disappointed on account of the first objective. Of course, the Persians would be short by an entire field brigade, a field brigade they would never get back. Arsaces was prepared to take his chances with Bessas on that.

At the start of the day, the scouts could see at a distance that a caravan train was moving along another trail that led down to a juncture that met with their own. The trail that the caravan was coming along would have passed through Scanda, still occupied by the Persians. Maurice thought it odd that the caravan showed no signs of stopping, though he could not decipher that it had any military purpose. It struck him as odd still that Persian civilians would wish to be anywhere near a Roman military band on the march in the middle of nowhere. Nevertheless, the tagma and the caravan approached one another until converging around midday at the juncture.

When they converged he advanced with his horse past the baggage train and past the marching soldiers up to Arsaces and his lieutenants who had already made contact with the caravan. Arsaces, whose family was of Parthian origin and who spoke Persian, was up ahead with a guard speaking on horseback with someone Maurice took to be the head of the caravan.

Pulling alongside Orbicius, Maurice asked, "What is it?"

"Silk," was his only answer.

"Silk?"

"It's a silk caravan. They port in Derbent and pass through Scanda on the way to Petra."

"What?!" Maurice asked, astonished and indignant.

"To sell to whom?" He asked.

For once, for one nearly ridiculous time, his administrative knowledge of the bureaucracies of a notary might actually matter.

The tagma was here. This was Roman land, and these were unregistered foreign vestioprates.

"Chapter 4, section 9," Maurice said.

"What?" Orbicius replied.

"The Book of the Eparch, Chapter 4, section 9...unregistered vestioprates, or alien strangers, selling silk stuffs...and I quote, 'shall be flogged, shaved and liable to confiscation.'"

Orbicius said nothing.

"Why don't we arrest them? Silk is precious. We're here—it's booty of war. Why isn't Arsaces ordering it confiscated. For that matter, why have they been approaching us since this morning? Why didn't they stay their distance?"

Again, despite the pleasantries of the night before, his suspicions of Arsaces were tinged. Almost involuntarily, he flexed. An image formed in his mind of the hell the eparch of the city could, and would, have brought on an ordinary, city-dwelling linen seller who dared exchange in unregistered silk. And those were Roman citizens, with rights!

These were Persian merchants in a land at war. He almost motioned his horse forward to arrest them himself when Orbicius stayed him and horse alike.

"Stop," Orbicius ordered, uncharacteristically, and in no uncertain terms.

"No one will be arresting our Persian silk merchants or confiscating their silk, Maurice. Not today."

When he did not continue, Maurice adjusted his horse so he could face Orbicius directly—his back faced Arsaces.

They considered each other, and no words were exchanged until Maurice could not stand it. He said, somewhat under his breath, "Him?" He tilted his head towards Arsaces.

Orbicius just looked at him.

"Is this about him? Is he filling his coffers?" Maurice asked, now somewhat angrily as it was increasingly difficult to have this conversation and not be noticed.

Orbicius finally spoke.

"Come alongside me, new Aetius."

Maurice did as he was asked.

"What you are thinking," Orbicius said, "is not so."

"Alright then, explain," Maurice answered.

Orbicius looked straight ahead as he answered, as if talking to the air, "The silk will not be confiscated. It will be purchased. The merchants will not be arrested, let alone flogged."

"What will happen to them?"

"They will be paid."

Maurice attempted a retort when Orbicius lifted his hand again to silence him.

"You heard me right. They will be paid...richly so." Maurice could not believe what he was hearing. "And, when they are paid, they will be let on their way back to Persia where they will acquire more silk and return with it to Lazica, to Suania, to Petra...where it will be sold, and they will not be arrested." Maurice, especially after the previous day, was red with anger.

He kept opening his mouth to speak, but—looking straight at Arsaces, who he felt sure was at the bottom of this—he could not find a way to speak the words he was thinking.

Orbicius went on.

"Arsaces isn't the best general, but he is from the Arsacids and retains connections in Persia, and he and his family are familiar with the Persian language and customs."

"He is here," Orbicius paused, "serving the Emperor's purpose."

"By stealing purple?" Maurice blurted.

Orbicius flinched and looked directly at Maurice.

"Be...quiet."

Maurice inhaled, then nodded, looking ahead again.

"No," Orbicius said, "Arsaces is here procuring the Emperor's silk and assuring that it has safe passage to Byzantium."

A moment or two passed while the words sunk in. While they did, Maurice watched. Arsaces had gotten down from his horse and was inspecting the cargo of some covered carts with the caravan leader. An orderly carried a bundle— likely containing payment. Another orderly carried a parchment, a bill, with a seal, a notary seal. It was a letter of safe passage.

"Whose money?" Maurice asked laconically.

"The Emperor's."

Maurice glanced over at Orbicius and said nothing until Orbicius understood he was still misinterpreting the situation.

"Look forward, Maurice, and don't look at me again. People will think we are having a conversation. The chiliarch," Orbicius said in reference to Arsaces, "spends the Emperor's money, at the Emperor's behest, to get the emperor's silk, which the emperor will have. Everything you see here is proper."

"The...emperor's...money?" Maurice said. The implications of it were almost too difficult for him to process.

"More accurately, we answer to the minister of the Emperor, Peter Barsymes, *comes sacrarum largitionum*—the minister in charge of the imperial treasury—and Barsymes speaks for the Emperor."

Once more, lacking another option, Maurice looked at Orbicius.

"One more time I remind you, we are not having a conversation. Look ahead," Orbicius said. He continued, "I know what you are thinking, but Barsymes does the Emperor's work here. This you can be sure of."

"How so?" Maurice asked, looking ahead as if talking to the sky.

"Arsaces is a traitor. A conspirator and a traitor whose conspiracy was to murder Justinian and replace him on the throne."

Maurice said nothing.

"Emperor Justinian forgave him and assigned him to Lazica."

Another moment of silence. The transaction before them seemed to be concluding and Arsaces was remounting his horse, directing the caravan's leader in the direction of the tagma's baggage train. The leader was shouting orders in Persian to the drivers who then started moving their caravan to join the train. The Persian merchant looked pleased. *Deeply* pleased. His scarf could not conceal his pleasure, even at a distance, at what he obviously took to be a highly favorable sale. His arms flexed under the weight of the small chest that held his payment.

A payment, Maurice thought, that could have been used to purchase more suitable equipment or to provide for better training.

What the hell are we doing here? He heard himself asking this in his thoughts, again.

"This is why," Orbicius was still explaining, "Justinian forgave him. It is why he was assigned to Lazica. It is why this military unit reports to the imperial treasury and not *magister militum per Armenium*."

When it seemed their conversation had ended and no words had been exchanged for a while, Orbicius said lastly, "It's also one reason we need notaries as much as we need soldiers in Lazica."

* * * * * * * *

Later, when the entire train had stopped and made camp, they ate. Rufus and Paphos sat with them. Maurice spoke to Orbicius, but without looking at him, "I'm speaking to the air."

145

No one said anything in answer.

"That was a lot of money," Maurice said aloud, as if to the air, as if about nothing.

"Everyone knows the product is worth its weight in gold," Orbicius said, also as if to nothing.

"Somewhere a lance is in a factory, un-purchased. Somewhere there's a tagma manning its second file with swords instead of lances. Somewhere there are line infantry, as much as waiting to die when we have the right equipment, but we choose to give them inadequate equipment. Somewhere there's a new recruit who is being deployed with his fears...but with six more months training he could be deployed instead with deadly habits that he could call upon in battle."

No one said anything. Maurice continued, "That's a strange choice to make. It is as if we pay for silk with our blood...or with our comrade's blood."

The words sat in the air for five or ten minutes while the four men ate, chewing their food. Eventually they finished and without saying much they began to excuse themselves to their tents.

Maurice was walking back to his own tent when Orbicius came up next to him and started talking. Once more, as if talking to the air, "Have you ever wondered what we are doing out here fighting in Lazica Maurice? What does the empire have need for of Suania? Of Scanda?"

"I never stop wondering. I'm almost consumed by wonder," he said, continuing on the way to his tent. They came to a stop together in front of it.

Orbicius started, "There are three known routes to Serinda. One is by sea, through Taprobane. It is difficult, poorly known, and sustained by strange networks of pirates, barbarians, Indians and Jews."

"Another passes through the middle of Persia and comes to Byzantium through Antioch. The Persians profit richly from this. Of all the routes to Serinda, this is the most temperate and best governed. There may be Persians, but there are few pirates, few brigands."

"The last is the route by which this caravan came today. It crosses the Hyrcanian Ocean on its way to Serinda where ships port at the Persian city of Derbent. The appetite for silk is insatiable. By one route is chaos, and by two routes, we pay the Persians."

"Orbicius," Maurice said.

"Yes."

"You are making me sick. After what happened yesterday, I'm going to be sick."

Orbicius lifted his hands and took Maurice by the shoulders, shook him once, and looked him in the eye, "How long have you been here, in Lazica?"

"A year, including the time in Hermonassa."

"And until today, you were like every common soldier. You were not privileged to know the reason why we answer to the count of the imperial largess. But yesterday you showed nobility. So today, I explain this to you."

Maurice shook his shoulders and stepped back, angrily, "Men died! You understand how. More men are going to die!"

Instead of responding to this, Orbicius just went on, "And I will privilege you once more so that you know one more thing."

Maurice considered Orbicius with something like disbelief until Orbicius broke the silence.

"Our mission is not just to facilitate Persian silk merchants who wish to patronize the Emperor. What you saw today is a tolerance, like the 'tribute' they paid Attila...you remember how Attila was paid tribute my fellow Flavius? It's just tribute. Our real mission is to secure the area from the Persians, so that we can open a *fourth* route to Serinda."

The words hung in the air, in the cold night silence between them until Orbicius broke the silence once more.

"Beyond Scanda, there is a road; it leads to Derbent. But, it crosses a gorge that cuts a northerly mountain pass, the Darial Gates. Scouts have been past there. We think it leads around the Hyrcanian Ocean. If it does—and if we secure Scanda—it's a route to Serinda and its silk. A route without Persians."

The enormity of Orbicius' words were so great that Maurice was left speechless.

"Of course," Orbicius concluded, "Chosroes knows this. Why the hell else would the Roman Emperor and the Persian Padishah allow both their empires' fortunes to be consumed fighting interminably over this godforsaken wasteland? Think of all the cities in Cilicia or Phrygia to tempt the Padishah—the coastal cities of Syria and the Levant—and yet he fights Justinian *here*. Think of all the great merchant centers in Mesopotamia to tease Justinian—yet he fights Chosroes here."

Orbicius shrugged in conclusion.

"Haven't you ever wondered? Why else would we fight in Lazica?"

At this, he left Maurice without another word and returned in the direction of his own tent.

He was walking away when Maurice called back to him, "Orbicius."

Orbicius stopped, turned, and faced his friend.

"All the time," Maurice said.

Orbicius looked confused.

"You asked if I wonder why we fight in Lazica. All the time, I wonder. Ever since I came here I have wondered. I have wondered and asked, and no one could explain...no one could tell me. So, I never stop wondering. But...it's the silk. It's all about the silk. And, if we don't do something about the silk, people, will keep dying."

They considered each other, motionless.

"I...I understand now," Maurice said. "Everything...everything we've been doing is *all* about the

148

silk." He nodded once more and turned his back, returning to his tent.

When their tagma returned to Archaeopolis, this assignment would be terminated. He would take possession of Terdete's eunuch, Euphrates, which was the tribute the rebel offered to Justinian, and return to Byzantium. The audience would be entirely formal and entirely transactional; his role as a notary was to seal the receipt of Terdete's token of surety. But the occasion provided an unrivaled opportunity for a face-to-face moment with the Emperor, a moment when Maurice could convey to the emperor what was going on in Lazica, a moment with a quality Maurice would not soon be blessed with again.

He shook his head at his own audacity. He paused for a moment and reckoned that he had—a day earlier—bombed a Persian *vasht* out of existence, so what would a few words out of place with the Emperor be?

One could be the beginning of a glorious career. Another might be the rapid end of the same. He shrugged to himself. Without thinking about it anymore, he retired for the night.

Chapter 7
Ambition of the Looms

To obtain admittance to the guild of silk merchants five members of the craft must testify to the eparch that the candidate is a person worthy to exercise the craft.

He shall then be admitted to it, he shall open a shop, and carry on business. His entrance fee to the guild is six nomismata.

To obtain a license to acquire the workshop of a silk merchant the tax is ten nomismata. The recommendation of the eparch is necessary.

...

Whoever attempts to carry on at one and the same time the trade of serikarios and vestiopratis shall be put on his election to choose one trade or the other.

Book of the Eparch

From the street side, leaning against the mulberry tree, Alexander could tell by the interior creaking of the building, the exterior reverberation on its walls, and even by the vibrations this commotion created—which he felt against the skin of his forearms—that Cyra was descending rapidly down a staircase into the serving room behind the service window. He lifted himself off the tree, rose up the few stairs, and walked past the gate and over the mosaic tile under the archway directly to the doors bypassing the service window. The doors opened almost immediately as he arrived; Cyra stood behind. They both had done this routine before.

Acquiring one another's eyes, they exchanged subtle nods. Cyra turned her back and walked into the service room with Alexander following her. She approached a counter and walked to the far side of it while Alexander moved to the stools on the fore side. Alexander took a place at one of them and removed a knapsack from his shoulder, placing it on the clear end of the counter away from some dishware on the other side. While he did so, Cyra started to call out through an open door to the day chamber where he could see the looms, thread, and figures of women weaving.

"Ana," she called out, causing the head of a bent-down young girl to turn upwards. Both the girl's hands were fully engaged in what looked like a wrestling match between her and the base-level cords of her loom. Her face cast a distressed look back at Cyra. Another woman, this one a nun, stood next to her, bent slightly at the waist and at a distance looked more than a bit cross, her ire directed at the young girl.

Cyra took stock instantly of the same affair and stopped herself. She then continued her address as to correct herself. "Oh, I'm sorry Anastasia. I know you're busy," she waved, dismissing both of them to their tussle, then she turned to Alexander and went on. "You must be so thirsty. How long have you been standing in the sun?"

"Well, I could use a drink," Alexander softly replied.

"Everyone is so busy here I can't even get the orphans to help me. They are up to their shoulders in work that's more important than anything a hegumenia might need."

Cyra turned her back to Alexander so that she faced a case of shelves against the wall and reached her arm towards a tall jar, an amphora. Just as she took hold of the handle she turned back to him and said, "You know I have cold eukraton, which you are welcome to of course. But, if you prefer", she said, slowing her words and adopting a slightly devious tone, "I have some olovina."

Alexander opened his lips to reply in the affirmative; he was thirsty enough, and just a touch of salt to his drink would make for a more satisfying beverage. For a monk, olovina would be a guilty pleasure that would be difficult to come across on almost any licit occasion he could hope to find himself in. He could trust Cyra to remain discreet, but he pursed his lips and thought about it twice then shook his head. "No thank you Cyra," he replied. "I really do appreciate it, but something makes me think I'm going to need all my senses about me. Let's just make it water this time", he said, careful to add the words to keep his options available next time.

Cyra released her grip on the amphora and nodded in acknowledgment answering, "Very well then, water it will be." She took hold of two ceramic cups from a shelf then shifted herself again to face Alexander, laying the cups down on the counter between them. A bowl of olives sat on the edge of the counter next to a stack of ceramic dishes. Cyra took two dishes from the stack, laying down one for Alexander and another for herself. While she filled the two cups with water, she bid Alexander to help himself to the olives.

They were sipping their drinks when Cyra motioned her chin in the direction of Alexander's knapsack. "I trust you don't mean to leave today without using that."

"Well, I don't imagine it should go any less used than in the last five times I paid Saturninus a visit," Alexander answered, laying down his cup. He pulled the knapsack nearer, clasped its cover, and stood to his feet before carefully placing its contents on the counter.

He went about fastidiously unpacking his sack, a result of long-standing repetition as well as of necessary care for several of the delicate implements. He set a velvet pouch onto the counter and carefully untied it. From the pouch, he removed additional small pouches, each one enclosed on the top by a folded surface and buttons. Unbuttoning the first, he retrieved a bronze metal arm. Opening the next, he took out a needle and a bracket. He closed the first two and returned them to the velvet pouch. He proceeded to the third from which he took a pair of bronze pans, a well finished wooden base, and a chiseled wooden pole. Finally, he retrieved a corresponding pair of chains from the remaining pocket. Returning all of the smaller pouches to their home, he placed the velvet pouch back into the sack. He retrieved still another small bag from which he unpacked seventy-two, small, bronze, flattened, weighted spheres—each marked as weighing one exagion; these he set out on the counter in nine stacks of eight.

He returned the bag to the knapsack and proceeded to assemble the items into an operating balance scale. As Cyra watched him construct his scale, he spoke. "The matter is going to be that while I can inspect the product, which I am sure it will be found superb, and while the eparch remains sympathetic to your ambitions, I think that Simeon is going to be a concern."

"I knew it," Cyra said. "He's a Jacobite, isn't he?"

Alexander paused to look up and answer her, momentarily resting a chain unevenly on a bracketed notch of the bronze arm, "Possibly." "My parents were Nestorians, and while I was graced to reject their error—thanks to my tutor in Berytus—Simeon seems to never tire of reminding me of my origin. So, you may be right. He did come from Derkoi at what some would say was an inauspicious time, and I understand Empress Theodora had him installed as an assistant to the eparch, a boullotes."

* * * * * * * * *

For millennia pagan peoples took for granted the existence of demigods—the progeny of unions between gods and women such a Hercules, son of Zeus and the mortal woman Alcmene; or goddesses and men such as Aeneas, son of Aphrodite and the mortal man Anchises—but the tectonic shift of pagan antiquity to the Christian era brought about by the enthusiastic followers of an enigmatic Jewish messianic figure presented a peculiar problem to the pagan mind:

This Christ was either a godman, or a man god,

Yet to pagan reckoning neither notion made any sense

As the Mediterranean world become less pagan and more Christian the paradoxes presented by the problem did not subside but grew in intensity so that whole regions defined themselves against one another by the variety of formulas locals preferred to make an account for what seemed an unsolvable riddle.

Gods and goddesses—Zeus, Apollo, Athena, Demeter—the pagan mind accepted as emanations of a divine One—manifestations of *principles* of divinity, though incomparably superior to men—they nevertheless held something in common with men in that they were *emanations* from the divine—belonging to the "many" who would be consumed inevitably along with the sages themselves and humankind, by Aion. None were the same in *substance* with the eternal divine, the "One".

Though Christianity filled a void left by empire in an incoherent montage of traditions and swept aside lingering superstitions and a confusion of competing cults, it struggled to distinguish between antique ignorance and ancient wisdom.

Where it came to making an account for the enigma of its own godman, these tensions came to a head. The tensions' effects were political, but their causes were philosophical. The Christian apostle John stated that Christ was the Logos— but more impossibly: the Logos "made flesh" and the gospel writers were unanimous that Mary, a Jewish virgin, bore this divine child. But was Mary like Leda or Europa and Christ like Hercules or Aeneas?

Julian the Apostate—the last pagan emperor in Byzantium, attempted to revive the old ways and wrote in defense of traditional Greco-Roman religion in "Hymn to the Mother of the Gods" over a hundred years earlier. Thirty-five years later Nestorius, a Syrian, was installed as bishop of Byzantium. Finding that sympathizers of Julian persisted among the imperial elite and encountering what he took to be a tendency to fuse the imperial cult with Christian teaching, he distinguished himself by putting his foot down on the matter and demanding that *the proposition makes no sense at all!* Jesus of Nazareth, Nestorius held, was a man, a human, a human being in a human body—and could not possibly be one in the same with Logos.

His message was popular in Syria and in Christian communities east of there in Persia and India, but was roundly rejected everywhere else in the Mediterranean world.

In time those in the north would unify around the Council of Chalcedon which condemned the Nestorians and held that Christ was a *man-god* : both human and divine; while Christians in Africa resisted Chalcedon, maintaining that the human body was no vessel that could contain divinity, with their own formulation and condemnation of the Nestorians, a formulation they called "miaphysite", they held that the god in Christ subsumed or even consumed the human nature of Jesus of Nazareth: to them he was the *god-man*.

Alexander's parents moved often but they had assured for him an excellent education and for all of his studies these disputes were utterly perplexing.

Only one thing was certain: while the Chalcedonians and miaphysites seemed able to agree on nearly nothing, there was one matter around which they united: Nestorius and his followers, the Nestorians, were condemned.

Which posed a problem since his own parents where Nestorian.

He had made up what he said to Cyra about his tutor—he really had no wish to put a stake anywhere in the question. Byzantines seemed to prefer the Chalcedonian formulation—Jesus of Nazareth, the human being in the flesh—was somehow God.

Did this make sense? Of course not

Was it his job to accept it? No

He was a monk—he was to obey

And obey he did.

Though the emperor himself was Chalcedonian and Chalcedonians clearly held the levers of power while enjoying the greatest popularity, the capital remained a contested place where Chalcedonians, miaphysites and Nestorians vied for power and ascendancy and these divisions expressed themselves everywhere in the imperial bureaucracy. Ironically Nestorians—hated by both sides, were often deciding-votes: king-makers.

The emperor's wife, Theodora, was miaphysite and raised the fortunes of miaphysites wherever it was in her power to do so. Though in the minority Nestorians and miaphysites were common despite Chalcedonian ascendancy and sympathized with their own. Outside the capital miaphysites remained centered in Alexandria and throughout Egypt and Africa, but their followers in Syria were known as Jacobites.

Simeon, the boullotes installed with the eparch by Theodora, was a Syrian Jacobite—like so many in Theodora's circle—a miaphysite. That would make him no particular friend to Cyra's cause—accounting for her concern. She took Simeon's evident animosity to be a matter of religious difference intruding on business affairs.

This was not an altogether unreasonable suspicion, but Alexander knew better.

* * * * * * * * *

Pausing for a moment, he inhaled and said, "But frankly, between me and you, I don't think that is what it's about."

Cyra looked up at Alexander; he was probably seven inches taller than she was though not an especially tall man himself. She locked eyes with him as if she had considered no other possibility and asked, "What is it then?"

Alexander let out a gentle chuckle. "You surprise me, Cyra. Normally, you are so, ... *so*, urbane"

Cyra just looked at him.

He widened his eyes, drew back his shoulders, and looked at her. She remained silent. Grinning and making his answer as breathy and spread out as possible so that the sound could be heard clearly by Cyra but no one else, he finally said, "Simeon ... wants ... a ... b-rrr-i-b-e", aspirating the last syllable.

Alexander allowed a moment to pass for what he took to be the obvious to sink in. Then, speaking in formal voice and aloud as if to pacify the ears of anyone overhearing, he said, "The eparch's boullotes expresses discomfort with what he perceives as an unauthorized establishment of serikoprates. He requires assurances that all forms have been followed and all procedures completed."

To Alexander's shock, Cyra was not having it. She shot back, "A bribe?!"

Alexander cringed. His hairs stood up, and he was sure he could see in his peripheral vision out the corner of his left eye a disturbance in what had been the rhythmic motion of nuns and orphans working away at the partially mechanized looms. He could feel their eyes looking at him and Cyra through the large open window in the wall between them. Tilting his left shoulder towards the door and exiting back to the street, he carefully lifted his right hand up to his pursed lips. He glanced back towards the working women and whispered, "Cyra, shush. This is a delicate matter, and delicate matters are precisely why *you* are in charge."

Cyra gave off a harumph. She turned her back towards the wall separating them from the workroom and paced towards the other side of the counter asking, "Who does he think he's protecting? With the war and the prices and the smugglers, how many factories has Justinian shut down?"

She turned back and faced Alexander directly but angled towards him so that his body blocked a direct view from the workroom to her face, "Seventeen?"

"Ahhh... seventy," Alexander answered.

"Al-mighty!" Cyra leaned forward spreading her arms, took a grip on both sides of the counter, and rested her weight on her shoulders. She stared down at the counter before looking up again at Alexander. Her face was ashen.

"There's no competition to protect, Alexander. Simeon shuts down the shops and traders, and Barsymes chases the smugglers and fleeces every one that's caught."

"Heh. True enough. Before she died, Theodora ordered those convicted stripped of their linen stocks and fined a centenaria of gold," Alexander added.

Cyra went on, "Very soon all the serikopratoi will be servants of the Emperor. Simeon will have a hard time collecting taxes when no one is left but public servants or smugglers."

Alexander grimaced just a little and replied, "It might be that you're not thinking about this in the right way."

He inhaled and went on. "That was an unfortunate term I resorted to a moment ago," feigning exaggerated formality, "and I wish to retract it and replace it with a new one. Jacobite or not, Simeon seems to my young eyes the kind of man who likes an argument, but he is very seldom persuaded by words. The factories you mention all understood this...I think. Now since they are closed, Simeon is seeking new candidates who understand his need for, *persuasion*."

"No one can know the Emperor's mind, and surely I don't, but in the short time I've been at this I've sensed a kind of subtext among other inspectors who've been doing this longer than I have."

"What is it?" Cyra asked. "What are you saying?"

"This needs to remain between us and were my parents not benefactors of Saturninus and were it not for our special relationship," Alexander said as he nodded towards Dalmatou, "I wouldn't feel comfortable sharing something that's just hearsay."

He stopped and waited for Cyra to respond.

Finally, never having lost eye contact, she did. "I understand. What is it? What you think?"

"From time immemorial, all manner of people have made a living—a highly profitable living—in the silk trade."

"A secret to no one," Cyra grunted.

Alexander sighed, "I'm not finished."

"Land traders must go around Persia. Traders with connections who are either brave, traitors to the empire, or hopelessly stupid, go directly through Persia. There are sailors on the middle ocean, sailors on the Red Sea, and even sailors to Taprobane and Sinhala. There are spinning and weaving workshops all about Egypt, Tyre, and Antioch. I lived near several in Berytus."

"All true but no state secrets yet, hmmm?" Cyra replied again.

"Not so long ago, silk was every bit as important as it is to us and New Rome today." Alexander leaned in a bit towards Cyra: "And being so important it sustained this industry for what? What do you think? Five hundred years? A thousand?"

Cyra replied, "Of course it's as important now as ever. What's changed? What's new *monk*?" The last she spoke with an edge of familiar deprecation.

"Purple."

Having uttered it, Alexander stood there saying nothing more.

For a moment, the two of them regarded one another. Alexander waited while the gears in Cyra's mind worked away at this. As the head of the nunnery, Cyra represented the unusual case of a woman with a complete education. She had done higher studies at the University of Constantinople. Obviously able at commerce, she was no dope. But Alexander still knew it might take a bit for her to put together the dots and the lines in the sketch he was trying to draw. Compared to the other academies, the University of Constantinople had a reputation for conservatism in what was already a conservative world and she surely could not count on her education to notice innovation unless, he figured, it was to condemn the innovation. After all, he probably would not of thought of any of this himself if he had not shared a few more drinks than were authorized to monks with his fellow mitotes when visiting a phousarkia while "on business" during appointed hours away from the monastery, and decidedly in violation of its rules.

After Cyra didn't answer him he spoke up, "For eons, back to Augustus, only the imperials wore purple. I don't recall that it was popular during the days of the old republic ... probably not. If I recollect right they said Julius wouldn't wear it. He had enough problems without rubbing his dictatorship in the eyes of a neutered Senate. Before then, the Etruscans—even as far back as the Etruscan kings—they wore purple."

"But they didn't wear silk," Cyra noted.

Alexander smirked, "Sure, they did. They *wore* it", he said scandalously.

"Ahh ... of course they did," Cyra answered. "What did Seneca say? How did it go? I remember: *'Silk! If materials that do not hide the body or even one's decency, can be called clothes...her husband has no more acquaintance than any outsider or foreigner with his wife's body.'* Yes, of course they wore it. They disapproved of it, they reviled it, *and they paid handsomely* for it."

This was the urbane Cyra that Alexander had come to know.

Her comportment changed. She had maintained a lean against the counter this whole time, but now she stood up, stepped back, and crossed her arms. Her muscles tightened in her high cheekbones around her nose; her pupils contracted: "Alexander, are you suggesting that civil inspectors don't approve of the nunnery assuming a place in the industry?"

Alexander let out a laugh: "Huh!? No Cyra, that's not at all what I mean." His enormous grin contrasted with her confused scowl.

In one part of his mind, he made the connection that if the humor of her misinterpretation was lost on her, as it appeared, then it definitely was going to be necessary for him to help her out.

"Cyra," he said, standing from his stool and taking a step towards her, "purple will always be imperial. That's one of those things that will probably never change. But, have you noticed that the imperials have..." he paused, rolled his eyes towards the ceiling, slunk back his shoulders, and turned his hands to either side, thumbs pointing to opposite walls, "what can I say? The imperials, they've," he paused, searching for the word, then settled on it, "diversified.

"That's it! That's what I mean to say. Our royals have diversified. It is still purple—it will always be purple—but since Justinian, since Theodora, since their friend Antonina..."

"The witch?" Cyra interrupted.

Alexander stopped at this interjection. He looked through the window at the workroom and glanced out the service window towards the street. His heart skipped a beat on seeing a pedestrian walking beyond the mulberry tree. *Please, God, I hope he didn't hear that,* he silently prayed, referring to the pedestrian who almost surely could not hear at such a distance.

"Antonina, the Mistress of the Purple," Alexander said impishly. "Perhaps it is something about her because I am to understand she did test the scent of fish."

At that, finally, Cyra laughed.

"All right, I think I follow you. The Emperor's Mistress of the Purple objects to the smell of fish, and anyone can see how she might wish to substitute something for purple. Is that what you're getting at Alexander?"

Alexander answered her, "Well what makes a suitable replacement for purple?"

At this, Cyra's eyes sharpened; she replied, "They are not mutually exclusive you know? Purple and silk. Just last week, I had Anastasia and the workroom embroider a purple silk terrycloth for the palace."

"What I said", Alexander shrugged, "they diversified— purple will never change—but the imperials have diversified," Alexander said.

"I'm a businesswoman and nun. You don't need to explain to me the merits of diversification while we discuss the expansion of this enterprise from linens into silk. I understand that completely, Alexander," she said, taking one step back on her right. She shifted her left shoulder towards him while she looked over it at him.

Breaking eye contact, she looked at the service window, and walked in the direction of the doors a few paces before stopping: "And all of this makes perfect sense." She said this with just a note of sarcasm in her voice. "The imperium wishes to diversify, to extend the arm of imperially managed commerce from the control of mere mollusky color purple to all the sublime varieties of silk." She stopped momentarily, holding a pregnant pause while fixing eye contact.

All the while she was talking, Alexander could not be sure if she understood better. Confidence began to lead him to believe that she did. His gut said otherwise, but he went with it. He presumed she understood.

At this, Cyra shed the look of calculation and merely looked at Alexander incredulously, "By diversifying into the silk industry, by increasing demand for this precious linen while locking down the channels that supply it—no less at a time as when nine years in the last twenty and for as many more as we can foresee, we are fighting with the very people who supply us with it—you are telling me that the Emperor, equal in wisdom to the apostles we are told, believes it fit to his magnificence to close down the silk workshops and merchants?"

"Yes."

The two of them stood alone in the room regarding one another.

Alexander's back was still to the workroom window, but he could sense from the hair on his skin a change in the tempo rising out of the window. He and Cyra were being noticed again.

For her part, Cyra was unfazed by any interest her nuns and orphans might be paying them. Finally, she asked, "Why?"

Alexander took three steps towards her before he answered. "Because they want it. The whole silk industry. *All* of it. Empress Theodora, I don't know, but I think she opposed it...but she's dead now. Thirty years ago, silk was a spectacle to the imperials, but now it's something that they understand. Plus, they are desperate. When Justinian's uncle, Emperor Justin, when he took the purple, Emperor Anastasius had left the treasury with 320,000 *pounds* of gold."

"Cyra, consider all of Justinian's wars—in Africa, Italy, Spain—all of his buildings—he has raised entire cities. And the harbors he's reinforced, the cities he's repopulated, and the plague we fought. This long, interminable war with the Persians...it isn't over. We have to win. If we don't, there must at least be an honorable peace. Such a peace may have to be bought. It will be expensive.

"The Emperor, by all accounts, is a man of great faith, but he needs coin. Lots of it."

"Lots of it," he repeated. "The imperials are people of war, people of the sword, but Theodora, she belonged to the circus and the theater and later the church in Alexandria. We are not supposed to remember her humble origins. But, it is said in quiet tones among some that after she returned from Alexandria and took her home as a reformed woman here in the capital she established herself in the protection of the Theotokos as a seamstress."

"I've only heard this. I can be sure I don't know, but some say that the distinction that drew the attention of Consul Justinian to a humble seamstress was that when she returned from Antioch and took up as a seamstress near First Hill she had brought back with her the gift from the Blues and her religious sponsors."

"What? Alexander, what?"

At this, Alexander turned his back to Cyra and paced forward to the window that separated the workroom. He stood in front of it. The nuns and orphans who a moment ago were almost surely joined in a conspiracy of silence took on a mode of uniform, intent attention to their tasks. Cyra walked forward with some weight in her step and came to Alexander's side, shoulder to shoulder and well inside his personal space. She was much closer than was ever appropriate for a monk and a nun, though there was no sensual intimacy about it. She looked up at him, craning her neck to the right and above, "What did Theodora bring?"

Alexander lifted his right arm and pointed at the loom that Anastasia and Vesta manned together, "One of those. The very *first* one of those. The first one, ever, in Byzantium."

The two of stared at the remarkable mechanical device. Whatever the commotion was earlier between the nun and orphan who manned it, it had long since cleared itself out. With two able laborers commanding the drawloom, it drew, wrapped, wove, and spread, over-and-over again. Though engaged in a symphony of eavesdropping moments earlier, it was impossible for any of the working girls and women to divine the significance of Cyra's and Alexander's intense interest in Vesta and Anastasia's drawloom.

"As I said," Alexander went on without moving his gaze from the rotating gears and spindles of the loom, "the imperials are military people, but in twenty-five years as Augusta, Theodora taught them about silk. It's the one industry that they really understand, and a very profitable industry at a time when a young dynasty seems to need a lot of money."

Alexander heard Cyra muttering the words to herself softly, finally understanding, "They want it all to themselves … *all* of it".

Chapter 8
The Storage Chamber

Should bales of cloaks be found in the storeshops of the dyers which do not bear the eparch's stamp the same shall be confiscated and the workman who had them shall have his goods confiscated.

Book of the Eparch

"Didyma!" Cyra called out loudly to the antechamber. She and Alexander had been aimlessly staring into the room for several minutes. Didyma, unpaired with any of the workers at the looms, was busily shuttling the large rolls of linen textiles that were stacked on a long table somewhere off in the far-right corner opposite where Alexander and Cyra stood, where she carried them over to each of the workstations whenever their warps were beginning to run short of raw fabric. She stopped midstream upon hearing Cyra call her name. Holding a wrapped linen in her arms, she looked up and made eye contact.

"Yes, hegumenia?" She called back.

"Finish your delivery and come here," Cyra answered her.

"Yes, hegumenia." Didyma answered again.

The nun carried her linen roll to a working station and laid it on a tray in an otherwise empty corner of the paved floor, which had been set aside as a space for raw linen. Alexander watched her as she stood taut for a moment to gain the attention of the older women, both of them nuns, who were working the warp-weighted loom. They were too distant for him to hear, especially over all the bustle of the workroom, but she made hand motions that led him to believe that she was explaining that there was some task she could not immediately do.

He confirmed his suspicion when she turned her back on the two nuns and began approaching. Behind her, one of the two nuns who had been managing the dangling weights on the loom took leave from her position where she had been placing completed sections of roll around the backside of the top beam. She moved over to pick up the linen roll that Didyma had left. She unwound it first and then rewound sections of it about the weights that she had been managing earlier. All of this time, her partner never diverted her attention from her work on the weave.

About this time, Didyma reached the space below the window from which Alexander and Cyra looked out at the workroom. The front room where Alexander and Cyra had been speaking together in stood four steps above street level, but the day chamber that served as the nunnery's workroom was a half level below that; it was effectively at street level itself. The door separating the two rooms opened to an unguarded staircase that fell seven steps to the floor. When Didyma presented herself at attention on the other side of the window, only her shoulders and head rose above the window sill to face Cyra.

Didyma was one of Cyra's trusted courtiers and despite her more humble dual roles, such as a porter, she had some administrative responsibilities.

"How can I be of service hegumenia?" Didyma asked.

Alexander doubted that she would have spoken so formally were he not present to observe.

Cyra did not wear a kamision, a simple tunic worn by monastics with a plain, light gray color that was free of any ostentatious patterns or stripes that might indicate rank or draw attention. Instead, due to her rank as a hegumenia, she wore a sticharion embroidered with a pair of vertical gold stripes on the shoulders, which unlike a kamision, designated rank. A bishop's sticharion would have two pairs of stripes, and a deacon would have none.

From Didyma's low vantage point, all she could see was Cyra looking down at her right side and pulling away at her belt, but Alexander saw that tucked behind her short belt Cyra had a pocket from which she produced a sliding key with three teeth. She handed it through the window to Didyma.

As Didyma took the key, Cyra instructed, "Monk Alexander is tasked by our eparch's boullotes, Simeon, to inspect the quality of our silk, so he can certify we are progressing to competence as a serikopraktoi and deem the item ready for purchase."

"I understand," replied Didyma. Didyma was showing respect and making it clear that she was listening. She knew Alexander and why he was here.

"Fetch the linens that Anastasia finished embroidering and return them to us."

"As you wish," at which Didyma gave a shallow bow. Cyra responded with a bow of her own. Didyma immediately proceeded up the unguarded concrete staircase to the door separating the day room from the front room. Alexander watched as she opened the door, closed it behind her, and proceeded to the circular staircase in the left corner of the front room, the staircase that Cyra had so thunderously descended from earlier when he was still waiting for her. Didyma ascended the stairs and disappeared into an aperture in the ceiling. Thereafter he could hear her make her way up still another circle of the staircase.

Due to the risk of fire and the general incapacity to fight city fires, lower floors tended to be valued more than upper floors on account of the fact that in case of fire one had a greater chance of escaping a lower floor with some property intact. Where it concerned the matter of storing the nunnery's valuable inventory, including both silk and other processed linens, a more complex assessment was necessary. In fact, Psamathia was an ideal location for textile work; the only rival location in the city was likely the region around the palace. This was due to the fact that Psamathia had formerly been an area with such a high concentration of wealthy and aristocratic families that most streets were paved, most floors were tile, and the ground floors (or *patos*) of most buildings were constructed of concrete or brick, as was Saturninus, where all three floors were made of brick with tile overlaid.

That helped to settle the question of where to store valuable products. Linens on a low floor were at greater risk of damage from flooding, especially from runoff from any of the city's hills down to the Propontis, Bosphorus, or Golden Horn. For that reason, unprocessed raw linen textiles were kept on the second level overnight and taken down to the day room every morning; any of the day's remainders would be returned again to the second floor. Processed linen in all their forms—such as carpets, clothing, cleaning wear, clothes, costumes, blankets, coverlets, cushions, sails, and nets—could be sold for a profit. These represented a significant investment in both the purchase of raw materials and of time, labor, and processing equipment. This included even those more coarse linens and not just the precious silk. For this reason, it was essential to protect them from theft, which was why at Saturninus they were kept behind the lock and key on the third floor—to which Didyma presently ascended.

Saturninus had been built from sandstone imported to Byzantium from a quarry, and its two lower levels were painted in shades of amber, burgundy, and maroon. The third and highest floor was unpainted and retained its natural white, wavy coloration. By contrast, Dalmatou was made primarily of brick and mortar.

When Didyma arrived at the second level, she stopped and walked to the table next to a closed, fractured, glass window. On a table in front of the window, was a silver lamp that ordinarily would be reserved for the nunnery church or various locations of the monastery. Unlike most other lamps in the building, which were ceremonially lit at sundown at the hour of vespers, the lamp-lighting hour, this lamp was lit by a nun at the hour of matins so that it could remain lit all day long. The expensive decision to use a silver lamp was to better assure that the fire would not go out during the day. Next to the lamp was a small basket lined by linen cloth and on top of which lay several candles, most of which had never yet been used. Didyma selected a used candle from the basket. She lit the candle with the lamp's fire, and—guarding the flame with her hand—carefully walked the staircase to the third and highest level of Saturninus. The rise from the staircase onto the third floor opened to a small foyer; the rest of the third floor was dominated by a closed (and locked) closet.

There was one narrow window on this floor that offered some lighting, and there was no attic—the room opened to a slanted, wood ceiling. Didyma approached the heavy, wooden door to the closet and set the candle on a small stand next to the closet doors. The doors were built of vertical, wood slats that were polished and carved with a chevron pattern. In the place of the knob, on both doors, were two circular pulls—slick, iron rings affixed to iron plates that were nailed into the doors on both sides. The two pulls were joined by an intimidating heavy, iron lock.

Standing at the door, Didyma leaned down to the lock and lifted the key. She held the key by a ring that looped around a screw clasp on a sickle-shaped bit. The key had three teeth of subtly varied height and were a slightly varied distance apart from one another. She inserted the key into an L-shaped hole in the locking plate; then, when it was inside, she maintained her grip on the key handle and swiped it in a rotating motion towards the corner. Hearing and feeling a hard, metallic clunk she saw the visible side of the bolt loosen and release.

She placed the key in a barely visible pocket in her kamision and then, with her free hand, pulled away at the loosened bolt, disconnecting it from its hinges. She then hung the lock on a hook in the door and opened the linen-storage closet. She retrieved her candle and took it with her into the closet, which had a few very narrow windows that were mostly used for ventilation and offered little by way of light. Didyma lit two clay oil lamps that hung from hooks on the wall to her left. Upon lighting the lamps, she extinguished her candle. One lamp bore a David and Goliath motif; she left it hanging on the wall. The other had a Christ-trampling-the-beasts motif; she lifted that one from the wall and carried it with her.

The nuns of Saturninus were actually being deliberately furtive in the choice of the term *closet*, for apart from the foyer into which Didyma had entered, the storage-closet encompassed the entire third floor. The word *closet* gives the sense—to covetous hearts—that upon breaking into a nunnery, ascending three floors, and breaking an imposing lock, one is not likely to find much to make the effort worthwhile. That was the intended impression.

The reality was somewhat different. In fact, the absence of an attic, though probably never planned for this specific industrial application, proved a notable feature because the floor was aligned with a series of shelves, and additional shelf space was created for the middle pair of shelves that rose above the ceiling towards its highest ridge at center. This caused these shelves to rise so high that there were several ladders set against various segments for workers to be able to reach the uppermost cubbies. Some linens were folded and placed in open sight in stacks inside the shelves; some were packed away in boxes, which were both shelved and strewn about the floor. Here and there were chests of various quality, and they too stored linens.

There was some rhyme and reason to the arrangement of the linens, but only up to a limit, and the limit too was deliberate and, like the name *closet*, furtive. Raw linens accounted for the space of three-fourths of the chamber. Raw linens were moved daily, early in the morning by orphans and novitiates, from the chamber to the day room for work on the looms. The process was "first in, first out," so beginning with the row of shelves on the left-most portion of the room from the entrance, workers removed the linens in bins intended to match the processing quantity of a day's work. They started from the front of left-most shelves, then moving in, came back the next line of shelves, and then moved back again on the third, and so on.

As new, raw linens were purchased, they were replaced in an orderly manner along the same line that they had been removed. This gave Cyra a reliable visual cue to guide the pace of her purchasing—as well as whether or not production was moving according to expectations. If the empty space between restock and removal got too big, she had to hurry her purchases so that a day would not arrive with no raw linens to weave. On the other hand, if she bought too much she might eliminate the empty space with excess inventory, which would have to be stored in boxes on the floor or in the worst case out in the open on the second floor. The earlier hegumenia had been haphazard in how she allowed linen to be stored and restocked. By imposing this careful order, Cyra saved money because she rarely ran out of linen to weave and generate salable goods, and she rarely overbought, and her workers were rarely idle, though neither were they too overburdened with the pressure to catch up for time lost when stocks ran short.

Off to Didyma's right, and slightly behind her as she entered the chamber, was a waist-high table where partially woven linens not yet complete were stored overnight. More often than not, this table remained empty as it was significantly more difficult to stop and restart a partial weave than it was to work just a bit longer to complete the exercise. Monasteries followed a strict schedule, and nuns were expected to conclude their work in time for evening vespers, but the presence of orphans at Saturninus made it possible to arrange for finishing touches to be completed almost every day before closing.

The remaining quarter of the chamber was for storing finished, processed linens and weaves. This section, rather than being organized according to the needs of the weaving process, was arranged topically according to the form of finished weave that was ready for a customer. Despite Cyra's ambition to convert the nunnery from a vestiopraktoi to a serikopraktoi, the great majority of its work and product remained that of ordinary linens made from cotton and wool. In this respect, Cyra had ordered her nuns to arrange the products in an order starting with the most base and inexpensive such as tunics, course blankets, and cleaning implements at the close end of the finished product section, while shifting products of higher value farther along the section that one walked until the most valuable products were found at the end. These most valuable linens were stored in locked chests, which were kept both on the floor and in shelves, except for linens, which may need to be stretched and hung, such as ceremonial articles of clothing for clergy, the government, or the military. Those were kept in a wardrobe at the end of the aisle that was sealed by a lock identical to the one that locked the storage chamber. Its doors were set deliberately on heavy, rarely-oiled hinges with springs installed so as to create a hideous, loud, metallic sound that would announce to anyone at a distance that the wardrobe was being opened.

Didyma approached the wardrobe, set her lamp on a hook, and unlocked it in the same way that she had unlocked the door to the chamber. She opened its doors and cringed a bit while it announced her deed with the characteristic screech heard by nuns and orphans throughout Saturninus. Back in the antechamber those who could hear checked over their shoulders at Cyra to see if she was bothered by this. Seeing that she wasn't, they went on with their work. Didyma, meanwhile, did not enter the wardrobe she'd just opened. Instead, she turned around and went back into the wider storage chamber. Known only to a few trusted nuns such as

Didyma, the most valuable products, those made of silk, were deliberately not kept inside the wardrobe, which to outward appearances would have been the most secure location in the storage chamber and the prized target of any thief.

Instead of being kept in the wardrobe, silk products were hidden in strategic locations about the finished product section, along points of the Greek letter μ, the first letter of the word μετάξι, or *metáxi* (Greek for silk), where they were hidden behind or underneath stacks of other finished linens in baskets that lay beneath the stacks. When observed in the dark, fire-lit chamber they were easily mistaken for a bottom surface but were in fact basket lids. Knowing this, Didyma approached an area about midway down the aisle and turned to her side where, in a tall shelf, were stacked several heavy soldiers' tunics wrapped together with a rope that also enclosed an envelope with their deeds of purchase. She lifted these aside, exposing a basket lining. She lifted it with both hands and exposed the shallow interior of the basket where Anastasia's silk embroidery lay protected by another cotton weave.

Didyma retrieved the entire bundle, cotton weave and all, replaced the lid, put back the cloaks, and closed the wardrobe, again cringing while it screeched. Locking it behind her, she returned to the door of the chamber, blew out the two oil lamp flames, exited the chamber and resealed its lock before returning to Didyma with the precious silk embroidery.

Chapter 9
The Balance Scales

Whoever dyes raw silk with blood or converts it into parti-colored purple, double, triple or two-thirds red, shall have his hand cut off.

Book of the Eparch

Palaces were built at the Tauros by Justinian the Great for his sister Vigilantia ... Antonina, the wife of the magistros Belisarius, who was the Mistress of the Robes for Theodora, the wife of Justinian, dwelled with Vigilantia here after she became a widow...

The so-called purple shops ... the purple garments were dyed there.

The Patria, Book 3

Didyma returned to the antechamber to continue her porter work while Cyra and Alexander resituated themselves at the counter. Alexander placed Anastasia's embroidery on his balance scale. In fact, what Anastasia had sewn was quite a bit more than that. What they had been calling, rather abstractly, an embroidery, was a small purse just a little larger than a hand purse. The purse was concealed inside a folded bed of coarse linens that Didyma had presented to Alexander. His eyes widened when Cyra unwrapped the folds to expose the purse. Upon seeing it, his heart felt that it skipped a beat. Cyra had dialed up the cageyness a bit more than usual for this visit—now he knew why:

It was a *purple* purse—a silk, purple purse.

Cyra was walking a tight line already, maintaining a shop that worked ordinary linens while trying to penetrate the silk market—and this while the emperor seemed dead set on consolidating all silk merchants into his own direct employ. He had not been expecting that anything from Cyra's workshop would be blattia: made from the purple-dyed textiles reserved by law for imperials.

"Where did you get the dye for this?" Alexander asked, still trying to process what he was seeing.

"The dyer workshops for blattia are in Tyre, Heliopolis, and Laodicea."

Pausing, he continued to examine the purse in his hands; it felt delicate, but that was part of the magic of silk; its delicacy concealed filaments of extraordinary strength, strong enough to hang and kill a man—a heavy man.

He went on, "I mean this quality? There's some lower quality you can get about the city, but..." Alexander realized something was wrong.

He studiously looked on either side of the purse, up and down, and fished his hands through the linen it came wrapped in. When it produced nothing, he lifted the whole body of wrappings, virtually starting to panic. *No, Cyra. I can't protect you from this ... no.* When he found nothing hidden underneath, he looked towards her with alarm.

"There's no seal. Purple ... no less purple *silk* without a seal?" He looked at Cyra with eyes that said *you can't be serious.* He went on, "Did Didyma leave it upstairs?"

Cyra shook her head no.

Alexander wasn't expecting this answer; this couldn't be.

"No seal? Where did you get this purple?" He asked with breathy exasperation.

With a firmness and confidence that surprised him, she answered, "It's not in great abundance, but imperial purple *can* be purchased inside the city."

Alexander looked at her suspiciously. "Cyra", he said urgently, glancing over his shoulder to check the workroom window. "You are already walking a dangerous line to have both silk and linens here. A few well-placed nomismata may persuade the boullotes Simeon to look the other way, but the sanction for dying imperial purple..." He dropped his head a moment and shuddered. Looking sideways over his shoulder, he whispered, "They can *sever* your hands for this."

"It's a serious crime. If someone found out that you were dying purple, then I suppose an ally could plead for banishment—if you thought that any better. But Barsymes is hell-bent on accumulating every silk merchant for the imperium. A nunnery ... you make no profit, so you are beyond his reach. You know that must gall him, right?"

"If you give him an excuse, you can throw yourself on the altar of Hagia Sophia, and it might ... *might* save your hands." He stopped a moment, looked down at her hands, and considered them before making eye contact again. "It won't save the operation. It won't keep you at Saturninus."

They held one another's gaze until Cyra spoke: "I understand your concerns Alexander." She continued, bluntly, "In the Buceleon, there is a dye shop. From time to time I acquire blattia there."

"Ahhhh," Alexander said with just a hint of relief while nodding in immediate recognition. Of course, he knew what Cyra was talking about, what a poor mitote he would be if he did not! He hadn't considered the possibility for good reason. The Imperial dye store would not normally sell nor commission work to a nunnery in Psamathia that lacked authority to cloth the purple.

Cyra, obviously, was sitting on some item of information she hadn't yet shared. Presently, he looked at her quizzically.

He finally broke the silence, "You are going to tell me what this is about?"

For a moment she held eye contact when finally, she answered.

"Sixteen," Cyra said simply.

"Excuse me?" Alexander answered.

"Sixteen nomismata. Sixteen *pounds* of gold Alexander." Cyra went on to say, "And that is only after we finish bribing the boullotes to look the other way while we sail this operation in two ships," she said, punctuating her words with emphasis.

"Alexander, with Barsymes on the hunt, with so few remaining merchants to fleece, how much do you think Simeon will demand to keep his silence? *Another* sixteen?"

Alexander let out a reflexive chortle, "Huh! Years ago. *Now*? Three times that."

Cyra for one second lost her composure. "Good God!" she said too loudly. She and Alexander both froze in immediate recognition of the *faux pas*. They both blushed, detecting a sure drop in the buzz of activity coming from the workroom as Alexander felt his skin crawl from the steely pincers of observing eyes and listening ears. He nodded his head in the direction of the front door and murmured his next words, mostly just forming the shape of the words with his mouth so Cyra alone would detect them:

"Should...we...talk...outside?"

Cyra merely looked back at him, barely resting her finger to point at the precious merchandise he had forgotten he was still holding in his hands, nodding "no" while murmuring and mouthing back to him,

"I...don't...think...so."

Instead, she approached him and situated a stool, so she could sit next to him on the same side of the counter. His head would block hers, so no one could see what they were saying.

"Sixty-four nomismata, Alexander.

"There are one hundred and fifty monks at Dalmatou; there are almost forty nuns and orphans at Saturninus. Almost two hundred people who we must feed, who also need clothes, fire, oil, everything. And raw linens, replacement parts, heddles, chords. These all cost money. How does a monastery survive on linens alone, and on top of it, come up with sixty-four *pounds* of *gold*?"

Alexander knew there was a slight exaggeration in this protest. While it was true that Dalmatou was supported by the work of the orphans and nuns of Saturninus, it also drew meaningful income from rents—the monastery owned several apartment buildings and collected rent from their occupants and—lesser known—it even owned a property that was rented out to a tenant who employed the premises productively as a phouskaria which ordinarily wouldn't be worth the extreme risk of scandal it represented—given that clerics where generally known to discourage and even condemn such indulgences by their flocks—but this tavern's location just outside the Hippodrome made for a particularly lucrative arrangement that suited the needs of everyone involved—while of course also doubling and tripling down on the potential for scandal for combining alcoholic drink with games and circuses, and the former so as phousa, the most déclassé form that it was known to be distributed in the capital. It was a rare case where he guessed Thaddeus kept even Cyra in the dark as to the origins of this remarkably reliable revenue, though she surely must have noted an unaccounted stream, she was just too astute to inquire after it. Just the same, her point had its merit. Margins after expenses from both textiles and rents would take a long time to amass sixty-four nomismata.

He answered her with the back of his head to the workroom window speaking lowly, "I understand the need for coin, but you must know this is dangerous business. Under-the-table purple Cyra? Does Thaddeus know?"

As soon as the words had left his mouth they both about laughed—almost a comic relief. Thaddeus wasn't the only clerical supervisor who kept secrets. He shook his own head at the remark while she almost in obligation said, "Of course not."

"Well enough then," he said. "But may I inquire as to the identity of the person who requires an *un*sealed, purple, silk purse from the good sisters of Saturnina?"

Cyra considered this.

"To begin with," she started, "it isn't really the purse that she needs. You still haven't looked inside."

She, Alexander noted, thinking to himself, *a woman, the customer is a woman.*

At her cue, he picked the purse up again, shaking his head at his own absentmindedness. The marvel of the silk purse and the alarm of its unsealed purple presentation had together distracted him from the obvious matter of its contents, which all along he could feel bulging inside. A silken string was strung around a stitched button on the front of the purse. He un-laced it and opened the cover of the purse and retrieved its contents. It was still another silk product, a skiadion, a kind of parasol with perforated bellows so it could be opened wide as a fan or made closed and compact for easy storage, such as in the case of this purse. Its bellows were dyed with different colors that they were varied and repeated in a series of four: purple, then burgundy, then a maroon red, then a maroon-yellow before purple again.

Regarding what he held in his hand, Alexander gave out a gentle chuckle, and without saying another word to Cyra he folded the bellows of the skiadion, placed it back into the purse, and proceeded to place the entire bundle on the right plate of his fully assembled scale, which sat on the counter between them. The bundle immediately weighted the scale down to its extreme bottom. Without hesitation he picked up three stacks of exagion and put them on the empty plate opposite the bundle, which served to partially rebalance the pair, but the bundle remained heavier.

"Twenty-four exagion. One third a nomisma…and that's the purse alone," he said to Cyra.

He added two more stacks, bringing the total to forty. At this point, the two plates were almost evenly weighted and he began adding one exagion at a time until at the count of forty-four the scale balanced.

He looked at Cyra and said, "A little more than six-tenths of a nomisma. With the purple though?" He lifted his brow as he spoke. "That will bid the price up quite a bit…" then he stopped, considering his next words, "…and without a seal? That, *might*, fetch a princely sum," he added ominously.

"Indeed," Cyra said knowingly, then went on, "*and* the embroidery. Have you considered the intricacy of the embroidery?"

Alexander knew she was right. While the embroidery was remarkable, there were already so many things about this unusual purse that he had not taken the time to consider. Once again, he took the purse in his hands and stood up. He walked to the service window, and, looking out towards the street, he lifted the embroidery to the sunlight, so he could make out details that might have remained hidden from view indoors when cloaked on dark purple hues. While it was such a small article and unlikely to be noticed by passersby, he was careful to conceal it from the street with his hands. It may as well have been a small gold bar.

Two features of the embroidery that struck him when he set it to examination. First, it was sewn with small knots which of themselves would not have been unusual except that these were rounded and plump and had body to them in a way he had not seen before. Secondly, the design of the embroidered knots was impressive in itself and showed considerable of skill on the part of the seamstress. The knots were stitched to depict a scrolling with spirals that alternated and reversed direction following a popular pattern of the acanthus leaves. The pattern extended like a scroll in a line all the way around the purse.

Bringing the purse back down level and turning again to face Cyra, he asked, "Who sewed this?"

"The orphan," Cyra answered.

"An orphan!"

"No," Cyra replied, "*the* orphan. I have only one orphan who excels at the drawloom, suffering the envy of her peers and superiors as a seamstress."

She turned and called through the window, "Anastasia!" Alexander saw a young woman and a child at a drawloom. They stopped their work and looked up at the front room through the window. "Come here. Monk Alexander wishes to speak with you."

That was a curious thing for Cyra to do. Summoning the orphan personally seemed unnecessary. Alexander had said nothing to suggest that he needed to speak with her, though in fact he had thought something close enough to it. He would go along with this and see what Cyra was up to.

A moment or two elapsed and Alexander could hear the girl walking up the stairs. He watched her come through the door, and while she did, he placed the purse on the counter and stood aside it, facing her as she approached. The thin girl had dark hair that hung down clean and unbraided past her ears and dark eyes. She stood tall enough to be a short woman, though she obviously was stick-thin and still a girl. She wore an unostentatious chiton and stood in their presence with the familiarity of someone who had lived her life in this place, but she betrayed a note of nervousness too. Cyra proceeded to speak to her, "Monk Alexander this is Anastasia. She recently entered her twelfth year. She's lived her whole life at Saturninus."

Though never having made her acquaintance before, Alexander was familiar with all the denizens of Saturninus and recognized her and addressed her thusly, "Anastasia. It's good to meet you."

She nodded at this and answered quietly, "Thank you, sir."

Cyra interjected to finish the introduction, "Anastasia, Alexander belongs to Dalmatau Monastery, I'm sure you've noticed him here before."

"Yes, I have."

"Besides keeping vigil with our brother monks, he is also in the service of the eparch, as a mitote. He inspects shops like ours to assure they meet with imperial standards. He's an important man to our work here. Do you understand?"

"Yes"

"I want you to answer a few simple questions he has about the purse and skiadion I asked you to sew."

"If you wish," she nodded to Cyra; Cyra nodded back. Anastasia spoke to Alexander, "I worked very long on both of those, sir. What do you wish to know? Is there anything about them that the eparch won't approve?"

Alexander sensed that she was wondering at the meaning of all of this and must be trying hard to conceal that she expected them to find something wrong with her work.

"Actually, on the contrary, they are remarkably well made, and you don't need to worry about the eparch's approval.

"You are always working on the drawloom," Alexander noted. "I didn't expect that someone as young as you would be set to such a task; the drawloom is more complicated than the other looms."

"The nuns seem to prefer the warp-weighted looms. It's how they learned to sew. I never got used to those looms, so the drawloom is all that I know," she said.

"I see. Tell me, Anastasia, how long have you been sewing purses?"

"Since I was five. They are one of the first things I learned to sew."

"Then you must be very good at it. Why did it take you so long to sew this one?" Alexander knew that might have come across judgmentally to a child and was probably the wrong way to put it even as the words left his mouth. He could see her lapsing into a bit of fear and defensiveness.

"I *can* sew a purse quickly, sir. But hegumenia warned me that this was very important and the fabric was expensive," her eyes strayed to Cyra for affirmation as she spoke. "She said Saturninus could not afford to replace the filaments if I erred. I only took so long because I was trying to be careful. I tried hard to see that there were no errors. I'm very sorry if you found errors."

"No, noooo, Anastasia. That's not it. I have weighed and inspected your work and it is of superb quality, worthy of imperial coin, and it has no errors—none at all."

She looked on him quizzically as if to say *what then?*

"In my role serving the eparch, I have seen many woven works: carpets, curtains, clothes, clothes, textiles, tents, sails...you name it. There was something about your purse that got my attention."

Her eyes pierced him.

"The stitches. Of all the woven textiles in Byzantium, your stitches are...an innovation." At this word Anastasia blushed. Innovation continued to be held in suspicion despite what was now the long and highly innovative reign of Justinian. Perhaps on account of his many innovations—many had had as much innovation as they could stand.

Alexander went on though, "While it's not at all new to me, I am impressed by the quality of the acanthus pattern."

At this she interjected, "Hegumenia said this had to be the finest pattern for the finest people. The finest pattern I've seen was at that Hagia Sophia when we went there for mass once. I tried hard to remember it and be faithful to it."

This made sense, "Did you learn the stitch pattern at Hagia Sophia too?"

"No, sir. I don't know where I learned that."

"You made them up?"

"The stitch we usually use is a knot stitch," Anastasia said, moving her fingers in front of her, recreating the motion used to make the stitch. "Hegumenia said this purse should be special though. I didn't mean to be presumptuous with innovation, but I took her to mean this purse should have something that should make it different from others. I practiced with coarse linens first to get it right, but I thought the knot stitches could be more...rich if I gave them body. So, I ran the thread an extra time through the loop with a needle."

"You did this to each stitch?"

"Every one."

"Marvelous," Alexander said absentmindedly.

At his exclamation, she looked up and brightened up, "You don't disapprove?"

"Of course not. I'm impressed. Someone of twelve years thought this up and applied it so well. Silk is precious, and purple is royal, but the knot stitch would leave little spaces between each stitch. Your stitch doesn't allow any space, so the weave rolls together under the fingers as if it were the scales of a magnificent creature—I might never know there isn't a base beneath it. It's done remarkably well, Anastasia. It gives the holder the illusion that he can *see* the pattern with his fingers, just by feeling it. I'm curious, what do you call this stitch?"

At this Anastasia seemed to freeze a bit, "Call it?"

"Do you have a name for this stitch? We cannot call it a 'knot stitch,' it's something new."

"I don't know, sir."

"Well, you created it, and I think you should have the honor of naming it."

Anastasia blushed a bit again, under both the unexpected honor but as well under the pressure. She glanced at Cyra who nodded with acceptance of this and then returned her eyes to Alexander, "May I hold the purse a minute?"

"Of course," he answered, handing it to her.

She took it gently in her hands and turned it over, but with deliberation and familiarity. She noted qualities about it that would be less important to the casual observer—if there could be a casual observer—of a purple, silk purse. She pressed the two edges and watched them expand after being flattened. She ran her finger along the bottom cleft of the purse and the seam it concealed, which anchored it together.

"The stitches are sewed to draw an acanthus. I hope that when the owner feels the stitches, that she might feel the plant and the pattern of the plant...even when she can't see it."

She looked at it for another moment and returned it to Alexander.

"Would it please you to call it a 'seed stitch'? The acanthus grows from seeds; it is drawn with this stitch."

She regarded him with inquiry.

Alexander held the little purse with its little seed stitches, running his fingers and thumb along them while he looked back at Anastasia. "Seeds. A seed stitch indeed."

"Yes—Anastasia's stitch will be known as the 'seed stitch,' the first one in Byzantium."

* * * * * * * * * *

Anastasia returned to her partner who had never left the drawloom and who remained waiting for her there the whole time. Alexander turned his attention back to Cyra.

"Quite an interesting young lady you are raising here, Cyra. I understand that she was...*left* here by her mother," he said modulating the tone of his voice on the word "left."

"What became of her, do you know?"

"The girl is an orphan," Cyra said with some emphasis, just a note more than might normally be necessary. "We don't know much of their parents."

Alexander continued to face her without saying anything.

"She is committed to our care because her mother died...plague."

"Do you know anything of her father?"

"Nothing."

"Remarkable. Such a skilled child."

Cyra said nothing in response. Alexander changed the subject.

"This is dangerous, but I understand. Tell me this though, who is the customer?"

"I can't say," Cyra answered.

He turned to her incredulously, "You can't say, or you won't say?"

"I can't."

Chapter 10
The Hànyǔ Interpreters of Dalmatou Monastery

At that time then matters stood thus between
the Romans and the Persians, both as
touching the war and in regard to silk.

Procopius of Caesarea
History of the Wars
Book VIII, Chapter XVII

Dalmatou Monastery
Psamathia Quarter
Byzantium

Tuesday Morning, *Trite*, "Third Day" by Byzantine
reckoning
Early in the "Fourth Watch"
—*many hours before sunrise and the night after Alexander's
meeting with Cyra*

28 March 551 AD
Julian Calendar

Alexander was dreaming. Against an iridescent, black-and-gray pallet there emerged a thick liquid from one corner. It spilled onto the pallet in a circular swirl, like a dye or paint. It consisted of several pastel colors, distinct at first, but they merged gently at one another's edges while swirling towards the center. As the dye spread, the pallet's flatness gave way to waves, which seemed to lift the pigments up and down like a fine cloth shaken by a servant before laying it down on a table for a superior.

In some places, the colors of the dye merged; in others it grew more uniform. All about, it increased in depth, simultaneously reaching towards Alexander and drawing away as if bidding him to follow. The waves of the pallet and the undulation of the dye became increasingly fierce until, in the leaking corner, they gave way to a misty disintegration. At first, Alexander could only perceive a bluish-white background. The disintegration grew until it shattered his field of view and Alexander found himself observing the waves of the ocean. In the distance, there was land. An island? The shore of the continent? He couldn't tell.

The vision of the waves beating against a shore began to take on a tactile nature, and he felt as though he was on a boat being kicked about in the water by uncooperative winds. He had a sense of a presence to his back of a figure who was hurriedly working with the ropes, struggling to adjust a mast. Alexander thought he could feel a fierce wind beating against his skin; there was shouting. It was both distant and blurry, like the vision of a dream. The last thing Alexander could detect seemed to be the outline of a primitive pier set against the beach and tall poles behind it bearing lit torches whose fire danced and kicked about by the force of the wind.

A man stood beyond the torches. Alexander could not make him out clearly but could see that he was mostly bald except for a long braid that fell along his back and over his shoulder. He wore orange robes with a black sash that crossed his chest. On his feet he wore sandals that were strung up to his knees. The man waved urgently at Alexander as if desperately trying to get his attention. In the confusion of his dream Alexander was surprised by a sense of recognition. He turned his head to say something to the man attending the masts behind him.

Just as he craned his head about his neck before his shipmate could come into view, he was woken by a sound. He shivered while he came to his senses under a strong, cool breeze that blew into his cell from outside.

Rising from his sleep, he was momentarily confused. Someone was sounding the xylon. Common in the monasteries of Asia Minor and Greece, the xylon was a gong-like plank normally struck with a hammer to summon monks and nuns to services. The monastery had three xylons that were used to signal different events. The wooden xylon had already been struck for midnight services earlier that evening. Alexander could tell from the clear glow of moonlight coming through his open window that it was too early for Orthros, but someone was striking the synakterion, a bronze xylon that normally denoted the commencement of morning services. As he sat up, he pushed aside the wooden shudders and tried to make sense of what was going on.

For a moment he wondered if this was a mistake. Perhaps one of the younger monks, a novice or one of the diakonetai—illiterate monks who usually served the monastery in roles of manual labor—had consumed too much wine. He quickly ruled out this possibility. An inebriated monk would beat the xylon erratically. No, he thought, the beating is rhythmic and purposeful. This recognition moved him to alarm. Something had happened: it was the middle of the night and all the monastery's inhabitants were being summoned to order. A robbery? Had there been thieves or violence? Fire? Then a dark thought, "Cyra's intrigues." He shuddered— *impossible*—whatever Cyra was up to, there was no reason to rouse the monastery in the middle of the night over it!

Alexander threw off the course, burlap blanket that had served as his bed cover. He quickly rose and put on his chiton, skipping other preparations. In nearly one motion, he slipped his feet into his shoes and was out the door of his monastic sleeping quarters. Moving down the aging wooden staircase, he passed under the apse into the trapeza, a large dining hall.

He took his assigned seat next to a sigmata, a semicircular table wedged into the wall; his placement at a sigmata distinguished him from other monks as being one of some education. The sigmata was set against the eastern wall of the trapeza, which was beneath a fresco depicting the blinded Apostle Paul on his knees on the road to Damascus under the glow of an angelic whose figure could barely be discerned inside a brilliant halo. Other monks took their seats, some along other tables against the walls and many more at the rectangular table in the center of the room.

He was by not the first of his brethren to arrive, but his anxiety at his slow response to the apparent emergency was alleviated by the sight of many more monks arriving after he did. There apparently was no fire and no indication of violence or a break-in. As he took his place among the cadre of literate brothers he allowed a moment's reflection to consider that most monastics must be like himself and habituated to daily midnight services and early-morning orthros at sunrise. They tended to sleep quite heavily in the short but dark nightly hours that separated the services—the same hours from which they had all been so suddenly wakened.

While he sat, he peered out of an east-facing window at the Katholicon, the monastery church, which was difficult to perceive in the darkness. Uncharacteristically, there were many lamps and torches lit, and in the flickering of their light he could make out the figure of Thaddeus, the monastery's superior and archimandrite of all the monasteries in the capital city of Byzantium. Thaddeus was flanked on one side by Joseph Nios, the oikonomos of the monastery. The two were rarely seen apart. To his other side were two men who Alexander did not recognize in the low glimmer of the torchlight. He could make out that one of them wore a paludamentum with two long-pointed segments hanging low beyond his knees; it was a military cloak worn by high-level officers. The other man appeared to be a soldier of some kind but was neither a scholae palatinae (an imperial guard) nor an excubitor (a bodyguard). He wore a distinctive purple palace fibula that fastened his cloak at the shoulder, which distinguished him from an ordinary soldier and implied some manner of connection to the palace—a hetaireia (imperial administrator) perhaps? What might that mean?

Whatever it meant, surely these must be messengers from the palace. Dalmatou Monastery was the oldest in Byzantium. Set in the eastern part of the Psamathia quarter outside Constantine's walls it had been founded by the Syrian Saint Isaac 170 years ago when some still living would have remembered Emperor Constantine moving the capital of Empire to what they then called New Rome, Nova Roma, Constantinople on the location of the ancient Greek Hamlet of Byzantium.

As Byzantium remained at the seat of Empire and Dalmatou Monastery was the superior of all the monasteries in the capital, visits by imperial officials were not uncommon. Nevertheless, in the two years Alexander had spent in this community he had never known imperial officials to call upon the monks with such short notice and least of all in the fourth watch of the night. Surely something urgent was afoot.

As the last of the monastery's inhabitants gathered, the rhythmic xylon ceased sounding. The low hum of whispers and the sounds of shuffling subsided.

Alexander was one of an order of monks known as lavriotai who differed from cenobites; the latter of whom both lived and ate together, spending nearly all moments waking and sleeping in the company of their brethren. The lavriotai, to which Alexander belonged, organized their monasteries such that their daily life was solitary, but social arrangements were organized around common spiritual purpose. The communities such as this observed considerable custom that cycled between moments of separation to individual activity: meditation, prayer, and moments of communal reconstitution such as this. The wax and wane of separation and reconstitution marked a particular harmonic quality to the lives of these monastics and was one of many such harmonics that laid and overlaid one another. Despite this gathering being unexpected and so untimely, it was still treated as if a minor choir section had gone off note with all the other choir sections doing their part to cover over the departure from harmony and return the body to its rhythm. While the trapeza had been lit dimly by a variety of lamps when he had first arrived, the lighting had grown stronger while he sat waiting. Designated monks, upon arrival at their stations, took to ritualistically and systematically lighting many hosts of candles on the tables and throughout the room.

Alexander's eyes adjusted while Thaddeus and Joseph, accompanied by their imperial visitors, entered through the main doors under the apse. While he watched them enter, Clement, a fellow monk and native of Italy, shared a seat at his sigmata. Clement motioned about either side of Alexander, lighting candles and pausing at each one to close his eyes. He dropped his brow, motioning softly with his lips the words of the prayer, and crossed himself before moving on to the next. Opposite Alexander and Clement on the opposing sigmata at the western end of the trapeza, another monk lit candles in a practiced manner oppositionally timed to Clement. He moved and lit candles while Clement prayed and lit his own.

With two candles remaining to light on the tables at both ends of this large hall, the archimandrite, his steward, and their visitors motioned and took a position on a raised podium at the head of the room. There they needed only to wait another moment for the final candles to be lit and those leading them to take their place and sit down at attention.

As Alexander fixed his gaze on the archimandrite and his party, he could see for the first time in the clear light the horologian, a clock that decorated the head of the trapeza. A sophisticated mechanical device, it was powered by dripping water concealed by the wall behind it and fed by a bladder contained in the attic beneath the wooden roof. The horologian proclaimed in decorative Latin scripted numbers—first hour of the fourth watch, about exactly what Alexander had suspected.

He let go a long sigh, too long apparently because it drew the attention and ever so scornful glare of the one of the diakonetai, Phillip, who sat nearby at the central table. Illiterate, these monks were expected to perform duties in the form of the manual labor. Usually of humble origins—the most common kind of origins even in Byzantium, they sat at separate tables, wore different schema, dwelled in separate kellia, and were even buried in separate plots from their literate, educated brothers. This separation of monks by class was on one hand necessary to bridge the gaping chasm that separated the worlds and manners of the literate and uneducated, but on the other hand it generated tensions that were difficult on a day by day basis to avoid—particularly in a monastery where necessity pressed the two groups and their work together so closely. Rare was the subtle transgression of a literate monk that would go unnoticed and unnoted by his prayerful but uneducated brethren the latter of whom felt that the former had it – pretty good – and were so given to holding their literate brothers to markedly high standards of obedience. Phillip was a fairly recent addition to the community at Dalmatou but took no time ascertaining the fissures among his brother monks.

Returning to his gaze to the archimandrite, Alexander brushed off the incident as he had so many times before. As he did so, Thaddeus beckoned upwards with both of his hands and spoke with a low but loud voice that could be apprehended in about every corner of the room: "In the name of the father, the son, and the Holy Spirit." With this motion and those words, all of the monks stood up from their seats and finished the prayer in unison with the archimandrite. He turned around and faced the wall behind him decorated in an elaborate fresco on an iconostasis and adorned on both ends with manoualia that each held about them three circular rows of candles.

Upon concluding their prayer, Thaddeus faced them again and motioned for everyone to be seated. He began to address them.

"Finally," Alexander thought. "Finally, we will earn what all of this is about."

* * * * * * * * * *

Before he had become a monk Phillip had spent a lot of time near Eirenaion on the Eastern shore of the Bosphorus, the larger body of Byzantium sat on the Western shore opposite Eirenaion. The close proximity to Eirenaion had left him with a lot of exposure to the order of akiometoi who inhabited the place. The akiometoi had been established a century earlier and were known as "the sleepless ones" as they were formed under the idea of perpetual singing. Their order broke each day into three eight-hour shifts where they replaced one another to allow for continuous singing. Phillip often wondered what allowance was made in their procedure to account for bodily needs. Sure, they had sixteen hours between shifts during which they might sleep, but eight hours of singing was too long to avoid relieving oneself. Who wouldn't collapse without some food or water?

Apart from that though it was pretty good set up. Many laborers had to work ten to fourteen hours a day, and even skilled laborers such as himself peddled their trades at appallingly low wages. His own father and been a skytotomos, a shoe maker, and had passed the skill onto his son, on to Phillip, though the wages were so impossibly low he had to find another way to make a living, and he had. Although his options were few, when fortune finally found him it was out on the margins. It all had worked pretty well until Barsymes. In any case though, he resented a bit that he could not help but admire the akiometoi who—despite eight hours a day of singing—lived in a comfortable community and had most of their needs met.

Relatively new still to the community at Dalmatou, Phillip had been made to understand that the monks there were organized into two groups: diakonetai like himself who were responsible for most of the labor about the monastery and educated choir monks who generally did not labor but offered their literate services to Providence through song. His mentor had not seen the necessity of explaining the roles of choir monks very well, so he was still under the impression that the choir monks of Dalmatou must follow the same rules and scripts as the akiometoi of Eirenaion. While he had always found the akiometoi somewhat annoying during his time on the Eastern shore, they were after all singing interminably, he found himself still more annoyed by the choir monks of Dalmatou who as far as he could tell enjoyed all the benefits of the monastic community including service by the hand of laborers such as himself, but who showed little evidence of performing for hours of "sleepless praise."

So as he sat waiting for Thaddeus to begin to explain why they had been woken and summoned at this unusual hour, he could not help but to be put off by the choir monk Alexander who sat at an honored sigmata against the wall off to his left and who looked disheveled and bewildered at the sudden interruption. Though Alexander had been with the monastery much longer than he, the former's inattentiveness to the rules of the place struck Phillip as a form of conceit. Here Phillip had to strain himself to learn to align to the order and rhythm of the community while this choir monk seemed to reckon himself above all that.

Thaddeus began to explain that the monastery had received an urgent message, and when he went on to say that the message came to Dalmatou from the palace, Phillip's heart skipped a beat. Despite his earlier concerns about monks' respect for order, he couldn't help but sulk and inched back into his seat. Through his discomfort, Phillip found it hard to follow Thaddeus perfectly clearly, but the gist of it seemed to be that the Emperor was hosting guests, ambassadors maybe.

Either way, they seemed to be of some importance, but due to some problem, the nature of which remained unclear, no one could understand the message these guests brought with them.

It all was very odd, but as Thaddeus wrapped up another monk spoke up questioning Thaddeus as to the urgency of their summoning. "Surely," he exclaimed quite loudly so that everyone heard him, "any ambassadors to the Emperor must've traveled a long way to arrive here from their foreign lands. What difference could it make to translate their words during the watch when in a short time the hours would commence and everyone would be fresh and clearheaded!"

Phillip lifted his head at this interruption and noted that it came from Clement, another choir monk. "Figures," he said under his breath.

Choir monk or not, Thaddeus did not look prepared to indulge the stakes at any length and merely answered, "The message has implications for our war with the Persians, and we are told it cannot wait. Now, with any grace, one will be found amongst you who can help...so let's not waste another minute."

At this, the choir monks started first each approaching the iconostasis where one of the palace messengers had established a document on a podium. Being illiterate himself until now, Phillip had for the most part ignored it, but he noticed as each of the choir monks walked up, they would note the document: some examined it closely, but most just looked at it with some confusion as if it were made of scribbles or a child's drawing. In each case, they eventually shook their heads negatively at the palace messenger who would acknowledge them, before returning to their seats.

This went on until Alexander and the other monks who shared his sigmata approached the iconostasis. Phillip was able to see that Alexander seemed to be craning his head to get a closer look at the document before arriving at the podium himself. Then, quite unlike the monks before him,

Alexander became noticeably excited. He looked to Thaddeus and Joseph Nios as he walked up to the document and nodded quizzically while pointing to it. He turned back to the palace messenger, and Phillip was able to read his lips to tell that he was asking the messenger where this document had come from.

Now that he was cued up, he could almost hear the words of the palace messenger as he watched him mouth them—something about the east, something about India. Now Phillip was interested. *What is going on?* he wondered. He strained himself to lean in, observe, and listen. The palace messenger seemed extraordinarily pleased that Alexander recognized the document's writing, but he clearly did not seem finished and was gesturing to Alexander to do something with it.

At this, Alexander gently peeled back the cover and exposed pages beneath, which Phillip was able to decipher illegible black scribbles against the gray white background. He could see that they held some meaning to Alexander whose eyes seemed to widen as he took the writing into his gaze; his right finger unconsciously rising to the page and pointing while he tried to sound out words. For a moment, it looked like he was struggling, and the messenger's face, full of hope a moment earlier, quickly drained and replaced all earlier inklings of that emotion with sullen skepticism. But Alexander, disheveled when he arrived, glanced down, shook his head, lifted his hand to the messenger, and even wagged it a bit correctively, insisting patience before opening his palm. The effect of which was to create an immediate look of annoyed confusion on the face of the messenger—though it was clear he was willing to proffer the requested patience.

The messenger looked as if he was about to dismiss Alexander when the monk began to speak. His words at first were a bit stumbling, two words, then three, then two, then stumbling on another one, and finally they began to flow. Alexander relaxed in front of the podium as his voice, reading the words on the page, became louder. While on one hand the orderly cadence of the sounds he was making was willful—his confidence gripped everyone present, it was abundantly clear that no one had ever heard the tongue spoken in which Alexander was now so forcefully speaking.

Everyone, except Phillip.

Until now, Phillip had never heard this tongue spoken except in lands beyond Taprobanê, a large island kingdom off the coast of India—to most Romans and Greeks it was the end of the civilized world. This was the tongue of a distant, almost alien people. Phillip was overcome with questions. *How had it come to be here? How had it come to Byzantium? To Dalmatou?*

Mesmerized by the force of his own understanding and transfixed by the incongruity of witnessing a kinsman, one who also came from Syria, speaking fluently in the tongue Phillip largely assumed he would never hear spoken again, he found himself rising and pacing forcefully past his fellow diakonetai, startling them by the act. He could barely hear their protests at his motion and he ignored the murmuring directed at him as he stepped out of order and pressed his way forward to the iconostasis. He came to a stop at a rise just below where Thaddeus and Joseph Nios both stood.

Thaddeus had been taken in some amazement by Alexander's unexpected fluency and had remained focused on the former the entire time Phillip approached. Now that Phillip stood just behind him, Thaddeus detected some commotion and looked around over his shoulder; his face rapidly transitioning between focused amazement, a note of confusion at the presence of a stray diakonetai, and followed immediately by some annoyance. Thaddeus did not even have to mouth the words, his face said it all: *What are you doing up here?*

Phillip was a burly man and an imposing presence. He had seen and survived a lot before joining this order of monks. Although he stood a step below Thaddeus, with his height he was still able to lock gaze, almost eye to eye, with the archimandrite. Still confused by Alexander's reading and a little intimidated by the archimandrite, Phillip raised his own hand, lifting a bent finger as his mind struggled to form the words that Alexander was speaking in the foreign tongue—words that he thought he would never speak again when he came to Dalmatou: *I understand this tongue. I understand what the choir monk is saying!* Was it the shock of hearing the language? Was it the fear of being discovered? Was he intimidated by the archimandriate? Whatever it was, it stoked a cold rush of adrenaline that he could feel spreading about his chest. "He..." Phillip said wagging his finger at Alexander, "he's saaaying it wrong. That's not how you're supposed to say it."

* * * * * * * * *

Phillip finished his correction a second time. When he had said it from the nave before coming up to the podium where Alexander stood, it was intelligible to no one, Alexander included. However, when he came within speaking distance and they faced each other eye to eye, the clarity of it, and of Alexander's own error, was immediately obvious. Phillip's pronunciation was tonal and alternated through several octaves in a way that Alexander was sure he could not easily reproduce without some practice. There was also some variance with the comparatively sing-song Greek they were both more accustomed to speaking, but as Phillip spoke the words the memories of his own instruction returned to him.

Alexander's parents, who had been attached to a Nestorian mission that was established deep inside Persia—indeed almost all the way to India where there were as many Indians as there were Persians, could not secure for him a Greek tutor. They settled for what they could find, and what they found was a woman his parents received as a maid from the Persians who was a refugee from some far-off country, east of India: Liang Ji. Perhaps because he had been so young, and language came easy to him, he learned this obscure foreign tongue, *Hànyǔ*, from Liang Ji. Liang Ji would have him spend all his afternoons in the church garden drawing the characters that he now read from a wax tablet. He only had her to speak with though, and that itself was long ago. He was never sure why his parents encouraged this. Perhaps they hoped he would be the first Christian missionary to the distant land Liang Ji had fled to them from.

Now, here was an illiterate monk who knew the language, who could speak Hànyǔ! And better so than could he, apparently.

Alexander nodded at Phillip in acknowledgment and recognition. Carefully, he tried to mouth the sounds himself. He and Phillip followed each other, together; he was able to correct some of the structure with Phillip leading him to do so, but he was sure he would need work on the tones.

Everyone watched their dialog unfold. It struck no one as odd that a roomful of monks and dignitaries were all observing two men speaking a language to each other that nobody recognized, let alone understood, yet they all looked on with rapt amazement. Realizing that Phillip perhaps had him bettered, Alexander stood aside from the podium and offered the letter to Phillip, gesturing to Phillip, then to the letter, speaking sincerely to this monk of lesser status, "Perhaps you can read this better than I?"

Phillip barely ticked his head towards the letter then reconnected eye contact, shaking his head. "No, no I cannot. I *speak* the language. Before I came here, I was a merchant. I did trade in the land where this is spoken, beyond Taprobanê, beyond India. I speak it—we had to, to conduct business there, but I cannot read it", Phillip paused, then stated absolutely, "I can't read."

The spell of it all began to clear, and the shape of the discovery started to crystallize within the archimandrite and the representatives he had hosted from the Great Palace.

Both Thaddeus and one of the palace messengers stepped forward towards Alexander and Phillip and stood on either side of them, the messenger motioning in from the wall where he had stood previously and Thaddeus from closer to the nave. They seemed to want to create an enclosure around the two, as Alexander noticed Joseph Nios step to the outer edge to allow them space. The other messenger, the officer, positioned himself the same but diagonally so that now three bodies blocked him and Phillip from the torrent of captivated, onlooking monks.

Alexander looked back and forth, first to Thaddeus, then to the palace messenger.

"What *is* this? What is this about? Why have you brought us here at this early hour to read this?" Alexander asked.

The foreign tongue and the letter had put some broad parameters around it so that at least now he had some framework or structure to make sense of what brought these visitors to Dalmatou, but it was still anyone's guess why this was so important that it could not even wait for sunrise.

The palace messenger spoke in a low but clear voice; Thaddeus motioned urgently for Alexander to be attentive.

"I beg your pardon that we could not be introduced earlier. I am Callinicus, cubicularius to Emperor Justinian", he spoke formally, "I am asked by our holy and God-led emperor on this occasion to act as dignitary for a foreign embassy. Accompanying me is Stilicho," he said, gesturing to the officer, "of the scholae palitinae."

"Together we are in the service of the Magister Officiorum, Peter Patricus. The letter you are reading is from an eastern prince, from a country..." Callinicus hesitated. "All we really know about it is that it comes from beyond India and it concerns the matter of silk", the last words he said with a heaviness that suggested a gravity that stood in contrast to the airy quality of the fabric.

"Silk?" Alexander interjected. Somehow, with all the commotion and intensity, the word was unexpected, and this despite it being the subject of the earlier afternoon's work. It was all almost too much to process. At once, Alexander recognized who Callinicus must be. He was actually being somewhat demure to introduce himself as the emperor's cubicularius—a eunuch acting as the Emperor's chamberlain and, usually, an adviser to the emperor but whose formal role was to lock the door on the emperor's bedchamber.

Callinicus, Alexander knew, was more than a chamberlain. He had recently risen to the post of *praepositus sacri cubiculi*—the grand chamberlain and highest-ranking eunuch in the emperor's service, which explained the purple! It also left no doubt as to who was in charge here, Callinicus's diminutive stature and heretofore modest presentation notwithstanding. The *praepositus sacri cubiculi* effectively managed the old post of the *comes rerum privatarum*, the count of the private fortune. He controlled Justinian's private accounts and, for all intents and purposes, served on the emperor's consistorium—a powerful man indeed.

He still didn't understand the meaning of the visit—but it was clear to him now it was something the Palace took to be of highest importance.

Callinicus continued. "Yes," he answered with emphasis, "silk is a great concern of the Emperor."

Alexander nodded, but it still did not add up with him. Almost despite himself, he spoke again out of turn, "But...Serinda", he stopped, recalling Callinicus's earlier reluctance to name the far-off land and noticing the slightest bristle from Callinicus when he uttered the word, then he chose his words more tactfully, "the country you are talking about—the place you think this letter comes from—it's *five thousand stadia* distant from here. Why wake us at this early hour and gather all these monks as if this were an emergency?"

Alexander wasn't looking in the direction of Thaddeus but he could feel the hairs raising on the back of his neck as though the hairs themselves could tell that the archimandrite did not approve of his follow-up questions. It did not matter; Callinicus did not hesitate with his answer, "Because, there are two ambassadors who brought us this letter, from Serinda...as you say. They are monks."

"Monks?!" This time it was all three: Alexander, Phillip and even Thaddeus who spoke out in unison.

"Yes, two monks, like you. But only one speaks Greek, and he is old and infirm. Just as you say, their journey was long, perhaps too long for his stamina. He lies on his deathbed this moment. We cannot waste time. We need to go. Peter Barsymes orders it. Both of you, come with us—we're leaving."

"Bar*sy*—mes," Phillip spoke up for the first time since their huddle began, saying the name with a breathy stretch in the middle that struck Alexander as being almost personal. Alexander looked towards him. The man had turned white as a ghost. *What was wrong*, Alexander wondered. "We must go see *him* now?" Phillip went on, and then he added, almost hopefully, "I thought you said you answer to Peter Patricus?"

Callinicus answered Phillip, "Silk is of highest importance to the emperor—it is a concern of the entire Consistorium. Barsymes, Patricus, and the emperor himself. The emperor knows no higher priority." In no uncertain terms, Callinicus concluded, "So *yes*. We must move. Who knows how much life remains in the old monk who brought this to us. We must leave right now."

As they gathered to leave, Alexander tried to digest what he had just heard.

This was bizarre. There were Moors raiding in Africa; they had recently killed a governor! The Goths remained entrenched in parts of Italy. A bitter war churned on against the Persians in Lazica—three fronts! He had heard of whole cities running out of their grain and bread supplies, and aristocrats grumbled about barbarians that the emperor was paying off with taxes they paid to keep their peace and their place, up by the Danube. The empire was still in grudging recovery from the loss of millions who died during the plague. In his role serving the eparch he had been able to observe up close as the prices of goods defied the Emperor's decrees they stand still, rising ever upwards in defiance.

All of these matters to trouble the Emperor's heart, but his highest concern is silk?

Callinicus's words echoed in Alexander's mind, *the emperor knows no higher priority*, the thought of it was ponderous: *silk ... no, higher, priority ...Silk?!*

Chapter 11
The Visitors in the Apokrisiarikion

Ta Patrikias which is behind Hagia Sophia toward
the east: as emperors passed by in procession with
their ladies when they wished to go to Hagia Sophia,
they would stop at this place.
It was a house built by Constantine the Great.

The Patria
Book 3, 204

There was between these two churches a hospice for
the relief of destitute persons and those in the last
extremity of disease, suffering in body as well as
fortune, which was built in former times by a God-
fearing man named Samson.
This also did not remain unscathed by the insurgents
but perished in the fire...The Emperor Justinian
rebuilt it in a magnificent fashion, and with a much
greater number of rooms...being assisted in these
pious works by the Empress Theodora.

Procopius of Caesarea
Buildings
Book I, Chapter II

First Hill
Palace of the Patriarchate
Southeast of Hagia Sophia
Byzantium

Later on, before sunrise
Still during the Fourth Watch

Tuesday morning, *Trite*, "Third Day"
28 March 551 AD
Julian Calendar

Lao Yi's body reclined in his bed, but his mind was only in periodic contact with it—and even then, only imperfectly so. It was night; the room was illuminated by several lamps. There were various figures occupying the room with him, which while accessible to his mind, presented themselves only as spectral ministers. He assumed they were his hosts. Also present was his junior brother monk, Hui-Shen. All of them would come and go, and he presumed the lamps were for their benefit, not his. He could not tell how often they were paying visits to him, but it seemed that he was briefly drawn out of the expanses of his dreams and into the confines of the room each time someone came in to check on his state or try to speak with him. Whenever he was pulled back to the room, he perceived the place as shrouded in a kind of ghostly, dark mist broken by the shadowy silhouettes of men. Sometimes they would adjust his sheets; other times one might wipe the sweat from his brow with a dry towel. Periodically, they would try to feed him by squeezing water, wine, or broth from a rag under his tongue, and often they seemed to be adjusting the lamps. Once in a while, it was Hui-Shen—he was sure—who would apply or remove an acupuncture needle from his meridians.

With its proximity to the ocean and a window for ventilation, the air in the room was damp and cool, and pleasantly so in the way that ocean air tended to be clean and bristled with salt. However, Lao Yi felt hot and dry. Though he could not make out the light from the lamps, the smoke they gave off was acrid and singed his throat. He was aware that Hui-Shen was sitting next to him during meditation, and after the sessions he could hear him muttering words about his master suffering from a deficiency of water. "My brother monk," Hui-Shen whispered, "you are growing old. The journey has been hard on you, too much heat—too much salt. You are losing water and your kidneys are deficient of *jing*. We must buttress wood and contain loss."

At this, Hui-Shen could be heard to sit up and away from Lao Yi, looking about the room with annoyance, "and damn this salty air. You have too much salt already" but he had no means of combatting it.

After these words Hui-Shen would sometimes make adjustments to this or that needle, remove or replace them. Even in his catatonic state, except for the part about the salty air which was the one redeeming quality of this place that Lao Yi could detect, he was prepared to agree with his junior monk's assessment and these brief returns to the edge of hypnogogic consciousness all served as strong reminders of just how thirsty he was.

It was always far more pleasant when he was lifted away from the plane this room seemed to occupy and taken to dream and it was such a burden and disappointment each time his body seemed to force his return. Indeed, on each return from subterranean realms of consciousness he found himself so thirsty he yearned that someone might squeeze more water into his mouth from one of the wet towels they use to clean his forehead—the water from two towels instead of one—as he never felt that he could get quite enough. And who knows maybe they were offering him water, properly— with a glass to drink it from, in large satisfying gulps, and he was just too far gone to accept it or notice, but just once if he could he would've gratefully mustered the strength to accept a glass of water instead of another needle.

This time as he came to there seemed to be more than one presence about him and still more entering into his room. There were several figures, he could not make out how many. Were these his ministers, his hosts? Had they come to move him? He hoped not. It seemed it would've been better to remain in this place, in this room on this bed, and die peacefully, rather than disturb a hopeless decline just so that another bed might play host to his soon-to-be-dead body. These men, these figures in the room, to them they were moving about in a reasonably well-lit space but to Lao Yi they were figures moving about in darkness. One of the figures pressed through from among the crowd and from the silhouette of his bald head and the crop of his robes Lao Yi sensed it was Hui-Shen.

Lao Yi remained immobile while Hui-Shen seemed to examine him, setting himself down on a stool aside the bed to do so. Lao Yi had a sense that his whole bed was being surrounded by these figures in the darkness and two figures, in particular, pressed closer, standing behind and to either side of Hui-Shen. They too, it seemed, had robes but there was something different about them.

Was it true then?
Was this it?
Had they come to attend to him as he passed away?

For a moment no one said anything. Hui-Shen simply sat on the stool and observed Lao Yi in the quietness of the room. He proceeded to lean closer, tilting his ear over Lao Yi's face, facing him directly and sniffing. After this he retrieved a brass depressor from his robes and used it in combination with his pointers to hold Lao Yi's mouth open and depress the tip of his tongue. Lao Yi was too weak to protest and, in any case, understood what his brother was attempting.

Reclining back to his stool Hui-Shen finally spoke, "your tongue is less cracked and flush than yesterday master.

I admit I am surprised, but you seem to be improving." Hui-Shen did not expect Lao Yi to hear this but let the words sink in while taking his elder monk's wrist up into his own hand and testing the pulse with three fingers.

When he was finished he stood and shifted about, apparently now his back to Lao Yi, he seemed to be addressing the two men who had stood beside and behind him.

Until this moment Lao Yi's entire presence in this experience had been transitory, as most of his experiences had been with prior visits since they arrived in this city. Coming in, feeling thirsty, drifting away, coming in, sensing figures move, drifting away, coming in, becoming aware of Hui-Shen and some manner of adjustments, then drifting again away...

But upon detecting that Hui-Shen was in conversation with the men who occupied the room with him, something alarmed him, and he felt something that had almost become a stranger to him—as if from a subterranean source the power of *will*, like an old friend, reasserted itself and thrust back into his abdomen.

His protégé Hui-Shen didn't know the language of Daqin, the vast empire their common master Xiao Yi had sent them to as emissaries. A young monk, Hui-Shen had been ordered to accompany Lao Yi on account his youth, strength and vigor, as well as his knowledge of medicine—all of which were on display and in fruitful use presently and all selected for specifically to complement Lao Yi's deficiencies in each area of the same. Besides as a necessary complement to Lao Yi, Hui-Shen had been sent with the hopes that he'd learn the geography, language and customs of Daqin in the tutelage of Lao Yi by way of the experience, as a kind of apprentice, in hopes he might be useful to his masters after Lao Yi departed.

Lao Yi—it was obvious enough now—was getting old for this kind of work.

But Hui-Shen didn't yet speak Greek, *E-lenika*, the language of Daqin.

So how is he talking with these people? Lao Yi wondered.

How was he carrying on conversation? Had he already learned the language in the short time they'd been here, or...

The thought disturbed him—how long had he been here?!

Had he lost his sense of time? Had they been here months and not just days, so long now Hui-Shen had had time to apprehend the language himself?

This would be good for Hui-Shen, and good for their mission if it wasn't too late to return ... but the thought of having lost several months or half a year of his life to unconsciousness was unsettling.

The problem transfixed him, and his puzzlement transformed itself into will and by the power of will he overcame the heavy sense of sluggishness that had long overcome him, and he stirred in the bed, drawing the attention of some of the figures who stood back, still in the shadows. His movements were too discrete to be noticed by Hui-Shen and the fellows he addressed, as they seemed occupied in conversation, but as he came to the ghostly dream-mist that had for so long shrouded the room cleared and cut into its place was the luminosity of the lamps—five of them—one on each wall and another standing above a surface emplaced off to his right, opposite the side that Hui-Shen stood at.

A split second after the mist gave way to luminosity, visual acuity returned. He could see!

What were a moment ago figures now came into clear sight. To his right were two men who stood back from the rest, by the fact that they were armed and wore helmets he concluded they must be attendant soldiers or guards. Standing back against the opposite wall just inside the entrance to the room was a tall, bearded man wearing a black, flowing robe that came around the top of his head and concealed some manner of squarish hat below it—a Daqin cleric? Between this man and Hui-Shen and those he addressed the space was crowded with two more men—one—a feminine looking man without a beard who wore purple, indicating imperial rank, and another who wore a white robe that was embroidered in green and brown colors with insignia he didn't recognize or understand, but which he suspected marked the man as an officer.

Finally—now with strength returning to him such that he could lift himself up from the cushions he lay upon for, *this must be the first time in how long?...*he was able to see that Hui-Shen was indeed making conversation with two men as he'd sensed.

These two—they also wore black robes like the two clerics behind them, but neither had his head covered. One man, standing to the left of Hui-Shen, was a bit taller, with broad shoulders, a thick, curly tuft of dark hair and what struck Lao Yi as a rather haggard beard, especially for a monk, while the other to Hui-Shen's right was a shorter, thin, clean-shaven and hair cut neatly to the scalp, but not shaved.

Propping himself up it was a moment to make out that he could apprehend the words being spoken between Hui-Shen and the two. Hui-Shen spoke with some energy that was in contrast to the gentle bedside manner he'd exercised a moment earlier during his examination. In the course of the moment Lao Yi realized that he could fully apprehend the conversation between Hui-Shen and these two men, but he had to press through the puzzlement because seconds later he understood why.

To his surprise they were *not* speaking in E-lenika, they were *not* speaking in the language of the Daqin—no, these men were speaking with Hui-Shen in Hànyǔ!

Before he could think about it he broke into their conversation, allowing the slightest bit of ironic correction to come through in his tone, "Hui-Shen, I am parched beyond words ... do you think this time it would befit you to serve your master with a full cup this time instead of a water-logged rag?"

At the unexpected sound of Lao Yi's voice Hui-Shen whipped around with a look of shock and the whole room stood in silence, their eyes in uniform both set and transfixed on the old monk, moments ago not far from death it seemed, but who was now lifting himself up by his own power.

* * * * * * * * * *

Twenty minutes later four monks sat together in the adjacent room around a table, the others loomed behind them. Hui-Shen had previously only had time to come to grips with Alexander and Philip's surprising ability to speak the common tongue—something he'd been led to believe by master Lao Yi was unheard of in Daqin, no one in Daqin, he'd been assured, could speak Hànyǔ! He had to digest this surprise while appraising the visitors of the dire state of his master and the reason he and Hui-Shen had become interned for so long as guests when they had an urgent embassy for the emperor. Now, as the four surrounded a table he was frenetic, on one hand trying to attend to his master's needs, on the other trying to explain the urgent purpose of their journey to these new visitors.

Fidgeting over tea he was pouring for Lao Yi, Hui-Shen said, "We are on a mission from the Emperor of the Liang".

"*Not* the emperor!" Lao Yi interjected, "General Hou may as well be the emperor..."

"...the prince" Hui-Shen self-corrected, "we are sent by Prince Xiao Yi, the emperor's brother".

"Emperor Xiao Guan is under *house arrest*", Lao Yi's proclamation was broken by a burst of coughs.

Recovering he continued, "and our prince, Xiao Yi, he has no authority on account of being the emperor's brother—his authority comes only from the fact that he remains governor of Jing province."

Hui-Shen was shaking under the excitement and the pressure and almost tipped over Lao Yi's tea cup as he filled it, burning himself.

All of this wasn't working—his Daqin hosts were having a hard time getting the handle of it, so he tried a different tact. The rulers of Daqin had sent them brother monks—he would try that venue.

Sitting himself down again, facing his tired and bewildered visitors, Hui-Shen said, "you said you are both monks".

They both nodded, the younger one said "yes".

"We also are monks, both of us, me and Lao Yi" he said—but before he could continue Lao Yi interrupted again.

"*Not* monks!" he pronounced loudly, Hui-Shen wondered if the entire conversation would go this way. They were in the presence of the purple. *Had Lao Yi no sense of the impropriety?* he wondered. *Would the imperial representative be understanding?* seeing as it was clear Lao Yi had suddenly and unexpectedly recovered, he hoped.

Alexander and Philip both rose in their chairs at the spectacle of Lao Yi's outburst, each entirely unsure of what to make of it. In this—so too—was Hui-Shen, *almost*...that is, his heart sank before Lao Yi could go on, and go on he did.

"No. *Not* monks. Outlaws!" Lao Yi yelled so loudly the onlooking guards and messengers stood on edge.

Hui-Shen tried to intervene before things got out of hand, "master...you have been long departed from us from the fever, surely you do not wish these men to understand..."

"We, are, bandits", Lao Yi interrupted ... starring straight into Hui-Shen's eyes.

Looking away from Hui-Shen he caught the eyes of Philip, "highway robbers", then Alexander, "pirates".

"Pirates of the highest order".

Coyly he addressed Alexander and Phillip, "perhaps you will join us?

"Who is your master? This man here?", he pointed to Thaddeus, "or him?" pointing to Callinicus in his purple, "what about the Emperor of the Daqin? Would he transform you from monk, to bandit?"

Lao Yi was determined with his tirade and Hui-Shen was on the verge of giving up, when Alexander, the younger Daqin monk, finally said something, "What brings you here then?"

Hui-Shen was relieved, thinking *this one is erudite and ignores my old fool of a master.*

Lao Yi would have none of it, "I already told you! We are thieves!"

"Then what it is you have been sent to steal?" Alexander pressed, retaining his composure.

Resigned, Hui-Shen stated, "My master ... has confused you. We are not *here* to steal anything".

The older Daqin monk Philip, who until now had been mostly silent except when they were introducing one another, drew a sly smile across his face at this, "I,...I understand".

Everyone regarded him.

"What's not to understand?" he asked to a silenced room.

"You are pirate monks, sent on the authority of an imprisoned emperor, to steal—*nothing*".

Then, truly sticking his neck out, he repeated himself for the others listening but who could so far not understand a word being said, this time speaking in Greek, "What our guest said is: they are pirate monks, sent to us on the authority of an imprisoned emperor, to steal—*nothing*".

His words hung in the air for a moment. Surely the lowest ranking man present he'd braved cutting what was obviously still thick ice—with a joke.

The silence lasted long enough for the fact of the uniform impropriety to sink in among two sets of monks of different faiths and vastly different lands, their guards, the

archimandrite and the imperial representatives all present—
Lao Yi himself led the way when everyone burst into laughter.

When the laughing receded it was Lao Yi who spoke
again.

"My brother Philip ... you are correct in your
assessment in aspects except one.

"You omitted that our mission is not to steal from our
guests ... our emperor Xiao Gang, through his brother Xiao Yi,
has sent us to the emperor of the Daqin—your emperor—to
offer us as outlaw bounty pirates ... we are to offer our services
to the emperor of the Daqin to make ourselves pirates against
the captive empire of the Liang."

Alexander stammered, "What? I, I don't understand"

Hui-Shen answered him, "Our nation is held captive by
an evil warlord—general Hou. He rules under the name of our
emperor, Emperor Xiao Gang, but he is emperor in name only.
He cannot command soldiers ... or for that matter: monks. So
he must command mercenaries instead.

"Lao Yi means that we have not been sent to take
anything from you or the land of the Daqin. Emperor Xiao
Gang sends us as outlaws against the regime that has
imprisoned him—so that we may assist the Daqin in
weakening the reviled warlord who imprisons the legitimate
ruler of the Liang."

At this, Philip spoke again.

"Your nation—the Liang—beyond India? That is
where you are from?"

"Yeees", Lao Yi replied lifting his cup of tea then
lowering it to the table, "we have journeyed all this distance to
offer ourselves as pirates for the emperor of the Daqin".

"I've been there", Philip responded.

Uncharacteristically, Alexander responded with
involuntary reaction that was, "What?! No one has been to
Serinda!"

Philip shook his head, answering, "brother monk, my
superior," at those words both Hui-Shen and Lao Yi

reacted...the dynamic between Philip and Alexander had been odd to both of them until now, as the older Philip had tended to defer to the younger Alexander, this was odd that an older monk understood a younger as his superior.

Philip made a bit of a show of looking around at the guards, Stilicho and Callicinus, then returned his gaze and fixed eyes with Alexander, "...thank God we speak a foreign language so in the plain sight of authority I can say this to you but there are things you don't know, things for which I owe you a full explanation, some *other time.*"

Chided, Alexander bid his silence and allowed Philip to continue.

Philip looked to Lao Yi and Hui-Shen, "brothers ... you visit this place which you and your countrymen call Daqin ... the Qin was the first dynasty of your own great country, so we know you are paying a respect to recognize a brother empire as an equal—Da, Qin—the 'Great Qin' ... let me say," Philip hesitated, glancing at Alexander, then at Callicinus, reminding and trying to reassure himself that only Alexander could understand, "...let me say that on behalf of Emperor Justinian, Emperor of Daqin, that we recognize and appreciate the honor stated in the spirit of the name you have recognized for us."

Alexander's eyes widened at the scale of Philip's presumption, to speak on behalf of the emperor, but he said nothing and Philip went on.

"Among the Daqin few people know of your country. Our maps go as far as India and even those who have maps only know your emperor's land as Serinda—the land beyond India, the land silk comes from."

Lao Yi and Hui-Shen were attentive.

"I may be presuming much but as one of the few of Daqin who has been to Serinda, let me offer on behalf of Emperor Justinian of Daqin, that we return the gift of recognition. Here—we are called Rome and this city, Constantinople or Byzantium, is her capital. Let us recognize the Liang, 'Great Rome'".

Not sure where Philip was going with all of this, but quite certain of the longer and longer reams of impropriety he was staking on his near lone-command of a foreign tongue and the implicit trust he was placing in Alexander to remain discrete with his knowledge of it, Alexander was becoming increasingly uncomfortable. Wishing to stop matters before they got too far he began to interrupt Philip in Greek, then stopped himself when Lao Yi's ears perked up—and he remembered the older foreign monk could speak Greek. Did Philip know Latin too?

Alexander ventured it *"Frater, quantum adduxeris specta, ante quam alea iacias.*[φφ]*"*

Philip barely nodded in acknowledgement but continued like he hadn't heard Alexander. "But, Rome—the 'great' Qin, is great—and Serinda, the Liang—is also great. You have come a long distance. I have been there—*I know*—how far you have come. Tell us, what can two monks offer to steal away from a land that, once lost, is so great that it decisively weakens the ruling warlord?

"Look at me and my brother", he gestured to Alexander.

"My brother is much more learned than me, this I admit, but surely he agrees with me that there is nothing we could do that might weaken our emperor and that is, ...God forbid...if we even *wanted* to. If your emperor wishes to weaken a rival, this is the stuff of the affairs of great powers and I, we, are not surprised. But a general who can hold an emperor under house arrest in a land as great as Rome—is both a great and terrible man. What can two monks like yourselves hope to do to weaken him? Won't any theft be like a pin-prick on the tough fur of a tiger?"

Alexander listened with a kind of roused ambivalence. Philip had ventured much with these words, too much already

---

[φφ] *Frater, quantum adduxeris specta, ante quam alea iacias,*
Latin: "Brother, look at the stakes before you throw the dice."

he was sure, but as he closed around his inquiry Alexander realized he'd come at it with some erudition.

Lao Yi answered.

"I have heard when I was last in Syria that the land of the Liang is called Serinda by those of you in Daqin," and while Philip nodded Lao Yi made a motion to Hui-Shen and the latter retrieved a pouch he was carrying around his tunic from under its belt, he opened it and lay its contents on the table in between all of them. It was a small, square cloth with an image of a dragon embroidered in its center. Hui-Shen unfolded it before all of them.

Lao Yi continued, "You call it this, you call the Liang, Serinda, because *Sī*ᵚᵚ, silk, is called in your language, 'Sericum' ... am I right about this?"

Philip and Alexander both nodded, each transfixed by the sight of the expensive and skillfully sewn silk cloth now on display—Alexander all the more so understanding as he did that this article, unless it was meant as a diplomatic gift for the emperor, technically ran afoul of the regulations governing import of blattion—purple—especially purple *silk*.

The silk alone was worth its weight in gold, but purple silk of this quality and the art that went into the design of the dragon and the cloth's carefully manicured edges had to make the artifact before them precious indeed. So light and simple, and yet so intimidating.

Philip, nevertheless, kept his cool and replied to Lao Yi.

"I have ridden with caravans that carry cargo across the deserts of Persia between India and Rome, Daqin, and over the great mountains that separate India from the Liang,...there are no deserts so vast or mountains so high—to carry this treasure here, I understand its value."

Lao Yi nodded.

ᵚᵚ **Sī**, Chinese for "silk"; written 絲

219

Philip continued, "but, in Daqin we have a governor, a man who rules over the silk, and all trade in the silk, by the authority of the Emperor. Perhaps you know of him, *Peter Barsymes?*" he articulated Barsymes name with a note of bile that did not go unnoticed by Alexander. The name, interjected in the stream of Hànyǔ, was detected by Callinicus who, though he couldn't understand, was paying rapt attention.

Both Lao Yi and Hui-Shen nodded their heads, "no".

"Well," Philip continued, "treasure that may change a man's life...is still pennies in the balance of empire. A long caravan of woolen linens or spice can pay for its journey through its wares. The same caravan bearing silk will not only pay for itself, it will generate fortunes many times. Still, these fortunes are merely fortunes on the scale of men."

Everyone was listening, but no one seemed to understand. Philip tried to explain himself.

"If I were a Persian brigand I could raid a hundred silk caravans, a hundred times and I might destroy ten-thousand fortunes of ten-thousand men. But in doing so I could no more than slap to the hand of one like Peter Barsymes—and to dispose of me I would be a gnat he may swat by paying off my bounty to the next three Persian brigands who would be too happy to oblige him."

The room was tense. Even the guards and messengers who couldn't understand what was being spoken nevertheless understood that Philip was saying something that was making everyone uncomfortable.

"Who did you call him? *General Hou?*", Philip asked.

Lao Yi nodded "yes".

"If your General Hou is like our Peter Barsymes", Philip said, "he wields the power of empire. He pays pirates to pirate to kill pirates! You can't weaken him with money, with gold, through theft... even stealing *silk* won't weaken him."

Everyone was quiet at this for a moment or two when Lao Yi eventually spoke.

"Brother ..." he hesitated now, "*monk*", ... the last word he said almost as if with a question mark after it, "perhaps we misled you. Here..."

He gestured to Hui-Shen to retrieve the silk cloth and give it to him. Though seated and speaking, he was still weak and unable to move too readily.

Holding the silk Hui-Shen had handed to him, Lao Yi offered it directly to Philip.

"Take it".

"What?"

"Take it," Lao Yi repeated.

"Take it ... it is yours", Lao Yi said again when Philip failed to take it the first time.

"I, I can't ..."

"Take it for your monastery then", Lao Yi leaned forward and pushed it with what little strength he had so that if Philip didn't take it, the precious article might fall to the floor. At this Philip instinctively gripped the silk from the old monk's hands.

Lao Yi spoke again while Philip held the cloth reverently, almost tremoring as he rolled the shape of its dragon between his fingers.

"You are correct that mere brigandry would do nothing to weaken, let alone stop General Hou. The land of the Liang," Lao Yi smiled, "Great Rome, is adjacent to two empires, the western and eastern Wei. Hou is no ordinary general. He is a warlord who commands armies of all four nations."

"What?" Alexander retorted, "how is that possible?"

"The general," Lao Yi shook his head, "is like no *man*. People say he came to power on account of sorcery.

"Our Emperor Xiao Gang is the third son of the former Emperor Wu, with his consort Ding Lingguang. Emperor Wu took to heaven only a little more than a year ago and general Hou seized power in the aftermath, imprisoning Xiao Gang".

"Did he kill Emperor Wu's first son?" Alexander asked?

"No. The emperor's oldest son, Xiao Tong, died long ago, some think ... at the emperor's hand."

"What?!" both Alexander and Philip gasped in unison.

Lao Yi explained.

"When their mother, consort Lingguang was buried, she was placed on a plot of land that a monk later learned was blessed with good fortune for Emperor Wu, but bad fortune for his son, Xiao Tong.

"Xiao Tong tried to dispel the misfortune with magic and ordered wax ducks buried with his mother."

Alexander and Philip both looked on with disbelief. Magic and sorcery were common in Byzantium, especially about the Hippodrome and the games, but the use of wax ducks struck both of them as utterly incoherent.

Hui-Shen seemed to detect this and interjected, "Xiao Tong believed that the excellent artisanship of the ducks would arouse the favor of the gods, and that as the ducks dissolved into the earth with his mother, that the dissolving wax would also dissolve his ill fortune."

With this explanation seeming to satisfy them, Lao Yi went on, "Emperor Wu came to learn of the ducks and was furious and Xiao Tong lost favor with his father. Several years later, Xiao Tong, still very young, mysteriously died. Xiao Huan, the emperor's second son, should have been made crown prince but Emperor Wu's anger at the sorcery was so great that he passed over his second son too, all the more to distance everyone from the injury of the sorcery, so that is how Xiao Gang became crown prince."

"This sorcery seems to have been a curse to Emperor Wu", Alexander said, "but what does that have to do with General Hou?"

"*Everywhere* General Hou goes there is magic—there is sorcery—there is power!" Lao Yi explained.

"So, you are right," he said to Philip, "not gold, not silk, not money alone—none of these would suffice to injure the powerful General Hou."

Philip, still holding the precious silk cloth in his hands, regarded Lao Yi again and said, "OK, then ... you still haven't answered my question. What are you here for? What did your emperor send you here for that offers any hope of challenging General Hou?"

Lao Yi leaned forward, took a sip from his tea, then reclined back into his chair and took a deep breath, finally he answered.

"You know nothing of the world at the end of your maps—to you 'Great Rome', the Liang, is ... Ser-Inda, the land beyond India, the place from which the precious thread, *Sī*, Silk, *Sericum*, comes from."

"Yes", Philip answered.

"Silk! It is so important, so precious—you name an entire unknown empire for it! An empire you know is as great as your own!"

Phillip and Alexander both nodded.

"Emperor Xiao Gang's brother, the governor of Jing province, Prince Xiao Yi, sends us, pirate monks, to you, to Daqin, to the great Qin, Rome ... to offer to steal from General Hou, for the pleasure of your emperor, Justinian, the secret of how to *make* silk.

"With what we may steal—together—your Emperor Justinian can make silk in his own land."

Alexander's heart beat in his chest at the gravity of what he was hearing, he looked at Callinicus, trying to guess at how much, if anything, he could make of what had been said.

Lao Yi slapped his tea cup on the table in a thump, punctuating his words, "It is not *silk* that brings us to you men, no. It is the *secret* of silk—that is why we are here."

"And that ... is how we, though we were once monks, are now *outlaws*."

Concluding, Lao Yi met Alexander with both eyes, "Is it by accident that two monks in Daqin speak the language of the land of Xiao Gang? I don't think so. Hui-Shen cannot succeed alone. Join us, let us be outlaws, together."

Chapter 12
Balaneus Divina

The so-called Basilike cistern was built by
Constantine the Great.
The great statue which sits on a chariot there is
Solomon, which Justinian the Great erected;
Solomon is holding his cheek and looking at Hagia
Sophia, as he was outdone by its size and beauty,
which is greater than that of the temple he built in
Jerusalem.

The Patria
Book 2, 40

Whereupon the emperor made very diligent enquiries
and asked them many questions to see whether their
statements were true, and the monks explained to him
that certain worms are the manufacturers of silk, nature
being their teacher and compelling them to work
continually.

Procopius of Caesarea
History of the Wars
Book VIII, Chapter XVII

The Augustaion
Byzantium

About sunrise
Prote hora

Tuesday Morning, *Trite*
28 March 551 AD
Julian Calendar

Sunbeams shone cutting above the ceiling of the Patriarchal Palace which housed the Apokrisiarkion, the guest quarters for pilgrims and foreign dignitaries to Byzantium, gently illuminating the nearly empty city square, the Augustaion, in the light of earliest morning so that shadows of buildings, statues and fountains were both sharp and oblique. The party emerged from the Palace onto the open square from where they'd been meeting. By now included in the party were Stilicho and Callicinus as well as their two Scholae Palatinae escorts from the Great Palace; Thaddeus the archimandrite and Joseph Nios who accompanied him, as well as Alexander, Philip, Hui-Shen and Lao Yi. They descended down a flight of broad steps which took them to the base of the square. Before them stood an fountain at the southern edge of the Hagia Sophia, which contained the cathedral baptistery, whose waters originated from the city aqueduct and flowed down from cisterns on higher ground until they were collected in the enormous Basilica Cistern above, which released water downhill into underground qanats where it flowed through tightly fashioned pipes that created pressure so that it the water could jet back through fixtures in the baptistery's base, creating marvelous streams.

The spray in the early morning air struck Alexander's face and though the droplets were small, they were still cool from the evening. He cast a glance sideways to notice the droplets were raining on the guests from Serinda as well. Hui-Shen motioned to wipe his face dry—Lao Yi looked as if he were refreshed and invigorated. The sight gave Alexander a moment of alarm—they were about to make an imperial audience; Lao Yi had been unconscious and in bed for weeks. Monks were expected to bathe twice a month and, perhaps providentially, he had visited the baths yesterday after meeting with Cyra.

They assembled for a moment, Alexander presumed they were about to enter the Chalke Gate which and it would be important that they make approach in proper order. Callicinus gestured to his guards who took positions at two extremes of the party, then motioned about so as to arrange all the remaining in pairs so that they would form a troupe. Alexander with Philip, followed by Lao Yi and Hui-Shen, followed in the rear by a guard. Then Callicinus and Stilicho each took a place besides Thaddeus and Joseph Nios respectively and in twos at the front. Callicinus had organized them into a dawn procession having hardly spoken a word—it was a bit of a wonder, but he was the emperor's chamberlain—order and silence were his mainstay. All the while that he did so another group of monks was gathering outside Hagia Sophia between the fountain and vestibule.

Opposite where they stood was an embankment that held back the enormous Basilica Cistern and standing atop the cistern was a statue of King Solomon standing in a chariot adorned in flowing robes, starring just sideways of where they stood, his gaze fixed on the Hagia Sophia.

It was the hour for Orthros and Byzantium was a metropolis of churches and monasteries, so the timing couldn't be more fitting to create an impression for guests. Callicinus kept them stopped at the base of the footsteps of the Patriarchate for a moment, it only took the moment for Alexander to realize why. In the walls of Dalmatou the only xylons Alexander heard were those of the monastery itself, their proximity so close that they dominated all other sounds and the walls of Dalmatou acting to dull the sound of those from churches nearby.

Here below the steps on the Patriarchate, the sounds of the city, like its main thoroughfares, converged, but the effect of their convergence was secondary to the orderly way that the sounds of morning prayers arrived into the square from afar. First Alexander heard the chimes of xylons emerging out of the north—and slightly east where the north east tip of Byzantium reached out into the Bosphorus as it led into the Golden Horn. There were several monasteries set against the sea walls running up that way where they terminated on the location of a large church at the northerly tip. It was the xylon of this church which was first to sound heralding the arrival of morning and the first to be heard entering the square.

Next, in sequence, then in harmony, followed a xylon from the next monastery south east of the first church, and then the next, stepwise, each on an approach to the Augustaion, each sound arriving in the square as if a giant had come to stand attention for the rise of the day—each one as much a presence as it was a sound, until the order of the sounds crossed behind the Patriarchate where the ambient xylons joined them.

While the arrivals of the morning matins from the north took everyone's attention, Callicinus used his lead position to direct the Scholae to orient the party so it was in front of and facing the Hagia Sophia, flanked back from the fountains. Moments later a xylon could be heard behind them from a church inside the walls of the Great Palace, joining the metropolitan chorus of Orthros, it followed the others in its sequence of notes when the suddenly, right before them, a burst of symphony erupted from the Hagia Sophia's interior, almost threatening to drown out the rest before the first notes subsided. Its echo bounced about the corners of the square where the reverberation was so strong Alexander found it momentarily dizzying.

Image on following page

The Augustaion in Byzantium

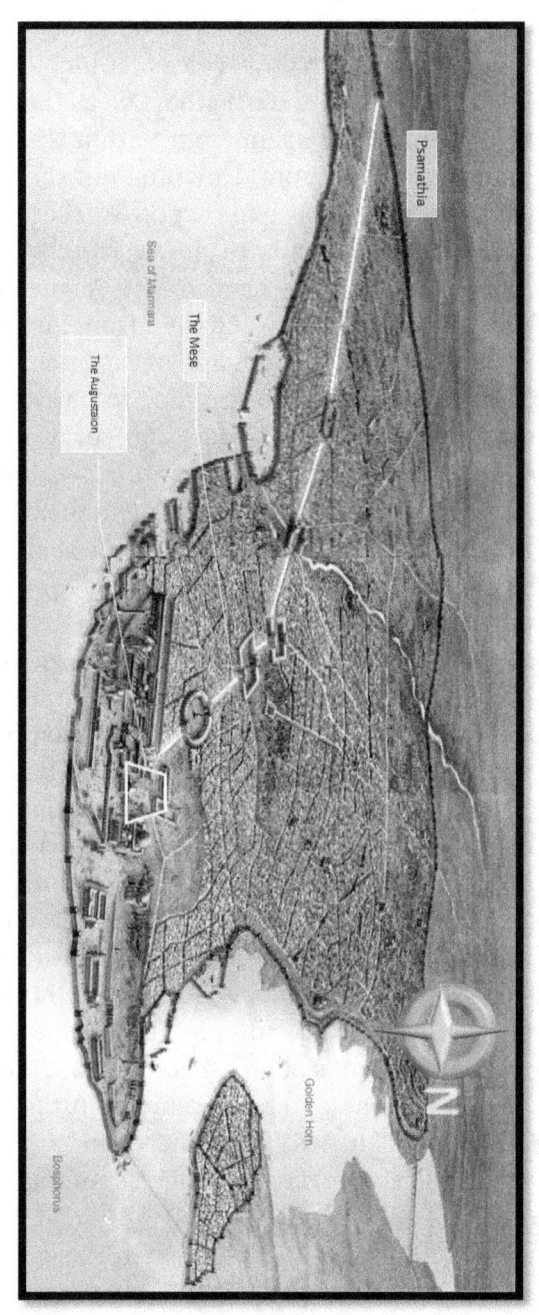

Psamathia

Sea of Marmara

The Mese

The Augustaion

Golden Horn

Bosphorus

N

The monks who'd gathered near the Hagia Sophia's baptistery moments earlier answered her song with notes of their own, singing with low voices, "Glory to the Father," drawing out the last note on "Father" so as their voices faced the note was taken up again from within the Hagia Sophia, which returned a loud hum drowning out the monks before softening again as they rose in response, "Glory to the Son".... While this went on sounds of newly rung xylons began to arrive at the Milon at the head of the Augustaion from the west, from center of the city and then from further away.

An impression was created of each nook and corner of the city emerging at the break of day to pay its respects and genuflect at city center. From the corners of his eyes Alexander realized that Hui-Shen and Lao Yi both seemed to be doing their part to try to participate in the rite. *Surely, they couldn't know the prayers?* he thought and being attentive to them he realized they were whispering prayers in Hànyǔ. Each had preceded with a series of movements that seemed to Alexander almost as if deliberate coughs, followed by the words "San Ching Jiao Tzu Wu Liang Tien Tzun", *honor to heaven, humanity and earth*, each inhaled then continued, "Yu Huang She Zui Tian Zun", *honor to the Jade Emperor*.

In a moment the ringing became subdued—this too, in order. First from the north, sound gave way to silence, oscillation to stillness; then the xylons of the Patriarchate were stilled, then those of the Palace, then the Hagia Sophia, finally the city itself quieted. The visiting sounds becoming increasingly distant until they faded to nothing and all that remained were the pink and blue hues of the early morning sun's rays on the clouds above. Hui-Shen and Lao Yi too took their cue and became quiet. For a moment the whole square and everyone in it was ensconced in a morning mist, penetrated by beams of dawn sunlight, standing still, together, in silence.

The stillness was broken when the troupe of monks who'd stood in front of the Hagia Sophia began their return.

Callicinus turned to face his party and was about to start with instructions when Alexander, remembering Lao Yi, gestured to interrupt. At his gesture Thaddeus, who had largely kept his distance until now, conceding the lead to Alexander in his office as interpreter, this time made a point of glowering at him, but Alexander was undeterred. They would see the emperor this morning, Alexander was sure that Thaddeus was more concerned with his subordinate monk acting out of turn than with their common presentation before the purple—it was the emperor and while he still hadn't had enough time to wrap his mind around the significance of it all, nothing about this strange mid-night interruption seemed minor. Alexander was willing to chance Thaddeus's disapproval. Callicinus recognized Alexander's motion so he indicated for closer quarters and Callicinus approached.

Callicinus had taken a greater measure of the mediums of communication with their guests that Alexander and Philip had already assumed. Alexander guessed that without anyone to translate for Hui-Shen communication had been laborious until now and Callicinus was eager to recognize Alexander and Philip as resources, not troublesome subordinates.

Alexander leaned in towards Callicinus for privacy. Callicinus was sensitive to the gesture and further closed the gap so that they spoke almost cheek-to-cheek, ear-to-ear, the hair on Alexander's neck told him of Thaddeus's discomfiture at his subordinate speaking directly with imperial office.

"We will see the emperor soon?", Alexander asked, the warm air of his voice turning to mist in the cool of morning.

"Of course," Callicinus replied.

"Hui-Shen has been in the Patriarch's care and is well groomed," Alexander went on.

"Yes," Callicinus answered.

"Lao Yi", Alexander said, drawing out the last syllable of the visiting monk's name and barely nodding his head in the negative, tilting his head now just aside so that with his left eye he could make contact with Callicinus's right.

Presently they both stood and faced each other, Callicinus connected both eyes with Alexander, understanding unfolded.

At once Callicinus motioned for the Scholae Palintae at the head of their procession and ordered him to Magnaura Hall where he was to make explanation under Callicinus's own authority that there would be a delay. When the guard was off Callicinus took a position at the head of the procession and led them all, but not to the Palace. Instead they passed diagonally through the center of the square to the Baths of Zeuxippos. Thaddeus flinched and seemed discomfited as they started their way there but seemed to relax as they made their way up the approach where they stopped at the Column of Justinian.

A pylon of bricks held aloft a statue of Justinian on horseback. Justinian seemed at once to stare down on them and face ahead to the horizon at their backs. One arm he held high, as if saluting those who approached, in the other arm he held an orb. His head was adorned with a Toupha[55] whose feathers seemed so exotic they could belong to a peacock. Callicinus brought them to a standstill for a moment beneath the column. To the left of where they stood was another statue which, like they, faced that of Emperor Justinian. The statue was comprised of three figures—a lead figure, hulky, heavily bearded, standing tall but head tilted low in a nod before Justinian, his hand enclosed around the hilt of a sword set into the ground before him. Next to him was another bearded fellow, genuflecting, the bulky tribal amulets Gothic kings were known to wear fell out from inside the tuft of his brow and hung low below his chin. Behind them both stood still another, this one keeping vigil over a cart pulled by a donkey

---

[55] **Toupha**, a helmet adorned with a tuft of fur or the feathers of exotic animals

which overflowed with treasures—tribute they would pay the emperor.

After a moment had elapsed for the sight to have its effect Callicinus made an announcement.

"Today—this morning—you will all make audience with Justinian, Emperor of the Romans—henceforth everything I say to all of you I require interpreted for our guests."

Callicinus paused and in the instant Alexander became aware that the pause was becoming uncomfortable Philip elbowed him to get his attention.

Callicinus had given an order. Alexander was the ranking translator, now Callicinius was waiting for Alexander to translate for Hui-Shen and Lao Yi.

Startled to attention Alexander shifted slightly. The senior monk he was expected to take the lead in translation though to this point his ability with Hànyǔ had served him better in listening than in speaking. Philip's more recent experience with the tongue endowed him with a greater capacity to manage its variant tones which Alexander was struggling to get a handle on. The moment already delayed and under pressure, Alexander tried to translate Callicinus's words.

He started, stammering a bit but began trying to translate for the guests,

> *Callinicus here, chamberlain to Emperor Justinian, requires that I interpret for you-and asks that you be attentive*

Hui-Shen and Lao Yi seemed to follow and casting an uncertain look at Alexander, motioned that he go on— encouraging him. *So far so good*, he thought, then continued, flushed now with confidence he stated the next words forcefully.

He attempted to render Callicinus's words to Hànyǔ,

Today—this morning—you will all make audience with Justinian, Emperor of the Romans, the Daqin

His moment of confidence was short-lived. Looks of confusion immediately came over both Lao Yi and Hui-Shen. Alexander tilted his head forward hoping they might offer a clue, was he on the right track? Could they make out his meaning? What had gone wrong?

Nothing, their looks told him nothing, nothing good anyway—Lao Yi almost looked like he was concealing a smile, Hui-Shen, ... *was the younger monk blushing?* Alexander was on task, and failing, and they hadn't even entered Magnaura Hall! He could feel hot sweat accumulating under his armpits and his heart started to beat in his chest. He turned a glance to Philip in desperation. Philip offered no support at all and didn't return his glance leaving Alexander to bear it alone— despite all forms and order, the older, burly monk stood, one arm crossing his chest defensively, the elbow of his other arm rested on top, his face wedged firmly in his palm.

Oh my God, what did I say?

"Perhaps," Alexander heard Thaddeus suggest, "we appoint you to *read* the ambassadors' letter, and allow Philip to, uh, do that talking. Would that please you Alexander?"

Philip on hearing this looked up and met Alexander's gaze. Alexander was almost pleading, and gestured Philip forward with a slight bow.

Philip immediately took control. Again, as Philip spoke, Alexander was gripped by how he could hear and understand the language and even read it, but was unable to use it to make intelligible sounds.

"I apologize for my fellow monk," Philip looked back at Alexander as he went on, "he meant no offense."

To this, Lao Yi made the most puzzling statement.

"Was it to us that he meant no offense," then pointing to the statue of the donkey that pulled the barbarian treasure cart, "or the donkey?"

"To you, he meant no offense to you", Philip replied with a barely concealed grin.

"Well", Lao Yi responded precociously, "we take no offense, but the donkey might require an apology."

At this Philip and Lao Yi enjoyed a laugh at Alexander's expense—their laugh was not shared by Thaddeus who looked on grimly or Callicinus who seemed intrigued but also in a bit of hurry for matters to move on. Alexander noticed Hui-Shen, though not laughing, seemed to be holding back a chuckle that made it impossible to share even an accusative stare. He flushed hot again with embarrassment.

What the hell did I say?

Wasting no more time Philip proceeded to translate Callicinus's words.

When Lao Yi and Hui-Shen both exhibited understanding Philip returned a gaze to Callicinus who recognized it and continued.

"Before you is the Column of Justinian, our emperor who you will see today.

"When you address him start with these words, 'Peace and mercy, happiness and glory from God be with you, high and mighty Emperor of the Romans. Wealth and health and longevity from the Lord, peacemaking and good Emperor. May justice and great peace rise in your reign, most peaceful and generous emperor.'

"You may address him as 'the great and high emperor who sits on the golden throne' or 'the most honored prince of the elder Rome'. You may ask 'How is the emperor, the spiritual son of the great and high emperor, and his children?' When addressing the empty throne next to the emperor you may inquire, 'How is the empress and mistress?' You may inquire polity of the archbishop who will be by the emperor's right hand, 'How is the most holy and ecumenical patriarch?' Also on the emperor's right hand will be his advisors, the consistorium, of them you may ask, 'How are the Masters and Proconsuls and Patricians?' You may lastly inquire of him 'How are the generals and the armies of the holy Emperor?', they will be on his left hand."

As Philip wrapped this up Hui-Shen looked concerned. Foreseeing his concern, he interjected before Callicinus started again, "I know it is a lot to remember. Don't worry, my brother monk Alexander and I, we'll help" and at this Hui-Shen relaxed.

"You will need to be well groomed to be presentable for the emperor, so we will make a visit to the baths", then Callicinus finished his preparatory speech by asking, "do you have any questions?"

Lao Yi answered Callicinus, startling everyone by answering in Greek, "are we to be like these men when we kowtow in the court of the Daqin emperor?", pointing to the statues of the barbarian kings offering tribute.

"You are ambassadors who mean friendship", Callicinus answered.

"True. But these are kings—they bear earthly wealth as surety of their friendship. We are monks. Will the emperor be pleased with the surety of spiritual men?" Lao Yi inquired.

Callinicus made a non-committal reply, "the emperor, I assure you, is most erudite."

"A good thing then," Lao Yi said, "because we cannot offer your emperor earthly riches—we bear only heavenly gifts."

Concluding the exchange, they made their way to the Baths.

* * * * * * * * *

Baths were open day and night, and many had their baths first thing in the morning before Orthros. It would have been out of form to be seen emerging from the baths just in time for Orthros when reverence was expected but now as the procession made its way in a small crowd that had been waiting inside passed by in the opposite direction. Lao Yi had been excited to meet the Daqin emperor. The journey to Daqin had been long and exhausting and while he endeavored to complete his mission in a full understanding of what was required, he'd harbored doubts until now about whether the mission could be fulfilled. The Daqin he knew, were real, but the emperor of the Daqin almost seemed like an abstract or mythical concept.

But after having been in bed for weeks he was relieved now that they were expected to bathe before making their audience with the emperor. Any other barbarian potentate would have the monk make audience in the raw. This was a good sign that the Daqin, as widely believed, were not barbarians. This was a very good thing, *a very good thing indeed*, he thought, sighing to himself.

Indeed, he and Hui-Shen bore no worldly tribute for this emperor. Rather, what they had to offer was far more valuable than earthly goods. Knowledge—*knowledge* that had kept and enriched his people for eons, all the way back to the time of Empress Leizu, Can Nainaiᵂᵂᵂ. In any other time, for any other purpose, and to anything less than the civilized ruler of civilized empire, a worthy sister empire to the Liang, the act he and Hui-Shen were about to commit would be a grave evil. They were monks now—but by the time they were finished with the Daqin emperor today they would be outlaws—renegades among their own people.

ᵂᵂᵂ **Empress Leizu, Can Nainai,** legendary empress—wife of the Yellow Emperor, credited by tradition with the discovery of silk and known in folklore as Can Nainai, "Silkworm Mother"

But now was not an ordinary time, he thought, *the legitimate emperor is under house arrest.*

And this is not an ordinary purpose, reminding himself of the words of prince Xiao Yi, *this is the only way to weaken General Hou—starve him of the funds his regime requires, to survive.*

The Northern Wei could not be adequate allies to defeat him—they were sworn enemies of the Liang, and Hou had subverted their regimes as well. The Persians were too far distant and busy with their own wars and in any case possessed none of the wet forested lands within their borders where the silkworm could thrive.

With no armies to defeat Hou—silk—was the only weapon that might work to stop him. Hou was a fearful power in his own right but if Hou cannot pay his soldiers, his soldiers would not fight. On the other hand—if Hou was not stopped, Lao Yi feared, the General cared only for himself and his own advancement—he cared not a whit for his own family, let alone the people he ruled. If he is not stopped all might degenerate into barbarity and silk would profit no one.

This is the right time, it is the right purpose, he assured himself.

The only remaining point was the question he was here to answer:

Could this Justinian be the right man?
Were the Daqin the right people?
Were they worthy?

When he had conspired to send Lao Yi and Hui-Shen to Daqin to offer the secret of the silk, Xiao Yi had considered that it would have been much easier to steal away the secret to the Huns who periodically still harassed the neighboring Wei on the norther frontier. In the time it took Lao Yi's embassy to reach the Daqin capital he would have crossed the empire of the Wei, been to land of the Huns, done away with the secret to some vile potentate, and returned to live his peace in the Wudang Mountains.

But this was unacceptable—the Huns were barbarians and *to give the secret of silk to anything less than a civilized emperor of a civilized people*, he thought, even under these dire circumstances, *would be an unforgivable sin against the Jade Emperor*ᵠᵠᵠ.

So this was the open question—was Justinian, emperor of the Daqin, civilized, as credited. What of his people? Even Hui-Shen was not privy that Lao Yi's mission was, in part—to judge the Daqin emperor and estimate his merits. *If he is found worthy of the secret of the silkworm?* Lao Yi shook his head at the gravity of the thought, murmuring to himself, "these are no earthly gifts we offer you today, ... Emperor Justinian, not earthly at all".

Finding Emperor Justinian and his people the Daqin worthy would be a great, and terrible thing—great, for being worthy, and for being the medium of the long-sought downfall of General Hou, but terrible too for it meant stealing away a secret which had kept Lao Yi's ancient people civilized and prosperous *for three thousand* years until now. After an epic stretch outlasting many great dynasties, Lao Yi would be found the man whose destiny was to go renegade and steal away this secret.

The plan and the orders were those of Prince Xiao Yi, but the burden would fall on Lao Yi.

Even still, a graver burden was possible.

What if Justinian was found not worthy?

ᵠᵠᵠ **Jade Emperor**, one of the representations of the first god in Taoist theology; known as Yuanshi Tianzun, he is one of the Three Pure Ones: the three primordial emanations of the Tao

What then?
How could two weak monks and a weak provincial governor ordinally addressed as a "prince" do to stop General Hou?

* * * * * * * * *

The building where the Daqin bathed was enormous. While inferior in architecture, it nevertheless rivaled the Daqin's extraordinary temple on the basis of size. The courtyard they crossed on the approach to the baths gave way to a broad colonnade held aloft by numerous columns. Callicinus, the emperor's chamberlain who led their group, marched them towards the right and Lao Yi could now see that there were two points of approach with Callinicus directing them to the rightward side. Men were exiting and passing their way on the right, to the left, in much fewer number, he saw women emerging from separate doorways.

Statues were everywhere. Lao Yi could only speculate at their significance. Some appeared to be of divine beings, others suggested the visages of sages and teachers. As they approached the entrance he could make out paintings that adorned the walls. On either side were winged men, *what the Daqin call angels?*

Flanking the angels were paintings of scenes whose significance he did not understand. To the left was a mostly naked man in a stream and another man washing him with others looking on. He had noticed a penchant among the Daqin to depict persons in varying lengths of nudity in their art—this did not seem to bode well for their status as a civilized people—but he reserved his judgment. On the right wall, to the right of an angel that seemed to guard the entrance, was an imposing figure of the head of a man—*the same one as in the image of the stream on the leftward wall?* This one had a halo—he checked the left—that one too had a halo—surely then, these images represented the same person. Was this a divinity of the Daqin? Lao Yi thought it impossible—*a disrobed divinity publicly bathing in a stream? But for the halo—surely the implication is that this man is divine?* If so, it still struck him as remarkable because the divinity depicted was considerably younger than the Three Pure Ones.

Before making entry they passed a large statue where a conical stone pillar gave way to the shape of the torso of a fierce looking, bearded man—the torso twisting out of the stone as if himself a whirlwind, holding a lightning spear in his right hand he hovered over two horses who challenged him. A divinity? One thing that struck Lao Yi was that the statue of the divinity seemed an older version of the haloed image of the man on the wall. Lao Yi resolved to inquire later about this with his Daqin interpreters.

The procession had come to a halt and Callicinus was negotiating with a clerk to make entry. Pointing to various among them and making explanation—Callicinus was speaking in Greek, explaining that four of their number were monks—*odd*, Lao Yi thought, *did he not consider us monks?* But as their conversation continued his reasons became clear— Callicinus explained to the clerk that he and Hui-Shen were ambassadors—ambassadors who would see the emperor today and would require special handling. The clerk asked for 10 obols which Callicinus produced.

* * * * * * * * * *

Alexander and Lao Yi emerged with their attendants from the frigidarium, the last step in the bathing process which entailed a cold-water bath, into a marble room with dry towels and cushions fashioned to create couches. On either side of a half circle of nearby couches sat two baskets, one each to hold Alexander and Lao Yi's clothing. They both stood for a moment to dry themselves and returning to the baskets where they began to dress. As they did so their attendants departed briefly but Lao Yi's returned quickly. His attendant, a eunuch, brought with him a wheeled cart upon which sat a tray where there were neatly arrayed a mirror, some combs, a brush, a few razors, two or three containers with balm, salve and oil, another with powder, a small tray holding soap, and an African red slip[+++] amphora which held water. The eunuch's cart had a tray on a second level below the top which held a plynos, a basin for collecting water and refuse, that protruded slightly from one side.

He drew the cart up next to Lao Yi so that the plynos faced him and began attending to Lao Yi even as he dressed. Lao Yi momentarily stopped dressing while the eunuch dabbed his face and beard with a towel and the eunuch shook his head, "You needn't stop—Calcinicus said we must make haste, you have an audience with the emperor"—he spoke in Greek and Lao Yi understood him and proceeded to dress.

Satisfied that Lao Yi's face was adequately dry he went on to apply some powder with a shaving brush—Lao Yi seemed to recognize the purpose of the shaving brush and stopped him, "there will be no need for that".

"What?" the eunuch protested.

"Hui-Shen is not far behind—he may wish for the razor not I."

The eunuch was nonplussed, "but you will have an audience with the emperor!"

Alexander decided to try to help and, recalling his faltering command of Hànyǔ and keeping in mind the eunuch, addressed Lao Yi in Greek, "the city was founded as capital over two-hundred years ago by emperor Constantine. The Greek tradition before Constantine was for men to wear beards, but Constantine wanted to draw a contrast of his 'New Rome' from the old—the old was in Italy, the new was at the cross-roads to Asia; the old was pagan or belonged to the

---

[+++] **African red slipware**, a common fine pottery form in the 1st through 7th centuries that was manufactured for export in modern Tunisia

Stoics and Epicureans—philosophs—the new would belong to the Christians. Christians set themselves apart from the old ways in one respect by shaving, so emperor Constantine shaved, and most leaders and elders have ever since. Our attendant is merely concerned with the impression you will make on emperor Justinian when we see him today."

It was a bit more explanation that may have been required but Alexander felt satisfied and was looking to make himself helpful, perhaps to redeem himself from his earlier failure at interpretation. Lao Yi listened to this and answered, glancing at Alexander but addressing himself to the eunuch, "I see," he said nodding, which the eunuch took to mean acceptance and immediately motioned towards him with the brush, but Lao Yi stopped him, lifting his hand and finger, wagging it just a bit.

"Laozi", he said, enunciating the difference in the "Zi" from the "Yi", which Alexander might otherwise have taken to be self-referential, "had both an earthly and a divine aspect. Laozi existed at the beginning of the cosmos and appears many times throughout—this is possible because the cosmos *is* his body and he transforms it—the cosmos into his body, his body into the cosmos.

"His left eye is the sun", Lao Yi said pointing to his left eye, "his right, the moon. His head is Mount Kunlun. His bones are the dragon, his flesh the creatures that walk on four legs. His beard," Lao Yi said, now stroking his beard, "are the planets and constellations."

Alexander did not know who this Laozi was, to whom Lao Yi referred, but presumed from Lao Yi's explanation he must be a figure of religious reverence—a foreign one such as the Persians' Zoroaster. He didn't know much of eastern saints beyond Persia but decided to take a chance.

"Emperor Justinian is known to be a pious man Lao Yi, and keeps several spiritual scholars close by, I think he may even know of the Indian saint, Βούττα***, but I do not think he will have heard of Laozi. On first appearance he may not recognize that you mean piety by your beard, it might be best to remain cautious."

Lao Yi's ears perked up upon hearing Alexander acknowledge Βούττα. This was unexpected but surely auspicious for the prospects of finding the Romans civilized. He didn't remain on the point though but questioned Alexander saying, "there is a man who accompanies us—he has not said much since arriving with you at my bed—he wears a cap covered with a black veil, who is this man?"

For a moment the question astounded Alexander, but it brought into focus how rushed and off-timed everything about this experience had been. Lao Yi was referring to the Archimandrite, Thaddeus, Alexander's superior who in any ordinary circumstances would have already have been formally introduced, probably by Alexander, to Lao Yi—especially in his appointed role as interpreter. Somehow in the dust up created by Lao Yi's abrupt recovery and his ability to traverse between Greek and Hànyǔ, the formality of an introduction had been skipped. Alexander realized with some dread that this fact was almost surely not lost on Thaddeus and was probably a cause for offense.

"That's the archimandrite, Thaddeus", Alexander said, "and I'm sorry, please forgive me that you were not earlier introduced. The cap, it's called a klobuk, it's worn by bishops and hieromonks".

"Arch-ee-man", Lao Yi enunciated tentatively.

*** **Βούττα**, Buddha, in Greek: Βούττα, was known to Greco-Roman society and minimally found mention by Augustine and the second and third century Clement of Alexandria, the latter in his *Stromata*, which Clement designed as a medium of Christian secret teachings via largely symbolic explanation

"Archimandrite", Alexander finished for him. "It means he is the abbot both of my monastery, Dalmatou, and of all the monasteries in the city."

"Ahhhh," Lao Yi said, "so you mean to tell me, Thaddeus—he is an important man? Your superior?"

"Well," Alexander flushed, "of course, yes."

"And so you are embarrassed because you failed to observe the formalities and introduce he and I, Thaddeus and me?"

Lao Yi's tone threw Alexander off guard. *Was this foreign monk, his guest, talking down to me?*, Alexander wondered, but he went on to reply, "well, indeed, and as I said—I am sorry, I apologize, I will introduce you all when we are all gathered again."

On this, Lao Yi pressed, "I notice that you, like Hui-Shen, do not have a beard, but Thaddeus bears one".

All at once the scale of Alexander's embarrassment had racked up in triplicate—the poor translation, the failure to make proper introductions, and now, he realized ... *rank*. Lao Yi was of higher, religious rank, than himself—and here he was advising Lao Yi to shave!

Seated and tying his sandals as they talked, Alexander paused for a moment and took his face into his left hand, pinching the wedge between his nose and his forehead.

"Your clumsy effort to demote me before your emperor is noted young monk", Lao Yi said in a way that projected both the realized authority of one just now discovering his relative rank, and a friendly, forgiving magnanimity along with a touch of humor.

Alexander looked up from his palm, then stood, facing the eunuch, ordering, "this man is of high religious rank in the land he comes from. He is an," Alexander paused, uncertain he had it right, but realizing it didn't matter went on, "he is an archimandrite. Prepare him for the emperor as you would Thaddeus."

The eunuch nodded at this, understanding, and he put down the shaving brush he'd been holding and pushed aside the razors.

* * * * * * * * *

As they exited the Zeuxippos and stood in the arcade where they'd first entered, Alexander spoke to Lao Yi.

"Lao Yi, I have a question".

Lao Yi regarded him and nodded, a subtle difference in body language was evident as it was clear Lao Yi was better apprised now of the rank-order of his surroundings.

"Earlier, at the column", Alexander said, gesturing in the direction of the Column of Justinian and the statues of the barbarian kings paying tribute, "when I spoke, I interpreted badly".

Lao Yi couldn't conceal a gentle chuckle on the last point, Alexander continued, "I learned Hànyǔ from my nursemaid, when I was a child, and my parents lived in Persia. She taught me to read using books and I only had her to speak with. I've never spoken Hànyǔ with anyone else, then or since."

"Ahh", Lao Yi said at this, understanding.

"I know Hànyǔ makes elaborate use of tones, we do not do this so much in Greek, but my command of tones is ..."

"Weak", Lao Yi finished his sentence.

"Yes".

"An understandable deficiency. We are grateful just the same—we did not expect to find anyone in Daqin with knowledge of Hànyǔ, let alone two, even if one of you can only read", Lao Yi said.

"I don't know how much more help I can be", Alexander said, "I am sure when you speak with the emperor you will either wish to use Greek yourself or rely on Philip whose spoken word is stronger than mine".

"Perhaps", Lao Yi said, "but our work is only started—it will not be long if you can read Hànyǔ that soon we will have you speaking it. In any case, what was your question?"

"Oh," Alexander said, having drifted off track, "yes, well ... what did I say? Back there at the statue, what did I say that was so funny?"

Lao Yi considered him neutrally like he was waiting for Alexander to finish his thought.

Alexander went on, "Obviously I said something—you, Hui-Shen and Philip all recognized it and laughed".

"Yes", Lao Yi said, "I believe you were trying to relate that later on this morning we would be making an audience with the emperor," Alexander nodded and Lao Yi continued, "but that is not what you said."

"Huh", Alexander breathed, "well, no. What did I say?"

"You said," Lao Yi cleared his breath then continued, "It's not so much what you said exactly, although it was a bit of that. It was," he paused, "the way you said it. You stated with some formality as if with great authority, "This morning", Lao Yi straightened his back and put on a show of stentorian pronunciation making long pauses between words, "the donkey, will, be, inebriated."

Alexander bobbed his head back a couple inches as if instinctively, opening his mouth to say something but unable to form words quickly enough, so Lao Yi spoke to fill in the space, as if he were a confused student, "there were no donkeys with us", he shrugged his shoulders, "so we assumed you must have meant the statue of the donkey. And I thought to myself that I had not thought it possible that a donkey could be inebriated—but then again, strange things are known to be found on long travels. Perhaps among the Daqin your herd animals are hard drinkers?"

Alexander smiled a bit, understanding that Lao Yi was making fun of him and light of the matter, he was grateful for the latter.

"Don't worry young monk", Lao Yi said, "in a short time, if your emperor proves worthy, Hui-Shen will have your tones all cleaned up."

The smile fell off Alexander's face on hearing this. "Proves worthy?" Did he hear that right? Was Lao-Yi teaching him tones? What was he talking about? Before he could probe for answers the others emerged from the Zeuxippos into the arcade and joined them. Presently Calcinicus began ordering them back into position to make entry to the Chalke Gate.

Chapter 13
The Consistorium

...the imperial treasurer is charged with the superintendence of this trade.

When Peter Barsyames held the office, they soon allowed him all manner of licence in carrying out his nefarious practices. He demanded that all the rest should carefully observe the law, and compelled those who were engaged in the silk factories to work for himself alone. Without taking any trouble to conceal it, he sold an ounce of any ordinary coloured silk in the public market-place for six pieces of gold, but if it was of the royal dye, called Holovere, he asked more than four-and-twenty for it. In this manner he procured vast sums of money for the Emperor, and even larger sums, which he kept privately for himself...

It is also said that Theodora, against her will, had been forced by the enchantments of Barsyames to become his friend; for this man had devoted great attention to sorcerers and supernatural beings...

Procopius of Caesarea
The Secret History

The Great Palace
Byzantium

Trite Hora, "Third Hour"
Tuesday, *Trite*

28 March 551 AD
Julian Calendar

While they assembled in the arcade of the Zeuxippos, Callicinus went about once again with quiet directions to restore them to an orderly procession. Before they made their way, he reviewed them as if they were a military troop, making minor adjustments to their robes and garments and assuring that each was presentable.

Satisfied, he took his place alongside Thaddeus and gave a sharp whistle that signaled to both guards to march and the procession made its way. The Augustaion served as a marketplace during the day and after the morning choir of xylons it was already bustling with more activity in the short time since they passed the Column. Merchants were making their way into the square, pushing or pulling carts and assembling structures from which they would soon sell their wares.

It was a short distance from the arcade to the Chalke Gate and the enormity of the structure made its presence felt nearly as soon as the party set on the move. The sun was rising from behind the structure and its bright beams obscured the detail while at the same time emphasizing its size. Hui-Shen had resided near the square for some time and proceeded forward, perhaps with some apprehension, but if so his face had a composure of blank affect. Lao Yi, Alexander noticed, marched ahead cross-ways to Alexander, and seemed to be trying harder to take in the sight of the Gate, struggling to do so against the brilliance the rising sun. Though he struggled, the old monk did not gawk like other newcomers to the capital. His affect was one of a person who was seeing—*about what he expected to see*, a point that would not seem to be much of a matter except for the fact that there could not be many places, anywhere, like the Chalke Gate. Most visitors for the first time to the Augustaion had no prior referents that would prepare them for it. The structure was intended to impress and intimidate dignitaries from far off, uncivilized lands.

Alexander noticed that Lao Yi was unperturbed.

Alexander's thoughts drifted to the question of where this old monk came from. What was a gentle, natural drift of thought in one moment, in the next moment gripped him.

All his life—and it was with some embarrassment that the thought struck him—he had scarcely given any imagination to what kind of place Serinda was. He had childhood memories of Persia and sketchier memories still of distant India where some Nestorians had returned after driving deeper east than his parents. Now he doubted his memories of India as he realized for the first time he had imagined it to be not so different a place from Persia.

What of Serinda? he wondered. Serinda was too far off, too mysterious, too unknown. Was it a civilized, if alien land, such as he largely remembered Persia? Or was it primitive and wild, like the lands north of here which in ancient days belonged to the Scythians but which now from time to time coughed up new manners of Huns and Goths?

He had no idea. Certainly, these two monks, while possessed of features reminiscent of his old tutor Liang Ji, were naturally more masculine. Alexander reflected for the first time that Lao Yi and Hui-Shen were nothing at all like the Persians he had known. Had he drawn upon his impressions of Persians to foresee the appearance of these two, then he had been altogether mistaken at the conjecture. Knowing so little of Serinda's *people*, he tallied up what few points of information he knew of Serinda, the land.

There was not much to tally.

It lay somewhere beyond India—north, or east, or northeast? No one really knew. Silk and, from time to time, other products—the occasional chest or statuette—all were known to originate from Serinda but could only find their way to Byzantium through long networks of intermediaries. What did Serinda accept in trade for its merchandise? Roman glass, he thought in answer to his own question. Serindians—*was that what they called themselves?*—traded silk, ivory statues, and fine furniture for glass.

And that was it. Serinda lies beyond India, produces silk, and has a taste for glass.

How odd to know more of the language of a place— better than anyone in the empire save the fluke coincidence of Philip who stood beside him—and yet to know nearly nothing whatsoever about the place itself, or its people.

Was Serinda great? In the way Rome was great? Was it a civilized land?

Alexander felt a cold rush of adrenalin in his gut. Odds were that in a short while the Emperor himself would be wondering at these same questions. As the Emperor was sure to find Alexander the highest-ranking kinsman with any working knowledge of the language of this distance place, he would expect Alexander to provide insights and answers.

He possessed neither.

The appearance of Lao Yi and Hui-Shen left him impressed with them as men of cultivation. Now that he thought of it, when was the last time Scythia had coughed up a monk? Monks, by and large, were known for *leaving* civilization to bring the fruits of enlightenment to barbarians. *Was Serinda sending its monks to civilize a more primitive Rome?* Lao Yi's account of General Hou seemed to rule this out, but the reversed orientation of this exchange–with Rome receiving monks from afar rather than sending them—was truly rare. More often, far off lands sent diplomats and aristocrats, lending status to Byzantium. Byzantium reciprocated by sending civilization and education—typically in the person of monks.

Two magnificent, marble, square piers were enclosed by columns that surrounded a pendentive containing an arch that lay superior to the gatehouse's doors. They passed through the open gates unhindered. Surely there were guards present on both sides and in positions both obvious and concealed, but no one ordered the procession to stop. Ahead and behind were found merchants and other individuals who were notable most of all for their lack of pageantry—many of whom wore simple white and grey chitons. Not everyone within the Chalke Gate or the Great Palace beyond was here to hold audience with the emperor.

As they walked into the gatehouse its two vaulted ceilings imposed their presence on those below with elaborate mosaic decorations that came into view, so they could see its interior was divided into two chambers. The images on their right, to the south, visually depicted the saga of general Belisarius leading Justinian's armies in Africa against the Vandals. The images on their left, to the north, shown an equally elaborate depiction of Belisarius and Narses sailing to Italy where they laid waste to the Goths. Over both frescos hovered the haloed image of Justinian. The commission of Narses, Alexander noticed, differed slightly as it was both Justinian and Theodora commanding him to take flight to Italy.

In the first chamber, the frescos depicted generals circled around a table in a tent, planning strategies, this image was followed by an assembly of armies taking orders at hilltops or digging ditches to thwart their opponents. Next, were seen skirmishes and a pitched battle. The images coalesced at their apogee where they came together in the interior pendentive, which found both Goths in Italy and Vandals in Africa vanquished.

Alexander grimaced on seeing this. True, the Vandals were surely done for, but the Goths were not yet crushed in

Italy, and even so battles raged against the Persians, especially in the wasteland of Lazica. Perhaps in obedience to the demands of artistic symmetry the emperor's artists displayed an excessive haste and confidence to foresee final victory in Italy, but as yet they had no stomach to set the story of Lazica to stone.

As they followed, Alexander noted that Lao Yi seemed to be attentively absorbing all the imagery.

Inside the gate the party stood for a moment while Callicinus performed some order of business with a guard detachment manning the inner side of the Chalke Gate. He motioned them to the left where they approached the Magnaura, the building that housed the Imperial Senate and the emperor's reception hall.

It was a short walk on a tree-lined path from where they entered to the outside walls surrounding the colonnade that led to the Magnaura. The high dome of the Senate was visible above its walls. When they passed under the archway and into the square colonnade, the basilica that housed the Senate came into full view. Until now, Alexander expected that most of what they had seen must have been familiar to Hui-Shen, but this would be the first time he might have set eyes directly on the Senate; Alexander could see that his head nodded upwards.

The building and its walls were constructed from red slip bricks from Africa and the colonnade's awnings were held up by marble columns that stood over tiled floors that encircled the courtyard. Mese Oak trees, symbols of power since ancient times, lined both sides of the path that lead to the steps up to the Senate basilica creating an effect of giant, bright green fans waving over either side, before the white marble of the Senate stairway rising to the building.

All of this impressed and was designed to impress the visitors who would arrive in the city for audiences with the Emperor and other authorities, but Alexander knew Hui-Shen and Lao Yi, who had come so far, could not be strangers to colonnades and courtyards.

Instead, what drew their attention was a feature of the Senate basilica itself: grand, towering *glass* windows. The foremost archway facing them had nine of its own—three atop three atop three—that stood over three vaulted entrance doors at the top of the stairway. Two more archways stood at either side of the foremost, they too with the same feature of nine windows. All about the basilica dome were more windows that would allow in sunlight at all hours of the day from wherever the sun hung in the sky. All told, the basilica was seven stories high and each window occupied the space of an entire story—these were windows that were taller than men! Glass windows were rare outside of Byzantium, windows of any size were rare anywhere, and windows that would not crush under the weight of such a great building must have been exotic, even alien, in the eyes of Hui-Shen and Lao Yi.

Making their final approach to the stairway Alexander noted when Hui-Shen's attention broke from the windows on the façade of the basilica. He leaned towards Lao Yi and asked a question; Alexander deciphered his whispers and lips, Hui-Shen was asking, "Where are the guards?"

This must have seemed strange to the visitors. Normally, in the heart of power, one would expect guards everywhere, but the stairway was bare, the path they walked, they walked un-escorted. Momentarily, both monks looked on either side. Beyond the trees that lined the pathway were grassy yards, thickly and randomly interspersed with still more trees. The odd horse was found calmly occupying space near this or that tree. At a distance some individuals could be seen walking about the colonnades but even if these were guards, and by the casual way they attended themselves that did not seem possible, the question could not be settled from at distance they were seen.

They made their way up the stairway and under the central pair of vaulted doors which were both wide open. Passing through they entered a narthex where, aside the door, a lone guard, a Scholarae, stood to their left—he seemed more a receptionist than a marshal. Recognizing Callicinus leading their party the guard said and did nothing to slow their approach. With direct sunlight entering from both the open doors and the combined twenty-seven windows of the three archways, the narthex was well lit. The floors were of polished marble and laid out in a diagonal checkerboard fashion. Six pairs of square columns divided the hall and lifted to heights high above the party; the hall itself stretched in either direction, terminating on either side with enclosed doorways. The columns and ceilings were decorated in elaborate detail with frescos of saints and Biblical figures. A central doorway stood immediately before them, and following Callicinus they passed under it.

The next room was most unusual. Circular in shape, it presented directly before them a marble staircase which terminated at a platform part-way up the opposing side. The party continued to follow Callicinus who led them up the first and central staircase, then the staircase to their left, which they climbed as it twisted around the circular chamber and where it terminated at the second level. He continued around so that they effected an encirclement of the room before arriving at another door. While they gathered, an odd thought crossed Alexander's mind. Here he was in the nerve-center of imperial power and this was the first door of the Senate building—in fact all the way since the Chalke Gate—that was closed.

As they stood together in front of it in silence, Alexander wondered what would happen next. No attendant was present for the closed door. Callicinus himself did not move to open it, nor even so much as knock. Was there a chime or mechanism to notify those on the other side that there was a party waiting? Alexander had no means of knowing but without a moment's passing he did not need to wonder anymore because there was a loud "clunk," and as if loosened from a hinge, the door fell open. Surely, they were being watched, but it was impossible to decipher from where.

Callicinus proceeded; the party followed behind, but before they had passed through to the next room, the chamber itself reached out through the doorway and greeted them. Immediately upon the door's opening, music entered the space where they stood and filled the air where a moment earlier there had only been silence. Beautiful notes of pipes, flute, and lyre tapped his ears. At first sporadically, then as they walked in through the arched doorway, the notes took on more clarity and rhythm.

This was the antechamber and the largest room by volume they had encountered. Square, it contained several stories and seemed to be designed to impress its occupants with their comparative lowliness. Its vaulted ceiling was held aloft on all sides by columns and arches. The marble floor was decorated with repeating octagonal patterns and on both sides but in no particular order that Alexander could discern. They were polished so smoothly they cast a reflection. Tall statues of saints, heroes, and officials gazed down on the occupants. Alexander was not certain whose visages were contained on most of the statues except for the final two at the terminal side of the chamber that stood on either side of immense double doors. On the left was Emperor Constantine, on the right stood a statue on whose base was labeled "a man of highest distinction" and below that, "Great Martyr." Though there was no other label, Alexander knew this to be Saint George.

It appeared that despite the early hour theirs was not the only party seeking audience with the Emperor that day. Ahead of them stood one group, military in nature and still another contingent he could not recognize but seemed foreign. He was seeking an identifying marker about the strange looking foreigners when he suddenly became aware that it was not clear how long they might spend waiting in this place, which for all of its accoutrements, lacked seating.

Courtiers moved about, some tending to the guests-in-waiting and others busy with unspecified matters of administration. A magister had finished with the first party—the strange foreign one—and was beginning to take attendance of the second, military party. Alexander noticed the magister as he made eye contact with Callicinus; the two nodded at one another in recognition.

Hope!

From the smooth, almost womanly features of the magister, Alexander presumed he must be a *cubicularii*, a eunuch chamberlain in the Emperor's service, which would mean he answered to Callicinus, the *praepositus sacri cubicularii*, the Grand Chamberlain. Surely, Callicinus would not let his guests stand about for some interminable period while they waited for their audience.

An instant later, the magister continued about his work and addressed the military party. Somewhat to Alexander's surprise the military party seemed represented for its capital audience by a fellow who seemed to be a youth. A calloused, tanned, and ruddy fellow to be sure, but Alexander was certain on taking an account of his youth that the military representative could not be a day older than fifteen.

Even so the lad held court with the magister confidently and, to Alexander's surprise, he noticed the fellow wore an eparch's chlamys on his paludamentum—designating him as a notary.

A military contingent whose representative to the emperor was a fifteen-year old youth, and a notary. Odd, he thought. *The plague and two wars have left grown men scarce.*

The magister and the young notary finished their dialog and Alexander was expecting the magister to continue his way to their party but was startled to see him turn his back and return to the front of the antechamber where he disappeared behind a screen. Disappointment almost swept over him at the seeming delay when the magister appeared again from behind the screen a moment later, this time on a podium high above and built into the wall where he took a rod and pounded it twice sharply on a drum in the floor.

The music that had filled the room silenced immediately and everyone turned their attention to the magister.

When all matters were brought to silence the magister finally spoke. Alexander was not sure how but by some means the acoustics of the room increased the volume of his voice so that the high-pitched, yet oddly masculine voice distributed itself clearly, reverberating to a slight echo.

"On behalf of the most honored prince of the elder Rome..." the magister paused between each sentence, keeping them short, allowing the echo to extinguish itself. "With the leading men and the whole people subject to them, I welcome you all to his audience."

He went on, "I am Stephen. Address me as Silentarius."

Stephen allowed a minute to pass before speaking again.

Stephen's next words were unexpected despite their predictable formality, "Today the Emperor is indisposed."

Alexander sense motion and disturbance in the audience before Stephen continued, speaking over it,

"He is represented in spirit by the *comes sacrarum largitionum* and the Emperor's own spiritual brother, Peter Barsymes."

At these words, the commotion rose to an audible murmur and risible shuffling. Despite himself, Alexander looked to both sides to assess how the surprise fell on the other two parties. Before he could fully take it in, his attention fixed on Philip who had been next to him, quietly minding himself the entire time. Alexander could not be sure why, or exactly when, but Philip had lost all color. He cheeks sulked and his eyes hung and even his pupils seemed to have turned grey. Was he ill?

Twice, a clang burst about the room when Stephen beat his staff against the drum, following it with a loud, eerie treble voice, "The Silentarius demands silence!"

When silence returned, he continued, "The Emperor's reception chamber requires absolute silence of its visitors. Do not speak until spoken to."

Again, Stephen extended the pause between sentences, using the silence to punctuate the importance of his words.

"When spoken to, reply in a manner as succinct as possible."

"The Emperor's spiritual brother represents the Emperor in person," Stephen said, "and you will address him in kind, 'How is the Emperor, crowned by God?'"

Stephen conveyed a few more instructions before descending again and stood while the three parties organized into a single file. The three parties passed through another room, the vestibule, enclosed on two sides by screens, the room itself too small to be a chamber but too large to be a simple hallway. At last they entered the reception hall.

The reception hall was built in the shape of a hexagon and was set below the dome of the building. The windows they had seen when approaching from the outside flooded the interior with sunlight. A chandelier was suspended by six chains set to each corner of the hexagon—cast in glass it split the sun's rays so that transient patterns of red, yellow, green, blue and purple appeared, dazzled then moved and disappeared unpredictably about the walls and floor.

A panel enclosed the center of the room and connected with the east-most wall on both sides, forming a U-shape. A throne was set on a dais that jutted out of the wall itself— being elevated above the floor and facing back towards the room at a height such that all accessible vantagepoints in the chamber were set below it. The dais extended below the

Magnaura's apse where frescos in the stone of the dome combined with glass to create a brilliant image of the Theotokos with Child looming above all the proceedings, illuminating them with the sun's rays. It had the particular effect of projecting from above where the Emperor stood on the dais.

Separating the apse and the dais was a large water clock built into the wall. Situated where it was, it left the impression that time itself flowed from the divine. A pit housing a low podium above a platform was carved out of the space below and in front of the dais so that the dais and the pit were enclosed together by the panel separating them from a terrace of five concentrically arranged, ascending tiers of seats. An effect was created so that everyone sitting, facing the Emperor in his dais in silent solidarity, sat nearly at his level, but those who sought to speak directly to the Emperor descended to the pit below, humbling themselves before the Emperor and everyone present.

As they made entry, Alexander observed that Stephen orchestrated the work of several ushers. The party of foreign dignitaries was set at the lowest row, the military party next, and Alexander's party third. At one time, this hall was house to the Roman Senate, and officially it still was, but Justinian had it repurposed as a reception hall for foreign dignitaries to punish the Senate for its involvement in the Nika riots. There was space enough to seat all the Senators of empire, but when everyone had found their place this morning most seats remained unoccupied.

Stephen's ushers had arranged the parties to occupy a central space together most directly opposite the Emperor's dais, leaving the seating on either side empty. Alexander's seat was in the first place on the opposite the corner-edge of the U-shape as it turned toward the terminal wall that held the dais so that he sat at about a 45-degree angle to Philip. It was a privileged position for observing others without being seen doing so as its corner provided him the ability to observe the rest of his party, the two parties in the tiers beneath them, the Emperor in his dais, and his audience in the pit without them being equally able to return his gaze with ease. Philip, still ashen-faced, remained at his left and gently bobbed forward and back nervously; by the look of his eyes he did not seem present but seemed to occupy a world of his own.

Alexander noticed with some curiosity that Stephen's ushers had moved the foreign monks, who had entered behind him, to the opposite end of his row rather than seat them in order of entry, leaving the seat to his right empty. By placing them on the opposite side, he figured, they were keeping the audience mostly confined to the central aisle.

There was one person at his right though. In the area of the lowest tier immediately against the same wall as the dais and occupying a larger area where ordinary seating had been cleared so that what remained was a corner platform, there stood a man dressed in an imperial paludamentum. Since he was standing, Alexander could see that he wore scarlet boots—denoting highest rank. Next to him was a heavy, wooden podium set upon with several large parchment sheets. It was Procopius, the Emperor's secretary. He seemed to shift nervously and fidgeted about with a quill, shifting his attention here and there.

Procopius and his wooden stand were at the far end of the platform. Nearer to Alexander and the continuation of regular seating was a broad oak table where there sat, on one side only, five magnificent chairs each one fit for a king, all on the same side of the table facing the dais. This area was reserved for the Emperor's Consistorium. No one sat there now.

* * * * * * * * *

Everyone took their seats. At no particular interval, there was a sudden, gushing rush of wind— Alexander had no idea what its source might be. The waiting silence was broken by a burst of sound from wide, base pipes followed by a flourish of music by a small line of unseen flutes that accompanied the entrance of a man onto the dais from an opening at the right side of the throne.

But it was not Emperor Justinian; it was Peter Barsymes, Count of the Sacred Largesses.

At his entrance, Alexander was almost startled by Philip who seemed to involuntarily grasp at his gut. Unable to avert looking, Alexander saw that Philip was clutching at his stomach, pressing a fist up towards his heart, and struggling to control his breathing.

"Are you alright man?" he asked.

Philip turned his head away from Alexander in answer. Lifting his free, left hand to wave Alexander down, he uttered something. Alexander thought he might have said, "Peace, brother." Whatever he had said it was evident he wished to be left alone.

Their conversation was short because everyone stood in observance of Barsymes's entry. Barsymes had long, flowing gray hair and a thick beard. He wore heavy robes of purple, green, and brown with hems colored in gold and silver. His slippers, like Procopius's boots, were scarlet. In every way, Barsymes presented himself as if he himself was the emperor, save one thing—he wore no crown. Instead, atop a porphyry table set to the left of the throne sat the Emperor's crown, encircled with pearl pendants.

Barsymes made a swift motion with his left arm, and the music that announced his entrance ceased immediately. Everyone sat down.

The business of imperial audience got off to a start. Alexander finally divined the identity of the foreign dignitaries when a chamberlain called to the platform Athanagild, of Hispania Baetica.

After some protocols were recognized, a conversation ensued between Barsymes and Athanagild. It seemed that Baetica was beset by revolts, which—to Athanagild's account—were creditable to the misrule of one Arian Visigothic king, Agila.

Athanagild had arrived with a party that included his two daughters, Brunhilda and the Galswintha—and their husbands, the Frankish Merovingian kings Sigebert and Chilperic. Barsymes wondered out loud at the vacuum that Athanagild risked creating by leaving his kingdom behind to make this embassy to Byzantium. Athanagild explained that his queen, Goiswintha, was capable to rule in his name, but that he was required for the embassy because with the empire already bogged down in several wars, no less than his personal presence might suffice to impress on the imperial court the desperation of their cause. Barsymes looked irked when Athanagild let slip some disappointment that he had been expecting an audience with the Emperor, not the Emperor's "spiritual brother."

He went on to explain that the usurper, Agila, compensated for incompetent and unjust governance by turning his subjects' attention to outward conflict and vain hopes of conquest and without imperial aid Agila's malign influence would spread from Baetica to Septimania. He explained his calculation that remaining behind and sending his daughters and their husbands in his name could at best only delay this outcome while it would risk failing to persuade the Byzantines of the justice and priority of their cause.

Athanagild claimed to have met Agila in battle twice and bested the latter both times, but—he insisted—the tyrant Visigoth king was deeply entrenched, and so his own disorganized assortment of fighting bands, though loyal and of high morale, were undisciplined and undersupplied. They made an inadequate force to expel Agila. He required—he begged Barsymes—to lend him a force with which to tilt the balance, defeat Agila, and return Baetica to peace, stability, and prosperity.

It was around this point that Athanagild's pleas were met with additional inquiries from Barsymes, but before Alexander could make them out he was put aside by a completely unexpected interruption.

Alexander almost leapt out of his chair when, with no warning whatsoever, the seat cushion in the empty seat next to him popped open as if thrown aside by a powerful spring!

An involuntary gasp shot up from his lungs through his throat. It was the intense solemnity of the circumstance and Stephen's earlier warning about silence that gave him the force of will to slap a free hand over his mouth and muffle his own shout.

Where a second earlier was an empty seat cushion, there was now an open shaft. The spring and hinges that the seat cushion had apparently been suspended upon were well oiled because their opening was almost silent but for the quick whoosh of air it displaced. Since the cushion enclosed the seat on all sides—top and bottom—anyone whose attention was caught by the motion would still at any distance see the blended cushion against the seat back and be wont to return their attention to the larger affairs at hand.

Alexander's eyes were fixed on the void occupying the place where a moment earlier there had been a seat. His wits returning, he looked around to see if anyone had noticed. Apparently *not*—the drama of Athanagild and Barsymes held their attention. It was only at the outermost periphery of his vision, at the top tier of seats, that he noticed Callicinus standing opposite his placement in the room and who seemed as he might be intent on Alexander and the newly animate seat next to him.

His own attention returned to the seat and the shaft it exposed when he heard breathing. Someone was coming up through the shaft—as if climbing a ladder! He was about to lay down the hand he had muffled his own cry with when a head emerged from the shaft. A woman!

If Philip were not struggling with whatever disturbance seemed to physically trouble him he surely would have noticed, but he remained vexed by some pain. Alexander's hand gripped his mouth more tightly, holding back his own gasps. His eyes, wide open in shock, were met with the piercing eyes of... *It couldn't be!* he thought.

Her eyes locked with his, she held one finger to her lips while the other hand gripped a ladder handle still inside the shaft. "Shhhh," she hissed. Then, lowering her finger, she mouthed her words as if exclamations, yet as with the skill of a mime—without sounding—so that he could read her lips saying "Danger! Do. Not. Make. A. Sound!"

Then she did something completely unexpected.

With the same free hand that a second ago she had used to hush him, she reached downward—there was no way to tell with what she struggled. Alexander imagined it was a belt or pocket in a confined place, but she managed to loosen something and brought it up again with her hand, tossing it into Alexander's lap.

It was a purse. The same purse he had examined yesterday with Cyra.

Anastasia's purse!

Again, with a mime's skill, the old woman mouthed, "Open it."

All of a sudden self-conscious of the hand covering his mouth, Alexander placed it on his lap. For the first time in what must have been two minutes, he inhaled. He imagined he must look blue. Trying to catch his breath, with two hands he unlaced the purse in his lap and revealed its contents. It was Anastasia's skiadion—with her clever embroidery.

His heart was pounding. *What was the meaning of this?*

He looked again at the head that seemed suspended above the darkness in the seat next to him. Once again, with a mime's skill, the woman mouthed, "Cyra sent me—you can trust me—be quiet—look natural." The last words she said waving her free hand—a bobbing head in a shadow where a seat cushion should be. She looked anything but natural herself.

Taking her cue, Alexander looked up once more, focusing his view on Barsymes and Athanagild. He tucked the skiadion back into the purse and tied the laces closed again. He left it in his lap, unsure of what might happen next.

Watching her in his peripheral vision, the woman—who was old but thin and lithe—slinked her way over the edge of the shaft acrobatically, as if with practice. Without turning around to face it and in one motion, she leaned backward while pulling the seat cushion towards her, up and over the shaft and there she sat herself down upon it.

Alexander was stunned.

Seated now at his right was Antonina—Mistress of the Purple, wife of General Belisarius. Keeping her in his periphery and doing his best to act naturally, he noticed one more thing about her—considering the minor acrobatics required to stealthily extract herself from the shaft it was unsurprising, though it was still most unwomanly even of someone of her age and above all entirely inappropriate given present surroundings—she wore trousers.

* * * * * * * * *

"You must trust me I do this sort of thing all the time," Antonina whispered in Alexander's ear while slipping her hand into his lap and whisking away the purse that sat there before shifting back to center in her seat. She sat still there for only a moment and then leaned over to Alexander again and continued.

"It keeps Peter off balance."

Alexander, despite himself, was perturbed by the personal familiarity she expressed when using Barsymes' first name.

"Justinian is a wreck, you know."

Did she just say that about the Emperor? Alexander was horrified.

And invoking the Emperor by his first name? She's talking about him like he's her nephew. Alexander was altogether nonplussed and could do nothing but sit in his seat and take it while Antonina kept dishing bits and pieces to him.

"He was bad enough after the plague. Most didn't survive you know—he didn't make it with all his wits intact. And then—Theodora..."

"I was in Italy when it happened. There was nothing I could do. He hasn't been the same since."

She droned off again before leaning back to neutral, her remark had surely been in reference to Theodora's untimely death three years earlier.

"With everyone working together..." She leaned in again to say, "the eunuchs, the excubitors, his niece."

She leaned back, leaving the sentence unfinished. She leaned in again, "Sometimes, some days—today, *hopefully,*" the last word she stressed, "we can get a good two hours out of him. Three if we are lucky."

"You'll need to make it quick though."

"That's the best that can be hoped for...three hours."

She set back again. They watched Barsymes and Athanagild exchange words. Matters did not seem to be going well for Athanagild. Antonina leaned in again.

"It seems to calm Justinian to walk in the gardens and make inquiries with his theologians, but while he does so Peter thinks he runs the place."

The place? Alexander wondered. *What is "the place"? What did she mean by that? The palace? The city? The empire?*

Antonina continued her rant, "He doesn't fear many, and he must comply with Justinian, but that's not enough. We have to keep him off balance...he claims to rule in Justinian's name."

She leaned back to her seat and almost immediately leaned forward again. This time Alexander deciphered that she wore a grin as she whispered, "And, poor Procopius over there," she was pointing at the Emperor's secretary—who was scribbling away frantically on the parchment with his quill and seemed pressed under with a great deal of stress. "He believes it!"

"He believes Peter rules in Justinian's name while he drives Rome into a ditch for his own profit. Procopius blames Justinian too. He thinks Justinian is bewitched. He may be right about that," her last words turned dark.

All this time Alexander had said nothing, simply sitting and trying to incorporate the bizarre turn events had taken. By now the gravity was settling in while the familiarity Antonina directed at him reminded him of Cyra.

Christ—that old nun knows people, he thought.

Finally, he leaned over toward her and returned a whisper.

"So who does Peet—who does Barsymes fear?"

Leaning back in the chair Antonina met Alexander eye to eye. She gave no answer, just an incredulous, if self-referential gaze as if to say, "Who do you think?!"

It was at this moment that Alexander realized he and Antonina were not alone. Their position on the elbow of the third tier had afforded privacy until now, but out of his left periphery he detected an interloper had tuned to their conversation; it was Lao Yi.

Antonina recognized this too.

Lao Yi for his part did not seem bothered as much as amused. From what Alexander could tell, the monk was holding back a laugh and not doing a good job of it. When

Alexander and Antonina both met him with their eyes, the monk lifted his left arm, which had been crossed over his right across his chest and placed it behind his left ear, as if to scratch an itch but then lifted it up and tilted it either way, waving at them, smiling knowingly.

Antonina wasted no time and responded to the gesture—*flirtatiously*. She tilted her cheek to one side, pursed her lips a bit while lifting Anastasia's silk purse to her cheek and stroked her skin gently with it two or three times before returning it to her lap.

Alexander, at times a monk at others a bureaucrat, sat for the first time in his life in the nerve center of imperial power and wondered, *What the hell is going on?*

* * * * * * * * *

Barsymes seemed on the edge of thanking Athanagild for his troubles and dismissing him. He was already reading a tribute for the latter—essentially funds to pay for their journey back to Hispania Baetica, a payment of sorts to cover the expense but a bargain for Barsymes who just wished for the embassy to go away—when with no warning Antonina stood up and called out to Barsymes, "Isn't this merely a matter of calculation?"

Barsymes visibly shook upon hearing her, and his response and her words drew the attention of everyone present back to the cause of the interruption.

"Anto-nina!" Barsymes called out in a rich mix of surprise and disapproval.

"Who let..."

She did not let him finish. "Peter," she interrupted, stretching out his name, slurring the sounds of its letters and emphasizing the familiarity with which she spoke, "the embassy from Baetica has not asked that we abandon the

Italian campaign and level Hispania. They merely ask for the resources necessary to tip the balance in their favor."

Barsymes regained his composure and stood at full attention at the edge of the dais facing Antonina.

The purple hue of his neck, cheeks, and forehead blended with the purple sash of his robes, "Antonina! Perhaps you haven't noticed—the empire suffers a shortage—of men!"

"Even if the embassy's request had merit..."

Alexander watched Athanagild visibly bristle at the "if". Barsymes continued, "...where would we find a contingent that might tip the balance?"

Alexander imagined the last words were spoken through gritted teeth; Barsymes was angry—he was struggling to control himself. It was as if he wanted to lash out from the dais at Antonina.

Antonina, he recalled, was wife of Belisarius—a very dangerous person to oppose. Barsymes must be angry indeed. *What did any of this mean?*

Barsymes was not finished. "I see," his voice shook, "it looks...it looks as if you have brought monks with you today!" He pointed at Alexander, Philip, Thaddeus, and their visitors from Serinda. "Do you suggest I call muster to the monasteries and pacify Baetica with holy men?"

If Antonina was intimidated she did not show it, but answered, "Peter, let us remember the Emperor, crowned by God," this time she contrasted her familiarity with Barsymes with the office Justinian held, "undertook the consolidation of Africa, Italy, and Hispania Baetica among other reasons to restore abundance. Surely a man in your position has noticed that raids by the Austuriani continue to hinder commerce with Libya while the war effort continues in Italy. And what of Lazica?"

From his left periphery in the lower tier Alexander detected motion at her mention of Lazica. It was the lad—the fellow representing the military party—Antonina said something that had caught his attention.

"I understand we receive nothing from Lazica except for bills. Invoices and bills."

Barsymes responded, "The empire faces challenges in all her eras and ours is no exception. What is your point Antonina?"

Alexander was struck by how far out of order the scene had become. No one was supposed to speak to the emperor or anyone present in his office on the dais, except from the platform in the pit. Barsymes obviously had no love to lose for Antonina, but even though he was empowered to do so he did nothing to silence her or expel her from the premises. He was furious with her—yet he indulged her.

"Barsymes, our spiritual prince," Antonina started. This time she addressed him with formality...was this to keep him off balance?

"How is the Emperor? How is the Senate?" she asked, reverentially, if a bit late.

"They are in good care Antonina. Please go on," Barsymes replied, impatiently.

She did, "I keep correspondence with Leander of Seville."

"Your wide range of correspondence is well known," Barsymes quipped, danger in his voice.

"He has reminded me in recent letters of Columella and *De Re Rustica*."

She paused for a moment until Barysmes answered, "That text is...ancient."

"Italy is ancient," Antonina said, "and she remains a fertile land. But how soon do you think we may expel the Goths and profit again from her commerce? A year? Five years? Ten?"

Barsymes was silent; Antonina continued.

"Baetica," she said, "is rich! While we wait to consolidate Italy and Africa—Baetica has vineyards, olive groves, and fish. When was the last time we received wine from Italy? When was the last time we received bread from Africa?"

Barsymes shouted in answer, "Would you have me divert armies from Italy and allow her to be overrun to make profit in Baetica?"

Antonina returned, "No! Agila isn't an Ostrogothic king or an Austuriani warlord. He's a usurper and petty criminal who is feared, but not loved."

Alexander watched while Barsymes bristled at these words, his skin returning again to shades of purple.

Antonina went on, "I would have you send a small garrison to assist Athanagild, so he may put down a petty criminal, and with peace restored, I would have you charge Athanagild to supply the campaign in Italy from Baetica, which is nearer to Italy than we."

When Barsymes said nothing she added, "Belisarius and Narses alike, would be well pleased."

"Who?" Barsymes respired, more than spoke. "Who would you recommend to lead this campaign?" Barsymes repeated, "did you come here to recommend that monk?"

Alexander was briefly horrified when Barsymes pointed directly at him. Philip, next to him, rasped sharply, not sure if he was the subject of Barsymes' accusing finger.

Looking anywhere for support, for the first time since this dialog began he connected eyes with Lao Yi— who read his thoughts and answered them with a shrug—as if he agreed perhaps Alexander should lead the expedition.

Antonina ignored them both, saying "I don't know. It's true—the city is short of men," she conceded. Then she suggested, "What about Liberius?"

Liberius! Alexander thought.

Alexander worked for the eparch—although the eparchy, which governed city affairs, was one office that had been among the many targets of Justinian's reforms and had gone without an actual eparch to lead it for decades. In recent years, Barsymes had installed Liberius in a new office, *comes domesticorum vacans*, and Liberius for all intents and purposes exercised the powers of the eparch.

"Liberius," Barsymes was choosing words, "is distinguished, but surely you have noticed that he's...he's almost eighty. Do you think he's the right man for this?"

Before Antonina could answer they were interrupted by a trumpet. There was commotion and Barsymes turned aside—everyone stood up. Callicinus announced loudly, "The Emperor approaches!"

Clearly surprised, Barsymes appeared to be thinking fast. He moved to conclude the matter hastily and looked to be trying to dismiss Athanagild before Justinian might re-appraise any judgment. Closing the audience he said, "We are grateful for your wise counsel as always, Mistress Antonina."

"It is ordered...a garrison of 2,000 under Liberius will accompany Athanagild and his embassy to Baetica. They will terminate the usurper Agila, pacify the region, and Athanagild will be commissioned to supply the campaign in Italy."

* * * * * * * * * *

The Magnaura   Second Audience

When Justinian finally arrived he came accompanied by the remainder of his Consistorium, who Barsymes joined at the oak table on the platform where Procopius worked. They were comprised of Peter Patricus, Master of Offices; Addaeus, Prefect of the East; Barsymes; Callinicus; and—this Alexander simply could not understand—Antonina.

Occupying the fifth chair at a table obviously meant for men—men of high office no less—sat Antonina, who, in her trousers, may as well have been wearing pajamas! Women in Byzantium and throughout the Roman world possessed liberties that were uncommon almost everywhere else. Alexander was no stranger to working with women in his inspection role as a mitotes. On account of a unique, Roman tradition of separate domain, a widespread system finding women holding skilled professions and important offices was possible in Rome while it remained impossible or else absent in Persia or India or among the tribes of Europe.

Precedent, customs, traditions, and sometimes old habits had long established whole arenas of commerce and sometimes governance where women operated without the presence or interference of men. Some of these were textiles, ceramics, and baking. The *Panis Civilis*, which had since ancient times supplied the entire city of Byzantium with daily bread and frequent rations of clothing, though it employed men, was largely the province of women and a system of female empowerment and enrichment, particularly where it was employed as a means of clothing and linen production and distribution.

Other modes of commerce such as masonry, tanning, plumbing, and logothete were restricted to men. Usually foreign trade and large-scale commerce, even in female wares, was given to men as women were believed to be better suited to a stationary existence than to the arduous and often dangerous travels of a merchant, but on local and smaller scales women managed the purchase and sale of their own wares. Within this female domain women were free to educate themselves and one another and to establish hierarchies of competence and governance. Eunuchs served an invaluable and irreplaceable role of mediums connecting these separate domains and facilitating their interoperation, and the emperor ruled absolutely above all—male, eunuch, and female. It was on account of this separation of domains that Rome in general and Byzantium in particular had something that could not be found anywhere else on earth:

A rich pool of female professionals and leaders

But nothing about this system or Alexander's experience was enough to prepare him to make sense of how

Antonina could be sitting there—in full sight of all those assembled—with the rest of Emperor Justinian's Consistorium, as if their equal—first of all because she was a woman, but secondly because she was dressed in trousers.

On the second tier just above and behind the platform sat some attendants. Patricus was attended by his son Theodore, Barsymes by a military officer Hephaestus, Antonina by Sophia—Theodora's niece, while Callicinus and Addaeus sat at the table together as if a pair, but had no attendants themselves.

Justinian began his proceedings but inquired first with Athanagild of whether he was pleased with the conclusion of his audience before Barsymes. Clearly seeing that Antonina had saved his embassy from an otherwise certain failure and not wishing to press his luck, Athanagild spoke kind words of Barsymes and his erudite handling of the Baetician party's petition. He expressed that he was eager to meet with Liberius and get back to Hispania Baetica, wishing the Emperor, his spiritual brother Barsymes, the Consistorium, and the Patriarch all good fortune.

The next party's audience was brief by comparison. As Alexander had come to guess, it was represented by the lad who identified himself to Justinian as Flavius Mauricius Arabissos. Alexander noted that Justinian took some interest in the lad's name. After some affectations of humility that the latter was clearly uncomfortable trying to navigate matters with the Emperor, another in his party risked the offense of interruption to explain that the boy had been heroic in military action and was awarded the title Maurice for his bravery. Justinian indulged Maurice and his struggle to explain this without seeming to take credit for it—but despite what Antonina had said about Justinian's incapacity Alexander suspected that he knew the young man's entire history before the audience began.

As to the Emperor's alleged incapacity—Alexander had never seen the man at this close distance. Physically he did not look well at all. Thin and gaunt, the scars left behind after surviving the plague were evident on his face, which was a sickly shade of grey. The crown that Barsymes could only stand next to, but not wear, sat atop Justinian's head. It seemed larger than the man himself, and as it leaned this way and that atop his head, Alexander expected he would fall forward under its weight and stumble off the dais into the pit below. Procopius, whose pattern until then had been to observe speakers as he scribbled notes, seemed determined not to gaze directly at the Emperor for any reason.

But though Justinian's physical powers seemed compromised—nothing about how he managed court would have left Alexander with any doubts at his mental capacity.

Once the niceties about the origin of Maurice's name were settled, the military party's audience with Justinian got underway. Maurice explained to Justinian that Bessus' lieutenant, John Guzes, had been successful in his missions to Apsilia and subsequently in the follow-up mission to Hermonassa. He said something about how he regrets to report that there were fewer—Alexander could not be sure he had made this out right—*streptons* than had been hoped, but Maurice explained that the ones they had, had been put to good use in Suania where under Arsaces command they were successfully employed to destroy an entire Persian garrison.

All through this report Justinian nodded, but he stopped there.

"And—who deployed the streptons?"

Maurice answered softly, clearing his throat, "Uh, me. The contents anyway, when we deploy—"

Justinian rapidly cut him off, "This is how you earned the honorific, Maurice? It was you who deployed the streptons?"

Alexander had no idea what they were talking about.

"Yes", Maurice started. Justinian interrupted him again.

"But was it not your duty to deploy the streptons? Few in the garrison knew about them. Why were you honored for doing what was expected of you? It is right to do one's duty," Justinian paused, then continued, "but unexceptional. As I recollect, the primary responsibility was..." Justinian leaned down toward Maurice who stood in the pit, "...burying their contents. Is that not right?"

"Ah, yes," Maurice answered, "and I did so, but..." A pause followed when he was uncertain, Justinian fixed eyes on him without breaking contact, "but, I do not think it was for that, alone, that my garrison honored me."

"We find that men are not often honored for the ditches they dig," Justinian said pursing his lips, "What was it then?"

Maurice took a deep breath and then started, "The Persian garrison we skirmished with—was larger than our own. We had fallen into retreat. There was confusion in the ranks. The Persians were closing on us and the fuse didn't light."

"That must have been disastrous," Justinian interjected. "How did you overcome this setback?"

Alexander watched—was Maurice biting his lip?

He answered the Emperor bluntly, "When I buried the contents of the streptons, I set up a back-up fuse and I had to think quickly when we were on the run, so I created a diversion."

"A diversion?"

Justinian was leading the poor soul on—surely, he already had intelligence and knew what he was going to say. Despite the reports of his ill health, he seemed to be playing with the young man and enjoying himself doing it.

Maurice spoke this time with confidence, "I do not think it's appropriate to say here, sir, in your court."

"I will be the judge of that. It's my court after all," Justinian answered forcefully, for the first time turning so his back was to Maurice. Then quickly, he turned—almost spinning back around, the crown almost fell off his head, fully tilting over one ear while Justinian finished, "Don't hold up our time. What was the nature of your diversion?"

Maurice swallowed—his Adam's apple making a visible bounce, then answered, "It was the heat of battle, and we were losing, Emperor—I had to think fast. We were on the run. The garrison was weakened, and it was possible to slow the Persians and buy time—but if the fuses wouldn't light all would all have been lost. I ordered the trumpeter to strip his clothes, cover his body in blood and dirt, run erratically as of after no purpose but to escape, but to terminate his flight at the location of the spare fuse, where he lit it."

Justinian initially said nothing at this. He straightened his crown, took hold of the bar on the edge of the dais, leaned forward and considered Maurice before sitting for a moment, as if to reflect on what he'd just heard. Standing again he addressed himself once again to the pit, "A innovative battle tactic, Maurice," Justinian said emphasizing the word *innovative*. Procopius, off in the corner, bristled in Alexander's peripheral vision, while the Consistorium and its attendants including Antonina let off a gentle laugh in unison—everyone that is except Barysmes and Addaeus.

Justinian stood up straight and appeared poised to bring the audience to a hasty conclusion, "We are grateful for your innovative battlefield thinking, Maurice. It appears the appellation is well earned. We are impressed with your mind for, strategy."

"Thank you, Emperor. I am honored," Maurice responded.

"I am made to understand you are a notary, not a soldier. Is that right?"

"Yes," said Maurice.

"We might think a notary had more a mind for letters than tactics," Justinian continued.

"Yyyes," Maurice said again, nervously.

"But soldiers often are not men of letters. Busy fighting—they do not often write," Justinian continued.

Maurice said nothing.

"Our manner of fighting—of making war—has changed much since ancient times, since the times of Julius. I think that it is important that we have a record to keep a memory of our changes, our *innovations*," Justinian turned toward Procopius when uttering the last word. Alexander thought that so odd.

"Otherwise," Justinian continued, "soldiers may slip back into old habits. The empire was halved, and halved again," Justinian emphasized the second time, also as he glanced back at Procopius, "in vain preservation of old habits."

Not knowing what else to say, Maurice answered "yes".

Justinian concluded, "I think you should consider putting your literacy to good use. Rome might be well served if someone in your position set our learning, our ways of war, to paper—so that lessons learned in blood needn't be learned again."

Maurice seemed shocked by the suggestion.

"I...I would be honored...Emperor, but I am...I'm just a notary, not a soldier, much less a general. It is as you say I have no mind or training for this."

Justinian considered him.

"Perhaps you lack training, but I'm not ready to agree that you have no mind for the work. I was not always emperor, but I ... came around to it. This is not an order. It's your destiny to decide. The court thanks you for your service. You and your party may leave. I have one request though."

Surprised, Maurice replied, "What? Anything Emperor."

"When, if, you do write the book on our innovations in the Roman way of war, while I do expect you will be thorough, perhaps keep as a state secret the Roman penchant for the use of nudity as a diversionary tactic," Justinian said, lifted one brow.

Maurice looked as if he was blushing and Justinian acted as though he expected Maurice to follow protocol and dismiss himself when Maurice interjected, "Emperor, there's one more thing."

"What is that?" Justinian asked, surprised. Alexander dreaded that they might continue down this uncomfortable, unseemly line of inquiry. He was quickly relieved of his apprehension.

"As a token of the restoration of friendship between Rome and the Abgasians, Terdetes sent with us a gift for your court."

Justinian stood there silently, bidding Maurice to finish. Maurice turned to his party in the second row and nodded. One of their members stood; Maurice returned his attention to Justinian.

"I present to the high Emperor Terdetes' gift of friendship, the eunuch Euphrates."

For a moment Justinian said nothing. Then when he spoke, he said, "Very well—the court can always use another eunuch. Callicinus will see to you, Euphrates, when we convene." Turning to Maurice he said, "Your service is appreciated—your friends have returned from Hermonassa and are where you first found them in Vlanga, near Eleutheriou."

At this, Justinian returned to his throne where he was intending to sit while the next party was introduced for an audience, but there was another disruption.

Maurice remained in the pit.

A chamberlain was waving at Maurice to move, but he remained until everyone became aware of the disturbance. Justinian, noticing too, stood up from his throne and approached the edge of the dais and addressed himself to Maurice, "Young man—your audience is concluded. What is this?"

Maurice was trembling now—he knew he was out of order. His own party was shifting about, waving and hissing at him to get off the platform and out of the pit. Justinian had to silence them with a wave of his hand and a downward flinch of his wrist. When they were quiet he repeated himself impatiently, "Our audience is over Maurice."

Maurice answered him, "Emperor, I have a question," he didn't wait for Justinian to stop him and continued, "Our mission in Lazica has burdened me with something I don't understand."

Justinian replied, "This isn't a school." Justinian let off a sense that his patience was being tested. "Waste no more time son, ask."

Maurice did so, "In Lazica—there is nothing. There are mountains and rocks; there are no roads. There is snow and ice; there are no farms or cattle. I watched a third of my garrison get slaughtered at the hands of the Persians. All of this was only so confusing to me. What I cannot understand is that—after the Persians had slaughtered us and after we answered them and slaughtered them in return—we made commerce with them. My own garrison commander— Arsaces—he purchased silk. From the Persians! Why do we kill the Persians, and they us, while we buy their silk?"

Justinian was quiet for a moment. Alexander was not sure who sweat more with anxiety, Maurice or his own shocked party who watched his outburst in horror.

Finally, Justinian answered, his answer did not bode well, "Your question is—audacious—Maurice." Alexander gripped himself for how this might end. Justinian continued, "But your heroic antics in battle have amused this court...they have amused my consistorium, and so while normally we might consider you lucky to be expelled from here without a night first in stocks for your intrusive inquiry into state affairs, I will make an exception."

Justinian proceeded to remove a deep purple sash from his imperial robes. He threw it over the edge of the dais down to Maurice. It was light, and with its slow fall Maurice had no trouble catching it, no matter that the gesture was so unexpected.

While Maurice held the sash, Justinian explained though it is mere fabric it would trade for several pounds of gold.

"If I meant for you to meet a quick end, I could gift the sash to you and you might feel yourself fortunate when I allowed you to leave the palace with it in hand," he said. "But I may be confident you wouldn't get far. With short work, a commoner or one of the circus factions would kill you and make away with an ordinary man's fortune."

"Maurice—you are young, and I am sure the loss of comrades must affect you—but Rome and Persia have challenged one another since the Seleucid's filled the vacuum left behind by Alexander. The losses you witnessed are all part of a long chain. It's been almost nine-hundred years that Rome and Persia have vied with one another—we are equally matched."

Maurice looked on silently while Justinian continued.

"Do you know what it means to be equally matched?" Justinian asked Maurice.

"No emperor", Maurice replied.

Justinian pressed his fingers together and tilted his head as he answered, "For two empires to be equally matched is something like the old gods," Justinian started.

"Emperor?" Maurice blurted, despite himself.

Justinian continued, "The old gods, being divine, where equally matched, and so were unable to overcome one another in their intrigues. What is man to a god?" Justinian asked, rhetorically.

Continuing, he said, "Man is like an ant. The finest soldier, the wisest philosopher—one does not crush an ant, he smooshes it. One does not defeat the argument of an ant, he ignores it. Such is the distance separating men from gods."

"Yet in order to defeat one another at their intrigues, gods—equally matched—were forced to enlist the support of men. Gods themselves had to win men to their sides. Why? Because men—with pin-prick bites no stronger than ants, were sufficient to tip the balance. What was at stake in the balance? By tipping the balance—men participated in overcoming gods."

"So here we find ourselves, Persians and Romans—equally matched."

"But only so long as Persia controls the silk. One thing, silk. By the silk, Persians enrich themselves. By the silk, Persians drain us. By the silk, our interminable fighting could go on and go nowhere, in Lazica and beyond, for another thousand years. Your children and grandchildren fighting and dying—because the Persians, while controlling the silk, are equally matched to us."

Justinian paused a moment and then started again, "The Persians harass us because they find our advances into Italy and Africa tentative and they believe our expansion is tenuous. They may be right. But the Persian grip on silk is half a millennium old, and it too, grows tenuous. Who controls silk—tips the balance. Who tips the balance controls the world. We do not fight the Persians in Lazica for land, farms, cities, or cattle. We don't even fight them for religion, enmity, or gold, though that is rumored to be so everywhere, and we are content with the rumor."

"But nor do they fight us for any of those things. The war in Lazica—Maurice—is a war over who controls the silk. The settlement of that war will be the settlement of destiny."

* * * * * * * * *

By the time their audience had come, much of the day had passed. The source of the sun's rays through the dome, which had begun when they arrived that morning in the east, had now shifted to the southwest. Alexander observed the water clock above the dais—*hespera*, one hour before sunset. To think all of this had started in the Fourth Watch the evening before!

Callicinus orchestrated ushers who in turn orchestrated Alexander, Philip, Lao Yi, and Hui-Shen to new positions in the pit. Several chairs were set up against the wall inside which allowed larger parties to address the Emperor, and the ushers situated Alexander and Lao Yi together in the center, standing with a podium at their side where Callicinus himself set the mysterious foreign letter that started all of this. Philip and Hui-Shen were placed in the chairs at the side. Alexander could see—he could even feel—that Thaddeus was none-too-happy to have been left seated in the third tier with Joseph Nios. Concerned with an economy of time and cognizant that the archimandrite could offer no more than formality to an occasion where time was pressing, Callicinus made the call to isolate them.

Alexander himself protested at first that he was set to interpret for Lao Yi. He was in no rush to repeat the donkey statue affair—but strangely—Philip would have none of it. Philip plead with Alexander to let him sit in the shadows and assured Alexander against the evidence of their entire experience together so far that he was fully competent on his own to interpret for Lao Yi. There was little time to settle the dispute, and Alexander found himself together with Lao Yi, facing Emperor Justinian in his dais from the platform in the pit.

Thank God Lao Yi speaks Greek!—Thank God he came too this morning, Alexander thought appreciatively.

Lao Yi and Alexander stood shoulder-to-shoulder, both facing upwards towards Justinian who seemed directly illuminated now by beams of light that shone above stretching from their source in the windows of the dome, over the terraced seating.

When it was time to start Justinian began first, addressing them:

> I understand that with us today is an unusual
> embassy of foreigners, so I will take a moment to
> familiarize you with certain matters of our custom.
>
> Callicinus, who has been your host, holds the office of
> *praepositus sacri cubiculi*, which makes him one of
> the highest-ranking officers serving us in the Palace,
> but I have also made him *patricius*, an honor
> denoting my sacred trust.
>
> He tells me that your embassy is most important.

Justinian paused then looked towards Callicinus who was at the Consistorium's table.

> *He* says your embassy is more important than any
> other.
> This is an extraordinary claim.
> More important than ambassadors from Chosroes in
> Persia. More important than an embassy from Totilla
> in Italy.
> We fight wars with these rulers. Wars that to this day
> claim the lives of thousands. We have razed Italy to
> the ground by war with Totilla.
> Callicinus has a history with me. He earned his
> reputation. He earned my trust. Much must be at
> stake for him to make such extravagant claims. What

does your embassy bring this court that persuades my trusted chamberlain that you are so important?

Until this moment, Alexander had been nervous, but that was only because he was concerned he would fail again at interpreting Lao Yi or Hui-Shen and embarrass himself in front of the court and the archimandrite. With what Justinian had just laid on him, his nervousness congealed with confusion until he stammered trying to say something—not at all sure what he was supposed to say.

Mercifully, Lao Yi stepped forward and spoke for them, addressing himself to the Emperor in Greek, "Greetings to the Emperor from the ambassadors of Emperor Xiao Gang of the Liang and on behalf of his brother Xiao Yi the Prince of Xiangdong."

The proper names Lao Yi used were as much as alien in this court; he expected that all those hearing, including Justinian himself, could not make them out.

"Emperor Xiao Gang is a pious ruler, and he sends to you two humble monks, Lao Yi." Lao Yi then gestured with two hands to his chest, giving a slight bow. "And Hui-Shen." Lao Yi passed his left arm straight behind him, gesturing to Hui-Shen.

Then—likely having rehearsed Callicinus's instructions from earlier by the statues when watching the first two audiences, Lao Yi ably stated protocol, "How is the Emperor, crowned by God?"

Justinian answered him, "Very good, ambassador of the Liang." *Liang, Justinian retained that*, Alexander thought.

"How is the most holy and ecumenical patriarch?", Lao Yi inquired.

"He is well, but could not today be with us, ambassador."

"How is the whole senate?"

Justinian smiled—slightly more with guilt than amusement, "They are pleased by your arrival and lend us their hall where we may receive you."

"How is the empress?"

Without warning, Alexander's heart shot up through his throat. A hot flush passed across his head followed by a dizzying lightness. His knees went weak. He felt sweat collecting in his armpits and the edges of his belly.

Until now Lao Yi had been doing so well!

Almost trembling, he watched Justinian, trying to divine his response to Lao Yi, fearing the worst, while Justinian fixed eyes with Lao Yi. Lao Yi was intuiting that he had made a *faux pas* but still attempting to apprehend the nature of his mistake.

"Ambassador Lao Yi, is it?" Justinian asked.

"Yes."

Alexander watched—this could not be good—Justinian looked as if he had aged ten years in the space of a few seconds.

"Callicinus informs me you have been in our city for months," Justinian forced, more than said. "Ye...yes."

It was the first time Alexander had heard Lao Yi speak since they had met, with anything other than perfect confidence.

"I must imagine you are not a particularly observant ambassador, for how is it that in all this time, it has escaped your attention that the Empress is dead."

Alexander looked up to the first tier of seats where Procopius wrote and the Consistorium observed from their table. Procopius was visibly trembling. Alexander did not think he could bear the tension while Lao Yi thought for a way out of this. All at once, Alexander wanted the whole ordeal to be over— to go into reverse—to have never happened—to be back in his bed brushed by cold night air. He longed to wake in the morning, attend matins, and get about the grind of the Eparch's work.

His instant of panic was broken when Lao Yi started again, bowing forward as he spoke, "Emperor, I am sorry. I meant no offense. Perhaps you were not informed that our visit has been so long because I did not arrive well. I am old. The journey was difficult for me, and I barely survived it alive. It was only this morning that I woke from a coma, and your monks and officials wasted no time bringing me to you. I beg your forgiveness."

No one dared make themselves the breaker of Justinian's momentary silence. The room became so silent Alexander could hear the soft dripping that powered the water clock. Justinian took a step backwards and sat down in his throne, then called out, with more sickness than force, "Callicinus."

"Yes, Emperor," Callicinus replied.

"Is it true?" Justinian held his head in his hand as if pressing against a throbbing ache.

"Yes, Emperor. The monk, Lao Yi, has been incapacitated since his arrival."

"Why," Justinian asked, holding his head even harder it seemed, as if trying to force thoughts and words, "Why have you waited so long to bring them into my audience?"

"Emperor," Callicinus plead, "the monk you speak with, Lao Yi, speaks Greek. The other monk, Hui-Shen, does not. We cannot understand their language. We only yesterday sought assistance from the archimandrite as an act of desperation to find someone who could speak with Hui-Shen when we didn't think that Lao Yi would survive another day. It was—like a divine act of grace—that when we finally found among the monks of Dalmatou two who speak their language. Lao Yi, as if by miracle, recovered."

Justinian sat in his throne for a full moment. Then by some wave of his hand ordered a chamberlain to bring him a drink. Doubled over forward between his knees, almost as if he might vomit and most unbecoming of an emperor, Justinian sipped at the chalice that was brought to him, separating each sip with long breaths. Alexander discerned Antonina making motions and signs. Another chamberlain brought Justinian a wet towel, with which he attempted to dab the Emperor's head. Justinian stopped him, took the towel, and treated himself with it instead.

Seeming to regain his composure, Justinian rose to his feet and stepped again to the edge of the dais, facing Lao Yi and Alexander.

For the first time he addressed himself to Alexander, saying, "You—you are a monk of Dalmatou?"

"Yes, Emperor—I am. I am also in the service of the Eparch. I am a mitotes—for linens and textiles."

Justinian spoke to Alexander again, "And you speak their language? I am made by Callicinus to understand these monks have arrived to us from Serinda. You speak the language of Serinda?"

"Ahhh," Alexander started before realizing he could not tolerate uncertainty, "Emperor I am able to read the language of Serinda. My brother monk Philip here—he has been to Serinda and I am humbled to admit he speaks the language much better than I."

Justinian turned his attention to Philip. "Rise," Justinian commanded. Philip did so.

"You have been to Serinda?" he asked Philip.

"Yes," Philip said, in no hurry to take liberty with words.

Justinian's reply was both unexpected and annoyed, "No one has been to Serinda."
Philip answered him in contradiction, "Emperor—it is true—I have been beyond Taprobane. It is how I learned their language."

"Hmmm," Justinian mumbled.

While Philip maintained his posture to stand on the platform, Alexander noticed that he compulsively looked out of the corner of his eye at the consistorium. Peering that way to guess at what he was looking at, he noticed that Peter Barsymes fixed on Philip in a manner that the other four were not.

Justinian addressed himself to Lao Yi presently, "What is it that brings you to us—that is more important than embassies from the Shahanshah or the king of the Goths?"

"Emperor, I believe the spokesman for the previous embassy was a young man who you called Maurice." Lao Yi paused; Justinian said nothing. "You answered your own question—when you answered his. Who controls silk, controls the world. Those were your words, Emperor."

Unexpectedly, Justinian laughed at this, "You offer us a means of securing Lazica from Persian control? Has a garrison from Serinda accompanied you here to ally with us?"

Lao Yi looked confused but remained unfazed. "Hui-Shen and I arrive from a great distance. I do not profess to know how you hope success in Lazica may help to acquire silk—though I do know that silk is made by the labor of the Han, the people of Emperor Xiao Gang, and we have never heard of Lazica. Our Prince, Xiao Yi, sends us to you with an immaterial gift—a gift he thinks you will find more valuable than any tribute we might have brought with us. It is by this gift that Xiao Yi authorizes us to offer you, that Rome may be free—forever—from the yoke of the Persians and their monopoly on silk. I think it is this that your chamberlain and our host Callicinus believe to be more important than embassies from Persia or the Goths."

Lao Yi waited. When no one answered, he motioned towards a table on the platform in the pit where the sash Justinian had thrown to Maurice now lay. Picking it up, he lifted it towards Justinian and spoke again.

"Emperor Justinian, Xiao Yi authorizes me to lend to you Hui-Shen—Hui-Shen knows the way. He can lead a party to what you call Serinda. He knows where silk is made and how to acquire its source. If you send a party with Hui-Shen to acquire the silk, then I will remain behind in your capital and instruct your assistants in constructing facilities where silk can be made in large quantities. Emperor Justinian, Xiao Yi authorizes me to make it possible that silk may no longer be acquired through a long journey to Serinda—across the toll of the Persians. He authorizes me to make it possible for silk to be produced here, in the land of the Romans."

When Lao Yi said this there was commotion at the consistorium's table. Barsymes rose, stood, and shouted, "This is nonsense!"

Looking accusatively to Callicinus, he demanded, "It's a trick. These monks have tricked you."

When no one spoke he went on, "The origin of silk has been a mystery for over two-thousand years. Did you know he was going to say this? Did you know that was the purpose of this embassy? You can't possibly believe this? No one knows how silk is made."

Most everyone in the hall remained in a state of shock. No one answered Barsymes, so Barsymes turned to Justinian.

"Emperor. Surely you can see this is subterfuge. It's probably a Persian trap. Why—why if they know the source of silk and how to make it, why haven't they just arrived with the secret to present to you here, now? What says the foreign monk? What account does he make?" Barsymes finished and remained standing, waiting Justinian's answer.

Justinian motioned with his left hand for Barsymes to sit. Barsymes started to answer, "I will no..." but Justinian shouted over him, "Peace! Spiritual brother. Sit."

Barsymes complied.

Justinian addressed himself now to Lao Yi, "The burdens of empire weigh on my brother Peter, Lao Yi. He is excited, but Rome is set upon by two wars and we dare not, we cannot, lose either. He asks legitimate questions. What would you say to mollify him?"

Lao Yi folded both of him forearms in the hem of his robes, looked down, took a deep breath, then looked up at Justinian and answered, "First, I will disclose how silk is produced. You will understand immediately that the knowledge of how it is produced is not by itself enough to produce it. Even with accurate knowledge of the production of silk—sacred knowledge not known even to most of the Qin—you cannot produce it. You will need to send Hui-Shen to acquire the means."

"Tell us then, get on with it," Justinian said.

Lao Yi inhaled, almost spoke, pausing mid-breath, then stated, "Silk is made by a worm."

There was a loud crash.

Barsymes stood again and pounded thunderously on the table as he did so. He was almost out of control and called, "Guards!" Justinian stood to shut him down, for once using the superior position of the dais to make a point of his authority.

"You will stand down, Peter. I am interested in what this monk has to say."

"But!" Barsymes protested. Realizing Justinian would not move, he quieted himself and sat down again.

Justinian sat and motioned for Lao Yi to continue.

"That silk is made from a worm should not cause such surprise. If I may Emperor, would it please the Emperor if I could step under the table?"

"What?" Justinian asked.

"The table." Lao Yi pointed to the table where the silk sash had been placed. "May I step under it? I will only be a moment."

"Monk, you would be correct to guess that in one-thousand years of our history no one has stood before an emperor of Rome in order to amuse him by suggesting that silk is made by a bug. You have my patience, but I am in no mood for a joke. Do you understand?"

"Yes, Emperor."

"Very well," Justinian said, "step under the table if it pleases you." He said this with some flourish, waving his hand.

Lao Yi quickly grabbed the stylus from the podium where the letter from Xiao Yi set. Then, with it in hand, he moved to the table, crouched, and crept under it.

Alexander had calmed enough since the misstep over mention of Empress Theodora that he was back to counting the ways this had been the weirdest day of his entire life. He watched as Lao Yi's robes shuffled and swished while he did something—under the table.

Stepping back and standing, Lao Yi spoke, "Ahhh—I found it, Emperor."

"What?" answered Justinian.

"It is too far for your eyes to see. May I toss it to you?"

This time it was Callicinus's turn to speak up, "Emperor, No!" Callicinus yelled. Callicinus obviously had a stake in their presence in audience today, but an ambassador throwing a stylus at the Emperor from the visitation platform was too much. Discerning that he might have miscalculated, Lao Yi corrected himself, and spoke to Callicinus. "I can offer it to you—instead."

Callicinus thought fast, "Give it to Alexander." Lao Yi obeyed.

Alexander held the stylus, examining it. Nothing was remarkable except that a spider's web was wrapped around it into a long tangle that dangled off one end.

Callicinus spoke to Alexander now, "Approach me."

Alexander did so, and Callicinus reached down from the tier—not so high above the platform as the dais—and they were able to connect so that Callicinus took the stylus from him.

Now it was Callicinus's turn to examine it. After a moment he addressed Justinian, "It's a web."

"A web?" Justinian said, questioningly.

"The monk," Callicinus went on, "twirled a spider's web with the stylus."

Justinian nodded then spoke, "You undertook this exercise to teach us barbarians that insects can make cloth? Do you have any other civilizing lessons for us, monk?"

Justinian's sarcasm did not bode well. Lao Yi may have pressed him too far.

"Only one, Emperor."

Alexander did not think that was the right answer. Justinian waited. Lao Yi continued.

"Wire. Thin, metal wire. You will find that if you shave an edge of metal so that it forms a thin wire and if you compare the strength of a similar bundle of a spider's web to the wire, the strings of the web are stronger. As you know, silk fiber is even stronger than that—a property for which it is prized. I think by this test you may know it is like a humble spider that spins a web; it is a humble worm that produces silk."

The Orphans' Dormitory at Saturninus

Psamathia Quarter
Byzantium

Tuesday evening, *Trite*
After *apodeipnon*

28 March 551 AD
Julian Calendar

Anastasia finished removing her chiton and affixed it on a hanger that she placed on a hook in the wall next to her bed and proceeded to put on a loose gown. She shared a sleeping room with the other orphans who were similarly preparing themselves for bed. It had been a long and exhausting day weaving and she looked forward to her head hitting the pillow with the slumber that she could feel in her joints. There were no windows in this room, but as she sat down on her bedding she could feel a sudden burst of wind slap against the outside of the wall. As close as Saturninus was to the ocean, when the nights were a commotion it made for some benefit to sleep in a room without windows. As long as the wind stayed outside the walls, its whistles and beats could be soothing and make for easier sleeping.

She had set herself down and was about to stretch her feet out to the end of the bed and lay her head down to the pillow when the door of the room burst open, swinging around its hinges and slamming against the wall. Anastasia could hear several of her orphan sisters gasp in surprise. For her part, she merely arrested her recline and leaned forward again so that her feet came to the floor while she looked towards the door to identify the interruption. She imagined that it must be common polite form in most times and places to knock on a closed sleeping room door towards bedtime, but this—of all places—was a nunnery. Throwing the door open like that was clearly out of order. *Who was it?* she wondered.

In just a second she had her answer.

It was Vesta.

Anastasia did not have to wait to find out for whom Vesta was seeking. She rose to her feet and stood, awaiting judgment. *What would it be this time?*

She did not have to wait long. Vesta was storming in her direction. In a few seconds, Vesta was standing directly over her. Though nine years separated them in age, it was perhaps just several inches that distinguished them in height—while Anastasia was not especially tall neither too was Vesta. It did not matter. When Vesta stood over her like this, she was like a demon in human form and the four inches that separated them may as well have been four feet.

Without greeting or hesitation, Vesta unceremoniously presented in two hands a wooden shaft that flurried before Anastasia's eyes to quickly for her to immediately recognize. "What is this?!" Vesta demanded.

Vesta was holding the object so close beneath Anastasia's nose that she tried to step back to gain a better perspective, only to nudge up against the side of her bed. She was forced to lean her shoulders back and crane her neck, staring down her nose in order to see what Vesta was talking about.

"A treadle," Anastasia said, in recognition and some confusion, almost as if a question.

"A *broken* treadle," Vesta answered accusingly.

At this—and despite her slightly increasing better judgment, which was training with a few years behind her age—Anastasia could not help herself. Repositioning herself to stand and face Vesta toe to toe, she addressed her elder almost as if a sassy younger sister might address her older, "Why did you break it?"

Vesta's face was already strained and grimaced. On hearing Anastasia, her cheeks and temples flushed purple and

Anastasia detected that for a moment Vesta clinched her back teeth, "I didn't break it. The heddle was wound too tight."

Anastasia reckoned this for a moment and quickly put together why Vesta must be in such a rage. She was already committed though and when she opened her mouth the words that followed came as if spoken by a devilish little imp, "Why did *you* break the heddle?"

Vesta did not even try to restrain herself; she just screamed at Anastasia, "I didn't break the heddle! You wound the heddle!" She thrust the broken treadle at Anastasia, almost forcing her back into the bed. She had to adjust her feet and spread her stance while falling back a bit to her left to support herself with her fingers pressing back from the wall to keep from falling. As she adjusted herself, Vesta continued, "You wound it too tight, so it broke the treadle fitting when I tried to finish the weave."

Anastasia pondered the snapped and broken treadle fitting that Vesta was presenting in front of her. She could visualize the whole thing. In fact, she had reset all the heddles before retiring from work for evening vespers. She knew that they were too tight when she had wound them, but time was running short. She did not think anybody would use the loom before morning, especially since it is normally a two-person job. She had intended to loosen the heddles in the morning before they started again. She wondered *why was Vesta looming this late in by herself?* Vesta must not have tested whether the heddles were too taut before she sat down and depressed the treadle with her foot. She was such a hot head she probably did not think when she noticed too much resistance, and instead of backing off and adjusting the heddles herself she probably just pressed harder until the fitting snapped.

Figures, she thought.

She did not think much more though. Vesta just pushed her aside and started collecting the linens from her bed. "What are you doing?" Anastasia asked, confused. Vesta ignored her and instead drew more linen from the bed and rapidly folded them into tight squares. "What are you doing?" This time she asked it more demandingly.

With several linens folded in a square, Vesta took Anastasia's small burlap pillow, placed it atop the linens, and thrust them at Anastasia, "You are sleeping on the bench tonight."

"What?"

"Put your chiton back on, get a coat if you wish, and then leave. Get out of here at once. Return in time for orthros." At this, Vesta pushed the linens into Anastasia so hard that in her confusion Anastasia absentmindedly took hold of them. Vesta turned her back and left, leaving Anastasia standing there holding a small pile of linens while everyone in the room stared at her.

* * * * * * * * * *

At the table of the Consistorium   After *apodeipnon*

Chairs had been placed on the open end of the Consistorium's table to make it possible for Alexander and Philip to meet with Justinian and his advisors at the conclusion of the day. While they ate deipnon*—which was no feast despite present surroundings, silk was hard business—they were served only a light course of wine and bread. Thaddeus and Joseph Nios had been included in the dinner party, but Callicinus had Lao Yi and Hui-Shen escorted elsewhere. Justinian wished to query Alexander and Philip privately. Alexander was skeptical to say the least that he could provide any information that might be decisive.

If Philip had seemed ill and distant throughout the proceedings of the daytime, he no longer remained ill; he had stopped his fidgeting. In the company of the Consistorium, he

---

* *Deipnon*—loosely deipnon was the evening meal

looked to be checked out altogether. He was a man trying his best not to be there.

A chair was established for Justinian at the head of the table, characteristically grander than the others. Procopius joined the party next to Joseph Nios. It would seem he had the privilege of sitting next to Justinian, an honor, but he yielded the honor to Alexander. Alexander did not know why, but one thing was certain: Thaddeus was not pleased with this arrangement, though there was nothing he could do about it. At the opposite end of the table from Justinian sat Theodora's niece, Sophia, who seemed about sixteen years old; she sat next to Antonina. Peter Patricus's son, Theodore, was permitted to be present but not afforded a seat at the table, instead being made to observe from the terrace above.

Barsymes, who had been eyeing both Alexander and Philip—Philip in particular—wasted no time jumping to accusations. "It's a trick. The whole thing is an elaborate plot— like Artabanes and Arsaces. They've been planning it for months. You should have them placed under lock and key until the truth comes out."

He looked at Philip. Philip averted his gaze. He then looked at Alexander and said, accusingly, "The truth will come out, it always does."

Justinian was undisturbed by the threatening treatment Barsymes aimed at the guests and went on like it was nothing, inquiring of Procopius, "The monk Lao Yi claims a worm produces the silk. It's a fabulous claim. No one has been able to produce silk anytime in memory. What did Pliny say of it?"

Procopius, whose knowledge was said to be encyclopedic, answered, "Pliny believed that down, removed from leaves with water and shaking, might yield silk. But no one has ever achieved this."

"Indeed not," Justinian finished for him. "I can hardly see why we would sustain hostilities in Lazica if silk could be produced by shaking down off wet leaves. Every commoner from here to Rome would be making silk in his own home."

When no one said anything, he pressed Barysmes, "Peter—if not from a worm—how do you suggest silk is produced?"

"Emperor," Barysmes answered, barely tempering his voice, "I admit no knowledge. But that makes me one in company with everyone—everyone!—for two thousand years. No one knows how silk is made...we only know that it reliably originates from Serinda. No one knows anything else of it."

Justinian looked as if he was about to say something when Barysmes continued, "What we do know is this. These monks—whatever their motives—elected to make their appearance here without the worm they claim makes the silk. They seek funding! It's a trick. They want money—they want the treasury's gold. Commission them and we will never hear from them again. Otherwise, if they really knew how silk was produced, why didn't they arrive with the secret in hand?"

Justinian inhaled and took a bite of his bread. Alexander noticed he did not sip his wine though he had been served with it.

"Perhaps," it was Antonina speaking now, "it's hard to steal this worm. It has been two thousand years that silk has come to us from the east. If it were easy—surely someone would have arrived with it sometime in two millennia."

Justinian set down the bread he was nibbling and addressed himself to Callicinus, "What of the letter? It bears a seal—but we do not recognize it?"

"That's right," Callicinus stated, "but the monk Alexander has translated it for us. It claims to be from the pen of the prince Lao Yi described, Xiao Yi."

"Meaningless scribbles. You've seen it with your own eyes Emperor. It's a trick, a plot—and these two monks are in on it."

To Alexander's surprise, Thaddeus stepped in and defended him—them, interjecting loudly, "Respectfully, I protest these accusations of my brothers—they are baseless. Alexander and Philip had no knowledge of this matter until this morning."

"Besides," now it was Peter Patricus, "if it is a plot..." He looked to Barsymes as he spoke, "we subjected them to a test."

A test? What test? Alexander's heart went cold. The only handle he had was that he could not imagine he would be sitting in present company if he failed the test. *What test?* His question was answered presently when Patricus continued.

Addaeus continued Peter's report, addressing himself to Barsymes, "We had the monk Alexander here read the document, and in a separate room we had the monk Lao Yi read it. Lao Yi's reading was more, ehh, fluent," he turned a sideways glance at Alexander, "but sentence for sentence they described exactly the same correspondence."

"You directed this Addaeus?" Barsymes asked. Addaeus nodded, "Peter Patricus ordered it, and I directed it."

"So good of you to inform me *now*" Barsymes concluded, his stinging eyes meeting with Addaeus, who lowered his own sheepishly.

Barsymes was not persuaded, "All that means is that they plotted carefully. Obviously this one is exceptionally well educated. That would not make them the first."

Alexander was sure he could have done without the backhanded compliment.

Justinian took a turn to speak, addressing himself to Philip, "When did you go?"

Philip did not answer. He just looked down at his plate with its untouched bread.

Justinian spoke directly and loudly, "Monk!" He snapped his fingers, "I'm talking to you." Taking a second to remember his name Justinian said sharply, "Philip!" knocking his knuckles on the table. Even with all of this, Alexander had to elbow Philip to break him from his spell.

"Tabrobane! Ah. Yes. Tabrobane. Emperor, I'm sorry." He shook his head for a moment. "It was six years ago. When the plague was almost past. Many sailors died."

Philip was able to hold Justinian's gaze long enough to say this before returning his eyes to his plate. He continued speaking, but as if talking to the air, "Many sailors had died in the plague. Normally—all the years before—they did not let Romans beyond Taprobane. We traded there with merchants from Sinhalla. But the plague was everywhere. They were short of men. I volunteered."

Justinian nodded then spoke, "And this is how you came to speak their language—they call it Hànyǔ?" "Yes," Philip said, "that's right."

Justinian addressed himself to Barsymes again, "I expect the Count of the Imperial Largesses to be sensitive to the lengths desperate and greedy men will go to foment coups or extort from the government—but if that is what this is, Peter—I think inventing a language is a new height of criminal achievement, don't you agree?"

"Emperor," Barsymes shot back, "they needn't have invented the language. Who knows where the foreign monks are from. The language can be real—but worms that make silk! That can't possibly be real. If it is like a spider, the fiber would be sticky. It would congeal to a useless blob. No one could harvest it."

"Peter," Justinian said, "I think...you have a point."

At these words, likely for the first time since the morning, Alexander saw Barsymes relax.

"And yet," Justinian went on, "I remember something."

Everyone tuned to Justinian who continued, "When Theodora was still with us, she was fond of butterflies. Butterflies start—as caterpillars. When they mature they weave. Peter," he looked at Barsymes to emphasize the point, "they *weave* for themselves a cocoon, a small bundle of fibers—very silk-like fibers. They remain inside this bundle for about two weeks until they emerge again…winged, and then they are butterflies."

Justinian paused. His head sunk a little and he continued, "Theodora loved this. She studied with Isidore to learn means of making spaces that butterflies were drawn to, so we often had cocoons and butterflies in the imperial palace."

Alexander waited. If Barsymes had an answer to this, he was thinking better of it than to say so.

Justinian started again, "I do wonder this though," looking to Alexander, "why not at least try?"

"I'm sorry Emperor, I don't understand," Alexander answered.

"Why didn't they at least try to bring the worm—this silk worm—here, to the capital. Peter has a point. Wouldn't it have saved a lot of trouble if they could just present us with the worm and its product? We wouldn't need to be here speculating?" He stopped and chuckled a bit. Alexander thought it odd to sit two feet from a chuckling emperor. "And…we wouldn't have my Count Barsymes over there accusing you of high treason."

Alexander thought better; he felt the stirrings of what his father called his "imp" coming up to vex the answer he was preparing. In any other moment, he would have stopped himself, but the lenient way that Justinian treated Barsymes' lethal threats disarmed his inhibitions. He answered Justinian, despite himself, with the truth, saying, "Lao Yi didn't bring the silk worm because he has…another mission."

That got Barsymes up again, "He admits!" Justinian waved, silencing him.

"Go on," Justinian said.

"He told me his mission is to determine if we are civilized. He said that he and Hui-Shen come from an ancient empire that has been civilized for thousands of years. The worm is sacred. That's why they can't give it to anyone. In their

304

language, the word for Rome is *Da-Qin*. When they call themselves the *Qin*, Daqin is a considerable compliment in their tongue—it means *Great Qin*. But, that Rome is great is only something suspected and hoped for. Lao Yi is here, Emperor, to divine if you are a civilized emperor and if we are a civilized people. He believes that if we are not, then his own empire will fall to an evil power because giving us the silk is the only thing that can weaken the usurper who holds his own emperor hostage. If their empire does fall, he hopes—his prince hopes—then in some respects it may live on in spirit, and they hope to transfer their spirit to a people worthy of it."

When his speech was met with silence, Alexander did not know what to make of it. That was until Peter Patricus finally broke in with a confidence, as if reading the minds of everyone at the table, except Barsymes, whose face had turned the color of a beet. "So, Lao Yi will stay behind as he suggested. The party we commission must include both of you," he said speaking at Alexander and Philip.

"Us!" they both protested in unison. Patricus went on, "You and Hui-Shen. We can probably arrange to take you to Antioch." He turned to Theodore, his son, who was watching the whole affair from the second terrace, "Theodore...who is that merchant? The one with new maps?"

"Ah, Indicopleustes, father, Cosmas Indicopleustes," Theodore answered.

"That's right. Cosmas. Incredible man—a fine resource to have on your side," he said, addressing himself directly to Alexander.

"On our side?" Alexander said, amazed that no one was even asking if he would volunteer.

"There's nothing to worry about Alexander," Patricus said, as if he knew him personally. "Cosmas knows the way. He has everything you'll need."

"Eh-em..."

The sound came from the end of the table, where until now the young Sophia had sat silently. "Not, *everything*, I think."

Patricus was bemused by the interruption and seemed skeptical that Sophia had anything of value to add. Once she held everyone's attention, she did not wait for him to shut her down, "How will they get through Persia? Three monks...won't that be suspicious? It's not as if the Emperor can write them a chrysobull for safe passage."

Patricus tried to brush her objection aside, "They won't travel as monks; they'll travel as merchants."

"But surely they can't go to Serinda alone," Sophia persisted.

"What do you mean? They won't be alone—they'll be together," Patricus answered her.

"That's not what I mean," Sophia said.

"What then?" Patricus asked.

She cleared her throat, then said precociously, half-winking one eye and twisting her cheek to one side as she spoke, "They are men."

When no one said anything she pressed on, addressing herself to Procopius, "when I was twelve we entertained an embassy from India. They gave me a drawing. Do you remember it Procopius?"

Procopius thought then answered, nodding, "yes."

"It's a curious drawing. Women in long dresses, their hair in buns tied together and held in place by sticks," Sophia elaborated.

"Yes," Addaeus chimed in, "I remember that."

Barsymes almost looked as if he were growling at Addaeus.

Sophia spoke to Procopius again, "They told me that it was a drawing of women, making silk. Is that what you remember Procopius? Did you record it?"

Procopius looked at the table and scratched his head, then nodded again, "I remember that too. You're right Sophia", he sounded genuinely surprised.

"I shared the drawing with the visiting ambassadors from Serinda. I asked them to tell me what was in the image. If it reminded them of Serinda," then she turned and looked directly at Justinian, asking, "and you know what they said?"

The two held eyes for a moment and Sophia continued, "they said, well—the old one—Lao Yi said, he said with no hesitation at all, that it is a drawing of women, tending silk worms, making silk. He was quite excited when he saw it and surprised I had it in my possession."

Except for an audible gulp from Barsymes who was returning to the color of purple, everyone at the table was silent.

Sophia continued, "What this means is that in Serinda, silk, is harvested, by *women*."

Silence again.

Sophia, allowing just a hint of annoyance in her voice, concluded, "They", pointing at Alexander and Phillip, "are *men!*"

"How will three monks—three *men*—secretly go about stealing away a mystery that Serinda has kept from us for two-thousand years? We will send them all the way past Tabrobane, all the way to Serinda, they will cross the world and if they are not locked out of the places where silk is made their intentions will be immediately held suspect because— it's obvious—they're men!"

Alexander looked at Peter Patricus and Thaddeus who both looked as if a child had just spilled wine on the tablecloth. Callicinus was blank faced, and Barsymes still resembled a beet. Only Antonina gave any indication of support for Sophia. Until Justinian spoke.

He said, "I think ... she might be right."

This time it was Peter Patricus' turn to pound the table, which he did, "What!?"

Justinian lifted a hand to quiet him, then started, "When I met Theodora she wasn't an aristocrat—she was not the daughter of a patrician or a general. She was a seamstress."

Everyone silently watched Justinian while he retrieved a memory.

"Had I married the daughter of an aristocrat, as many urged, there are likely many things I would not understand today, and I might hear Sophia's words differently."

Now he addressed himself directly to Peter Patricus, "Peter, you know that men don't go anywhere near a loom. What man knows anything of weaving? How will our monks, when they are in Serinda, how will they approach areas that are closed to men?"

At this, Thaddeus interjected, "Emperor, you are not suggesting my monks travel across Persia and India with a woman?"

Justinian answered, "Brother archimandrite, I am not suggesting anything. I have no answer to this puzzle."

Turning himself to Alexander, Justinian concluded, "I am giving you an order, monk. Return to Dalmatou and pray on this tonight. Tomorrow, tell me how you will travel to Serinda—you, brother Philip, and our guest Hui-Shen...with a woman. And it cannot be any woman. You must take with you one who understands silk."

Chapter 14
The Chrysobull of Propontis Tower

Yet if Paradise did exist in this earth of ours, many a man among those who are keen to know and enquire into all kinds of subjects, would think he could not be too quick in getting there:

for if there be some who to procure silk for the miserable gains of commerce, hesitate not to travel to the uttermost ends of the earth, how should they hesitate to go where they would gain a sight of Paradise itself?

Cosmas Indicopleustes, 550 AD

Propontis Tower
Dalmatou Monastery
Byzantium

Prote Hora, "First Hour"
Sunrise
Wednesday, *Tetarte*

29 March 551 AD
Julian Calendar

The highest floor of Propontis Tower was enclosed on all sides by an exterior circular porch and covered from above by an apse below a dome. There were no glass windows, and it was open to outside air, which entered through portals arranged in an octagonal pattern around the tower's perimeter. The monks of Dalmatou used the space for storing goods that were best left exposed to the continuous ocean winds or else which could tolerate outdoor weather and were best kept far from wandering eyes and loitering hands. In no particular order—and in some contrast to Cyra's meticulous arrangements—material was set all about the circular edge of the tower against a partition separating the porch from the interior. At the far end most opposite the Propontis were several large cubicle bales of straw, each piled two deep and two high in a row four bales long along the one side.

Anastasia created a space for herself by extracting one of the bales and laying it to the side so that a nook was opened between a center-facing bale and the edge of the tower. She

 fashioned a pillow for herself with linens from a wooden chest and used sheets to cover herself and protect her from the cold. Cold night air gave way to salty morning air; the hum of night insects gave way to a pre-sun silence that was now giving way again to the choirs of chirping and cawing birds. Beams of morning sunlight, cut by the horizon, illuminated the tower with rays that reflected off the walls causing a light purple glow on the back of her eyelids. The gentle accumulation of stimulations finally combined with a bit of congestion, and she was barely aware of herself. Occupying that early morning space between alertness and slumber, she gave no thought to where she was. Anastasia sneezed—she sneezed in her sleep, just once, sneezing herself awake.

When, upon sneezing, there was a sudden stir from the other side of the hay bale, towards the center of the tower room. Anastasia became sharply aware of herself, her

presence, location, and surroundings. In her sleep, she had almost—only almost—forgotten that she had slept in the tower that evening. But this was unexpected; the stirring was followed immediately by a rustling.

"Oh my God," she silently swore, "someone is in here." Then in vain hope and assuming it was a monk, "Did he hear me?", squinting her eyes and gritting her teeth she plead to the air, "I'm in such trouble!" Thinking as quickly as her mind would allow she rapidly concluded she had no option except to remain still. There was nowhere to run, and any movement would give away what little remained of her secret hideaway. Fighting to control her breathing to a bare, slow inhalation, she listened in horror to the unmistakable sound of approaching—slowly approaching—footsteps.

Should I move? Should I look?

No, she answered herself, commanding her body, *stay still!* as it struggled against her, trembling under the sheets.

Gaining some command she became still, lying motionless under the sheets, gritting her teeth. She pressed her head into her makeshift pillow and allowed as much as she could for her sheets to cover her head, hoping against all probability that the interloper would mistake her for a bundle of unfolded linens.

The footsteps stopped. She held her breath. The silence in the tower was broken by the loud caw of a crow that must have been fifteen feet away at the ridge on the tip of the roof of Dalmatou. The crow stopped its noisemaking and the sound was replaced by distant waves. Anastasia was holding her breath, willing her body to remain motionless. It seemed a whole minute passed. There was nothing, no sound, but then in a man's voice and heavily pointed tone emerged the words...

"Who the devil are..."

The words, her lack of breath, and the tension broke Anastasia's will to remain still. In one fluid movement, she lifted her whole torso, waist to head, all upwards to a sitting position. Unable to help herself, she let out of sharp rasp as she inhaled. She startled the man who had spoken; he hopped back a foot defensively. His motion added to Anastasia's tension and she followed her rasp with a sharp cry, involuntarily dropping her hands to the surface of the hay bale. Using her wrists, palms, and heels, she shunted herself backwards into the corner that separated the hay and the tower partition.

For one tense moment Anastasia and Alexander made eye contact. Both were completely shocked to encounter the other, and neither was sure what to do next.

Alexander broke the silence. Letting down his defensive posture, he took one step closer, saying, "*Ana— sta—sia?*" he said, drawing out her name in a surprised, higher pitch, "What are you doing up here?"

When she did not immediately answer, he followed up with another question, "How?" he shook his head in a sharp sideways node, "How did you get up here?"

Long ago—the first time Anastasia had taken refuge in the tower—she had considered the possibility of getting caught. That evening she did not get much sleep. She was so apprehensive that something— exactly like what was happening might now—might come to pass. Instead, she ran scenarios through her head: scenarios of escape, scenarios of capture. She had even strained to think of alibis, some of which, at least at the time, seemed persuasive. That's what she'd told herself anyway. She'd never had to test her alibis except with the monks she imagined herself confounding them with. This time—it was a real monk. It had been a long time, and she had grown complacent because no threat ever appeared.

Now, face to face with this monk in the tower, cornered and caught, she drew a blank.

Again, it was Alexander who broke the silence, "Anastasia, it's okay. Nothing will happen to you—at least not on my account," he stopped there, considering his words. "Tell me...why are you sleeping up here? Shouldn't you be in Saturninus with the other orphans?"

When she still did not answer, Alexander pressed her once more, "Truly—I mean no harm. I have more important things to worry about than orphans hiding out in towers at sunrise."

Not sure if that would persuade the scared girl, he added, "Here. If you won't speak, at least come out of there. You look terrified in that corner like I'm some monster that's come to get you. Don't be ridiculous I don't bite. Now come. Come out."

Then to disrupt their bad start, he changed tact and stepped out of view himself, returning to the center of the tower room. Anastasia listened to the few departing footsteps. There was a shift and a creak, as if he had found some place to sit. Presently he called after her, "Here. I'm out here. I'll wait for you. Come out whenever you're ready."

It was at this moment that Anastasia finally felt that it was safe to relax and breathe normally. Becoming conscious of how she had bounded between gasping after air and holding her breath, she held a hand to her chest and took several long inhalations and exhalations. Catching her breath, she looked ahead to the narrow path through the hay bales— a path that the space just outside of which she knew was blocked by Alexander. Still hoping for some means of escape to present itself she looked up—nothing. There was no climbing out. She would just be on top of a hay bale and unable to escape. To her left was the partition separating the tower room from the exterior porch. She did not think she could scale it, and even if she could she would simply find herself on the outside of a dead-end, circular porch with nowhere to go but around or down.

The desperate thoughts of escape would not easily let up. For a moment she wished she could back up time, back up to that space just before she sneezed, to the soft purple hue that was beginning to wake her up. *If only. If only I had woken up earlier!* she thought. She could be safely down the stairway or in the ventilation shaft by now, beyond discovery or capture.

But this was desperation giving way to thinking. Taking another breath, she thought more. Now she wondered how long Alexander had been in the tower. Five minutes? An hour? The thought gave her shivers. Even if she got away, even if she could distract the monk, or if luck saved her and he was called away by a superior, he would certainly tell Cyra.

The enormity of it settled in.

I'm caught.

The last thought Anastasia had before she lifted herself to exit her little nook was strange: regret. Fear was replaced with regret. Now the monk, and soon Cyra, would know her secret. That was too bad. Sometimes it was not such a bad thing to get into trouble; it gave her a reason to sleep alone in the tower with the salty, ocean air. To wake and watch the sun rise over the water's horizon. Once they knew how she had found this place they would close off her means of entry. She regretted that because she liked it up here.

Standing up straight, she spotted Alexander who had established himself on a chest in the center of the room. When she approached him, he motioned to a kneeling bench that would normally be used for prayer or meditation. It was not usually among the merchandise that the monks kept in the tower, and she did not remember seeing it when she entered the evening before. Alexander must have brought it with him when he came up this morning. Was he up here praying? If one was going to pray, it was as good as any place to do so she imagined. Alone, up high, the sun rising over the ocean.

As Alexander motioned her to the bench, she did not follow his meaning. Her first words were filled with puzzlement, "You…you want me to pray?"

Alexander's face immediately shone surprise at her question, which as quickly gave way to a soft laugh. "No," he smiled at her, "you're shorter than me. I thought you could sit on it while we talked. You can sit on a chest if you like, but your feet won't touch the floor."

Anastasia hesitated.   "What's wrong?" Alexander asked.

"In Saturninus", she said, regarding the bench, "we are not allowed to sit on prayer benches. If we are caught sitting on them they strike our knuckles."

Alexander didn't immediately respond to this and she added, "I thought that was always a rule with churches— never to sit on prayer benches. Only kneel."

Alexander looked at her and shrugged, "well, we aren't in church, are we?"

Anastasia tilted her head with a dint of surprise, "ah— well, we're on top of a monastery and you're a monk! We almost may as well be!"

Then for a moment she was shocked at herself by the familiar way she'd addressed herself to the monk, like he was an older cousin. She fought the urge to clamp her hand on her mouth and instead squeezed her fist a few times.

Alexander detected her change in composure—she suddenly held her eyes wide open and he could see the motion of little fingers below her sleeve. He answered her, smiling, "Well, it's my bench. Actually, it doesn't even belong to the monastery. It was carved in Persia and it belonged to my family. They let me keep it when I arrived here. They don't let us keep many things, but they made an exception for a bench. It's mine though and I—say you can sit on it."

"Good enough?"

Understanding him, and for the first time disarmed by his non-threatening manner and accommodation, she took his lead and pulled the kneeling bench to her calves where she positioned it and sat down facing him.

"Now—let's start again," he said, "what on earth are you doing in the tower? How did you get in here? You didn't go through Dalmatou...surely someone would have seen you."

Anastasia apprehended that the puzzle of how she got here was at least equal in interest to Alexander as the infraction of her presence in the first place. She realized he was trying to make sense of how she might have come in through the front door of Dalmatou—then through any halls or passages or stairways where the monks reside—and somehow do all of this without being seen or heard when surely someone would notice a child who had no place in a monastery.

She was about to answer him, to explain the door on the side of the monastery, the passage it led to, the ventilation shaft and the access it provided to the staircase that led to the tower, when a force rose up inside her, and she stopped momentarily. Again—it felt like a kind of regret, especially when the monk seemed so inviting, so interested, and so nonthreatening. She wanted to tell him. It had all been a secret discovery that she had kept to herself for years. It was a prize that she sometimes wanted to share but dared share with no one. Now, finally, she could share it with someone, not with a friend but someone who did not seem prepared to punish her for it.

She understood that in sharing it that she would lose this escape. She would be trapped again in the walls and hallways and closed doors of Saturninus.

What must have been a brief glow gave way to sadness. She could tell from the way he looked at her that Alexander had detected the change.

He spoke again, "Are you hungry? I'm sorry—I'll be right back." He stood up from his chest and walked to where the staircase opened into the tower and retrieved his sack— the same he had with him two days ago when she saw him in the shop visiting Cyra and inspecting her embroidery. He sat down again, opened it, and retrieved a tightly wrapped cloth bundle. He unwrapped it and handed the contents to her. It was dry bread.

She took the bread. Up to this moment she had not thought to be hungry—the morning had had too many peaks and shocks. The sight and slight scent of the bread mixed in her stomach and she felt something like pangs. She thanked him and began nibbling at it.

Alexander was watching her while she ate, and she him. "Oh!" he said, picking up the knapsack that he had discarded a moment earlier. He rummaged about inside it until he found something. Removing it carefully from the bag, he handed it to her.

It was her purse—the purse with the embroidery.

"Do you know where I got it?" he asked.

"No," she answered curtly, breadcrumbs dropping from her mouth.

Alexander was sheepish in how he answered. With no possibility that anyone could see or overhear them now, he looked over one side of his head anyways, as if scanning for spies. Returning his attention back to her he went on, "The Senate."

Anastasia almost spit out the crust she was chewing, "The Senate?"

"I know, I know," he said, shaking his head. "You...you wouldn't believe me if I explained how. Besides, it's a long story. But it seems that Cyra sold your purse to someone pretty important."

"Pfffht!" Anastasia chortled. Speaking through a childish giggle, she asked, "What were *you* doing in the Senate?"

Alexander shook his head and placed his hand briefly to his brow before letting it down again, "It was ridiculous. I have no business in the Senate! But there I was, and to my shock and surprise there too was your purse."

They considered each other for a moment. Alexander went on, "So I might as well be asking you what was *your* purse doing in the Senate?"

Anastasia did not answer. Alexander asked again, "What are you doing here Anastasia? How did you get here?"

* * * * * * * * *

Anastasia explained everything. The door, the passage, the ventilation shafts. Her bout with Vesta and the previous evening's banishment. Alexander listened. He interrupted her with a few questions. He was curious as to how long she had known about these secretive means of ingress, what other hiding spots they may expose, and how long she had been at this. She even told Alexander that she had discovered that Didyma kept Cyra's keychain on a hook high up on a wall at night when she retired. Didyma had been selected for the duty of key master in part because she was tall, and the hook was too high for Anastasia to reach, but she improvised by using a nearby stool. With those keys, she found her way around all manner of nooks and porticos that were normally off limits.

"Years!" he said, "You've been coming up here for years and no one has discovered you until now?"

"No one. Not until today," she replied.

"And scampering around the shafts?", he asked.

"Yes", she answered.

Despite himself he looked either way, "and…surely you overheard discussions—discussions people thought were private?"

Anastasia said nothing but answered with a slow, narrow nod. Alexander seemed to be smiling, but put his face in his palms.

The flow and positive energy of their exchange suddenly expired. It was replaced once more by regret.

"I won't be able to come up here anymore will I?" she asked.

318

When Alexander did not immediately answer, she asked, "Are you going to tell Cyra?"

"Are you afraid of what Cyra will do?" Alexander asked her in return.

She did not think long, answering, "Not really. Cyra won't let me come up here again, and she'll probably shut off the ways I sometimes escape. But, Vesta..."

"Vesta?" Alexander interrupted.

"Yes—Vesta. Vesta will *kill* me. And after she kills me, she'll make my life miserable. And then..."

She did not finish, so Alexander tried, "And then what?"

"Where will I go? Now everyone will know," she answered.

"You know..." she started up again. Her voice trailed into silence; they connected eyes.

"What? Do I know what?" Alexander asked when she did not finish.

Anastasia was conflicted. They had established some rapport. She felt as if she could trust the monk—if he had meant any harm he was doing a good job concealing it. But, her head was slowly nodding back and forth as if to say *no* while her mouth tried to mumble words. What resulted were barely audible *ahs* and *uhs*.

Alexander beamed a smile back at her, slapping his knee, "Anastasia you look ridiculous. What are you trying to say?"

There was something about the remark that made her stop.

It was so—familiar. Monks were supposed to maintain some distance between themselves and most laity. Alexander made regular exceptions when doing his work as a mitotes. The orphans were also expected to keep their distance from the monks. Anastasia knew that some were approachable and welcoming, but Alexander spoke to her as if he were a friendly uncle, not a welcoming monk tailoring away at a bracket with no more to offer than a smile and a pat on the head.

She answered him, "Cyra will probably make it impossible for me to come up here again, and I don't think I can live with the misery Vesta will put me through."

She said nothing else. Alexander turned a cheek slightly, saying, "And…"

"There are lots of other doors in Saturninius, and at Dalmatou."

Again, she followed this with nothing. Alexander again prompted her, "And…"

"If no one were to tell Cyra or Vesta, then I might…then maybe I will stay out of the tower if you don't want me to return here, but then I could see what's behind other closed doors."

Once again, they sat quietly.

Anastasia became aware of her heart thudding in her chest, not fast, but hard. She tried to read her own intuitions of what this monk would make with her disclosure. She was thinking too fast. Was that a miscalculation or a tremendous act of trust? She didn't know. Either way, he could tell Cyra of her intentions. Then Cyra might be sure that every door was always locked, that the keys were always laced to someone's body, and that a supervisor's eyes were always locked on Anastasia. She could not explain this act of trust to herself. *Why did I tell him that?*

When Alexander finally addressed her, he seemed to change the subject.

"You know, it's a strange thing," he said.

"What?" she asked.

"In three days—you and I have had three encounters."

"What?" she asked, "I count only two."

"Yes," Alexander said, "but I'm counting my encounter with your purse yesterday, in the Senate.

Monday, you and I met with Cyra, and I inspected the fine work of your purse and embroidery. Tuesday—

yesterday, a powerful stranger presented me with the same purse when I was summoned to the Senate. This morning, well," he looked around, gesturing to their surroundings, "here we are." A moment passed, and he added, "I think that's very odd. Don't you?"

"I guess," she answered.

Some time had passed; the sun was well above the horizon. Realizing that it probably did not matter that Alexander meant to escort her to Cyra, she still spoke as if he were more of a playmate than an elder, as if he might let her go back the way she came, to the staircase, the ventilation shaft, and back to the porch where Vesta would be expecting her. Thinking this, she nodded only barely in the direction of the sun, saying, "I should probably go soon."

Once again, a silence posed itself into their conversation and this time Anastasia was the one to break it, "Are you..." She had to force the words, not believing she was going to ask this, "going to let me go or are you going to take me to Cyra now?"

It was Alexander's turn. He started by saying what she expected, "You are right about that. I have to take you to Cyra. I'm sorry."

She nodded at him, almost with her whole head and neck so even her chest bobbed forward and back nervously.

"But I don't think this is going to go the way you may think," Alexander said.

These words were unexpected.

"What do you mean?" she asked.

"Well," Alexander answered, "there are at least two advantages to what I'm thinking. And even if you agree to it, it will still require Cyra's approval?"

"What?" Anastasia asked, "I still don't know what you mean."

Alexander replied, "I think I can arrange it so that you won't get in trouble with Cyra...or Vesta."

"What?" she asked again, "How? Why?"

"And," Alexander went on, "I think I can arrange it so that you don't need to worry about the doors of Saturninus being closed off to you anymore."

"What?" Anastasia asked, challenging, looking for other words to say but not finding them.

"Do you know where silk comes from?" Alexander asked.

"Silk?" she asked, startled at the sharp change in topic.

Alexander nodded, "Yes, yes. Silk. Do you know how it comes to the city?"

"Sailors, ahh, merchants, I don't know" she started.

"No, that's not what I mean. Do you know where silk is made?" Alexander asked.

They met eyes again, saying nothing.

"Anastasia, the reason I was here in the tower this morning is that I was sent to consider a problem."

"What problem?" Anastasia asked.

"Emperor Justinian has commissioned a party, but the party is incomplete."

"Emperor Justinian?" Anastasia remarked, "...what party?"

"He requires that in order for it to be complete, our party needs another member...one who knows about silk. A seamstress. He means to add a woman to our party, but we don't know how that is possible."

Anastasia was confused, "What are you talking about? What are you saying?"

Alexander answered her, "I would be lying if I told you that it will be safe. It won't be safe. But we need someone to join our mission."

"Mission?!" she asked, raising her voice in confusion, almost objection.

Her apparent protest seemed to slow him down.

"You know," he shook his head back and forth, "it's so funny—you are so young. You're too young. But if you were any older, it would probably be impossible, and if you were any younger, you couldn't help us. "I can't think of anyone worse, and yet I can't think of anyone better."

A few seconds separated his words.

"Anastasia, the emperor, Emperor Justinian, is sending some of us to Serinda. But we need someone who can help us."

She starred at him blankly.

He continued, "I think you are the one. I think you can help us—in Serinda. Would you like to—join our mission—and go with us to Serinda?"

* * * * * * * * * *

The Magnaura   The table of the consistorium
                                      After *apodeipnon*

Stephen the Silentarius led them back through the vestibule to the reception hall. This time no one was in the dais and no one would speak from the platform in the pit. Justinian, Procopius, the entire Consistorium as well as Theodore, Peter Patricus' son, and Sophia were all gathered. Antonina was present—this time not in her pajamas but dressed in the blattia—in purple designating a patrician with a rank on the Consistorium. Cyra and Thaddeus both attended. Thaddeus was furious about the arrangement but was powerless to stop it. Justinian had appointed the decision to Alexander, not the archimandrite.

In the privileged place next to Justinian—where Alexander had sat a day earlier—sat Sophia, at a far corner from Peter Barsymes, to whose far side sat Antonina.

Unlike yesterday, Justinian did not look well at all. Sophia was holding a cup for him, bidding him to sip from it and seeming to whisper supportively in his ear. He seemed to be a man burning away at his reserves just to hold himself up in his seat. After Sophia whispered something to him, he looked to be willing himself to connect with Alexander and addressed him.

"You've returned."

"Yes," Alexander answered.

Sophia lent Justinian the cup again. He sipped from it and then started again, "Have you returned with a resolution to our puzzle?"

"I have sir," Alexander answered affirmatively.

At his answer there was a stirring. Peter Barsymes shifted visibly, leaning forward and holding his body straight while connecting eyes with Alexander, disbelievingly. A moment earlier he had been comparatively relaxed. Alexander wondered if he had been counting on failure. To count on such a failure would have been quite reasonable after all.

"We are pleased," Justinian said. Then, taking another sip from the cup Sophia held, he waved a hand weakly at Alexander, "Go on, go on. Don't hold up. What is it? How have you resolved our puzzle?"

Alexander stepped to one side, opening a space between himself and Thaddeus; he nodded to Cyra.

Stepping between them, the highest point of her head rising no taller than the middle of Alexander's chest, walked Anastasia.

Justinian considered them with a glassy look in his eyes, and Alexander addressed his words in the general direction of Justinian, but recalling the drawing she'd shared yesterday he met eyes directly with Sophia, "For the Emperor, in answer to our prayers, I present the chrysobull of Propontis Tower."

"This is Anastasia. She resides at Saturninus and weaves silk and linens. She is Cyra's charge."

Allowing a moment for this to sink in, Alexander, eyes still fixed with Sophia's, added, "Anastasia is the chrysobull we need, the chrysobull we prayed for—so that now we may make haste to Serinda."

Appendices

Time and Chronology
As Justinian and Theodora Knew Them

By the time of Justinian and Theodora several systems of reckoning time were in use, chief among them were the year of the current Olympiad (which was falling out of use as the Olympics had been recently abolished, but which still retained a utility as a reliable benchmark going back 1200 years), the reign and year of the current emperor as well as a number of inconsistent syntheses of cosmic calendars representing attempts to synthesize pre-Christian, pagan reckonings of historical and pre-historical time with the ascendant reckoning attributed to the Hebrews by contemporary Christian popularizers.

For our treatment of Justinian and Theodora it is our ambition to represent them and their world with the utmost faithfulness without creating an excess of burden on the reader, with hopes to transport the audience into the enchanted world Justinian and Theodora occupied. It is not possible to achieve any of these goals without adequately accounting for a Byzantine reckoning of time so that we may understand their chronology both as they understood it and as they lived it.

A somewhat fascinating coincidence is that the current, dominant system of calendar: the BC AD era system or Anno Domini system of dating was devised in 525 AD by Dionysius Exiguus of Scythia Minor at about the time Justinian and Theodora married. That system didn't come into wide adoption however until three centuries later. The systems in use during their time were the aforementioned.

As more than one syncretization of pagan and Hebrew reckonings existed, for simplicity and consistency we select one and hold to it throughout the series, our method is as follows.

The Patria (1:55) records that it was in the 5838th year "of the creation of the world" that the city of Byzantium received the name "Constantinople". We know the year Emperor Constantine consecrated Byzantium as Constantinople was 330 AD and we take 330 AD to correspond to 5838. The Patria in the same passage claims that this was also in the second year of the 265th Olympiad— but finding as the 265th Olympiad was in 281 AD and its second year was 282 AD, we take that to be an error of medieval chronological record-keeping, which is not unusual and we ignore it—instead we find that 330 AD was in the second year of the 277th Olympiad and we retain this as the year corresponding to 5838 in Byzantine chronology.

Using this as our point of reference we presume for purposes of this series that Justinian was born in 484 AD – sources differ on this and some suggest he was born as early as 481 AD but we will hold 484 AD to be his date. 484 AD under the prior reckoning is the 5992nd year of the creation of the world, and we derive from there that Theodora was born in 6005 (497 AD), they were married in 6033 (525 AD) and for purposes of Serinda, our eastern monks arrive on the scene in 6059 (551 AD).

In at least one reckoning of Byzantine chronology all of history and pre-history was divided into eras numbering 532 years each and the Byzantines of Justinian and Theodora's time regarded themselves to occupy the 12th such era which, fittingly, they held to be the "Byzantine Era". This holds some significance as in modern times we hold that the attribution of "Byzantine Empire" to Justinian, Theodora and those who would follow them is retrospective and that they and their contemporaries understood themselves to be Roman and an organic continuation of what was until 476 AD the Roman Empire in the west and the east, but by the time of Justinian and Theodora remained intact only in the east.

But time is as fitting a dimension as space for locating identity and acknowledging that both Justinian and Theodora probably understood the chronology of their own lives as particle to the Twelfth Era, the Byzantine Era, it seems quite appropriate to understand them as uniquely Byzantine in a way that earlier Romans, east and west, were not. It so happens that the final year of the Byzantine Era to which Justinian and Theodora reckoned themselves to belong ended in 887 AD. In 2018 AD, as Justinian and Theodora would have understood it, we are today in the 7528th year of the creation of the world and the 66th year of the Fifteenth Era which will come to an end in 2483 AD. Our current era in their time began in 1952.

Byzantine Epochs			AD/BCE of Last Year of Era
Year of Creation: 5497 BCE			
First	1	532	4964 BCE
Second	533	1065	4432 BCE
Third	1066	1598	3900 BCE
Fourth	1599	2131	3368 BCE
Fifth	2132	2664	2836 BCE
Sixth	2665	3197	2304 BCE
Seventh	3198	3730	1772 BCE
Eight	3731	4263	1240 BCE
Ninth	4264	4796	708 BCE
Tenth	4797	5329	176 BCE
Eleventh	5330	5862	355 AD
Twelfth (Byzantine)	5863	6395	887 AD
Thirteenth	6396	6928	1419 AD
Fourteenth	6929	7461	1951 AD
Fifteenth	7462	7994	2483 AD

With this understanding of Byzantine chronology we take one thing to be an interesting coincidence. Most modern scholars of the subject find the estimation by Dionysius Exiguus for the year for the birth of Jesus of Nazareth, 1 AD, to be an error and our best accounts instead suggest that he was born at some time between 6 BCE and 4 BCE (recall that there is no year 0 in this system). With this adjustment it is interesting to note that almost exactly 532 years elapse between the actual year of the birth of the historical Jesus of Nazareth, and the ascension of Justinian and Theodora to the throne in 527 AD – the length of one full era as Byzantines computed them.

Glossary of Byzantine and Some Chinese Terms

African red slipware, a common fine pottery form in the 1st through 7th centuries that was manufactured for export in modern Tunisia

Amphora, a tall jar with two handles and a narrow neck common in the Greco-Roman world for storing and holding beverages

Autexousion, legal emancipation of a minor son from his parents (especially his father); usually between 16 and 18 years of age although variable if the child married, took monastic vows, owned his own workshop or joined the military

Basilikoi, officials who accompanied foreign embassies and dignitaries, who brought them into audiences and meetings, provided for their needs and arranged for safe passage

Battle of Maurica, known to various historical accounts as the *Battle of the Catalaunian Plains*, *Battle of the Catalaunian Fields*, the *Battle of the Campus Mauriacus*, the *Battle of Châlons* or the *Battle of Maurica*; it occurred on June 20, 451 AD, about 100 years before the events in this narrative

Blattia, plural of blattion—originally meaning the color purple, in late antiquity and the earlier Byzantine days of Justinian and Theodora, it had the connotation of the highest quality purple that was reserved for royal or imperial use

Boullotes, an assistant to the eparch who oversee one or another bureau or regulatory body in the eparch's purview – corporeal punishment was imposed on a merchant who refused entry of a boullotes or his representative (i.e.: a mitotes or a legatarios) to a workshop

Βούττα, Buddha, in Greek: Βούττα, was known to Greco-Roman society and minimally found mention by Augustine and the second and third century Clement of Alexandria, the latter in his *Stromata*, which Clement designed as a medium of Christian secret teachings via largely symbolic explanation

Chartoularioi, in both Byzantine government and church affairs, chartoularioi, or chartophylax, the latter term more appropriate for the church, acted as tertiary officials and functionaries with a variety of responsibilities for fiscal, archival or other affairs including some military applications; their responsibilities may range from the relatively simple courtier to heads entire bureaus, often called "sekreton" or "secreton"

Chiton, basic tunic worn by both men and women of all socio-economic strata

Comes sacrarum largitionum, the count of the imperial largess – minister in charge of the imperial treasury and a member of the Emperor's Consistorium

Comitatenses, Roman or Byzantine field army which came to replace the legions in later Roman and early Byzantine times of late antiquity beginning around the time and under reforms of Diocletian who specifically designed the comitatenses as mobile field armies whose mission, training, equipment and structure differed from *limitanei*, the other primary organizational form for large military units, who were assigned to guard the border or "limit" of empire; driven by the changing military landscape in late antiquity which increasingly came to favor mobile units while incorporating archery, artillery and the horse, the comitatenses were a means and ends to military force re-organization and modernization that continued through Theodosius who merged cavalry and infantry units and up through the time of Justinian, by whose era Rome's legendary legions were already an artifact of the distant past

Consistorium, the highest advisory body in the imperial service—closely akin in function to a Presidential Cabinet—technically separate from the Senate, during the time of Justinian the role of the two bodies effectively converged

Daqin, Chinese word for Rome. By the time of the early 7th century we know the Chinese knew the Byzantine Empire by the word "Fulin" (Chinese: 拂菻), however it is not certain that the name Fulin had come into adoption before 618 AD, about 70 years after the events in this story. Before that, the *Weilüe* (Chinese: 魏略, "A Brief History of Wei")which was written by Yu Huan, a historian of Cao Wei during the Three Kingdoms period between 239 and 265, records information about societies west of China including India, Parthia and the Roman Empire, the latter of which Yu Huan describes as "Da Qin"(Chinese: 大秦), "The Great Qin". The *Weilüe* includes in particular descriptions of sea-based routes by which one may travel from China to Roman regions. We presume for the start of our story that the term Fulin was still in use.

Daugava, a waterway used in late Roman times and throughout the Middle Ages by the Byzantines to access Russia, the Baltics and Scandinavia.

Deed of Purchase, deeds recording the details and exchange of property and rights in a legal transaction typified by a deposit or disposal of money and an exchange of money or property; they followed formularies—that is formulas or templates, "model books" for documents which in different times and places were more universal or more local that were produced by chanceries and notaries—6th century law schools are believed to have fomented the spread of uniform deeds in the Byzantine world

Dekarch, a leader of a 10-soldier squad (a decharchy)

Depotatoi, medical corpsmen – units in a Tagma of eight to ten whose role was to recover injured soldiers and unhorsed cavalry from the field of battle

Empress Leizu, Can Nainai, legendary empress—wife of the Yellow Emperor, credited by tradition with the discovery of silk and known in folklore as Can Nainai, "Silkworm Mother"

Eparch, The Eparch of the City, effectively the governor and supreme judge of Byzantium and chief of police responsible for law and order, second only to the emperor

Eukraton, a beverage common in monasteries which substituted for wine usually served as a hot drink made by boiling water with pepper, cumin, or anise - it was usually a staple during fasting periods

Exagion, a unit of weight intended to match the weight of a solidus, a gold coin originally minted by Diocletian where there were 60 solidi to a Roman pound but by the time of Justinian the conversion had been increased to 72 such that one weighed one exagion and 72 exagion weighed 1 pound; by the late Roman and early Byzantine era the solidus had taken on the name nomisma

Excubitor, a small group of elite troops created by Leo I as a special imperial bodyguard under the command of a *comes excubitorum* which was a position that rapidly took on considerable importance in the regime

First Watch, the first nightly watch ended around 10 PM, so as much as four hours prior to 10 PM, but after sundown—if described as "later" as here, then probably between 8 and 10 PM

Hegumenia (Greek: ἡγουμένη), female form of hegumen (Greek: ἡγούμενος), title for the head of an eastern orthodox monastery

Hekantontarch, a commander of a hundred soldiers (a hekatontarchy)

Hetaireia, a military unit of uncertain provenance but which in some way was attached to the emperor—it is likely that they were responsible for the administration of certain estates held by the imperial government, including properties about the palace

Horologian, a Byzantine time keeping device—usually a water clock or sundial

Hyrcanian Ocean, the Caspian Sea as it was known to the Byzantines—its geography was poorly understood and the Byzantines had no clear sense of where it ended

Iconostasis, a high barrier in churches and similar sanctuary buildings that was used to create a reserved or protected space in religious buildings of late antiquity; it was superseded later in the Middle Ages by the use of open templons and low screens

Jacobite, local (Syrian) term for a follower of what was late (7th century) described as the monophysite or miaphysite movement of Christianity centered in Alexandria but popular in Egypt and Syria; that movement then as to this day at some odds with the larger northern body of eastern orthodox and Catholic Christianity both of which are regarded as Chalcadonian based on agreements they made against the doctrines of the Jacobites (monophysites) at the Council of Chalcadon regarding the nature of the incarnation and the Trinity

Jade Emperor, one of the representations of the first god in Taoist theology; known as Yuanshi Tianzun, he is one of the Three Pure Ones: the three primordial emanations of the Tao

Jing, in Traditional Chinese Medicine jing is the essential fluid of the physical body that contains the life force; sometimes described as the "essence of Qi (Chi)" it is both the material basis of the body and the fluid container of the life force—it works with the life force Qi and Spirit, Shen and together with these three is recognized as one of the "three treasures"—said to be stored in the kidneys and "prenatal jing" which one is born with cannot be replenished—a loss of jing can cause premature aging and death

Kelliotes, kellia, a monastic cell

Logos, (Greek: λόγος) – when translation is attempted, often translated as "word", such as in the most common English translation of the Gospel of John, "In the beginning was the (λόγος) Word...", or when Saint Jerome translated the New Testament into Latin, "In principio erat *Verbum*...", and contemporary Spanish translations, "En el principio era el *Verbo*..."

Arguably—each of these translations are in error and the correct rendering of logos is for translators to retain the word in its Greek form, *logos*, so as to urge readers and thinkers to ascertain it as a distinct concept, apart from "word", which for its part is a different word altogether in Greek: λέξις, transliterating as "lexis";

Found in Plato's writings and those of his followers for centuries afterwards, and believed to have predated Plato and possibly originating from out of the Bronze Age, logos may be most simply understood on a human level as the dark, precognitive space—just prior to and beyond the reach of language, that *creates* meaning by selecting words in party to the action of mind, before words themselves are formed as cohesive, verbal thoughts—or more generally as *the source out of which the mind forms meaning*, for example the font from which an artist imagines an new image or a musician intuits a composition for a musical score;

In contrast to words and other symbols and acts of art which themselves *are* meaning—logos is an elusive, inchoate noun—that thing which *creates* meaning and a philosopher may speculate that this act of creation is of its own nature *ex nihilo*

On a metaphysical level, logos is the aspect of Plato's fecund and infinite, divine "One", which Plato held to be unknowable to its emanations—emanations such as gods and goddesses, angels and demons, men and women, animals, plants, the four elements and matter—but emanations destined in Plato's universe to reunite with the One; though the One is unknowable, lying as it does even beyond Plato's "Realm of the Forms", the logos is an aspect of the One which renders as intellectable both the One and the process of imminent return to the One, to its emanations; in Plato's complex ontology emanations, otherwise lost to confusion and chaos, may come to know about the One, because the logos renders the One intellectable to them

Logos found particular refinement as a concept for fusing together Hebrew and Greek thought in the writings of the Jewish thinker Philo of Alexandria in the early first century; in the Christian era, particularly in the Johannine tradition beginning with John's non-synoptic gospel and echoed from Irenaeus to Justin Martyr to Clement of Alexandria and Origin all the way to Justinian himself, the logos was appropriated out of the Platonic tradition where it was equated with Christ as divine-made-incarnate, just such as we find stated in the Gospel of John;

Though it has fallen out of popular use in the awareness of contemporary Christians of all sects, the logos lay at the heart of Byzantine Christian spirituality and references to it are frequent in Byzantine writings and art, including those of Justinian himself[λ]

Apprehension of the roll of the logos in the *ex nihilo* act of creation of meaning in a Platonic, fecund, infinite universe is a precondition to understanding the minds of pre-modern, pre-scientific people, but more so it would be difficult for people in modern times to understand the most divisive issue of Justinian and Theodora's era without first understanding the place of the logos in the minds of people in Late Antiquity—the dispute between European "Nicene Christianity" and African, largely Egyptian miaphysitism

The conflict between Nicene Christianity, also known as "Chalcedonian Christianity" which descends to us today as Roman Catholicism, Eastern Orthodoxy and Protestantism, versus monophysitism or miaphysitism, which is preserved today as the Coptic Orthodox Church, is a division that literally set Justinian and Theodora apart from one another, as a couple, while paradoxically this personal division also

---

[λ] See *On the Person of Christ: the Christology of Emperor Justinian*, Trans. Kenneth P. Wesche, St. Vladimir's Seminary Press, 1991 – Justinian wrote copious letters to monastics and clerics staking out positions on the intersection of philosophy and Christian theology – the substance of these letters make clear that he was especially concerned with implications of Christ, as Logos

accounted for their ability *as a couple* both to seize and hold power over a divided empire, together, for decades

Of some interest to the particular cultural intersection at the heart of this novel, *Serinda*, is that when early translators of the Bible first translated the text into Mandarin Chinese, when confronted with the same problem as western translators who faced the Greek logos and elected to replace it with "word", Chinese language translators opted instead to translate logos to Mandarin as "Tao" so that when rendered in Chinese the first verse of the Gospel of John reads, "In the beginning was the Tao and the Tao was with God, and was God"

Manoualia, large brass candle stands, usually placed on either end before the iconostasis or templon and intended to represent the pillars of fire that guided the Hebrews on their journey in the desert

Melchite, local term for Chalcadonian (Eastern Orthodox or Catholic) Christians in Syria who used the term to distinguish themselves from the majority Jacobites (monophysites) and Nestorians

Mese, literally meaning the "middle" road, this was the central avenue and main street of Byzantium; it began at the Milion which was symbolically the initial milestone of empire which originated in the Augustaion Square in front of the Hagia Sophia and stretched from there towards the city center where around the south west base of Third Hill in an area called the Philadelphion it forked with one branch extending north west to the Gate of Adrianople and the other branch extending south west to the Golden Gate, this second branch subdivided shortly beyond Dalmatou at a juncture called Sigma where one branch continued to the Xylokerkos Gate, also known as the Gate of the Source or the Pege which was planted with trees and had a source of water (pege) that locals held to be miraculous

Misthios, an apprentice

Mitotes, one class of legatarios, the word was broadly applied for both civil and military officials responsible for overseeing the operations of variousdepartments of the Byzantine bureaucracy who usually answered ultimately to the Eparch and who were considered his assistants in the conduct of regulation; mitotes were legatarios who were inspectors responsible for the quality of silk linens

Neorion, a merchant market relocated to the Harbor of Julian by Justinian with a colorful history of enchantments

Nestorians, a Christian movement centered around Antioch in Syria that developed in the early fifth century that tended to punctuate the human nature of Christ while denying what other Platonist educated Christians called the *hypostatic union* of the *divine Logos* with the human person of Jesus; in addition they rejected the use of the term Theotokos, which means Mother of God" as a reference to Mary and preferred to substitute it with Christotokos which means "Mother of Christ"; they incurred the ire of other Christians who accused them of propounding the existence of two sons of God rather than one Son of God; besides a violence their opponents perceived the Nestorian theology to commit on a seemingly more Platonic understanding of the Christian vision their opponents also objected that Nestorian beliefs implied that Jesus liberated himself to become Christ rather than that being Christ, he lacked the ability to sin; the movement was uniformly rejected by the antecedents groups which would eventually come to be the modern Orthodox, Catholic and Coptic Christian movements at the Council of Ephesus in 431; despite this rejection they retained a strong presence in some parts of Syria, Persia, Northern Arabia, and across Central Asia to India and even into China

Oikonomos, a cleric responsible for managing the property, income and expenses of a religious body or institution such as a church or monastery; in a monastery this role might be known as a steward and was generally second to the hegumenos—the Council of Chalcedon (451) had required this appointment but it was not extended as a requirement to monasteries until the Second Council of Nicaea (787).

Olovina, while it is difficult to be conclusive because most surviving literature from the Byzantine era is naturally a product of the upper classes and literate ranks and therefore infected with certain slants we nevertheless get a sense that while wine and other liquors were both common and popular in Byzantine times and places, beer was not so popular; though one factor that may serve to support the idea that beer's unpopularity was merely a quality of the bias of surviving literature are reports of a wine like drink made from barley called olovina, which is an old Russian word for beer - it was used disparagingly to refer to a drink popular with "semi-barbarians"

Opsonion, referred to as a provisions allowance, a sum that soldiers received when on campaign in addition to their ordinary salary (roga)—although it technically could be granted in cash

Orphanage, orphanages had an important function in Byzantine society—one should exercise caution not to project modern assumptions onto the past—orphanages occupied a significant structural place in early modern western Europe, but generally have not been a significant fixture of society prior to that—though they were an important institution in Byzantium; called orphanotrophos, they were under the direction of a orphanotropheion and while sometimes independent, were usually administered by a monastery; orphanotrophos served the blind, crippled and elderly; orphans could stay in them until they were old enough to marry and orphans had rights that were recognized in law

Paludamentum, a form of chlamys which by the sixth century had many forms and applications to designate that the wearer bore this or that formal office, where the paludamentum was a chlamys designating a high-ranking military officer, as opposed to other versions for huntsmen, riders, civilian officers and a purple chlamys which was exclusively worn by the emperor

Panis Civilis, the Roman custom of bread distribution which was preserved in Byzantium by Emperor Constantine who ordained it there on May 18 332 and which continued until after the reign of Justinian in 618— along with the distribution of bread officials could also distribute wine, meat and various linens including clothing

Pous, a unit of length similar to a "foot", 31.23 centimeters and derived from the Greek "foot"—used in documents describing the Hagia Sophia; at 400 meters above the Kodori River, the *base* of Tsibilium fortress was at 1280 pous by Byzantine reckoning, which is about 1312 English feet high, a quarter-mile at the fortress's base

Prandiopratai, merchants who imported and sold foreign, but especially Syrian silk fabrics

Psamathia, the quarter in the southwestern corner of Byzantium between the Constantinian and the Theodosian walls; originally occupied by aristocratic mansions in the fourth and fifth centuries they came to be replaced by monasteries

Rasophore (Greek: ρασοφόρος), title given to an eastern orthodox nun, in the modern era of the lowest rank, but less stringently so in antiquity—the name is derived from a napless woolen cloth garment out of which developed the cassock—the title is used in a similar fashion to "sister" in Latin / western monastic convent traditions

Sagia, plural form of sagion, which could variously refer to a cloak worn by soldiers in the sixth century infantry or to a heavier form used for blankets and tents

Scholae Palatinae, imperial guard; created by Diocletian, by the 5th century they had been reduced to a largely ceremonial role including carrying out Palace business, reporting to the Magister Officicorum, their guard role had been transferred to the excubitors—wealthy families often paid for their youths to hold an office in the Scholae Palatinae

Sī, Chinese for "silk"; written 絲

Skiadon, a term which took on different meanings at different times—as used in late antiquity of Justinian and Theodora it was a parasol or sunshade but in later times it came to mean a conical hat with a broad brim that was popular among imperials and those of high rank.

Strepton, a bronze tube used by Byzantines to contain flammable liquids and chemicals—later, just a hundred years after the era of Justinian and Theodora, this would be combined with a pumping device called a *siphon* which when combined with a strepton made for a pre-modern flame thrower of legendary effectiveness, reported by their allies, their enemies and the Byzantines themselves to be "Greek Fire", or literally "liquid flame"—in its more advanced, "flame thrower" manifestation its use is not recorded before 678 AD when it was deployed to repel Arab invaders with astonishing efficiency; but the 6th century *Strategikon of Maurice*, contemporary to these events, as well as other sources make it clear that incendiary weapons, even "bombs" were known and already in use by the Byzantine military at this earlier date—this was especially so in the prosecution of siege warfare where explosive devices where particularly valuable for tilting the balance of power to the side of the aggressing party

Tagma, refers to a military regiment—the word came into adoption around the 4th century and is common for example in the contemporary Stratikon of Maurice, although it took on a more formalized meaning in the fundamental organizational structure of the Byzantine military around the 8th century; prior to that, however, it was in widespread use to refer to various specialized regiments, the first of which were the scholai and excoubitoi, but later came to include at least two units specifically associated with the city of Byzantium, one for wall regiments and another for regiments that guarded prisons and various city sections; one record holds that there were four cavalry and two infantry tagma in Byzantium, each with 4000 soldiers

Taprobanê, Sri Lanka as it was known to the Romans, Greeks and Byzantines

Taxis, a Byzantine concept that permeated most aspects of life holding that human society was a mirror of the cosmos and opposite the abhorred concept of ataxis, or disorder; from taxis followed realities of etiquette, precedence, ceremony, rank, class and ways of life

Tetrarchy, by the 3rd century AD the Roman Empire was too large to effectively govern and defend and was beset by one crisis after another which often boiled over on account of delays between the onset of what could have been a minor crisis, and the centralized, executive correction, because news traveled slow and information was incomplete and inaccurate; to stem this problem and others the Emperor Diocletian instituted reforms which divided Rome into four "dioceses", administrative zones ruled by a tetrarch—this was the first separation of Italy from Byzantine, eastern Rome and set the foundation that provided for the structure of the later east/west split which would result in the relative rise of Byzantium that corresponded to the decline of the Latin, Roman west

Toupha, a helmet adorned with a tuft of fur or the feathers of exotic animals

Trapeza, a refrectory in eastern monastic communities

Typikon, foundation charter for a monastery or nunnery

Vasht, a smaller division in the Sasanian Persian army

Vestioprates, (plural: vestiopratai; Greek: βεστιοπράτης) a supposed occupation for the 6th century inferred based on contemporary John Malalas' use of the word *bestion* to designate clothing that was handed out as part of the *Panis Civilis* and the later (after the 9th century) use of the term for merchants of fine luxury garments primarily composed of silk but inclusive of other fine linens

Xylon, called a semantron after about the 11th century, prior to which it was known as a *xylon* or a *rhabdos sidera* ("iron rod")

www.ingramcontent.com/pod-product-compliance
Lightning Source LLC
Chambersburg PA
CBHW061323170626
46817CB00001B/288

* 9 7 8 1 9 4 9 2 3 5 0 6 7 *